THE MAGAZINE AND ITS MAKERS
VOLUME 1

Edited by John Locke

Off-Trail Publications

Elkhorn, California

For their many generous contributions, the editor would like to thank Douglas A. Anderson, Mike Ashley, Stefan Dziemianowicz, Doug Ellis, Ed Gobbett, E.A. Grosser, John Gunnison, Dave Kurzman, Will Murray, Rob Preston, Dan Roy, Morgan Wallace, and especially Norm Davis.

GHOST STORIES
The Magazine and Its Makers
Volume 1
Copyright © 2010, Off-Trail Publications
ISBN-10: 1-935031-09-0
ISBN-13: 978-1-935031-09-3

OFF-TRAIL PUBLICATIONS
Castroville, CA 95012
offtrail@redshift.com

Printed in the United States of America
First printing: July 2010

Contents (Volume 1)

(Many tales in GHOST STORIES credited the author and the narrator with separate bylines. However, these were listed inconsistently within the magazine. In this contents page, we've standardized the credit by listing the presumed author first, and the narrator, if any, second. The story headings within preserve the original attribution.)

Contents (continued)

The History of *Ghost Stories*
By John Locke

THIS WILL NOT BE THE HISTORY OF GHOST STORIES, which are as old as human consciousness. This will be the history of *Ghost Stories*, an odd magazine issued by one of the most successful magazine chains of the 1920s, Macfadden Publications. *Ghost Stories* ran from July 1926 to March 1930, as a Macfadden magazine, after which it came under the control of Harold Hersey's Good Story Magazine Company, running from April 1930 to December 1931/January 1932, for a total of 64 issues. It had different aims than its contemporary, *Weird Tales*, but nevertheless failed to achieve the soaring flights of fancy found in *Weird Tales*, against whom it is bound to be compared. Neither was it a tremendous financial success. As Hersey said of the Macfadden run: "It had a short period of prosperity and then began to lose ground."

Still, *Ghost Stories* proves to be a deeply fascinating magazine, for unexpected reasons. It had a variety of editors, eight that have been identified, a high number for a magazine that lasted six-and-a-half years. They are roughly divided as six for the Macfadden run, with an additional two for the Hersey run. The instability, particularly during the Macfadden years, suggests that the magazine was an undesirable assignment, tossed around the editorial offices like a hot potato. The benefit of this, now, is that it offers an unusual insight into both the personnel and the operation of Macfadden Publications, much more than might be available from a long-running magazine with a stable editorial reign, a characterization that applies to most of Macfadden's bestsellers. *Ghost Stories* represents Macfadden's middle-ground; neither was it a long-running success, nor was it a quick failure, like the company's handful of weak attempts to enter the pulps.

The field of authors who contributed to *Ghost Stories* gives further insight into Macfadden's operations. The high caliber of the talent demonstrates the editorial standards that had to be met by freelancers. And because many of the *Ghost Stories* regulars, like Edwin A. Goewey and Harold Standish Corbin, were Macfadden staffers, we get a look into the editorial personnel, and also a view of how the content of Macfadden magazines was generated.

Rather than fold case studies of the talent into this introduction, we've provided separate biographical sections that fill in the backgrounds of all of the editors and cover artists, and all of the authors included in this collection.

We should point out that this is not the first time the history of *Ghost Stories* has been recorded. Will Murray has written about the magazine several times. The most thorough examination to date is Mike Ashley's introduction to *Phantom Perfumes* (Ash-Tree Press, 2000), one of the rare anthologies drawn from *Ghost Stories*. Ashley provided a comprehensive survey of the fiction in *Ghost Stories*, whereas our approach evolved to examine the magazine as an exemplar of the Macfadden magazines and organization. So there will be new information here, both in this introduction and scattered through the talent biographies.

It all starts with Bernarr Macfadden, the health and fitness evangelist who started *Physical Culture* in 1899. The magazine motored along steadily through the first two decades of the 20th Century, a leader in a niche field. Then, in 1919, Macfadden introduced *True Story*, a new concept in magazines. Rather than print fiction, which most mainstream magazines of the era did in whole or in part, *True Story* specialized in real-life experiences submitted by ordinary readers. "Truth is Stranger Than Fiction" read the banner on the cover of early issues. (In truth, some of the stories were written by Macfadden's editorial staff or submitted by professionals; and the actual reader submissions were rounded into shape by the staff. But Hersey insisted that, "The readers, contrary to sophisticated opinion, *do* write the stories.") Real-life experience was emphasized in several ways: the stories involved ordinary moral and emotional issues; they were narrated in the first-person, and thus are categorized as first-person confessionals; they were illustrated not with art but with staged photographs which fooled some readers into thinking the events of the story had actually been captured on film. The magazine was a great hit and within a few short years subsidized a major expansion of the company, making Macfadden one of the most successful publishers of periodicals for several decades.

In 1922, Macfadden hired a former Baltimore newsman, Charles Fulton Oursler, as Supervising Editor of the chain. Oursler and the eccentric Macfadden appeared to be complete opposites. Oursler was erudite with literary ambitions, and apathetic to matters of health; whereas Macfadden was earthy and practical. Nonetheless, this genuinely odd couple formed a mutually-beneficial symbiotic relationship, as if mind and body had united to form a complete organism. Macfadden had a capable man of letters to guide the expansion of his empire into areas for which he possessed no natural instincts; Oursler had a magazine-lover's playground, and an unresisting market for his copious literary output. Macfadden was set on a path that he thought would serve as a platform for political power; Oursler was on his way to becoming a famous editor and author. Oursler's stamp on Macfadden's magazines would be significant.

Since early boyhood, Oursler had loved the world of stage magic, though he lacked the talent to become a successful magician himself. He helped establish the Demons Club of Baltimore, an organization for magicians. Through his interest in theater and vaudeville, he became acquainted with famous magicians like Thurston and Houdini. With Houdini, he shared an interest in debunking occult frauds like fortunetellers, crystal-gazers, and mediums who claimed to make contact with the departed—ghosts. Oursler had already turned his magic-inspired musings into commercial fiction, publishing a series of entertaining weird mysteries in *Mystery Magazine*. Oursler's interest in magic lasted a lifetime and, though he was ever a professional and highly competent journalist, editor, and author, the haunted half of his imagination always seemed to be looking for opportunities to express itself.

Oursler initially caught Macfadden's attention when he supplied four items for the first issue of *Brain Power* (September 1921), a cerebral companion to *Physical Culture*. Macfadden hired Oursler as a consultant, then brought him completely into the fold by appointing him Supervising Editor in June 1922. *Brain Power* languished on the newsstands and was quickly, though temporarily, renamed the *National Pictorial Monthly* (and after that, *National Brain Power*). The April 1922 *National Pictorial* published an article by Howard Thurston, titled, "Do Dead Men Ever Tell Tales?," a consideration of the scientific validity of spirits. The May issue followed up with a new monthly column, *True Ghost Stories*, headlined: "Actual Experiences With Specters, Spirit Voices, and Prophetic Dreams—a New Department to Which All Our Readers are Invited to Contribute." The first column included editorial comment and "David Belasco's Story." A blurb at the end of the column read: "They saw a plume of flame rise from the Corpse. This is one of the

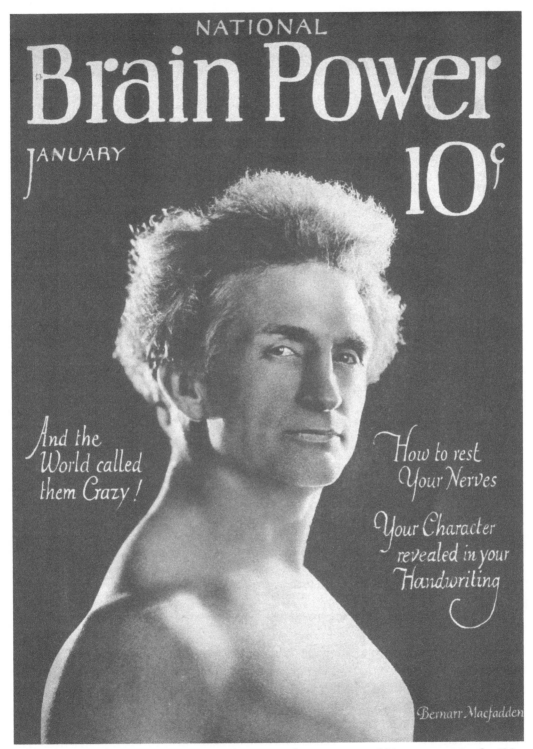

Nobody was calling him *crazy after the tremendous success of his company in the '20s. Usually adorned in the Emperor's New Clothes, BM's visage was a common sight on Macfadden covers. The publisher is the product.*

extraordinary TRUE GHOST STORIES which have come to us in answer to our appeal. They will be published in the June number." Editorship of the column was kept mysterious; the magazine referred to the column's "ghost editor." But there's no doubting his true identity. *True Ghost Stories* had melded consultant Oursler's occult interests with Macfadden's first-person confessional style.

As Supervising Editor, Oursler set to work immediately to get Macfadden's first weekly on the market. It was a thin tabloid called *Midnight* (later *Midnight Mysteries*) that debuted with a date of August 19, 1922. According to Macfadden's then-wife, Mary, Oursler said that *Midnight* "evolved from the theory that people who went to bed at a normal hour would want to know about the terrible things that happened in New York while they were asleep." The magazine contained plenty of pin-up photographs, including, and especially, on the covers. The content took a rather horrorful view of New York, with articles about prostitutes, death in the electric chair, jazz addicts, and other subjects that appealed to voyeuristic impulses. It also included a fair amount of supernatural fiction, some supplied by Oursler.

Neither *Brain Power* nor *Midnight* lasted long. *Brain Power* stumbled along under various titles and formats into 1924. *Midnight* fared worse, pressured into an early exit after several months by a summons from the New York Society for the Suppression of Vice. It was remembered in the Macfadden offices as "Fulton's Folly." But with his interest in the supernatural, Oursler was on to something, had he possessed the foresight or the means to act on it fully. In "Editorial Prejudice Against the Occult," in the October 1922 *The Writer*, Henry S. Whitehead wrote:

> Said a famous editor not so very long ago in writing to one of his contributors: ". . . but my dear fellow, if you are aiming to enlist against you the suspicion—nay, the actual *enmity*—of the average editor, send him a Ghost Story, a Fairy Story, or a Dream Story. If you want to be absolutely certain of such an effect, make it a Dream Story!"
>
> These three classes of stories may be said to merge into what is generally understood under the caption, "The Occult." And "the occult" in this general sense of the term is banned by most magazines. Authors who "try one on an editor" are apt to get their tales back in haste; yet there is the well-known fact that readers revel in tales of this general type! Moreover, there is hardly an author of note who has not done good work in this field, or at least tried his hand at "the occult."
>
> . . .
>
> Why, O why, do not the magazine editors give the people what they want?

It fell to another company to act upon Whitehead's ideas. In 1922, Rural Publications, Inc. was established by J.C. Henneberger and J.M. Lansinger. They hit the newsstands with March 1923 issues of *Detective Tales* and *Weird Tales*. According to Henneberger, the idea for *Weird Tales* came through discussions with writers yearning for a market for "the realms of fantasy, the bizarre, and the outré." Whitehead's article may also have been an inspiration—the timing is perfect, anyway. Whitehead was true to his convictions. He contributed many stories to *Weird Tales* from 1924 until his death in '32. *Weird Tales* became the leading publisher of fantasy fiction, and printed many tales of the supernatural.

Weird Tales wasn't the first venue for fantastic fiction, though. The Munsey pulps specialized in it during the teens. Street & Smith had attempted a magazine of the fantastic

July 1919. The magazine that launched an empire.

in 1919, *The Thrill Book*, but the concept had been poorly executed and the magazine went off the market after sixteen issues. It remained to *Weird Tales* to find a formula that would endure.

Macfadden was to issue other failures: *Beautiful Womanhood*, *Muscle Builder*, and several others that failed to take root. But when the company adhered closer to the mainstream of confessional magazines it had created with *True Story*, success came more assuredly. *Dream World* (1924), *True Romances* (1925), and *True Experiences* (1925) had long runs. Macfadden imitators populated the newsstands with first-person magazines. Macfadden issued the first true-crime magazine in 1924, *True Detective Mysteries*, and it became as influential in the market as *True Story*.

Meanwhile, the all-fiction pulp field steadily expanded during the '20s. Macfadden toyed with the idea of a western-fiction magazine in 1924, then finally entered the arena in late-'25 with the awkwardly-titled *Fighting Romances from the West and East*. It was in the larger, prestige size usually reserved for "respectable" magazines, rather than the standard 7x10-inch pulp format. It wasn't the first all-fiction magazine to take this approach. In 1923, Rural had tried it with *Weird Tales* (unsuccessfully) and *(Real) Detective Tales* (successfully). Doubleday enlarged the size of *Frontier Stories* with the issue of November 1925, the same date as the first *Fighting Romances*. Gernsback introduced *Amazing Stories* in the large size (first issue, April '26). So a small trend was underway.

The title, *Fighting Romances*, is telling. Macfadden drew much of its income from female readers. In addition to the romance magazines, *True Story*, and even *Physical Culture*, were distinguished by content that directly appealed to women. The female subjects on most covers were a dead giveaway. *Fighting Romances* was an attempt to keep both genders entertained. It looked like an action magazine, but it included romantic stories. For *Fighting Romances*, "romance" was defined as the romance of the outdoors *and* the romance of love-interest. The unlikely editor was Walter W. Liggett, a self-professed radical journalist who had been job-hopping among the major New York newspapers since 1923. Macfadden's motive in hiring him is unclear, but Liggett had just made his initial forays into fiction-writing so *his* motives are a little easier to fathom. As will become evident from perusing the talent biographies in these volumes, the Macfadden editorial offices in the '20s were a watering hole for accomplished, literate people. It probably had a reputation within publishing of being a place with a large staff, ever-changing enough to allow for ready employment to a person of general qualifications. At any rate, Liggett's role as editor ended after only a few issues, with staffer Harry A. Keller taking over. (Editorship of the lesser Macfadden magazines is difficult to pin down with precision. Editors were not highlighted within the magazines, and editor listings in the writers' magazines could be unreliable. See, for example, our Harold Standish Corbin biography re: *True Strange Stories*. Liggett's editorship of *Fighting Romances* is established by the initial listings in *The Author & Journalist*, and confirmed by the reminiscences of author Walter J. Norton in the February 1928 *A&J*.)

The eighth and last issue of *Fighting Romances* was dated June 1926. The first issue of *Ghost Stories* was July 1926, and there are several reasons to believe that when *Fighting Romances* was killed, its resources were simply rolled over into *Ghost Stories*. The timing of consecutive months is the most obvious; also, *GS* was another large-size magazine; its initial editor was Keller; and Liggett stories, which had appeared in *Fighting Romances* through the end of the run, continued to appear in *GS*. (The June 1926 *True Detective*

Fulton Oursler's first new magazine for Macfadden. This issue included his horror story, "The Stone Yard of Satan." Midnight's reliance on scantily-adorned women and scandalous material soon forced it off the market, after which it was known in the Macfadden offices as "Fulton's Folly."

12   Ghost Stories

Mysteries has full-page ads for both the June issue of *Fighting Romances* and the July issue of *GS*. The *Fighting Romances* ad promises a July issue, which suggests that the transition from *FR* to *GS* may not be entirely clear-cut, or perhaps that was simply some errant ad copy that slipped through.)

The Author & Journalist, June 1926, announced *Ghost Stories* as "a new Macfadden publication, using tales of weird and supernatural type," the language obviously meant to invoke comparisons with *Weird Tales*. We might speculate that three factors combined to create the new magazine. First, Oursler's dormant desire to present the public with occult material, a desire that hadn't disappeared with the failures of *Midnight* and *Brain Power*. Second, the staying power of *Weird Tales*, despite financial difficulties. Third, the continuing desire to publish a fiction magazine, despite the failure of *Fighting Romances*. Oursler's 1929 biography, *The True Story of Bernarr Macfadden*, states unequivocally that *Ghost Stories* was Bernarr Macfadden's idea, but that book was written to assist Macfadden's political aspirations and gives Macfadden credit for every company success. Fulton Oursler's son, Will, in his book *Family Story*, confirmed what seems to have been common knowledge within Macfadden circles:

> My father's interests were many, his paths diverse. Magic and magicians were still a very real part of his life. At Fulton's suggestion, primarily because of his own interest and extensive reading into the occult and the supernatural, Macfadden started a magazine called *True Ghost Stories* [sic].

The first issue of *Ghost Stories* could have been assembled quickly by the ready group of professionals in the Macfadden offices. The cover painting, of a ghost with fangs, looks like it was painted in an hour, at best. It's almost a recruiting poster, the ghostly pointing finger resembling the "Uncle Sam Wants You" motif of World War I. Oursler was as productive as he had been for the inaugural issue of *Brain Power*, with four contributions. The "George William Wilder" editorial was probably his; the "Arnold Fountain" story, "He Fell In Love With a Ghost," was a reprint from *Midnight*; he had an article under his "Samri Frikell" byline; and, as with *Brain Power*, he conjured up the first segment of a serial, in this case, *The Phantom of the Fifteenth Floor*, which could have been an original or a rewrite of an existing piece. *Phantom* was the only item to ever appear in *Ghost Stories* under his real name. Fiction was also supplied by other known Macfadden staffers, Liggett, Grant Hubbard (another serial), and Edwin A. Goewey. Other short stories came from Emil Raymond, who is another possible staffer, as the bulk of his known work appears in *Ghost Stories*; and Hubert V. Coryell, son of deceased Macfadden stalwart John R. Coryell (1851-1924), who was an insider though not confirmed as a staffer. A Frank R. Stockton story was a "classic" reprint. Two names, Al Clifton (short story) and Ann Irvine Norment (article), have no publishing records and were probably staff pseudonyms. Which leaves only two shorts written by genuine freelancers, Eugene A. Clancy and Jack Bechdolt. Clancy's and Bechdolt's contributions, minus illustrations, only account for about 10% of the magazine's content. The rest was generated in-house. Which goes to show the value of a creative staff. Instant magazine. Ninety percent staff-written doesn't represent the entire run, however. A thumbnail estimate indicates that at least 30-40% of the magazine came from the Macfadden offices. A more accurate estimate would require researching the backgrounds of all the many unfamiliar names who appeared in the magazine.

From a distance, *Ghost Stories* bears some resemblance to *Weird Tales*, but the comparison is superficial. *Ghost Stories*, during the Macfadden run, never overtly competed with *WT*, though there was some similarity of content. For example, *WT* ran Seabury Quinn's stories of psychic detective Jules de Grandin from 1925 forward. *Ghost Stories* had similar series, Victor Rousseau's Doctor Martinus, Robert W. Sneddon's Mark Shadow, and W. Adolphe Roberts' Hugh Docre Purcell. But *WT* was a pure fiction magazine; *Ghost Stories*, in blending Oursler's occult interests with the first-person confessional style of Macfadden's bestsellers, created a unique product. Will Oursler incorrectly remembered the magazine's title as *True Ghost Stories* (above); as did Mary Macfadden in her memoir of Bernarr Macfadden. It's a common error, given the many Macfadden magazines that did include *True* in the title. But *True Ghost Stories* could never have been the title of this magazine. The other *True* magazines wanted the reader to think that the stories were nonfiction, whether they were or not. *Ghost Stories*, because belief in an afterlife is a spiritual matter, implied that the truth of the stories was for the reader to decide. The carefully worded language of "In Touch with the Unknown," the first issue editorial (reprinted herein), is a case in point; it establishes its authority not in facts, but in the beliefs of others. The approach hobbled the content of the magazine, though. *Weird Tales*, because it included outright fantasy, offered a limitless imaginative realm to its writers; readers were only being asked to believe in the story while they were reading it. *Ghost Stories*, by constraining its stories within the realm of the plausible, or not too far beyond the edge, prevented its writers from topping each other with imaginative daring. Also, like its *True* brethren, *Ghost Stories* took aim at the women's market. The preferred subject of the cover paintings was the image of a haunted or terrified woman; and many of the stories had a love angle. For all these reasons, the magazine was held in low standing by the growing numbers of (predominately male) fantasy fans at the time, and continues to be regarded as an item of dubious merit. It doesn't even rate highly within the Macfadden orbit. In all the many books written about Bernarr Macfadden, *Ghost Stories* receives little attention; it's a minor entry among his larger accomplishments. Fulton Oursler's autobiography probably would have had more to say about it, but Oursler died in the midst of writing the memoirs and had only advanced the narrative to 1925.

Ghost Stories may not have appealed to genre fans, but it does seem to have sparked an occult trend in magazines. For instance, *Mystery Magazine* underwent changes in mid-'27. The title was changed to *Mystery Stories*; Clinton A. Faudre replaced Robert Simpson as editor; and a new direction was announced. "We should like to get in touch with writers on such subjects as Numerology, Astrology, Dreams, Chirography, Palmistry, etc." and "We are especially interested in ghost stories and other occult tales which have unusual ideas and seem plausible." In fact, *Mystery Magazine* had previously welcomed occult stories, but their "new direction" showed a heightened emphasis.

Tales of Magic and Mystery, edited by magician Walter B. Gibson, debuted with a December 1927 date. Gibson solicited stories "touching upon the strange, the bizarre and the unusual, ghost stories, horror stories, etc. It will also use articles on magic and miracles of the past and present, as well as spirits, spiritism, etc." The low-paying magazine survived a mere five issues.

Macfadden went to the well a second time with *True Strange Stories*, which managed eight issues from March through November, 1929, at which time it was met with the economic downdraft of the Wall Street collapse. The initial developer was staffer, and frequent *Ghost Stories* contributor, Harold Standish Corbin. He originally announced the magazine as simply *Strange Stories*. As he wrote in the September 1928 *A&J*:

> Strange things happen all around us. We want the strange, the weird, the grotesque, the arabesque, the outré, the bizarre, the extravagant and the odd! The strange coincidence that could happen but once in ten million times yet which does happen and is convincingly told. The incalculable surprises of life, whether in an incense-soaked temple to Buddha, or in the seventh-story back room of a Hester Street tenement, or in the palace of an Eastern monarch. In fact, happenings out of your own quiet life or at the ends of the earth. It is queer things that happen to human beings of which we want to tell. In these strange stories, the facts or plot may seem incredible, but the matter of telling must carry conviction. They will be told so logically and convincingly that at the end, the reader will sit back in thought and at last exclaim: "That certainly was a queer one!"

Corbin was careful not to include occult material in his solicitation. "We must not encroach on the field of *Ghost Stories*." Gibson was soon hired to take over the development, and edited the eight issues. However, he steered the magazine back into the *Ghost Stories* arena. The first issue, for instance, included stories like "The First Time That I Died," "Two Fierce Spirits Warred Within His Soul," "Cursed by a Voodoo King," etc. In the third issue, Gibson pitched in with the article, "Why I Am Called a Witch."

Mystic Magazine, which debuted November 1930 from Fawcett Publications and only lasted four issues, was a clear imitation of *Ghost Stories*. It was large-size, slanted toward women, featured staged photographs, etc. Fawcett's staff supplied articles on "psycho-analysis, astrology, palmistry, numerology, telepathy, clairvoyance, etc." Solicitations were made for "articles on clairvoyance, clairaudience, vampirism, ghosts, hauntings, spiristic phenomena, interviews with accredited mystics, Hex murders, spirit drawings, telepathy, adventures in the occult in foreign lands, and many other subjects which are allied."

Another short run, *Mind Magic*, issued by Shade Publishing, ran from June to September, 1931. It was described as "devoted to actual experiences of a supernatural or psychic nature," and also solicited "ouija-board and astrology stories based on facts." It changed title to *My Self* for two final issues, adding this to the solicitation: "Occult fiction is used, but stories should not be told merely to provide a thrill or horrify the reader. The purpose of the magazine is to awaken an interest which will lead readers to investigate occult matters seriously."

The trailing edge of this wave was Clayton's *Strange Tales of Mystery and Terror*, which *was* a direct competitor to *Weird Tales*. A standard pulp, it lasted seven issues scattered from September 1931 to January 1933. The initial solicitation read: "All stories must contain strong angles of mystery or terror, and they may cover the whole field of the supernatural and weird—vampire, obeah, mafia, ghost, reincarnation, spells working themselves out, werewolf, etc." ("Mafia" was probably a nod to the currently-successful gang pulps.)

In early 1927, Oursler had a surprise Broadway hit with his gimmicky play, *The Spider* (co-authored with Lowell Brentano). He immediately resigned Macfadden to pursue his long-held dream of supporting himself solely as an author. Harold Hersey, who had met Oursler after World War I when Oursler was new to New York City, was hired away from Clayton Publications to be the new Supervising Editor. However, Hersey "resigned" at the end of

Fawcett's Mystic Magazine *was a clear imitation of* Ghost Stories. *It combined occult features with staged-photo illustrations. This November 1930 issue is the first of four.*

the year, and Oursler returned unexpectedly to his old job. The details of the "switch back" were never fully explained by either man but, as subsequent events will show, no bridges had been burned. (The novelization of *The Spider*, written by Oursler's wife Grace, and published in eight installments, December 1928 to July 1929, became the longest running serial in *Ghost Stories*.)

As for *Ghost Stories* throughout the Macfadden run, under both Supervisors, the editorial approach remained consistent, but instability was in evidence in other areas. The first 25 issues were 8½x11½-inch 96-page magazines, similar to other Macfadden titles. With the August 1928 issue, it became a standard 7x10-inch 128-page pulp. The illustrations changed from staged photographs, which wouldn't reproduce well on the cheaper pulp paper, to the line-art common in pulps. The cover price remained an unvarying 25¢, as it did throughout the entire 64-issue run.

Format changes are usually indicative of a struggle to rescue a failing magazine's fortunes, and that's probably most of the story here; the pulp format was cheaper to manufacture, and positioned the magazine on the newsstands with the all-fiction pulps and away from the women's magazines, aiming for a different audience. But there is another wrinkle. Two months after reducing *Ghost Stories* to a pulp, Macfadden introduced *Red Blooded Stories*, an adventure pulp. Macfadden was making its first tentative moves toward exploiting the growing pulp field, and *Ghost Stories*, not successful enough in its large format, must have been the beginning of the experiment. *Ghost Stories* lasted eight issues as a pulp. *Red Blooded Stories* lasted a mere five issues, then changed title to *Tales of Danger and Daring*. With issues dated April 1929, both *Ghost Stories* and *Tales of Danger and Daring* switched to large size, further linking them as part of the same experiment. Macfadden made other forays into all-fiction magazines in 1929, but none were successful.

The new large-size *Ghost Stories* wasn't quite the same as the old one. It was 96 pages, but a half-inch broader in both dimensions. It was also printed on pulp paper, so the staged photos were not to return. This new format lasted out 1929, nine issues. It reverted to a pulp again with the January 1930 issue. The only concession to the original format was a 50¢ one-shot, *Spirit Mediums Exposed* by Samri Frikell, which reprinted a number of the Fulton Oursler *Ghost Stories* articles published under his pet penname. Large-size and 96 pages, it was printed on better paper and included photographs. *Spirit Mediums Exposed* is copyrighted 1930, but not otherwise dated. The cover is by Dalton Stevens, who painted many *Ghost Stories* covers starting in February 1930, which gives an approximate date for *Spirit Mediums Exposed*, since Macfadden was soon to be rid of *Ghost Stories*.

Before considering its new home, we should note another sign of instability with *Ghost Stories*, the editorship. A complete examination of the *Ghost Stories* editors is included in two separate sections, THE EDITORS and EDITOR AND WORD-RATE DATA, but to reiterate the main points, *Ghost Stories* used an unusual number of editors, particularly during its three-and-a-half-year run at Macfadden. This does give some insight into the Macfadden operation, where stories were selected by a vote among the readers, not by editor discretion; where editors were expected to be multi-skilled, to put magazines together, and to supply copy as needed, so that editorship was more a matter of assigning the available man to the job rather than the right man. As Fulton Oursler's brainchild, he would have been the natural editor for *Ghost Stories*, but as Supervising Editor, he had too many other responsibilities. That *Ghost Stories* never established a stable regime in his absence indicates that the magazine became of diminished importance in the company; it could be handed off to whomever had idle hands.

At any rate, as 1929 played out, shifts in Macfadden's ambitions were underway. Attempts to expand the company's line into the all-fiction field ceased for the time being. Instead, the company quietly financed Harold Hersey's new pulp publishing venture, the Good Story Magazine Company. After the failure of Macfadden's own pulps in 1929, Good Story addressed Macfadden's (and Oursler's) itch to be invested in the field. Hersey's pulps hit the newsstands in the final quarter of 1929; then, throughout 1930, several Macfadden magazines, including *Ghost Stories*, migrated into Hersey's control. *Ghost Stories* became a Good Story pulp with the April issue, with no change in format. The red Macfadden label on the cover was replaced by a lookalike label with the Macfadden name removed; most readers wouldn't have noticed that the publisher had changed. Good Story eventually put out 19 issues over 1930-31.

The inaugural Hersey issue led off with the first installment of a Fulton Oursler serial, *The House of Sinister Shadows*, published under the Samri Frikell byline. The story received the cover illustration, launching the Hersey era in style. Few readers would have caught them out, but the serial was actually a rewrite of Oursler's novelette, *The Mystery of the Seven Shadows* (*Mystery Magazine*, August 15, 1919). Oursler beefed up the text to add suggestions of genuine supernaturalism, a feature that *Seven Shadows*, which resolved its weird mystery with a rational explanation, lacked. It's possible that the Frikell-bylined *Spirit Mediums Exposed* was on the newsstand at the same time, to serve as a cross-promotion.

In the Hersey era, many of the regular freelancers continued to appear in *Ghost Stories*, Gordon Malherbe Hillman, Wilbert Wadleigh, Victor Rousseau; as did staff-editors Harold Standish Corbin, Edwin A. Goewey, and Stuart Palmer. Presumably, Hersey inherited unpublished inventory with the magazine, which would account for some of the continuity; Hersey may also have wished to continue using authors the readers were accustomed to; and some of the regulars may have been under contract. New names like Hugh B. Cave and Conrad Richter began to appear. It's unlikely that Hersey would have maintained Macfadden's edit-by-committee approach—he ran a much smaller shop—but he was never forthcoming on that point. Hersey's imprint starts to show itself in stories like Jack D'Arcy's "The Gospel of a Gangster's Ghost" (November 1930). Hersey and Good Story had made quite a stir with their introduction of the gang pulps, e.g. *Gangster Stories*, *Racketeer Stories*; so it was natural that Hersey would invite a new subgenre, the gangster-ghost story. Nevertheless, *Ghost Stories* was fading from sight. As Hersey said of its fortunes: "I did my best, but I was vain indeed to imagine that I could succeed where so wise a publisher [Macfadden] could not."

Stuart Palmer had been a Macfadden editor as early as 1928. He supplied numerous stories to *Ghost Stories*, as well as *True Strange Stories*. He continued to appear in *GS* after Hersey took over, which probably means he transferred to Good Story with the magazine. Palmer was announced as the new editor of *GS* in the August 1931 *Author & Journalist*. His solicitation announced the first major change in direction since *GS* began:

> Please call the attention of contributors to the fact that our policy changes at once to thrill fiction, away from true ghost and sweet stories. We require short-stories of 4000 to 7000 words, with atmosphere, horror, and chills; novelettes of 15,000 to 25,000 words, and articles, the latter upon assignment or after discussion with the

editor. No natural explanations are desired; nor occult or S.I.S. phenomena dope, but stories of the Benson, Machen, Wells, Doyle types. No articles to appeal to spiritualists, haunted houses or Egyptian mummy stories. We want grue and horror, but it must be deftly and lightly handled.

His own story in the July 1931 issue, the grim "White Witch of Stoningham," is probably the best example of what he was looking for, and indicates the magazine was going after the no-pussyfooting *Weird Tales* readers. It was a very promising development, but also a challenge since it required attracting a disparate readership from the current *Ghost Stories* audience. But since that audience must have been shrinking, the new direction was left as a desperate move to rescue the magazine. There are strong clues indicating when Palmer actually took over. The Hersey-era cover art of Dalton Stevens (then briefly, George Wren and Carl Pfeufer) shows a continuity of style, and subject matter, e.g. ghost images, women's faces. (See the COVER GALLERY in Volume 2.) The last issue of this period, August-September 1931, is the first bimonthly issue, another sign of slowing sales. The following issue, October-November, is probably Palmer's first. It retained the logo and the standard banner which had been used since the first issue: "Uncanny, Spooky, Creepy Tales." But the cover art was a radical departure, its experimental theme differing not only from previous issues, but from the vast majority of pulp covers. Stuart Leech's Art Deco design substituted symbolism for narrative illustration. And the acute angular features of the ghost face are genuinely scary, befitting the new direction. Leech's cover for the next—and final—issue isn't quite as extreme, but it does capture a scary pair of eyes and continues the modernistic approach.

Palmer's ambitions, however, were being thwarted by bigger business decisions, even as his initial issues were being put together. In the late summer of '31, Macfadden bought some of the assets of the failed Radio Science Publications (formerly Mackinnon-Fly), including *Amazing Stories, Complete Detective Novel Magazine*, and *Wild West Stories and Complete Novel Magazine*. This was Macfadden's last serious attempt to enter the pulp field. The new magazines were published under the name of a subsidiary, The Teck Publishing Corporation. When Macfadden withdrew financing from Good Story several months later, it was surely related; Good Story was failing and Teck made it expendable. Hersey responded by purchasing Good Story's assets from Macfadden. And thus did *Ghost Stories* become the outright property of Harold Hersey. It would be convenient to assume that Hersey's ownership of *GS* freed him to allow Palmer's new direction, but the timing doesn't support such a conclusion. The last issue of *GS* was a Good Story magazine, and the changes had been underway prior to Hersey's acquisition. Hersey continued to publish a number of Good Story pulps under new publishing imprints, but *Ghost Stories* was not to be one of them. It wouldn't have mattered much. In the summer of '32, Hersey sold off his magazine assets to a new firm. And thus did *Ghost Stories* become the property of Jay Publishing. Jay should best be remembered for continuing *Gangster Stories* as *Greater Gangster Stories*, and for producing the '30s true-crime magazine, *American Detective Cases*. The August 1933 *Author & Journalist* reported that Jay was "open for material to be used in a magazine of ghost stories. It may be in the first or third person and in lengths up to 10,000 words, but should be fairly convincing." Obviously, they were looking to exploit their ownership of the *Ghost Stories* brand, but their plans were never consummated. And thus did *Ghost Stories* fade from history.

The Editors

WE TYPICALLY THINK OF A MAGAZINE PUBLISHER as having a well-defined organizational structure: the company publishes magazines, the magazines have assigned editors who shape the content with their taste, judgment, and carefully-cultivated relationships with writers. A great editor possesses skill at balancing commercial with literary or journalistic aspirations.

There were numerous editors in the first half of the 20th Century whose association with a magazine defined an era, for example, Ray Long with *Cosmopolitan*, Bob Davis with the Munsey pulps, Cap Shaw with *The Black Mask*, George Horace Lorimer with *The Saturday Evening Post*. Upon Lorimer's death in 1937, the *New York Times* editorialized: "His name will be associated with an institution largely of his own creation." The editor was himself a creative force.

However, the Macfadden Publications, who issued *Ghost Stories*, wasn't run like the typical magazine publisher. The chain was marketed to the public as a reflection of company founder Bernarr Macfadden (1868-1955). An evangelist for health and fitness, a believer in his own greatness, and a creature of ambition, the label "A Macfadden Publication" appeared on the cover of every magazine. The label carried a subliminal message: Macfadden is a giant and this is a product of his great energy. Macfadden was the message and Macfadden employees were the messengers. All of the fame sat in one chair. Thus, Macfadden Publications had no foundation for famous editors and magazines with distinctive editorial regimes.

Macfadden had modest success with his original magazine, *Physical Culture*, established in 1899. In 1919, he introduced the first confessional magazine, *True Story*, featuring ostensibly reader-submitted first-person accounts of real-life experiences. It was a huge success and before long money was rolling in. Macfadden established a publishing empire, and introduced many more magazines, all of which highlighted his philosophy, featured his photograph, sold his many books on health and fitness, and turned him into the publishing giant of legend. But he needed someone to manage the increasingly chaotic offices which overnight teemed with editors, salesmen, secretaries, and all the personnel that growth begets. In stepped a former Baltimore newsman and aspiring author, Fulton Oursler, who became Supervising Editor of the company in June 1922, and remained as such for most of the next two decades. Oursler became well-known as Macfadden's top editor in the '20s, and even famous as *Liberty's* editor, after Macfadden acquired it in 1931. So we begin with a slight contradiction.

Oursler's contribution, in addition to overall management, included creating new magazines, and writing copious amounts of copy under his own name and several pennames. What distinguishes him from the Lorimers and Longs was that most of Macfadden's magazines were mass-market products lacking in genuine literary aspirations. Macfadden attempted to enter the "high class" field, on Oursler's urging, with the purchase of the failed *Metropolitan* in 1923, but the experiment failed after two years, and it was back to business. Most of Macfadden's successful magazines would follow the first-person confessional formula, which may have produced democratic copy, but fell well short of literature.

In fact, Macfadden editors were not given the freedom to select the stories for their magazines. Submissions were passed around readers in the office, scored individually, and the composite high scorers were published. As the process was described in a writers' guidelines leaflet: "Every manuscript receives careful consideration. Whether it comes from an unknown outsider or whether it is a contribution by a member of the editorial staff, it undergoes the same careful scrutiny by a trained corps of unbiased readers. In some instances the manuscript is read by as many as eleven persons before its fate is decided, including a board of ministers and an attorney." A Macfadden editor was more of a manager, making sure the issue got out on time, than a creator. Once the format of the magazine was established, the editor's job was little more than filling in the blanks every month. Harold Hersey described the nuts-and-bolts of a Macfadden editor's responsibilities in his 1937 memoir, *Pulpwood Editor*:

> The editor selects the best [story] situations for use as illustrations, standing over them while they are being photographed in the studio with living models. He writes the blurbs, the captions, the announcements; arranges the sequence of stories; sees to it that the serials have dramatic breaks at the close of each installment so that the buyer will want to follow the narrative in the succeeding issue; handles the reader departments and the fan mail.

Oursler created *Ghost Stories*, and more so than for any other Macfadden magazine, its content reflects his personal interests. However, bearing the larger responsibilities for the company, he was never the hands-on editor. It became, simply, one of his charges as Supervising Editor. He resigned the company for seven months in 1927, and was replaced as Supervising Editor by old friend Hersey. Oursler soon came back, Hersey left, and eventually, after Hersey established his own Macfadden-financed pulp chain, *Ghost Stories* became a Hersey publication. Thus Oursler and Hersey both had two periods with *Ghost Stories* under their supervisory control.

What follows are brief biographies of Oursler, Hersey, and the editors who actually had hands-on responsibility for *Ghost Stories*. As a special case, we've also included George William Wilder, the byline listed for editorials in the first fourteen issues of *Ghost Stories*. The sources which establish the names and dates of service for each editor are listed in the following section, EDITOR AND WORD-RATE DATA.

If the editors were given little latitude in shaping the qualitative content of the magazine, the obvious question is, what is the relevance of these biographies? We will not be able to match editorial tenures with shifts in the magazine's policies because the policies were static, at least until the late stages of Hersey's second period. To answer the question: as a minimum, these editors still contributed to the history of the magazine, even if their contributions were unusually constrained. There is also a secondary benefit to this survey. The examination of this one magazine, *Ghost Stories*, gives us is a microcosm of the Macfadden editorial offices, to a greater extent, perhaps, than other Macfadden magazines. There are eleven names in the chronological list below (including Hersey twice). If we throw out Oursler, Wilder, and the first Hersey, we're left with eight editors in a five-and-a-half-year period, a high degree of instability not generally found with other Macfadden titles. As examples, John Shuttleworth, a Macfadden reader, took over *True Detective Mysteries* from Harry A. Keller in late '27, and was still editing the magazine in the '40s; Helen J. Day, a Macfadden stenographer, took charge of *Dream World* in early '27, and edited it into

1934. These two examples would lead us to believe that promotion from within was the rule; that the company followed the prevailing one-editor-to-a-title model typically found in the business. But what the *Ghost Stories* instability suggests is the topsy-turvy nature of the Macfadden offices, where a title could be moved from desk to desk, depending on the workload and the number of active titles. Isabel Lundberg is an interesting case, on the opposite end of the spectrum from Shuttleworth and Day. Our only evidence that she edited *Ghost Stories*, or even worked for Macfadden, comes from a single February 1930 letter. Perhaps the responsibility fell to her because she was a new hire—low editor on the totem pole—and no one else wanted the magazine. Her experience suggests that *Ghost Stories* was a second-tier title in the company's offerings, more than a liability but less than a prize.

The unexpected conclusion reached from these biographies is that Macfadden Publications, despite its lack of literary legacy, was not run by mediocre minds. The editors, without exception, demonstrated a high degree of professional competence and accomplishment in their careers. Bernarr Macfadden and Fulton Oursler should be credited for many wise hires; how that credit should be shared between them is another question. Despite the obvious talents of these editors, however, few of them would be likely to cite their Macfadden experience as the high watermarks of their careers. Macfadden was probably considered a well-paying company for an editor, but still a magazine factory not capable of fulfilling dreams of self-expression.

Another conclusion is that the Macfadden offices were a crossroads. The biographies show numerous instances when these individuals knew each other before their Macfadden employment, and crossed paths afterwards. The company had effects well outside its boundaries.

The editors (listed chronologically):

Oursler, Fulton [Supervising Editor, Macfadden Publications, 1921-27, 1928-41]
Keller, Harry A. [editor, 1926-27]
Wilder, George William [editorial byline, 1926-27]
Hersey, Harold [Supervising Editor, Macfadden Publications, 1927]
Roberts, W. Adolphe [editor, 1928]
Bond, George [editor, 1929]
Wheeler, Daniel E. [editor, 1929-31]
Lundberg, Isabel [editor, 1930]
Howland, Arthur H. [editor, 1930]
Hersey, Harold [Publisher/Editor, 1930-31]
Palmer, Stuart [editor, 1931] (biography included in THE AUTHORS, Volume 2)

The editors (profiled alphabetically):

Bond, George (Doherty) (October 23, 1903 - May 25, 1986) [editor, 1929]: Bond was a prominent Texas literary figure who took a brief detour to New York to work as a Macfadden editor. He studied at Southern Methodist University (1920-24) under the guidance of Professor Jay B. Hubbell of the English Department, who had established a strong poetry curriculum. Hubbell initiated a national undergraduate poetry contest to be judged by nationally-known poets. As a sophomore, Bond's "Sketches of the Texas Prairie" won the inaugural contest (1921-22), taking first place in all three divisions (National, Texas, SMU).

In 1922, he married Mildred Elizabeth Martin.

In 1923, Bond was elected president of the Texas Intercollegiate Press Association. In the Association's annual awards, he won two third-places, in the Best Poem and Best Short Story categories. In 1924, while still a student, he became a founding editor (with Hubbell and two others) of the highly-regarded literary magazine, the *Southwest Review*. After graduating, he remained a primary editor and taught English at the university. Throughout the '20s, he published poems in national and regional publications.

In 1927, Bond moved to New York City, where he joined Macfadden's editing staff. We have no evidence to indicate what other Macfadden titles he worked on. He appears to have edited *Ghost Stories* for the majority of 1929. As a peripheral note, he was the editor of record when fellow Texan, Robert E. Howard, placed his only story in the magazine ("The Apparition in the Prize Ring," April 1929, under the name John Taverel).

After the Depression hit, Bond returned to Texas to help run the family farm, ending his New York adventure. He also returned to school in Texas, earned his doctorate, and began a permanent career as a teacher at SMU. For many years, he chaired the English Department. He returned to editing the *Southwest Review*; he also edited the *Dallas Morning News* Book Page. As a professor, he became an important mentor for student-writers, many of whom went on to pursue literary careers.

He died at the Baylor University Medical Center, and was buried in Hillsboro, Texas, just south of Dallas.

Hersey, Harold (Brainerd) (March 29, 1893 - March 17, 1956) [Supervising Editor, Macfadden Publications, 1927; Publisher/Editor, *Ghost Stories*, 1930-31]: Harold Hersey had a long career in magazine publishing and editing. He, like Fulton Oursler, presided over *Ghost Stories* at two separate periods. Indeed, he and Oursler were the only two people to have supervisory control over the magazine. The difference is that *Ghost Stories*, created by Oursler, reflected Oursler's interests, whereas for Hersey, the magazine was simply one of a stable. We wrote extensively about Hersey's life and career in "Harold Hersey: Tales of an Ink-Stained Wretch" (*City of Numbered Men: The Best of Prison Stories*, OFF-TRAIL PUBLICATIONS, 2010), and will not repeat all the details here. But the outline is as follows.

Hersey was born in Bozeman, Montana. Harold's father, "Doc" Hersey, a seeming jack-of-all-trades, became a newsman. The family relocated to Washington, D.C., around the turn of the century, and while Mrs. Hersey and two daughters stayed at home, Harold accompanied his father on far-flung reporting jobs. The elder Herseys divorced in 1906, and Doc died in '07. Harold worked at the Library of Congress for eight years while earning a degree at night at George Washington University. On the side, he wrote poetry and published amateur magazines.

In 1915, he relocated to Greenwich Village to write poetry, publish, and live as a Bohemian. After a stint in the Army during World War I, he returned to civilian life in 1919 looking for a real job. A chance encounter with W. Adolphe Roberts led to him being hired to edit an experimental new pulp for Street & Smith, *The Thrill Book*. The experience ended badly, but he soon rebounded, joining William Clayton's new publishing company as editor. From 1919-27, Hersey learned the pulp trade; and, as the company grew, Hersey assumed the position of chief editor.

In 1927, Fulton Oursler left Macfadden to become a freelance author. On his recommendation, Macfadden hired Hersey to fill his position. Under Hersey's charge were all the Macfadden confessional magazines like *True Story*, *True Detective Mysteries*, and *Dream World*, as well as *Ghost Stories*. For various ill-defined reasons, Hersey resigned the position in December 1927, and Oursler returned.

Hersey's next major step was to launch his own chain of pulps, the Hersey Magazines, which included *Flying Aces*, *Western Trails*, and *The Dragnet*. They debuted in the summer of '28. A year later, Hersey left the company to found yet another chain, the Good Story Magazine Company, this time financed by Macfadden. Good Story's most noteworthy product was the gang pulps, *Gangster Stories* and *Racketeer Stories*, which inflamed bluenoses and were a surprise success with the public. Both the Hersey Magazines and Good Story issued a dizzying variety of new titles, including many short runs, which left Hersey with a reputation for failure.

During Good Story's first year, several Macfadden magazines migrated from the parent company to Hersey's control. Thus did *Ghost Stories*, with the issue of April 1930, fall into Hersey's hands for a second time. In late '31, Macfadden withdrew his support for Good Story. Hersey took sole control. *Ghost Stories* was one of the victims as Hersey shed titles in a struggle to survive, finally selling his magazine assets in 1932.

Hersey tried to establish himself as a publisher several more time in the '30s, without any lasting success. He published his magazine business memoir, *Pulpwood Editor*, in 1937. From 1941 until his death, he continued to publish and edit as an employee of H-K Publications (humor, crossword puzzle, WWII novelty magazines), Charlton Publishing (popular music magazines), and then with H-K again.

Howland, Arthur H(oag) (July 25, 1873 - April 2, 1952) [editor, 1930]: Born in Mechanicsville, New York. Attended Hackettstown Preparatory School, New Jersey. Received a B.A. from New York University, 1895. Received a B.D. from Drew Theological Seminary, 1902; was ordained as a Methodist minister, but never took a pastorate. Did postgraduate work at Free Church College, Glasgow; the University of Marburg, Germany; and Oxford. Taught Rhetoric and Hebrew at De Pauw University.

Howland entered magazine work in 1908. Among the magazines he edited were *The Christian Herald*, *The Circle Magazine*, *The Forum*, and *The Square Deal*, a magazine devoted to social justice. A blurb in the July-August 1908 issue of *The Editor* listed Howland's fiction requirements for *The Circle*, which concluded with: "Wants no muck-raking, and will not emphasize the seamy side of life. Likes philanthropic movements in its work, and anything of an elevating nature."

He appeared to marry late, perhaps at the age of forty. He and wife Beatrice had two sons.

He was managing editor and publisher of *Psychology* until 1930, a period that may have lasted ten years or more. An ad in the March 15, 1930 *New York Times* announced a "Frank, Scientific" lecture on the "Psychology of Sex" by Howland, a "recognized authority on normal and abnormal psychology."

In 1931, he published the noteworthy *Joseph Lewis: Enemy of God*, a biography of the president of the Freethinkers of America. He spent his later years in mission work in New York City. He died at home in New York City, survived by two sons and three grandchildren.

Howland's connection to Macfadden appears to date from early 1922, when he took on the editing responsibilities of the *National Pictorial Monthly*, a temporary renaming of *Brain Power*. Later in 1922, he published several articles in *Midnight*. Though known primarily as a nonfiction writer, he published a smattering of fiction and poetry. The timing of his editorship at *Ghost Stories* suggests that after his position at *Psychology* ended, he used Macfadden for employment while working on *Joseph Lewis*.

Keller, Harry A. (*b.* 1894) [editor, 1926-27]: Biographical details are in short supply for Keller at this point, although we have a fairly good map of his career in publishing. He was apparently born in Philadelphia. He published an article in the October 1923 issue of *Metropolitan*, which may indicate he'd joined the Macfadden staff by then. He emerged as an editor when *True Detective Mysteries* debuted in early 1924, the third of Macfadden's "true"-style magazines, after *True Story* and *True Romances*. In 1926, he supplemented his duties by taking over *Fighting Romances from the West and East* from editor Walter W. Liggett, probably an attempt to salvage a failing magazine. Its eighth issue, June '26, proved to be its last. *Ghost Stories* debuted with a July issue, inheriting the resources devoted to *Fighting Romances*, presumably including Keller as editor.

Keller's reign as editor of both *True Detective Mysteries* and *Ghost Stories* ended in mid-'27, with *TDM* going to John Shuttleworth, who would be its long-term editor, and *GS* going to W. Adolphe Roberts. Keller may have left the company at that time, because he no longer shows up as editor-of-record on any Macfadden magazines. His next two years are unaccounted for. Enter the Mackinnon-Fly Company. They began as the Novel Magazine Corporation in 1925, publishing a single pulp, *Complete Novel Magazine*. In mid-'28, aiming at expansion, company co-founder Bergan A. Mackinnon, Jr. (with H.K. Fly) resigned his 20-year position as circulation manager for *Pictorial Review*; *CNM* was renamed *Wild West Stories and Complete Novel Magazine*; and *Complete Detective Novel Magazine*, *Screen Book* (film novelizations), and *Plain Talk* (primarily nonfiction) were created. By mid-'29 the company had been renamed after its founders, and further expansion was in store. This is when Keller resurfaced, as their primary editor. After the company purchased *Brief Stories* from Harper & Brothers, Keller was installed as editor. He may have been recruited by W. Adolphe Roberts, editor of the Harper & Brothers incarnation of *Brief Stories* since October 1928. Keller also took over the editing of *Complete Detective Novel Magazine* from Mackinnon, and added *Wild West Stories* to his responsibilities. On top of that, he created a new love pulp, *Complete Love Novel Magazine* which debuted with a January 1930 cover date. By the end of the difficult year of 1930, Keller was gone, replaced by Joseph Cox. A year later, Macfadden took over the struggling company, reforming it as a subsidiary, Teck Publishing.

Keller must have retained friendly ties with management, because his first-known magazine story appeared in the April 1932 *Complete Detective Novel Magazine*. It hinted at his new mission in life. A series of Keller novels soon began appearing: *Death Sits In* (1932), a murder mystery; *Sacred Sin* (1932), "an authentic picture of American nudism"; *Debtors' Holiday* (1933); and *Yesterday's Sin: A Nudist Novel* (1934). We might surmise that the writer's life failed to meet Keller's expectations, for the only remaining stories from his pen were shorts in the April 1935 *New Mystery Adventures* and the October 1936 *Wild West Stories and Complete Novel Magazine*. Instead, he returned to editing in late-'34 with a new magazine, *Official Detective Stories*, published out of Chicago. As a pioneer in the true-crime field with *True Detective Mysteries*, he must have looked like a great hire. His itinerant career had finally solidified. He edited *Official Detective* into the early '60s when, presumably, he retired.

Lundberg, Isabel (Cary) (June 10, 1903 - May 6, 1991) [editor, 1930]: Mrs. Lundberg may have been the least involved of any of the known *Ghost Stories* editors. Her sole connection to the magazine comes from a February 1, 1930 letter to August Derleth which she signed as editor.

She was a native New Yorker, a 1925 graduate of Vassar College. In 1930 she was married to Ferdinand Lundberg (1902-95), a *New York Herald Tribune* Wall Street reporter who had come to New York from Chicago in 1927. He became a prominent nonfiction author. The couple divorced in 1942.

Isabel is known to have worked as an editor on *Cosmopolitan* and *The Smart Set*. The last issue of *The Smart Set* was dated July 1930, so the foreseeable demise of that magazine may have led to her employment with Macfadden.

In the '40s, she appeared in *Harper's*, and other intellectual magazines.

"Isabel Lund" was used as a byline on two known stories for love pulps in 1943. Could this have been Lundberg picking up some extra income?

She earned a Ph.D. in 1957, then taught sociology at Hunter College, New York University, and the Fashion Institute of Technology. She died of lung cancer in Manhattan, leaving no survivors.

Oursler, (Charles) Fulton (January 22, 1893 - May 24, 1952) [Supervising Editor, Macfadden Publications, 1922-27, 1928-41; creator, *Ghost Stories*]: Fulton Oursler was a key figure in the rise of Macfadden Publications in the '20s and '30s, responsible for the creation of a number of magazines, including *Ghost Stories*. We wrote a detailed description of Oursler's life and career in "Fulton Oursler: The Magician Editor" (*The Magician Detective: and Other Weird Mysteries*, by Charles Fulton Oursler, OFF-TRAIL PUBLICATIONS, 2010), and will only touch on the relevant highlights here.

Oursler was born to a poor family in Baltimore. He was an avid reader as a child, both of the classics and popular literature. At age six, he was mesmerized by a magic act performed at Sunday school. Thus were his two main interests, writing and magic, set for life. At age seventeen, he landed a position as a reporter for the *Baltimore American*; he eventually spent six years as a music and drama critic (1912-18). On the side, to help support his young family, he freelanced to magazines, primarily nonfiction, but had some small success writing for the emerging pulp detective field, *Detective Story Magazine* and *Mystery Magazine*. Several of his magic-infused stories for the latter are included in *The Magician Detective*. Oursler was a founding member of a magic club, the Demons Club of Baltimore, and met famous magicians like Houdini and Thurston, but he lacked the panache to succeed as a stage performer.

In 1918, Oursler was hired as a reporter by *Music Trades*, a small New York City trade paper. He was soon promoted to managing editor. In 1921, his friend, Harold E. Bessom, former editor of *The Black Cat*, where Oursler had placed a couple of stories, had been hired on contingency to develop a new magazine for Macfadden Publications, *Brain Power*, a cerebral companion to Macfadden's flagship, *Physical Culture*. Bessom recruited Oursler to help with the outline. After Bessom was hired as editor, Oursler supplied four items for the first issue, two articles, a column, and the first part of a serial. Bernarr Macfadden was so impressed with Oursler's abilities, he eventually recruited him away from *Music Trades*. "I shall call you Fulton," he said, and "Charles" was forever after dropped from Oursler's name. By the summer of '22, Oursler had risen to the post of Supervising Editor of all the Macfadden magazines.

Macfadden had made his name with the modestly successful *Physical Culture*, and his vast fortune with *True Story* beginning in 1919. The immense profits from *True Story* allowed the company to grow rapidly. Under Oursler's leadership, magazines similar to *True Story* would follow, like *True Experiences*, *True Detective Mysteries*, the first true-crime magazine, and *Dream World*, a love story magazine. When Macfadden took over the higher-class *Metropolitan*, Oursler's literary works were serialized in its pages, helping to establish him as a name author.

Oursler never lost his love of magic. Houdini became a friend and the two shared an interest in debunking occultist frauds like fortunetellers. They both had a desire to believe in a verifiable afterlife; paring away the fakers was part of the search for truth.

Macfadden's confessional-magazine style and Oursler's interest in spiritualism merge together in the creation of *Ghost Stories*. While the magazine mixes fiction with "fact," the stories are told in the first-person. In content, they range from true-blue ghost experiences, to stories of shyster "crystal gazers," making *Ghost Stories* an uncanny reflection of Oursler's interests. He provided material for the magazine, of course, primarily articles on spiritualistic matters written under the penname Samri Frikell. However, as Supervising Editor of many magazines, Oursler had wide responsibilities. There's no evidence he ever personally edited *Ghost Stories*.

Oursler had a lifelong interest in drama, and, in 1927, had a surprise Broadway hit with the play *The Spider*, co-written with Lowell Brentano, of the Brentano's, Inc. family publishing firm. *The Spider* was a tour de force of novelty, weirdness, gimmicks, and spooky music; a murder mystery revolving around a stage magician's act. With the success of the play, Oursler immediately resigned the Macfadden company to pursue a career as a freelance author. Harold Hersey, who Oursler knew from his early days in New York, was hired away from the Clayton publications to fill Oursler's job as Supervising Editor. However, onerous alimony payments to Oursler's first wife, and lawsuits stemming from *The Spider*, resulted in Oursler's return after seven months.

In the late '20s, Oursler led Macfadden's diversification into the booming pulp magazine market, although Macfadden's pulps, like *Red Blooded Stories* and *Flying Stories*, were unsuccessful. In 1929, Macfadden subsidized Harold Hersey's new pulp venture, the Good Story Magazine Company. Throughout 1930, Macfadden magazines migrated into Hersey's orbit, including *Ghost Stories*, which debuted as a Good Story publication with the issue of April 1930. That issue led off with the first part of an Oursler serial, *The House of Sinister Shadows*, under the Samri Frikell byline, a last hurrah for Oursler in the field of pulp fiction.

Oursler's fiction writing turned up instead in hardbound mystery novels, the first of which was *About the Murder of Geraldine Foster* (1930), written under the penname Anthony Abbot.

In 1931, Macfadden purchased the popular national weekly *Liberty*, and installed Oursler as editor. *Liberty* was a leading voice in the '30s on many significant issues, the New Deal, crime and gangsterism, and the war threats brewing overseas. Despite his tremendous responsibilities, Oursler relocated to Hollywood in 1932 to write screenplays, while running the Macfadden operation remotely. The Hollywood adventure was unsatisfying, though, and Oursler was back east in March 1933—running Macfadden from his Cape Cod home.

Trips to the Middle East in 1936 and '38 slowly converted Oursler from a lifelong agnostic into one of the Christian faithful. He began formulating the idea for a popular biography of Jesus. Meanwhile, his stewardship of *Liberty* had made him one of America's best-known editors. In 1941, Bernarr Macfadden was forced out of his own company due to financial improprieties; with his mentor gone, Oursler resigned soon thereafter. In 1944, he reemerged as editor of *Reader's Digest*. In January 1947, his plainspoken biography of Christ turned into a long-running radio show, *The Greatest Story Ever Told*. His book of the same name was a 1949 bestseller.

When he died, Oursler was partially finished with his autobiography, having completed the chronology through 1925. It was eventually finished by Fulton Oursler, Jr., from his father's notes, and published in 1964 as *Behold This Dreamer!*, taking its title from Fulton Oursler's first serious novel.

Roberts, W(alter) Adolphe (October 15, 1886 - September 14, 1962) [editor, 1928]: Roberts was born in Kingston, Jamaica; his father was English, his mother, Jamaica-born of English parents. His father was Anglican chaplain of a British regiment. Walter was raised on the family coffee plantation. He was educated in his home near Mandeville, Jamaica, by his father and private tutors. In 1902, as a mere sixteen-year-old, he became a reporter for Kingston's *Daily Gleaner*. He jumped ship to a spin-off, the *Leader*. When it went under, he sailed for America, arriving in Baltimore on August 15, 1904. He first passed through New York, working for the *New York Herald Tribune*. Then he went west, and worked on the San Francisco *Chronicle*.

He sold his first stories to *The Overland Monthly*. Our earliest known freelance publication for him is a poem in the July 1906 *Munsey's*. He sold poems to *The Outing Magazine* and *Sunset*. Our latest known sales in this period are to *Overland* in 1909. He traveled in this period. He had several pieces in the *Los Angeles Times*. The first (September 24, 1907) was a poem, "A First Day in Los Angeles," which opens: "Roving, roving, ever restless, drifting on from strand to strand . . ." The last (April 12, 1908) was an article on West Indian proverbs which appears to be derived from material collected in his *Daily Gleaner* days. These pieces suggest a Los Angeles residence for this period. He also traveled, dates unknown, through Mexico and Central America, "where he held down all kinds of queer jobs and even took part for a brief space in one of the frequently recurring revolutions."

He returned to New York in 1911 and got a job as assistant editor of the *National Sunday Magazine*, a syndicated newspaper supplement. He was a member of Greenwich Village's literary renaissance in prewar years. His *New York Times* obituary described him as "a lightly bearded and Bohemian Village character," and "one of the finer chess players in New York." During the winter of 1911-12, he lived at Madame Katharina Branchard's "house of genius" at 61 Washington Square South, which had been home to a large number of writers, artists, and musicians. One of his friends was poet Alan Seeger, later to become known for his WWI poetry. Roberts kept a partly fossilized Indian skull in his bookcase. On Seeger's suggestion, the two delighted in telling the Madame that they drank from the skull. (Seeger joined the French Foreign Legion and was killed at the Somme in 1916. Roberts memorialized him in poems and articles.)

Between 1914 and '16, Roberts worked in *The Brooklyn Daily Eagle's* Paris bureau. He became a war correspondent when the conflict broke out. One of his colleagues was famed commentator H.V. Kaltenborn. A 1920 newspaper profile of Roberts reported:

> He was almost shot for a German spy during the first part of the war, because he appeared too near the front without his papers. He was only saved by the fact that he is a very French-appearing and fluently French-speaking person, added to the fact that two English correspondents, who had similarly broken the rules about proper papers, had been mistakenly shot for so doing just before he was caught—an incident which made the powers who do such things more wary, no doubt.

An *Author & Journalist* profile reported:

> He was on the battlefield of the first Marne before the fighting ceased, and pushed on with the French forces to the Aisne. Special missions took him many times to the front, and to Spain and England. Interviews with Clemenceau and other Allied leaders brought him to the front rank of correspondents.

In the summer of 1913, Roberts met Margaret Sanger, the birth control pioneer, in Provincetown, Massachusetts, a Cape Cod fishing village that catered to New York artists and writers. They began an on-and-off affair that lasted for several years. Sanger was married with children at the time, but a free-love idealist. Roberts never received the permanence he sought from the relationship as revealed, for instance, in this February 1916 letter: ". . . you are wrong, wrong, dear heart, in considering any reasons why we should not love each other important. We do love and should refuse to sacrifice even the smallest fraction of anything so beautiful and sweet." They both traveled extensively during this period, Roberts on assignment, and Sanger to avoid prosecution under obscenity laws for her 1914 magazine *The Woman Rebel*. Roberts' poetry appeared in *The Woman Rebel*. When Sanger established *The Birth Control Review* in 1917, he acted as Managing Editor, and was listed as Literary Editor into 1919. He contributed at least article and one poem to early issues of *Birth Control Review*. Despite the transitory nature of the relationship, they remained friends for many years. In 1917 Roberts married an American woman, Katharine Amelia Hickey (*b.* 1877). It's not clear whether Roberts' affair with Sanger coincided. We should note, also, that Sanger introduced Roberts to Harold Hersey in 1919. Hersey became her lover in time, and also helped edit *The Birth Control Review* (1921-22), which is quite a lot for two *Ghost Stories* editors to have in common.

While in France for the *Daily Eagle*, Roberts' work continued to appear in the *National Sunday Magazine*, poems and articles. This period is useful for tracking the shift in his byline. All his early work was signed "Walter Adolf Roberts" ("Adolphe" appears to be the correct spelling). The last known use of Adolf appears in the April 19, 1914 *National Sunday Magazine*. In the May 3 issue, he appears as Walter A. Roberts. In December 13, he's Adolphe Roberts. By the June 6, 1915 issue, he used Walter Adolphe Roberts, which became common for the rest of the decade, except for *The Birth Control Review*, which listed him as Walter Roberts. He appears to have settled on W. Adolphe Roberts in 1921, and that remained the name he was known under for the rest of his career.

Roberts' first known pulp story appeared in the September 18, 1915 *All-Story Weekly*. Thereafter, he occasionally appeared in the pulps—*Snappy Stories, Breezy Stories, The*

Parisienne, The Popular—with short stories and poems. He was hired by Street & Smith in the latter half of 1918 to edit *Ainslee's*. "Ours is a magazine without a serious purpose," he wrote. "All we ask of a story is that it be entertaining. We don't aim to uplift, and we shrink from spreading culture." Privately, he referred to it as a "trashy" magazine. Harold Hersey, who was introduced to Street & Smith by Roberts, described *Ainslee's*, under Roberts' guidance, as becoming "a much talked about periodical." Roberts edited *Ainslee's* for two-and-a-half years, during which time he rejected ten thousand short stories, he estimated, and five thousand poems. *Ainslee's* was known to be unusually hospitable to poetry, publishing as many as a dozen poems per issue. He maintained a high standard, and did not think of poetry as "filler," as was the case with so many other magazines. *Ainslee's* featured such well-known poets as Edna St. Vincent Millay, Harry Kemp, Richard Le Gallienne, and George Sterling. Roberts published a collection of his own works in 1919, *Pierrot Wounded and Other Poems*. It was issued by the firm that had been publishing Harold Hersey's books for two years, the Britton Publishing Company, suggesting a personal connection. Like Hersey did with *his* 1919 collection, Roberts included a poem about Margaret Sanger.

In 1921, after leaving Street & Smith, Roberts became president of the Writers' Club of New York, which involved him in the seemingly endless obscenity controversies from this era. He participated in anti-Prohibition protests. He became a U.S. citizen in 1921. He also was an associate editor of *Hearst's International* under Ray Long, although the timing is unclear. Harold Hersey followed a brief tenure at Street & Smith with the position of chief editor at William Clayton's pulp chain. When the company issued *Ace-High Magazine* in 1921, Roberts was present in the first issue with the start of a nonfiction series, *American Kings*, which ran for at least six issues and profiled a variety of Central American rulers.

In early 1922, Macfadden Publications planned to increase the amount of overt fiction in their magazines—e.g. *Physical Culture*, *True Story*—and hired Roberts as fiction editor for the group. There are two potential explanations as to how Roberts may have become known to Macfadden. Fulton Oursler began a consulting arrangement with Bernarr Macfadden in late-'21 and became Supervising Editor of the chain in June '22. Since Oursler and Roberts shared a mutual friend in Harold Hersey, the possibility of Oursler meeting Roberts, and recruiting him, exists. The second possibility is that Roberts was recruited by Arthur H. Howland, then on the Macfadden editorial staff, and a fellow associate of the Writers' Club. Roberts traveled to the continent in February 1923 to act as European editor for Macfadden's newly-acquired *Metropolitan* magazine. One wonders whether this may have contributed to his 1923 divorce from Katharine. His byline appears in *Metropolitan* as late as the December 1923 issue. While in Paris, he wrote his first novel, *Austin Bride*, and returned to New York in late '23 to have it published. The book never appeared. He may have been with Macfadden through most of 1924, as no alternative employment has surfaced. Upon leaving Paris, he subleased his apartment to four other writers, so perhaps he returned to reclaim it.

A movie lover, he appears to have relocated to the Los Angeles area, perhaps with fond memories of his earlier visit; 1925 shows him to be involved in film journalism. He edited a film-fan magazine, *Movie Monthly*. He also wrote a column, *Confidences Off-Screen*, for *Motion Picture* magazine. The column appears as early as the December 1924 issue, and as late as September '25. He also provided articles for *Motion Picture*, and at least one piece of fiction. *Motion Picture* started 1925 with Roberts' mystery serial, *Whose Hand?*, set in the film industry. It became his first published novel in early '26, under the title *The*

Haunting Hand. The *New York Times* dropped the axe, calling it "too stupid and hackneyed to be even the least bit impressive," although a regional review found favor, pointing out, "it is apparent that Mr. Roberts knows something about the cinema industry." (Roberts' collected papers include photographs of him with various movie stars, dated 1925-26.)

In late '25, Roberts started a new literary quarterly, *The American Parade,* a "magazine in book form." Its focus was "the glittering pageantry of American life—the circus going by the door, whether it be on the definite subjects of books, the theatre, motion pictures, art and music, politics or sports." Several Macfadden associates appeared in its pages, including editor Harry A. Keller, and future *Ghost Stories* contributor, Gordon Malherbe Hillman. It included a fair amount of poetry, of course. The magazine died after four issues, which were dated January, April, July, and October 1926.

After the failure of *The American Parade,* Roberts may have returned to the Macfadden editorial staff. The earliest known evidence of this is an article he bylined for the June 1926 *True Detective Mysteries,* then edited by Keller. Roberts started appearing in *Ghost Stories* with the second issue (August 1926). The story, "Told by a Talking Table," was bylined "By Hugh Docre Purcell, as told to W. Adolphe Roberts." Purcell was a fictional name, in the custom of *Ghost Stories* bylines. (Purcell was Margaret Sanger's mother's maiden name; perhaps not a coincidence.) He purportedly was an amateur psychic investigator— "But I'll say frankly that I haven't made up my mind whether I actually have been in communication with the spirits of the dead." The story concerned a ghost in the subway. Roberts eventually contributed nine stories to the magazine, and two serials. His seven-part serial, *The Mind Reader* (July '27 - January '28), was published as a hardbound mystery in 1929, and concerned Purcell's investigations into a Svengali-like mind-control specialist.

After the majority of his *Ghost Stories* appearances had found print, Roberts' name appeared in the record as the magazine's editor. This is another candidate for the date at which he joined the editorial staff. He edited *Ghost Stories* during 1928; and also edited Macfadden's *The Dance* for an equivalent period.

In late 1928, the pulp *Brief Stories* was purchased by Harper & Brothers, and moved from Philadelphia to New York. Roberts was hired as editor in October. (Harold Hersey had been a buyer for *Brief Stories* in mid-'28 and may have tipped Roberts off to the opportunity.) Roberts summarized the magazine's requirements: "We will use human-interest fiction with a romantic appeal and a melodramatic climax—adventures that might happen to anyone—the surprises of real life." Of note, Roberts ran the serialization of Fulton Oursler's 1929 novel *The World's Delight,* a story of old New York. After nine months, Harper sold *Brief Stories* to the McKinnon-Fly Company, and Roberts was out, replaced by Harry A. Keller. This essentially marks the end of Roberts' magazine career, and the start of his new career as a serious novelist and historian. He mined his experience as newspaperman and pulp magazine editor for the protagonist of his 1931 novel, *The Moralist.*

Roberts' second and last serial for *Ghost Stories* appeared later in 1930, however, when the magazine was under the control of old friend Hersey. *The Devil Doctor of New York* ran from October through January 1931. The blurb accompanying the first installment reads: "A young scion of Pennsylvania Hex Murderers carries their fiend formula to the Metropolis." And what more do you need to know? Roberts may have prevailed upon Hersey to buy the story in a time of need (Roberts' first serious books didn't start appearing until 1931); or, the story may simply have been part of the inventory Hersey acquired when the magazine was transferred to his new pulp chain, the Good Story Magazine Company.

In 1931, Roberts published a novel, *Mayor Harding of New York*, based on contemporary New York scandals. The byline was Stephen Endicott, and the publisher, Mohawk Press, offered a prize to anyone who could unmask the real author. A second Endicott novel, *The Strange Career of Bishop Sterling*, followed in 1932.

Roberts' last known pulp story is a short, "Dark Honey," in the August 1932 *Harlem Stories*, an extremely obscure magazine.

As a serious writer, Roberts published numerous novels and nonfiction works, primarily about the history and characteristics of the Caribbean, especially Jamaica, Cuba, and even New Orleans. Novels like *Sir Henry Morgan, Buccaneer and Governor* (1933), *The Single Star: A Novel of Cuba in the '90s* (1949), and his New Orleans trio (1944-48), were based on extensive travel and research. His best known historical work was *The Caribbean: The Story of Our Sea of Destiny* (1940). He lectured extensively on historical subjects and Jamaican politics.

In the '40s, he wrote several books about the U.S. Navy. His co-author on *The Book of the Navy* (1944) was Lowell Brentano, Fulton Oursler's co-author on the hit play *The Spider* (1927).

In 1936, Roberts founded the Jamaica Progressive League, an association of Jamaican-Americans dedicated to Jamaican independence; a movement which realized its goal mere months before his death. He was involved in a number of Jamaican organizations, including the Jamaica Historical Society, The Poetry League of Jamaica, and the Natural History Society of Jamaica. He was considered the dean of Jamaican writers. He received many awards for his service to literature and his native country. In 1955, Kingston gave him the Key to the City. In 1961, Queen Elizabeth honored him with the Order of the British Empire.

He passed away in his sleep from a cerebral hemorrhage, in London, where he was consulting with his publisher about his newly-completed memoirs, titled *These Many Years*; his ashes were returned to Jamaica and interred in the Mandeville Parish Church yard. The memoirs have never been published; the manuscript languishes still in the National Library of Jamaica as part of his collected papers. We didn't consult it in preparing this brief, so any lingering questions raised here may have answers buried there.

By the time of his death, his association with Macfadden and *Ghost Stories*, and with movie magazines, had long since been dropped from his resume. He was remembered as a serious novelist and historian. *The Daily Gleaner* memorialized him as an "outstanding Jamaican." His name is inscribed on the marble memorial in Poets' Corner, Royal Botanical Gardens, Kingston.

(At some point, Roberts was naively classified as African in heritage, which, if true, would have made *The Haunting Hand* the first mystery novel written by a black man. The classification was probably an assumption based on Roberts' Jamaican birth and advocacy of Jamaican independence. Roberts had a richer view of his homeland: "National cultures are not founded upon race, but upon a synthesis of the strains involved. . . . It is as mischievous to argue that Jamaica is a Negro country as it would be patently silly to say that it is Anglo-Saxon. Jamaica is itself." Roberts described himself as a Celt, although his Jamaican origin was of far more interest to him than his British background. In 1954, he wrote a prominent bookseller of African-American literature: "Please be advised that I am not a Negro, or of Negro ancestry. Will you please remove my name from your list."

His protestations notwithstanding, in some quarters he retains the African classification. Booksellers still demand premium prices for his "pioneering" novels; and, amusingly, some academic works express puzzlement over the lack of black characters in his mysteries, as if he labored under some Freudian complex.)

Wheeler, Daniel E(dwin) (March 1, 1880 - December 1972) [editor, 1929-31]: Wheeler was a native New Yorker, the adopted son of a mail carrier. He had varied accomplishments in publishing, of which his editorship of *Ghost Stories* comprises one small chapter.

In 1908, he edited and annotated the ten volumes of *The Life and Writings of Thomas Paine*; he also helped edit and compile the bibliography for *The Works of Charles Dickens, with the Life of Dickens* for The University Society (New York). In 1909, he was Managing Editor for the Young Folks' Treasury (The University Society). He was also President of the American Womanhood Society (NY).

Wheeler's creative impulses revealed themselves in a number of poems he sold to Street & Smith pulps from 1914-20. Most appeared in *Top-Notch*; a few others appeared in *New Story*, *Detective Story*, and *People's*, etc. In 1918, he was an editor for S&S's *The Popular Magazine*.

In 1916, he published an Abraham Lincoln biography for juvenile readers as part of Macmillan's *True Stories of Great Americans* series.

For some period, he edited the house publications for Thomas A. Edison, Inc., resigning in early 1922.

Wheeler's *Ghost Stories* editorship overlaps George Bond and Arthur H. Howland, illuminating the shifting responsibilities in the Macfadden offices. In his introduction to *Phantom Perfumes*, Mike Ashley cites correspondence between Wheeler and August Derleth at various times from 1929-31.

In April 1931, Bernarr Macfadden bought *Liberty*, adding it to his burgeoning empire of publications. At some point in the ensuing years, Wheeler served as fiction editor. He had a short story in the September 2, 1933 issue. (We should note that a J.N. Wheeler edited *Liberty* in 1925, but no connection between the two Wheelers has been established.)

In 1935, globetrotting journalist Lowell Thomas started *Saga*, "The Adventurers' Magazine." Though listed as editor, the actual work was performed by Wheeler. In the following year, Wheeler was President of New York's Adventure Society, an organization established to "stimulate interest in travel, exploration and adventure." This may have grown out of his position with *Saga*.

Our remaining credit for Wheeler is as editor of *The Manual of Child Development* in 1955, again with The University Society.

Wilder, George William ["In Touch with the Unknown"]: This name was the byline on editorials in the first fourteen issues of *Ghost Stories* (1926-27) and appears unlikely to be the name of a real person. The only other known uses of this name are on three editorials in other Macfadden magazines of the period: *Metropolitan Magazine* (April '23) and *True Detective Mysteries* (November '25, June '26). It was likely a pseudonym for one (or more) of Macfadden's editors.

The leading candidate is Supervising Editor Fulton Oursler, whose full name, "Charles Fulton Oursler," is suspiciously similar in sound to "George William Wilder." As a novelist, Oursler often based characters on people he knew, creatively disguising their names.

For example, a character based on his attorney, Arthur Garfield Hays, was named Tyler McKinley Grant, both names formed from the last names of U.S. Presidents. It would be in character for Oursler to disguise himself in similar fashion.

Oursler churned out a variety of material for the magazines under his authority, fiction and nonfiction alike, writing under several names that we know of. Perhaps the strongest piece of circumstantial evidence is that the last known Wilder piece corresponds closely with the date of Oursler's resignation from the company. Oursler wrote Bernarr Macfadden in May '27 asking to be relieved of his duties, but probably didn't leave until his replacement, Harold Hersey, could be brought in; and Wilder's final appearance came in the August '27 *Ghost Stories*, many weeks after the copy would have been composed. After Oursler's departure, editorials were bylined "Robert Napier." (Oursler returned to his previous job after about seven months, but the Napier byline continued on all editorials.)

A secondary candidate for Wilder's identity is Harry A. Keller, who had an article under his own name in *Metropolitan*, October '23, and thus may have been employed with the company that early; he was also the inaugural editor of both *True Detective Mysteries* (1924), and *Ghost Stories*.

(George William Wilder is not to be confused with another peripheral name in the pulps, George Warren Wilder [1866-1931], who was typically known as George W. Wilder, as was his son, George W. Wilder, Jr. George Warren Wilder, Sr. was President of the Butterick Publishing Company when the pulps *Adventure* and *Romance* were introduced.)

Editor and Word-Rate Data

THE FOLLOWING TABLE contains a list of every known reference that indicates the editorship of *Ghost Stories*. The primary value of this data is to illustrate that Macfadden Publications was less formal in attributing editorship to magazines than most companies, and that *Ghost Stories* in particular was subjected to a high degree of editorial instability. Macfadden's editors were moved back and forth between assignments, and were limited in influencing the shape of the product.

We've also used this table for a secondary purpose, to show the listed word-rates, and associated data. See the key for detailed explanations.

SRC	DATE	SRC2	L	RATE	EDITOR	NOTES
AJ	26-06	LMT		"Macfadden rates," pub		initial announcement
GS	26-07					1st issue
AJ	26-09					no listing
AJ	26-12					no listing
GS	27-01	SO			Harry A. Keller	Joseph M. Roth (mg)
AJ	27-03	HML	B	2¢ pub		
WD	27-04	WM		2¢ acc	H.A. Keller	
AJ	27-06	HML	B	2¢ pub		Hersey becomes Sup Ed
GS	27-07	SO			H.A. Keller	Joseph M. Roth (mg)
AJ	27-09	HML	B	2¢ pub		
AJ	27-12	HML	B	2¢ pub		
GS	28-01	SO			W. Adolphe Roberts	Joseph M. Roth (mg)
AJ	28-03	HML	B	2¢ pub		
AJ	28-05	LMT				Roberts becomes editor of GS
AJ	28-06	HML	A	2¢ acc	W. Adolphe Roberts	
AJ	28-09	HML	A	2¢ acc	W. Adolphe Roberts	
C	28-11-27	Derleth			George Bond	
AJ	28-12	HML	A	2¢ acc	W. Adolphe Roberts	
GS	29-01	SO			George Bond	Edith L. Becker (mg)
AJ	29-03	HML	A	2¢ acc		
AJ	29-06	HML	A	2¢ acc	Henry Bond	
GS	29-07	SO			George Bond	Camille MacAdams (mg)
C	29-08-07	Derleth			Daniel E. Wheeler	
AJ	29-09	HML	A	2¢ acc	Henry Bond	
C	29-10-31	Derleth			Daniel E. Wheeler	
WD	29-11	WM		2¢ acc	Daniel E. Wheeler	
AJ	29-12	HML	A	2¢ acc	Henry Bond	
GS	29-12	SO			D.E. Wheeler	Camille MacAdams (mg)
WD	30-02	WM		2¢ acc	D.E. Wheeler	
C	30-02-01	Derleth			Isabel Lundberg	
AJ	30-03	HML	A	2¢ acc	D.E. Wheeler	
C	30-04-07	Derleth			Arthur H. Howland	from Macfadden
AJ	30-05	LMT				Hersey editor of GS
WD	30-06	WM		1-2¢ acc	Arthur H. Howland	

SRC	DATE	SRC2	L	RATE	EDITOR	NOTES
GS	30-07	SO			Arthur H Howland	Edith L. Becker (mg)
AJ	30-06	HML	A	1¢ up acc	Harold Hersey	
AJ	30-09	HML	A	1¢ up acc	Harold Hersey	
AJ	30-12	HML	A	1¢ up acc	Harold Hersey	
GS	31-01	SO			Harold Hersey	
WD	31-01	WM		1-2¢ acc	Arthur H. Rowland	
C	31-01-06	Derleth			Daniel E. Wheeler	from Good Story
C	31-01-15	Derleth			Daniel E. Wheeler	from Good Story
C	31-01-20	Derleth			Daniel E. Wheeler	from Good Story
C	31-02-13	Derleth			Daniel E. Wheeler	from Good Story
AJ	31-03	HML	A	1¢ up acc	Harold Hersey	
C	31-03-31	Derleth			Daniel E. Wheeler	from Good Story
AJ	31-06	HML	A	1¢ up acc	Dan Wheeler	
C	31-06-16	Derleth			Stuart Palmer	Macfadden letterhead
GS	31-07	SO			Harold Hersey	
C	31-07-07	Derleth			Stuart Palmer	Good Story letterhead
WD	31-08	Lichtblau			Dan Wheeler	
AJ	31-08	LMT		1-2¢ 30d	Stuart Palmer	new policy
C	31-08-13	Derleth			Stuart Palmer	GS to be discontinued
AJ	31-09					no listing
AJ	31-10	LMT				discontinuation announcement
GS	31-10/11	SO			Harold Hersey	
AJ	31-12	HML	B		Harold Hersey	not in market
GS	31-12/32-01					last issue

• Key •

SRC (source)

AJ	*The Author & Journalist*
C	correspondence
GS	*Ghost Stories*
WD	*Writer's Digest*

DATE (y-m-d; slash indicates bimonthly issue)

SRC2 (detailed source identification)

Derleth	Author August Derleth's papers contain a number of rejection letters from *Ghost Stories*, signed by the editor.
HML	Handy Market List: A quarterly, comprehensive listing of freelance markets listing basic data like publisher, address, editor, word-rate, etc.
Lichtblau	An article by Joseph Lichtblau
LMT	Literary Market Tips: A monthly feature describing the editorial requirements of various magazines.
SO	Statement of Ownership: A block of legally-mandated text identifying a magazine's ownership and management, including editor. *Ghost Stories* ran this block ten times, approximately twice a year.
WM	The Writer's Market: A monthly feature describing the editorial requirements of various magazines.

L (list)

The Author & Journalist subdivided magazine markets into three classes:

A   Mainstream periodicals that paid market rates with a pay-on-acceptance policy.

B   Less desirable markets which paid low rates, had a pay-on-publication policy, or accepted little freelance material.

C   Trade publications.

RATE

Listed word-rates, and payment policy (publication or acceptance). Macfadden was a big publisher but, for a period, they paid authors on publication, a policy more likely to be found with smaller, or fly-by-night, publishers. Macfadden's pay-on-publication policy created conflicts with authors since their income was held up indefinitely. Including the data here shows when the policy shifted.

30d   30 days

EDITOR

Listed editor; Managing Editor (mg), if different from literary editor, is listed under **NOTES**. Misspellings, abbreviations and nicknames have been retained to show the origins of previous misinformation on this subject.

NOTES

Additional details listed in the source, or other explanatory information. "From Macfadden" or "from Good Story" indicates the source of the correspondence. This is only interesting because Macfadden letterhead was used after *Ghost Stories* was transferred to Good Story, showing how the resources of the two companies were mingled.

Statistics

Based on classifications from the *Science Fiction, Fantasy, & Weird Fiction Magazine Index: 1890-1998*, by Stephen T. Miller & William G. Contento (CD, Locus Press, 1999).

ISSUES (July 1926 - December 1931/January 1932)	**64**

NON-SERIALIZED FICTION

Short stories	517
Novelettes or longer	12
TOTAL	**529**

SERIALS

2-part	12
3-part	5
4-part	13
5-part	8
6-part	6
7-part	2
8-part (*The Spider*)	1
TOTAL	**47**

Total items of fiction (complete serial counted as one)	577
Total items of fiction (serial part counted as one)	719
Average items of fiction per issue (serial part counted as one)	11.2

MISCELLANEOUS

Nonfiction items	148
Editorials	44
Poems	1

TOTAL ITEMS	**911**
Average combined items per issue (serial part counted as one)	14.2

The Authors (Volume 1)

FOLLOWING ARE BRIEF BIOGRAPHIES, AS THE SECRETIVE PAST PERMITS, of the authors whose stories are collected here. A few of the names will be familiar to modern readers; many will not. The main purpose here is not to rank these people in the grand scheme of history, or to necessarily restore unjustly forgotten legacies, as it is to give an impression of the caliber of people drawn to the magazine. In a surprising number of cases, we find that *Ghost Stories* contributors possessed strong intellectual and literary achievements, either at the time of their contribution or in the form of potential yet to be demonstrated. Like the *Ghost Stories* editors, they're a distinguished group.

Many of the stories in the magazine were bylined by a narrator and an author. With one known exception (noted in the Guy Fowler bio), the narrators of the "as told to" stories in the magazine could not be matched to real people, confirming our suspicions that they were names invented to lend the illusion of true stories.

The bulk of the information comes from newspaper reports, obituaries, and public records. The online FictionMags Index, and published and private indexes, provide much of the publication records. Douglas A. Anderson encouraged us to include Leonard Cline, and provided significant help with his biography, as well as with the biography of Edmund Snell.

Note that this section only includes the biographies of the authors collected in this volume, with the exception of Gordon Malherbe Hillman, who has stories in both volumes and is profiled in Volume 2.

Bigelow, C.B. (dates unknown) ["The Ghost Light"]: No information. Only known publication.

Cline, Leonard (Lanson) (May 11, 1893 - ~January 15, 1929) ["Sweetheart of the Snows"]: Cline was born in Bay City, Michigan, but grew up in Detroit. After his father's death in 1904, he, his mother, and older sister moved to Ann Arbor. He attended a Jesuit high school in Montreal. In the Fall of 1910, he began studies at the University of Michigan, Ann Arbor. He dropped out after three years and married a Michigan woman, (Mary) Louise Smurthwaite (1893-1980), in October 1913. Within several years two children were born, a daughter, Mary Louise (1914-95), and a son, Leonard Lanson (*b.* 1916). Cline went into newspaper work, and wrote poems on the side for poetry journals. His first book was a collection, *Poems* (The Poet Lore Company, Boston, 1914). He worked for *The Detroit News* from 1916-22, starting as a reporter, and ending as an arts editor. His life to this point uncannily mirrors Fulton Oursler's, several months his senior, who rose from reporter to art critic for the *Baltimore American*.

In early 1922, H.L. Mencken lured Cline east for a job on the *Baltimore Sun*. On the side, Cline sold material to *The Smart Set*, *The Nation*, *The New Republic*, and other magazines.

Louise divorced him in 1924 for adultery. She kept the children and stayed in Baltimore. Cline's second marriage, to a Detroit woman, writer Katharine Doolittle Gridley, had its origin in the *Detroit News* period. They had no children.

After Baltimore, Cline went to New York to join the staff of the *New York World*. He shared an apartment with novelist James M. Cain. Cline's boss at the *World* called him a "wonderfully good reporter when sober." From New York, he went to the *St. Louis Post-Dispatch*, serving as literary editor, then returned to New York prior to the publication of his first novel, *God Head* (1925), in August 1925. Set among Finnish settlers of Michigan's Upper Peninsula, and incorporating legends from the Finnish epic poem, the *Kalevala*, the protagonist of *God Head* seeks to become a superman.

Cline then moved on to the *Chicago Daily News* before moving to Greenwich Village in the summer of 1926. His second novel, *Listen, Moon!* (1926), a well-reviewed burlesque about an aging literature professor involved in a treasure hunt on the Chesapeake. Cline was building a strong literary reputation. He also branched out into playwriting, co-authoring *Daisies Won't Tell* with Owen Winters, a former University of Michigan classmate. It was sold to Broadway producers, played in Boston and Stamford in December 1926, but never made it to the Great White Way.

Also in December '26, the Clines bought a five-acre farm with house near Willamantic and Mansfield, Connecticut. They named it Chicory Hill.

May 1, 1927 gives the first indication that Cline's promise was about to take a turn for the worst. He and a friend from New York, Wilfred Irwin, had "been spending several days in boisterous seclusion" at Chicory Hill. Irwin was an insurance salesman with an interest in literature. He also shared with Cline a propensity for excessive drinking. On the 1st, Mrs. Cline left the estate for New York, presumably to flee their bad behavior. Later that day, Cline called the police and had Irwin arrested following an altercation which apparently lasted six hours. Irwin was the larger of the two, and the police noted that Cline was badly battered. Both men were intoxicated. The following morning Cline showed up at the jail, claiming that it had all been a misunderstanding. He paid the fine and Irwin was given a suspended sentence.

The Chicory Hill drinking party apparently resumed. Mrs. Irwin came up from Brooklyn for a weekend, departing on Sunday, May 15. A few hours later, Cline called for an ambulance. The orderly who arrived found Cline with a shotgun in his hands, and Irwin with a severe wound in his side. Both Cline and Irwin claimed that it had been an accident. Irwin was rushed to the hospital, and Cline gave his own blood to Irwin in a transfusion. Nevertheless, Irwin died after sixteen hours late Monday.

Mrs. Irwin told the coroner that when Cline drank, he had jealous hallucinations, that he imagined a "flirtation" between Irwin and Katharine Cline. The evidence easily refuted the claim of an accidental shooting: Irwin had been shot at close range; shells were found in the yard; windows of the home had been shattered.

Cline's reputation was sufficient to make the death, and its legal aftermath, a national news story. While languishing in jail awaiting trial on first-degree murder, the press erroneously reported that Cline finished his third novel, *The Dark Chamber*. Actually, he had completed it before the shooting, but worked on other novels, stories, and plays while incarcerated. *The Dark Chamber* is a fantasy of a man who becomes obsessed with delving into his ancestral memory. It's revered by connoisseurs of weird fiction. H.P. Lovecraft praised it as "extremely high in artistic stature."

In September 1927, while the ink was still wet from the good reviews for *The Dark Chamber*, Cline went on trial. After a jury was selected, in a surprise, Cline pleaded guilty to involuntary manslaughter, which prevented the full facts of the case from becoming public. He was sentenced to a $1000 fine and a year in jail. Around January, he appeared to fall apart. The serious writing stopped. He had a religious crisis, and renewed the Catholic faith of his youth. Katharine, who had attended the trial and was visibly emotional at times, deserted him and moved back with her parents in Detroit. Cline was released early for good behavior in July 1928, after serving ten months. He lived at Chicory Hill with an artist friend.

Many of Cline's jail-written stories were produced for the pulps in early-'28, to raise money for Chicory Hill's expenses. All were published under the penname Alan Forsyth, an abbreviation of his maternal grandfather's name, Oscar Fitzalan Forsyth. The first known story to reach print was a five-part serial, *The Cult Murders*, which began in the July 28, 1928 issue of *Detective Fiction Weekly*. Other tales appeared in *Mystery Stories*, *Complete Detective Novel Magazine*, and *Air Trails*.

"Sweetheart of the Snows" hit the August '28 issue of *Ghost Stories*. It bears some resemblance to Algernon Blackwood's story "The Glamour of the Snow." In letters to his daughter, Cline mentioned the story: " 'The Lady of Frozen Death' [original title] is a ghost story, which will appear, quite appropriately, in *Ghost Stories* magazine. When, I know not and care less." (April 12, 1928); and "As for the ghost story, darling, I haven't taken the trouble to get a copy for myself. I felt rather badly about that story. It was a good idea, and if I had handled it properly it would have made a beautiful, fantastic piece. But when you begin to try to get money for your writing, you have to make it cheap." (July 9, 1928).

After his release, Cline freelanced and also wrote for *Time*. In the summer of '28, he reconciled with his first wife, Louise. They planned to remarry when Cline got his finances squared away. In late-'28, he took a studio apartment in Greenwich Village because he was having trouble working at the farm.

On Tuesday, January 15, 1929, he threw a party to celebrate the $400 sale of a scenario co-written with Louis Lacy Stevenson, a syndicated newspaper columnist and long-time contributor of detective stories to *Flynn's*. At the event, Cline complained of heart pain. It was the last place he was seen alive. In the following days, a maid knocked on the door, received no answer, and peeked in to see him laying on the bed. She assumed he was sleeping because he often worked late on manuscripts; she'd been instructed not to disturb him. On Sunday, other tenants eventually deduced that he was dead. Heart disease was the official diagnosis.

Manuscripts were piled about the apartment. A miniature Christmas tree lay on the floor where it had fallen off a table, with broken ornaments scattered. The manuscript of a completed short story, "Shuffle-Thump, in the Dark," sat on the table. The story turned up in the March 1929 *Mystery Stories*. One last serial found print: *I Come Creeping* (*Detective Fiction Weekly*, August 24 - September 21, 1929). A handful of unpublished stories remained.

To quote from "Darkness" in his 1914 collection *Poems*:

> Late in the morning, still abed,
> I lie a-wearied, and my head
> Is filled with dreams, that I were dead—

Corbin, Harold Standish (March 4, 1888 - May 6, 1947) ["Sardonic Laughter"]: Corbin was a member of an old Connecticut family, the middle child of three; he traced his lineage to Myles Standish of the Plymouth Colony. Putnam, Connecticut was his residence as a teenager, where he was active with boys' clubs and a church choir.

His career shows many jobs in the newspaper business, including printer, but the sequence and durations are unclear. His first jobs were undoubtedly with local papers. He was on the editorial staff of the *Windham County Observer*, where Putnam is located. He started as a reporter for *The Worcester Telegram*, Massachusetts, about 25 miles north of Putnam, then worked his way up to city editor. Later, he was assistant Sunday editor for the *Syracuse Telegram*. The big city beckoned. He was on the staff of *The New York Herald*, and then *The Herald Tribune*.

In the World War, he was a lieutenant in the infantry.

On January 9, 1925, he married Charlotte Mennen Hatterman of Brooklyn, where the marriage took place. At that time, he was editor of *Mooseheart Magazine*, the organ of the Loyal Order of Moose, headquartered just west of Chicago in Mooseheart, "the Child City of the Moose," a large-scale orphanage made up of the children of deceased Moose members, which is still in operation. (No trivial publication, *Mooseheart Magazine* had a monthly circulation of 763,000 in 1927.) Corbin's first known published fiction appears in 1925, two short pieces for *The New Yorker*. About that time, he joined the Macfadden editorial staff. He contributed an article to the April 1926 *Physical Culture*, "The City Where Children *Rarely* Die," the story of Mooseheart. In 1926, as late as July, he was the editor for *Physical Culture*. Starting with the February 1927 issue, Corbin made many contributions to *Ghost Stories*, most under his own name; several times, he had two stories in an issue, but the second was always bylined with a pseudonym. His tales for *Ghost Stories* constitute the bulk of his known career as a fictionist. He had stories in another Macfadden title, *Flying Stories* (1929). He had very few published stories outside of the Macfadden orbit, e.g. *Complete Stories* (November 1927), *Real Detective Tales and Mystery Stories* (March 1928), *Brief Stories* (January 1930) when it was edited by W. Adolphe Roberts. He had a short story in the rare one-shot pulp, *Wall Street Stories* (March 1929). In 1927, the Sunday magazine of *The New York World* began soliciting for original short story submissions. Out of 6,000 submissions, Corbin's "The He-Man" was the first one selected and appeared in the September 11, 1927 edition.

Macfadden announced a new magazine in late '28, *Strange Stories*, to be edited by Corbin. The *Author & Journalist* solicitation (September 1928) read: "We want the strange, the weird, the grotesque, the arabesque, the outré, the bizarre, the extravagant and the odd!" It hit the newsstands as *True Strange Stories*, lasting for eight issues from March to November 1929, with Corbin as the sole listed editor. However, the story of *True Strange Stories* is more complicated. Walter Gibson, future author of the *Shadow* novels, wrote extensively about *his* editorship of *True Strange*. He took over the magazine while still in development and, in consultation with Fulton Oursler, produced all eight issues, and provided copy. His recollections are not in dispute. This says less about Corbin, who probably spearheaded the initial development, than it does about the challenges in unraveling the true history of the Macfadden magazines.

We've found only two published stories after Corbin's last *Ghost Stories* appearance (February '31). One was the cover story of the September 1931 *Moose Magazine* (retitled from *Mooseheart Magazine* in 1930). He also had an article in the January 1940 *Moose*. He had either become a contributing editor to *Moose* after his Macfadden tenure, or had maintained his ties all along.

The second piece of fiction was a romance sold for newspaper syndication in 1934. That was the year he joined the staff of The United Feature Syndicate, editing the syndicate's picture page. He was still with the syndicate when he died in 1947 after an illness of several months. He was survived by his wife Charlotte, a sister and a brother.

Dyalhis, Nictzin (Wilstone) (June 4, 1873 - 1942) ["He Refused To Stay Dead"]: Dyalhis' modest output includes about a dozen stories in an 18-year span. Eight were published in *Weird Tales*. His presence in *WT* has made him the object of avid attention from researchers, but biographical details have remained elusive. He's sometimes regarded as having a mysterious background but, in truth, his history yields as much information as most of his low-producing peers.

He was born in Massachusetts. His father was a native of Massachusetts and his mother was from Guatemala. He married, about 1912, to Harriet Lord (*b.* ~1874). At the time of his World War draft registration, 1918, the couple resided in Chautauqua, far western New York. In 1920, they lived 17 miles to the south, in Sugar Grove, Pennsylvania, with Harriet's mother.

His writing career appears to have started late in life, as he was nearing fifty. His earliest known publications are two eight-page westerns that appeared in *Adventure*, 1922: "Who Keep the Desert Law," October 20; and "For Wounding—Retaliation," November 20. In his introductory remarks in *Adventure's* column, *The Camp-Fire* (October 20), Dyalhis made himself sound like quite an experienced adventurer, if an undersized one:

Sugar Grove, Pennsylvania.

By profession I am a chemist. In years nearly fifty—in heart, about sixteen—my wife's mother says I've never grown up! One way she's quite right, for I am one of these sawed-off, hammered-down, weazened-up runts weighing—when I'm fat-and-sassy—from five to ten pounds over one hundred.

A long time ago I went to the South-west. My intentions were good—I was going to assay all the ore west of the Rockies!

Rex Beach wrote a book once called *Pardners*—in that book an old-timer says: "Thar's two diseases no doctor has any right meddlin' with—one's hoss-racing, t'other's prospectin'." He's quite right! I know! Assaying? Pooh-pooh! An old man, with more pity on my ignorance than I deserved, took me with him on the desert.

Bitten at a tender age, what hope remained for one thus afflicted?

Sure, I've done lots of other things since, but—I went one trip snapper-fishing in the Gulf when only a "kid-of-a-boy." I took one trip and only one "down-de-bay" out of Baltimo' on an oyster-dredger in the bad old days of the "pungy," the "bug-eye," and the "brogan-canoe"! I've signed out on more than one "tall water" cruise, but I invariably turned up missing before the return trip. Because why? Prospectin' was good somewheres up-country!

I've prospected for gold, silver, platinum, tungsten, several of the commercial minerals, and, above all, for gems and precious stones, including pearls (fresh-water variety), also, turquoise and ruby (domestic and foreign). Did I ever strike it rich? I'll say I DID! I'm worth exactly eleven million seven hundred thousand dollars—in experiences which otherwise I might never have had! Money? How do you get that way? I'm dead broke!

"Never made any?" Oh, yes, I did—but I used it! What am I to do when Winter comes? Before next snow-fly I'll be on the trail again. Following that—I should care! And the worst of it all is—my wife aids and abets me in my sins! And she's no slouch with a pan, a dry-washer or a jassacks! She can tie all "them" hitches—hackamore, hobble, diamond and squaw. Also, she knows a dang-sight more than I do about pearls.

He may have paid a price for his adventures as his WWI form reveals: "One eye gone; Other one good." That, and his age, no doubt disqualified him from service.

His first story in *WT* was the novelette, "When the Green Star Waned" (April 1925); another story appeared in October. He would never have more than two stories published in a single year. His lone *Ghost Stories* entry was nearly the last to appear somewhere other than *WT* (the last ones being a pair of gang stories, "The Whirling Machete," *The Underworld Magazine*, December 1933, and "Gangland's Judas," *Complete Underworld Novelettes*, August 1934). His *WT* stories reflect a belief in the occult, often involving reincarnation or travels in the "astral plane." They appeared at scattered intervals, the last published in the September 1940 issue.

In 1930, Harriet was a patient at the Warren State Hospital, a mental institution in the vicinity of Sugar Grove. Dyalhis remarried, and resided in Maryland, dying in Salisbury.

Eckley, Constance Bross (April 22, 1897 - April 20, 1967) ["A Ferryman of Souls"]: Born in Portland, Oregon; birth name, Constance Kingsbury Bross. By 1910, the family was living in Indianapolis; but references to Portland and the Pacific Northwest in "A Ferryman of Souls" suggest she grew up in the region long enough to remember it. She left Indianapolis to attend the University of Chicago, class of 1920. Her father, Ernest Bross, a career newspaperman, was editor of the *Indianapolis Star*. On October 26, 1918, she married, in Washington, D.C., Harold James Eckley of New Rochelle, New York, a 1917 Cornell graduate. The couple immediately moved to London on behalf of Harold's employment with the U.S. Shipping Board, which would have hindered Constance from finishing college at the time. In London, she took employment with the Information Service of the Allied Maritime Transport Council. By 1920, the couple was living in New Rochelle. Harold entered employment with a brokerage. In 1921, he was with the Traffic Department of the New York Telephone Company. One daughter was born to the couple in 1920, another in 1921.

Constance must have set her sights on a literary career, for a 1924 book, *History of Indiana From its Exploration to 1922*, described her as "creating an enviable reputation for herself as a writer." However, we know of only two magazine publications, a short in the July 1920 *Breezy Stories*, and the story collected here. In later years, she worked for newspapers and industrial publications in New York and New Jersey. At one time she was a correspondent for the Salisbury *Daily Times*, in eastern Maryland, where she apparently lived. For thirteen years, she was a reporter for the *Wilmington News-Journal*, and also contributed a twice-weekly column, *Circling Sussex*.

Harold was dead by 1965. At her death, Constance was married to J. Edward Brown, and bore the name Constance Bross Brown. She died of emphysema at home in Georgetown, survived by her husband, two daughters, ten grandchildren and three great-grandchildren.

Eddy, Muriel E(lizabeth) (January 19, 1896 - January 30, 1978) ["True Ghost Experiences: The Beheaded Bride"]: Muriel Elizabeth Gammons was born in Taunton, Massachusetts. Part of her childhood was spent in California. The remainder of her life was spent in

Providence, Rhode Island. She met Providence native Clifford Martin Eddy, Jr. (1896-1967) through a mutual interest in creative writing. They married in 1918 and had three children. Both Eddys stayed active in writing. Clifford published short stories in the pulps, including several in *Weird Tales* in the mid-'20s; he was a ghostwriter for Harry Houdini. Muriel sporadically published poetry, articles, and stories in a variety of publications; and was a prolific letter writer. The youngest child, Ruth Muriel Eddy (*b.* 1921), founded the Rhode Island Writers' Guild in 1950. Both parents served as president, especially Muriel with two decades of service.

The Eddys are best remembered for their friendship with fellow Providence writer and *Weird Tales* star, H.P. Lovecraft. They met him in 1923 and remained among his small circle of friends until his death in 1937. Lovecraft assisted Clifford with his *Weird Tales* stories; and, potentially, may have advised Muriel on her *Ghost Stories* piece. Muriel wrote a number of remembrances of Lovecraft, the most comprehensive of which is *The Gentleman from Angell Street: Memories of H.P. Lovecraft* (1961).

Fowler, Guy (March 4, 1893 - October 20, 1966) ["The Ghost from the Flying Circus"]: The most detailed biography of Fowler was found in his obituary in the *Eureka Humboldt Standard*. Fowler spent his last years in Eureka, on the northwest coast of California. The obituary makes a number of exaggerated claims about his life, so the *EHS* will be noted as a source whenever used.

Fowler was born in Bowling Green, Kentucky, the son and grandson of preachers. The *EHS* notes that he entered newspaper work at the age of sixteen (~1909), "at a salary of five dollars per week." They note that he was a World War I Army Air Force pilot, a fact bolstered by his many aviation stories, including "The Ghost from the Flying Circus." In the '20s, he worked for the *New York Herald Tribune*, and other New York newspapers. Further, the *EHS* notes that "in his earlier years [he] was a familiar figure on New York's famed Park Row, where the giant daily newspapers were consolidated."

His earliest known fiction was in Macfadden's *Fighting Romances from the West and East* (1926). Most of his modest fiction output appeared from 1926-31; seventeen items were in Macfadden publications, five were in other disparate magazines including *Boys' Life*, *Submarine Stories*, and *Brief Stories* when it was in the hands of former *Ghost Stories* editor W. Adolphe Roberts. *Ghost Stories* and Macfadden's *Flying Stories* were his major markets.

Fowler had nine stories in *GS*. They covered a variety of topics. The first, "The Curse that Crossed the World" (October 1927) had a French Foreign Legion background. "The Phantom Pilot" (November 1927) was a sea story. "The Weird Affair Near the Pole" (June 1928) was set in Alaska. "The Ghost of Flying Hawk" (August 1928) was about an Indian. "Ghost Patrol" (October 1929), a police incident set in Atlanta, was co-authored with James A. Belflower, a police reporter for the Atlanta *Georgian*; it's the only known case where both names in a *Ghost Stories* "as told to" byline were real people. Two of Fowler's *GS* stories involved aviation, "The Ghost from the Flying Circus" and "Keeping Faith with Dusty" (June 1930).

The bulk of his aviation material appeared in *Flying Stories*. He was a continuous presence in the magazine in 1929-30, with three serials and an article. He also appeared in Macfadden's *Red Blooded Stories* with an aviation short (November 1928). It's curious that he never appeared in the air pulps, as he would have been a natural. But since most of his fiction appeared in Macfadden magazines during a specific period, he may simply have been writing as a member of the editorial staff; his non-Macfadden record doesn't demonstrate a strong commitment to freelancing.

Two stories which lie outside of his fecund period are "Trail of the Mavericks," *Action Stories*, November 1936, and "Copy Boy," *Detective Fiction Weekly*, December 24, 1938.

In the late-'20s, Fowler began writing with a Hollywood connection. The first known example is his *GS* short, "The Ghost Tiger" (December 1927). Its photo illustrations were taken from Paramount's famous wildlife documentary *Chang*, which had its general release on September 3, 1927. This was in the middle of a period when *Ghost Stories* was using movie tie-ins (see COVER GALLERY).

From 1928-31, Fowler authored seven film novelizations for Grosset & Dunlap. The most famous of the subject films was the WWI aviation drama *The Dawn Patrol* (1930). Two other novelizations had WWI aviation themes, *Lilac Time* (1928) and *The Sky Hawk* (1929). *The Finger Points* (1931) had a newspaper background.

He had an article, "Floyd Gibbons Goes Movie" in the August 1931 *Complete Movie Novel Magazine*. The proliferation of film connections at this time suggests that he may have relocated to Hollywood. He's definitely living there by 1942, but the intervening years couldn't be documented.

Fowler appeared a number of times in Walter Winchell's nationally-syndicated column. The earliest known example is June 7, 1937; the latest is September 22, 1958. In most of the appearances, a poem by Fowler led off the column. Often, the theme was nostalgia for New York. In other cases, Winchell notes changes in Fowler's career. It's clear from the citations that the two were personally acquainted, and probably friends. They probably met in the late-'20s, when Winchell was rising to fame as a columnist for Macfadden's *New York Evening Graphic*. It suggests that Fowler may have gotten his introduction to Macfadden Publications through employment with the *Graphic*.

References to Fowler's Hollywood years are scattered. In 1942, Fowler was a member of a committee set up by the film studios to coordinate publicity for their War Bond drives. That year, he published a syndicated article, "Hollywood's Britons." An ad for *The Star Weekly*, which printed the article, noted that "Guy Knows Hollywood." In 1944, Fowler joined the publicity department of the Republic film studios. Later, he reminisced of his time with Republic: "we like to laughed our heads off at some of the business. We had respect for it, but we ate food instead of film and slept sleep instead of previews." Winchell noted in his March 22, 1948 column that Fowler was on the editorial staff of the *Valley Times*, North Hollywood. In 1949, Fowler was established with a column, *All in a Day*. He was still in Hollywood in 1950, but Winchell noted in his May 17, 1951 column that Fowler was the new managing editor of the Bartlesville, Oklahoma *Examiner-Enterprise*. By 1953, he was back in Los Angeles. Both of his parents died in Los Angeles that year, his mother on February 6, his father on July 3. It may have severed his connection to the area.

Fowler's remaining years were spent in the Eureka area. Winchell's September 22, 1958 column led off with this Fowler poem:

BROADWAYITE IN CALIFORNIA

Here where the redwoods spike high drifting fog,
They seem to dwarf the Empire State back home. . . .

But I still enter mem'ries in my log,
The way a man will do—condemned to roam.

A Tree in Brooklyn grew into a book
When I was there a thousand years ago. . . .
I wonder now how central Park would look
In some small grove out here where redwoods grow.

I see St. Patrick's on the Avenue
Each time I walk in these cathedral wilds. . . .
I still recall a Village rendezvous—
The pristine white at noon in any Child's.

Humble I stand where ancient timbers rise. . . .
And old Manhattan's skyline fills my eyes.

By 1959, he was a staff writer for the *Humboldt Times*.

Nineteen-sixty-one was a bad year for Fowler. On February 17, the *EHS* reported on a spectacular auto accident, in which Fowler's car sheered off a fire hydrant, careened through a service station, setting a gas pump on fire, then veered back across the highway before finally coming to rest against a motel. Fowler blamed a brake failure. Six weeks later, on April 1, the *EHS* reported that Fowler had been arrested for drunk driving after hitting two cars in front of a tavern. He was obviously having problems. To make matters worse, his wife Gerry died in August.

The date of his retirement isn't known, but in his last position, he covered City Hall and the Board of Education for the *Humboldt Times*. His column, *All in a Day*, continued to appear in the *Arcata Union* and the *Humboldt Beacon*.

Five weeks before his death, Fowler was stricken with heart trouble. He died in a Eureka hospital undergoing treatment. He had nearly completed a biography of the WWII commander, General Russell E. Randall.

Fowler referred to himself as "the last of the tramp reporters"; it was to be the title of his last book. A "tramp reporter" is an itinerant newsman who performs temporary work for small-town papers.

The *EHS* obituary described Fowler as "moving picture writer and friend and associate of the legendary great and near-great in American politics and cultural life," which, considering the record, sounds like an exaggeration. They claimed that "he wrote countless movie scripts," which isn't true unless the scripts all went unfilmed. The *EHS* also seemed to think that his film novelizations were actually the original works inspiring the films. They claimed that he was the "author of many biographies, including Clark Gable and Al Capone." Other than the film novelizations, he had no books published under his name; so unless these biographies were pseudonymous (unlikely), they don't exist. Clark Gable appeared in *The Finger Points*; that as close as we can get. Another claim was that "he had worked on most of the nation's major newspapers," but there's no record of any major newspaper work outside of New York. Our conclusion is that Fowler was the victim of shoddy journalism by the author of the obituary; or that he had been "improving" his record for the pleasure of the locals. From the coverage of his death and funeral, it's clear he was held in high esteem, something of a local legend.

He was survived by one son, William, and several grandchildren.

Gregory, John Miller (*b*. October 4, 1887) ["Talking Glass"]: Gregory was born in Atlanta. He co-authored a play (ca. 1906) titled *The Exodus*, which posed a solution to the "Negro problem" by relocating blacks to a new state carved out of the western territories. For a time, he worked for the Fields Minstrels. By 1910, he had written a number of successful plays for the legitimate theater and vaudeville. His magazine appearances start in 1911 with a short in *Young's Magazine* and in 1912 with several stories in *Top-Notch*. He also wrote newspaper commentary and edited a magazine called *Town and Farm*. By 1914, he appears to have relocated to Chicago. Four comedic plays were copyrighted in the '20s.

Gregory had quite a number of stories published in magazines from the mid-'20s through the early-'30s. His best markets were *Top-Notch*, *The Popular Magazine*, and *Ace-High Magazine*. He had three appearances in *Ghost Stories*. In the later years, he hit a number of lesser pulps, *Air Adventures*, *The Dragnet Magazine*, *Eagles of the Air*, *Man Stories*, and *Miracle, Science and Fantasy Stories* with the enticingly-titled "Fish-Men of Arctica."

In 1942, he worked for St. Francis College, Loretto, Pennsylvania.

Hillman, Gordon Malherbe [profiled in Volume 2]

Hurst, Mont (dates unknown) ["The Wolf Man"]: No biographical details could be confirmed, but from a review of his brief publishing record, we would characterize him as a Texas writer and humorist with a sub-interest in weird fiction.

The earliest known published work was a short story for *Mystery Magazine* of April 15, 1924. In magazines, he published a handful of short stories, articles, poems, and epigrams, appearing in, for example, *Laughter* (October 1925), *Lariat Story Magazine* (February 1926), *True Gang Life* (September 1939), and, the latest we know of, *Mother's Home Life* (November 1949). In addition to his one appearance in *Ghost Stories*, the weird stories include "From an Old Egyptian Tomb" (*Mind Magic*, June 1931), "Bayou Horror" (*Murder Mysteries*, March 1935), and "Ghost Gloves" (*Fight Stories*, Fall 1944).

His earliest known book is the *Tip-Top Minstrel Book* (1925). He also published several one-act farces with ethnic themes, e.g. *The Family Budget: A Hebrew Play in One Act* (1929) and *Chickens for the Lodge: A One-act Black-face Comedy* (1933). His last known publication was a short book, *Melody in the Night* (1952).

Kelly, T(homas) Howard (1895 - July 24, 1967) ["The Ha'nts of Amelia Island"]: Kelly was born on historic Amelia Island, about thirty miles north of Jacksonville, Florida. Amelia is the southernmost of the Sea Islands, narrowly separated from the mainland by a network of intracoastal waterways. The island would provide one of the two main themes running through Kelly's life.

Kelly must have been a prodigy because he seems to have skipped college and gone straight into the publishing world. In 1914, a T.H. Kelly, presumed to be our Kelly, edited *The Black Cat*, in Salem, Massachusetts. Fulton Oursler, supervising editor of Macfadden Publications from 1922 forward, had been receiving rejections *The Black Cat* during this period, which could have provided Kelly an entree into the Macfadden orbit later on. In 1915, our Kelly, for certain, was working for The United Press, his entry into the newspaper field.

When the United States entered WWI, Kelly was handed the second major theme of his life. He served as a private in the 26th Division, AEF. He was a legendary go-getter, with a "reputation for getting the French to give him almost anything he asked for." He turned his experiences into a novel in 1920, *What Outfit, Buddy?*, detailing the observations of Jimmy McGee, fighting yank. In a brief introduction he wrote:

> A great many impressionable young men who become soldiers overnight and go to war feel strongly inspired to write books about their adventures. I felt the same way before the newness of the life on the western front had been rubbed away by constant friction with some of the more monotonous things of war, such as hunger, cold, mud, cooties, and other romance-destroying agents. I buried the idea of writing a book just before my division was called upon to stand between the Boches and Paris during the trying days of July and August of 1918. It is very good for me that I detached myself from the desire to write a war book about that time. Experience proved that it was necessary to give all my available time to the business of fighting the *guerre*.

The war had overwhelmed his desire to write, but only temporarily. . . . The "trying days" were the three-week Second Battle of the Marne, that did so much to turn the tide against the Germans. Kelly's best friend was killed in the battle, and buried in an unmarked grave in France. In 1921, he accompanied the friend's mother to the Armistice Day ceremony at Arlington Cemetery. As the casket of the Unknown Soldier passed by, she fainted and had to be taken back to her hotel. She later confided to Kelly that she had become convinced her son was the soldier in the casket. Kelly poignantly described the incident in a Memorial Day newspaper piece (*Chicago Daily Tribune*, May 25, 1958). He was to write a number of WWI pieces over the years. He also published several more books on the subject, e.g. *The Unknown Soldiers* (1929), *Roll Call From on High* (1936).

His career in the '20s is difficult to characterize, as he seems to have been involved in a number of writing-related activities. He was a newspaperman; his stories appeared in *The New York American* and *The Herald Tribune* in the '20s and '30s. He published an article and three stories in Macfadden's *Midnight* (and *Midnight Mysteries*) in late '22. A short story, "The End of a Paris Night," for Macfadden's newly-acquired *Metropolitan* (August 1923), suggests a WWI theme.

In 1923-24, he had a number of articles published in another Macfadden magazine, *Movie Weekly*, with titles like "If Your Income Was $500,000 a Year Would You Punch a Time Clock Every Morning? That's What Mary Pickford Does" (April 26, 1924). In the March 4, 1923 *Movie Weekly*, Kelly wrote that the KKK may have been responsible for the death of William Desmond Taylor, a Paramount director whose unsolved 1922 murder provoked much controversy; in response, Kelly received anonymous death threats, worthy of an article in another issue. At any rate, two of Kelly's stories were turned into feature films in 1925. *Lover's Island* was a romance. It appears to have been based on a seven-part serial, *Dream Lights*, published in Macfadden's *Dream World* from October '24 to April '25. Set on Florida's fictional "Tiger Island," *Dream World* described it as a "A Thrilling Romance of Southern Shores." The film was released in December '25. The other film, *His Buddy's Wife*, from a story in *The Smart Set*, involved a World War vet who falls in love with the wife of his presumably dead war buddy.

Kelly had two stories in early issues of *Ghost Stories*. The one not included here, "Guided by a Spirit Hand" (September '26), was about the ghost captain of the freighter *Amelia D.*

In 1927, Kelly was married and living in Westchester County, outside of New York City. The following year, after James R. Quirk bought *The Smart Set* and *New McClure's Magazine* from Hearst, Kelly edited both magazines into 1929. He also worked for *Cosmopolitan* at some point. His fiction output was sporadic; he did hit the war pulps (*War Stories*, *Over the Top*, *Battle Stories*) on occasion. One senses that he tapped out his personal experiences in creating stories, and didn't have anywhere to go after that.

In 1934, Kelly was still living in New York, but spending his winters in Fernandina Beach, the main town on Amelia Island. In late '35, he organized an expedition for wealthy treasure-seekers to search for Captain Kidd's pirate loot on the island. The venture had been inspired by old folk tales, the same ones, obviously, that inspired his story included here. "Even if we don't find any gold, it ought to be fun," Kelly announced, as part of the pre-hunt hoopla. There was no post-hunt hoopla, which pretty much tells the story.

As early as 1930, Kelly was writing for the pharmaceutical trade. In 1936, he was executive editor of *Drug World*, and associate editor of *American Druggists*. In that year, he remarried, to Mercedes S. Peine of Chicago; the fate of the previous wife is unknown. The marriage seems to have prompted a move from New York to Chicago. Mrs. Kelly was a frequent name in the Chicago society pages. In Chicago, Kelly became involved in the brewing industry. He was a member of the United Brewers Industrial Foundation and, for twenty-five years, associated with the Rahr Malting Company. He was president of the Kelly Company, possibly a public relations firm.

He died at his second home in Fernandina Beach, survived by Mercedes, a daughter, and three grandchildren. Today, he is considered Amelia Island's leading literary figure.

Liggett, Walter W(illiam) (February 14, 1886 - December 9, 1935) ["The White Seal of Avalak"]: Liggett was a nationally-known journalist who took a detour through the world of fiction, including a brief period during which he worked at Macfadden Publications. He was involved in a number of controversies which tarnished his legacy, and his daughter, Marda Liggett Woodbury, published a biography of her father to set the record straight. *Stopping the Presses: The Murder of Walter W. Liggett* (University of Minnesota Press, 1998), gives away the ending in the title, but so be it. The book provides a detailed description of Liggett's life, from which we drew much of this outline. Additional information came from newspaper reports; Liggett's association with Macfadden, unmentioned in *Stopping the Presses*, is documented by several items in *The Author & Journalist*.

He was born on his father's farm near Benson, Minnesota. No ordinary farmer, his father became the first dean of agriculture at the University of Minnesota. His mother was a progressive, active in women's groups. It was a family of readers. Walter grew up in St. Paul, but spent his summers in the country. His sports were football and boxing. In 1904, he entered his father's agriculture college at the university. The following year, at age 19, he left school to become a newspaperman. He reported for papers in Minneapolis, St. Paul, Duluth and Fargo.

He went to Seattle, and landed a position as managing editor of the Skagway *Alaskan* in 1909. Skagway is located north of Juneau, on the Inland Passage. It was a boom town during the Alaskan gold rush (1897-1898). When Liggett arrived, it was dirty and unruly, populated with conmen and gangsters. The town was ten miles from the Canadian border and, during his time in the Yukon, Liggett became well-acquainted with the Royal Canadian Mounted Police (RCMP). Skagway was a big influence on Liggett's life; not only did he marry a local girl, Norma J. Ask, he was to write of the Yukon, and the Mounties, on many occasions.

Liggett's last job in Skagway was as express manager for the White Pass & Yukon Railroad. In October 1910, Walter and Norma moved to Tacoma, Washington, where Walter took a job with the *Tacoma Ledger*. Then he and another reporter bought a newspaper in southeast Washington, the *Pasco Progress*. Joining the advancing temperance movement, Liggett advocated for liquor controls in the paper's pages. Why a newspaperman would oppose the consumption of alcohol is another question. In 1915, the *Progress* was sold, and Liggett returned to St. Paul, to join the *St. Paul Dispatch*.

The Nonpartisan League was a progressive political organization that grew out of a coalition of North Dakota farmers. On Sept 20, 1917, Liggett covered a speech by Wisconsin Senator Robert La Follette at a League event. La Follette's antiwar comments inspired the audience—and Liggett—but incited a public backlash against the League. Liggett quit the *Dispatch* and joined the League as head of publicity. When another antiwar Leaguer, Charles A. Lindbergh Sr. (the aviator's father), ran (unsuccessfully) for Minnesota governor in 1918, Liggett wrote speeches for him. He also worked for papers in Bismarck and Fargo, North Dakota. As a counter to the establishment press, and on behalf of the League, he organized a string of weekly farmer-owned newspapers in North Dakota. His involvement with the League ended in October 1919 owing to a difference with other executive.

Liggett quickly rebounded. In December, he landed the post of North Dakota's Deputy Commissioner of Immigration. He was based in Washington, D.C. for the next two years, arriving just as Prohibition took effect. Immigrants were important to the north Midwestern economy because of the amount of uncultivated farmland. However, this localized need butted up against anti-immigrant arguments coming from American labor. On January 3, 1921, Liggett testified before the Senate Immigration Committee in opposition to a protection bill.

In late 1921, on the recommendation of a Maryland Senator, Liggett headed the American Committee for Russian Famine Relief, in response to a looming crisis. Harding's Secretary of Commerce, Herbert Hoover, suspected Soviet sponsorship of the organization and asked the Bureau of Investigation to investigate Liggett. Liggett sent a telegram to Harding in protest, and asked that the American Relief Administration, headed by Hoover, be investigated by Congress. In due course, Liggett was cleared by a BI investigator. Liggett often described himself as a radical, but never a communist.

In late spring of 1922, Liggett moved to New York City to take a position as city editor of the socialist *New York Call*. Norma, who didn't share her husband's political leanings, remained in D.C. Liggett fell in love with Edith Fleischer (*b.* 1901), a young *Call* reporter who did share his views. He obtained a Mexican divorce from Norma and married Edith in July 1922. The couple had two children: Wallace (*b.* January 1924), and Marda (*b.* September 1925). The *Call* failed in 1923, the result of political infighting.

Between 1923 and '26, Liggett worked for four New York newspapers, the *Sun*, the *Times*, the *Post* and the *News*. During this period of job-hopping, he began moving outside the newspaper business. In 1925, he obtained an advance from *Collier's* for a series on the Mounties, and traveled to Ottawa. The articles began running in September. His first known published fiction was a short story of the Mounties in the August 1925 issue of *The Frontier*. It would be about this time that he joined Macfadden. He was the initial editor of Macfadden's first all-fiction magazine, *Fighting Romances from the West and East*;

presumably this was the assignment he was hired for. *Fighting Romances* lasted for eight issues (November 1925 - June 1926), and featured well-known pulp-adventure authors like Arthur Guy Empey, Murray Leinster, William Merriam Rouse, Nels Leroy Jorgenson, and James Perley Hughes. Liggett had shorts in five of the issues. The bulk of his fiction drew from his northwestern experiences and knowledge of the Mounties. He also sold pulp material to outside markets: *Mystery Magazine* (March 15, 1926), *Flynn's* (April 24, 1926). He didn't last long as editor of *Fighting Romances*. In short order, Harry Keller took over. The last issue of *Fighting Romances* was June 1926, and the first issue of *Ghost Stories* was July. It appears that all of the resources of *Fighting Romances* were rolled over into the new magazine, including Harry Keller as editor. Liggett appeared with shorts in the first two issues of *Ghost Stories*, indicating that he was likely still with the company. "The White Seal of Avalak," in the first issue, fits neatly into Liggett's fictional oeuvre, with its Arctic setting and RCMP protagonists. "The Voice that Came Through the Night," in the second issue, is about a man who deserts his wife; it has a North Dakota setting but is not specific in its details. Liggett had lived in Greenwich Village; with the second child on the way, the family moved to Brooklyn; in the summer of 1926, they moved to Cape Cod, which undoubtedly marks the end of the Macfadden period. Liggett must have maintained cordial relations with the company because he made two more known appearances in Macfadden magazines: *Red Blooded Stories* (November 1928), *True Strange Stories* (July 1929).

The question arises as to how Liggett came to be working for Macfadden, which at that point in his career seems to be a complete anomaly, both because it was a mass-market magazine publisher, and because he was made a fiction editor, two areas for which he had no track record. We can't answer the question with certainty, but several possibilities suggest themselves. The most unremarkable explanation is that he applied for an advertised position, or simply walked in off the street. His career demonstrates a knack for picking up professional employment without much difficulty. A related possibility is that he came looking for work on Macfadden's *New York Evening Graphic*, the sensationalistic daily newspaper established in 1924, but was ushered into the magazine offices instead. A third possibility is that he was introduced to the company by a mutual acquaintance, a common practice in the industry, especially with Macfadden. Under this theory, the likeliest missing link would be Fulton Oursler's personal attorney since the summer of 1925, Arthur Garfield Hays. Both Hays and Liggett were active in the same New York left-wing causes, and the probability of them knowing each other is high. If Hays knew that Liggett was job-shopping, he could easily have introduced him to Oursler. The weakness in this theory is that no linkage could be established prior to Liggett's employment at Macfadden.

Whatever the cause, Liggett had left the newspaper business. At Cape Cod, he wrote three books for the Macauley Company: *Frozen Frontier* (1927), an adventure story of the RCMP; *The River Riders* (1928), an adventure story that dealt with abuses in Minnesota's logging industry; and *Pioneers of Justice* (1930), a history of the RCMP.

He remained politically active. In 1927, flush with advances from Macauley, he worked for a month on the case of Sacco and Vanzetti, two anarchists sentenced to death in Massachusetts for a 1920 armed robbery that left two guards dead. The case was highly controversial, and in 1927, the execution date drew near. On August 10, Liggett presented an appeal to the governor of Massachusetts signed by numerous writers and artists; the appeal called the impending execution a "legalized lynching." Liggett, with four others, organized the Citizens' National Committee for Sacco and Vanzetti. Liggett went on a speaking tour to generate support. Arthur Garfield Hays was a member of the Committee; he also worked on the appeal of the death sentence. All went for naught, though, as the pair was executed on August 23.

In 1928, Liggett worked for the election of Alfred E. Smith in his race for the Presidency against Herbert Hoover. Another lost cause. In late-'28, the Liggett family moved to Chevy Chase, adjacent to D.C.

On the side, Liggett continued to supplement his income with fiction sales. He hit *Everybody's* four times in 1927-28, with boxing stories; and hit *Mystery Stories* four times in the same period; he sold to *Complete Stories*, *Detective Fiction Weekly*, and *War Novels*. He even had a serial, *Girl of the Northland*, in *Sweetheart Stories*, 1928. His last known pulp story was a novelette of the Mounties in the August 10, 1932 *Short Stories*.

Tom Mooney, a San Francisco labor leader, and Warren Billings, a labor activist, were convicted of a bombing in 1916. Another controversial case, which Liggett had been following for years, and writing about. The case resurfaced in 1929 with new evidence. Liggett helped draw national attention to it with an article in the May 1929 issue of *Plain Talk* magazine (published by B.A. Mackinnon and H.K. Fly, who also produced the pulps *Complete Novel Magazine* and *Complete Detective Novel Magazine*). Liggett and Hays were members of the National Mooney-Billings Committee (as were Sinclair Lewis, Clarence Darrow, H.L. Mencken, and other notable figures).

The Mooney article led to a series in *Plain Talk* on the efficacy of Prohibition. The first article appeared in the September 1929 issue. Beginning with the December issue, Liggett focused on a different city or state in each article. The titles betray the attacking tone of the pieces, and show that the once pro-temperance Liggett had reversed course:

> "How Wet Is Washington?," December 1929
> "Bawdy Boston," January 1930
> "Holy Hypocritical Kansas," February
> "Michigan, Soused and Serene," March
> "Minneapolis and Vice in Volsteadland," April
> "Georgia—Godly but Guzzling," May
> "Whoopee in Oklahoma," June
> "Ohio—Lawless and Unashamed," July
> "Pittsburgh—Metropolis of Corruption," August

In the December piece, Liggett claimed that Washington, D.C. was "wetter now than ever before," that there were twice as many liquor outlets (speakeasies, etc.) in the city as before Prohibition. The thrust of his meticulous research was that Prohibition was unenforceable and had fostered widespread corruption in government, conclusions we take for granted today but which were controversial while Prohibition was still the law of the land. Liggett's charges made headlines, especially in the target areas; local officials fought back with vigorous denials, and accusations that Liggett was being paid by the "wets." His timing could not have been better. In the midst of his series, Congress opened its long-awaited hearings to determine whether the Eighteenth Amendment required modification or repeal. On February 12, 1930, Liggett became the first witness to testify, before the House Judiciary Committee. He delighted the audience with lurid observations like these:

Detroit is in the grip of racketeers, gangsters, crooked politicians and grafting cops. I know of drunken revelry, a wild party, given by Dennis Murphy, a gambler, at a Grand Avenue roadhouse, at which a Governor of Michigan, a Chief of Police and four judges were present with gamblers, criminals, bootleggers and politicians, all fraternizing together. There were hootchie-kootchie dances. Next day they all said they would enforce the law.

The audience had to be continually rebuked by Committee members for applauding Liggett's remarks. He got his biggest round when, after three hours of testimony, he concluded, "My honest opinion as an American who is proud of his country, is, that if there is ten more years of this law, you will have the country ruled by a gang of underworld rats."

Plain Talk's editor, G.D. Eaton, died in June 1930. Liggett took over, planning a ten-part series on old nemesis Herbert Hoover, but the magazine folded after a couple of issues. Liggett moved the family to Chicago to investigate organized crime for the *Chicago News*. In late-'30, they moved on to San Francisco. Liggett worked on the Mooney case and started gathering material for a book on Hoover. Then it was back to New York to finish the book. *The Rise of Herbert Hoover* was published in February 1932, in time for Hoover's reelection campaign. The publisher was H.K. Fly Company, former publisher of *Plain Talk*. The critical biography ostensibly dismantled "the Hoover myth," demonstrating that Hoover's reputation had been constructed by publicists.

In 1932, Liggett appeared regularly in national magazines. He published articles on Hoover. He wrote articles on farming for *Scribner's* and the *American Mercury*. He did a series on the aviation industry for *Popular Aviation*. Trying to establish a successor to *Plain Talk*, he set up a new monthly magazine for Dell, an opinion journal with a touch of satire, *Spotlight* (first issue, June 1932). Dell pulled the plug after a couple of issues and Liggett tried to continue it on his own as *National Spotlight*. A year later he produced another unsuccessful magazine, *Liggett's Searchlight*.

Liggett returned to Minnesota in July 1933 and the newspaper business, running the Bemidji *Northland Times*. He resigned after a month. At the Minneapolis Athletic Club, he met and was charmed by Floyd B. Olson, who had been elected governor of Minnesota in 1930 as a Farmer-Labor candidate. Olson encouraged Liggett to establish a Farmer-Labor newspaper in Rochester, Minnesota, seventy miles southeast of the Twin Cities, and arranged financing. In October 1933, Liggett purchased the defunct *Red Wing Organized Farmer*, reopened it as the weekly *Midwest American*, and eventually moved it to Rochester. Running a local paper may seem like a step down for Liggett after attaining national prominence with his anti-Prohibition articles, but it was the Depression, and Liggett seemed to enjoy the nuts and bolts of putting out a newspaper.

He quickly turned against Governor Olson, repeatedly accusing him of machine politics, cronyism, and being in cahoots with Twin Cities racketeers and bootleggers. He also blamed Olson for the political sin of using Farmer-Labor to advance his political career while selling out its principles. To carry on the campaign against Olson, Liggett moved the *Midwest American* to Minneapolis at the end of 1934. On June 23, 1935, Liggett was indicted for abducting two teenage girls; the charges were later amended to include sodomy. The purported crime occurred during a March 22, 1934 stay by Liggett in a Minneapolis hotel; the charges smelled of frame-up. The defiant Liggett kept up his charges on Olson. After the indictment, every issue of the *Midwest American* printed a list of the ten reasons why Olson should be impeached. Liggett also went after Olson's cronies including, most notably, Isadore Blumenfield a.k.a. Kid Cann, a career criminal and the top dog in the local liquor trade. On October 24, with Liggett's trial impending, Kid Cann offered a bribe, suggesting that Liggett's legal troubles could be taken care of. Liggett refused. Later that night, he was cornered by Cann and a gang of thugs, severely beaten and hospitalized. When the trial opened on November 5, Liggett was still bruised and battered when he defended himself. The case was covered by the *New York Times*, *Chicago Tribune*, Associated Press, and other prominent outlets. A jury acquitted Liggett after a twenty-hour deliberation.

He continued his attacks on Olson. Then, on December 9, 1935, Liggett was gunned down in the alley behind his Minneapolis apartment as his shocked wife and children looked on. The shots came from a passing car. Edith identified Kid Cann as the gunman. Cann went on trial January 29, 1936. Macfadden's *Liberty*, edited by Fulton Oursler, sent Will Irwin to Minneapolis to cover the case. Cann brought forth a number of alibi witnesses and was eventually acquitted. The murder of Walter W. Liggett was never officially solved. A lot rested on Edith's identification of Kid Cann, and if she was wrong . . . let's just say that Liggett had amassed an abundance of enemies by the time he was killed.

Broke and exhausted, Edith moved the children back to New York, to stay with relatives. She made a meager living from writing for newspaper supplements and true-crime magazines. She had one known fiction sale, a short story in the February 1937 *Coronet*. It would have been logical for her to try the pulps, but no examples are known. Olson died of cancer in 1936. Edith died of heart failure in 1972. Kid Cann linked up with the mob in Las Vegas and Miami. He died a millionaire in Minneapolis in 1981.

Marinoni, Rosa Zagnoni (January 5, 1888 - March 26, 1970) ["The Green Monkey"]: Born in Bologna, Italy. Her mother was a poet and artist, her father a newspaper war correspondent and drama critic, her uncle a leading Italian poet. In 1898, Rosa, an only child, moved with her parents to New York City while her father covered the Spanish-American War; the family never went back. In July 1908, she married Antonio Marinoni, also a native Italian, in Brooklyn. He was a professor at the University of Arkansas who would eventually head the Department of Romance Languages. After the marriage, he took Rosa back to Fayetteville, Arkansas, home of the university, where she remained for the rest of her life. Rosa took classes and began to write. She was also an active citizen, campaigning for women's suffrage; before and after WWI, she was associated with loan drives and the Red Cross. Beginning in 1922, she and her husband led summer tours of Europe for several years.

In 1926, Rosa fell down in her kitchen and injured her leg. Doctors told her she might never walk again. She recovered completely, but the sobering experience caused her to focus completely on her nascent writing career. Eleven months into this creative outburst, she had written 94 short stories, 475 poems, and a novel. She wrote from 8 to 14 hours a day, every day producing a short story, several poems, or progress on a novel. By the early '30s, she had written some 3,000 poems; most were brief or epigrammatic. Her output soon became legendary. Heywood Broun joshed in his syndicated column: "If Mrs. Marinoni will agree to let a single weekend pass without one short story, novel, saga, sonnet, epic, or lyric, I'll pass up all my columns for that same period." By the time of her death, she had published poetry in more than 500 magazines around the world, published 1,000 stories in 70 magazines, and written over 5,000 poems.

These awesome numbers come from her family, which has preserved her papers. Her prolificacy is not in doubt, but the roundness of these numbers suggests some seat-of-the-pants guesswork. Current indexing of commercial magazines reveals only a bare handful of stories and poems, which probably means that the bulk of her published work ended up in literary magazines and newsprint. For example, her short poems were a frequent presence in the *Chicago Tribune* daily column *A Line o' Type or Two*, from 1925 into the '60s. She had at least four stories in *Ghost Stories*, her earliest known stories for the pulps. (Two were bylined Rosa Zagnoni. A possible fifth was published under "Lilith Shell"; see separate bio.) She has two known appearances in *Sweetheart Stories* in the early '30s, and probably made other sales to the love pulps, but these are underrepresented in current indexes.

She also published 12 volumes of her poetry, as well as other books, including a series on the Ozarks from 1956-67. In the introduction to her 1929 collection, *Red Kites and Wooden Crosses*, the poet William Stanley Braithwaite wrote of her: "She is what I call an ironic psychologist. She knocks shams, hypocrisies, superstitions and false illusions into cocked hats; she does it not as a politician but as a poet."

Professor Marinoni died in 1944. Two years later, Rosa married another professor from the Department of Romance Languages; he died in 1953.

Throughout her career, she accumulated many honors. In 1936, she was named Poet Laureate of the Ozarks. In 1953, the governor made her the second person to be named Poet Laureate of Arkansas, a title she held for the rest of her life. In Italy, she was known as the most widely-known Italian-born poet abroad, and received honors in Turin and Milan in the early-'60s.

She is fondly remembered for encouraging aspiring writers, for making a difference in many lives. She held regular poetry meetings in the living room of Villa Rosa, her Italian-style house a half-block from the university campus. One pictures her serving tea, wearing her customary cape, still speaking in an Italian accent. In 1990, Villa Rosa was placed on the National Register of Historic Places.

In 1948, she helped establish October 15th as Poetry Day in Arkansas. Every year, she selected three outstanding state poets for recognition. In 1969, by proclamation of Arkansas' Governor Rockefeller, every October 15th was declared Rosa Zagnoni Marinoni Day.

She died in her sleep, age 82, at home in Villa Rosa. She was survived by a son and a daughter (two other children died as babies), eight grandchildren and six great-grandchildren.

Her local paper, the *Northwest Arkansas Times*, memorialized her passing: "We're not apt to see her like again. . . . [She was] a woman of extraordinary accomplishment. . . . an accomplished connoisseur of life. . . . Arkansas and the Ozarks are better places for having had her as a friend."

Mumford, Ethel Watts (June 23, 1876 - May 2, 1940) ["The Specter in Red"]: Contemporaneous newspaper accounts of Ms. Mumford's life and career—and there are many—scrupulously avoid mentioning her birth date or age. Her *New York Times* obituary omits all mention of these details. A survey of available official documents yields a range of birth years from 1873-79. The above given date of June 23, 1876 represents a reasonable consensus, but should be considered provisional. It, at least, makes the date of her first marriage (at age 18 rather than 16) more plausible.

She was born in New York City, the daughter of Dickson Given Watts (~1845-1902), a Kentuckian, a charter member and twice President of the New York Cotton Exchange, a scholarly businessman whose essay, "Speculation as a Fine Art," is considered a classic.

A child of obvious gifts, Ethel's mother Mary made sure she received the finest education. As a teenager, she finished her education studying painting at the Julian Academy in Paris. Afterwards, she spent a year traveling Europe and the Orient, and another year in Japan. She was described as "tall, athletic, witty, vivacious, beautiful, clever" and pictures of her from the time do nothing to contradict the relevant parts of that description.

In 1894 she married George Dana Mumford, lawyer and "capitalist." Her career as a writer and artist began in earnest. The marriage was fraught with difficulty, however. Mr. Mumford was jealous of her devotion to literature and art, and uninterested in her writing. He wanted a full-time wife, not a full-time professional. She insisted she could balance the two, but there was to be no meeting of the minds. In 1899, she moved to San Francisco, taking their only child, three-year-old George. She sued for divorce on grounds of desertion. When it was granted in 1901, she returned to New York, a free woman. She vowed not to marry again unless she met a man who understood her need to write and paint. Another round of travels began: a year in the South Seas, and extensive journeys through the U.S., Mexico, and Latin America.

Eventually, a Wall Street broker, Peter Geddes Grant, emerged to meet her spousal standards. He was delighted by her talents. They married in 1906. Her name became Ethel Watts Mumford Grant; she published under that name intermittently but eventually "Ethel Watts Mumford" predominated. She continued to travel, splitting her time between New York and Scotland, where her in-laws lived.

One of her early works was a play, *The Scenario* (1898), set in Mexico and Paris. Many of her earliest publications were written in San Francisco. These included short stories written for newspapers and magazines, which often reflected her international experience; and her first novel, *Dupes*, a story of New York society life published in 1901. She produced constantly, writing fiction, poetry, articles, songs, vaudeville sketches; painting and book illustration. Her stories appeared in numerous national magazines. She wrote a literary column, *Novelettes of the New York Streets*, for the *New York Evening World* during 1913-14.

She emerged as a successful playwright in the teen years. To get serious about drama, she read 2,000 manuscripts to learn technique, picking comedy for her specialty. Ever the wit, her plays ranged from the merely humorous to the farcical, and were performed on the Broadway and London stages.

She could be unpredictable, though. Her story, "Easy," appeared in *The Grim Thirteen* (1917), a collection of stories by successful authors repeatedly rejected by the leading magazines for being too grim. The *Los Angeles Times* described "Easy" as "easily the most sordid in the book."

During WWI, as a member of the Vigilantes, an organization of leading writers and artists dedicated to serving the country, she contributed patriotic articles and poems. The opening stanza to her "A Song for the Ships" (1918) reads:

> Bless the Seas with your myriad ships,
>   America, my own.
> Call them forth to the longing seas,
> Flaunt their sails to the urging breeze,

And bring the Hun to his begging knees
In his cursed Danger Zone!

Mumford stories reached the silver screen four times from 1920-25; three were from magazine stories, the fourth from a play.

In 1925, she published a book on palmistry, *Hand-Reading Today; A New Angle of an Ancient Science*.

A 1928 newspaper column described her as "always on the go—either coming or going, packing or unpacking."

Though known as a quality writer, Mumford made numerous appearances in the pulps, especially as her career extended into the '20s. She had a serial in *Women's Stories* (1914), poems in *Adventure* (1919), short stories in *People's*, *Western Story*, *Detective Story*, *Short Stories*, *Flynn's*. Her two shorts in *Ghost Stories*, both 1927, come as her career seemed to be winding down. Her husband, Peter, died in May 1929, and her known publication record is thin after that date, until her last known publication in 1935.

A resident of Sand Point, Long Island, she died in a New York City hospital, survived by her son.

Shell, Lilith (dates unknown) ["Who Am I?"]: Known publications under the name Lilith Shell are few. They include a short in *Thrilling Tales* (May 1927), and a poem in *Complete Stories* (February 1928).

Lilith Shell may have been a penname for Rosa Zagnoni Marinoni, who had four stories under her own name in *Ghost Stories* (see separate profile). Marinoni lived in Fayetteville, Arkansas, the wife of a University of Arkansas professor. She began writing in 1926 and was a prolific poet. The first citation we could find for Lilith Shell is a poem in the July 10, 1926 *Fayetteville Democrat*. Another Arkansas and poetry connection was a noteworthy Lilith Shell article, "Folk Songs Furnished Most of Mountain Entertainment," in the March 11, 1928 *Arkansas Gazette*. At first glance, the WWI theme of Shell's "Who Am I?" may seem off-trail for Marinoni, but Marinoni's father had been a war correspondent, and she had volunteered with the Red Cross during the war, either of which may have made the subject matter attractive to her. In addition, the story is not vivid enough in its details to suggest that the author had any firsthand knowledge of the war.

At any rate, for *Ghost Stories* to have published two female poets with a Fayetteville connection would have been quite a coincidence.

Sneddon, Robert W(illiam) (June 19, 1880 - March 8, 1944) ["Painted Upside Down"]: Born in Beith, Scotland, a doctor's son. He read voraciously as a child and was torn between being a writer or an engineer. At Glasgow University, he studied the arts and the law, the latter at his father's urging. He served a law apprenticeship in Glasgow and Edinburgh. He also lived in London and Paris. He sailed from Glasgow to New York on the S.S. *Caledonia* in June 1909.

He became a writer of both nonfiction and fiction, short stories, editorials, book reviews, propaganda articles during WWI. His first published work was a series in *Judge*, "The Cynic's Examination Papers." In his first three years as a writer, he exclusively wrote humor. His first published short story was "Little Golden Shoes" (*The Forum*, August 1912), a story of Russian New York. His second was "The Red Diary" (*Snappy Stories*,

February 1913), the first of many tales of French life for the magazine. Harold Hersey claimed that Sneddon had been discovered by William Clayton, by virtue of featuring him in *Snappy Stories*, at times on a monthly basis. While this cannot be literally true, since Sneddon had already been publishing for four years, his 1914 *Snappy Stories* series, "Paris in Profile," may have significantly raised his profile.

Sneddon struggled to sell his work for many years. He became accustomed to sending stories to ten different markets before eventually making the sale. "To most of us," he observed, "success is a matter of dogged obstinacy in the face of obstacles. . . . I have tried the same magazine three times with the same story and sold on the third time out."

He was known to be much stronger on characterization than plot. Of fiction writing, he advised, "Write only of what you know. Observe and absorb. Do not be in a hurry to make immediate use of your observations. You will be surprised to find what a complete picture you may make of a patchwork of impressions acquired mostly unconsciously over a period of months. The mind is a very active worker, even when it seems most latent."

Interested in the theater since childhood, Sneddon wrote a number of short comic plays. Some were published, a few were performed, most notably *The Might-Have-Beens*, a fantasy which drew comparisons to *Peter Pan's* author J.M. Barrie.

He published two novels, *Galleon's Gold* (1925) and a mystery, *Monsieur X* (1928).

He appeared in *Ainslee's* in 1918, which undoubtedly acquainted him with future *Ghost Stories* editor, W. Adolphe Roberts; he appeared twice in *The Thrill Book* (1919), which led to friendship with another future *GS* editor, *Thrill Book's* editor Harold Hersey. In the '20s, he appeared in Macfadden's *Metropolitan Magazine*, and its successor, *Macfadden Fiction-Lovers Magazine*. He appeared in the fourth issue of *Ghost Stories* (October 1926) with "In Terror of Laughing Clay," which featured psychic investigator Mark Shadow, Sneddon's fictional co-author, who would feature in three of Sneddon's six *Ghost Stories* appearances. One of Sneddon's non-Shadow stories, "On the Isle of Blue Men" (April 1927), was so shocking—the "blue men," tentacled sea creatures, capture a woman for breeding purposes—that *Ghost Stories'* editors rewrote the ending to allow the woman to escape.

Sneddon appeared in many mystery and detective pulps in the '20s through the '40s with fiction and non, particularly *Mystery Magazine/Stories*, *Clues*, and *Detective Fiction Weekly*. He was no stranger to Hersey-edited pulps, including "The Gangs of Yesterday," a nonfiction series he contributed to *Racketeer Stories*. He wrote and published up to the end of his life, several of his later stories appearing in Popular's *New Detective*. Two weeks before his death, the *New York Times* published a letter by Sneddon, in which he expressed his disgust with Congress; their actions in the face of certain war issues were "too sickening and disquieting for words."

He died of a heart attack in New York City, his wife Helen surviving him.

Snell, Edmund (September 5, 1889 - 1972) ["The Black Spider"]: British writer Snell was born in Lambeth, in Greater London. He served in France and Italy during WWI, 1914-20. He married Marjorie Anne Griffin in the Spring of 1917. They had a son and a daughter. He listed his various other occupations as shipbuilding clerk, assistant on a rubber estate, and actor; his recreations as badminton, travel, and amateur theatricals.

He appeared in an American magazine as early as the February 1922 *Metropolitan*. He burst into prominence in 1923 with his first book, *The Yellow Seven*, a tale of a sinister

Chinese organization in British North Borneo, "an island of mystery to which the Darkness of Africa is like noonday." It was serialized in American newspapers, ads for which call him The Kipling of Borneo, and provide a dramatic glimpse into his background: "His earlier life was one of adventure in earth's strange places. A soldier in the World War, he took up the pen when the conflict ended and already he is the literary sensation of England." The sensation must have peaked early, for he seems to have as quickly sunk into the ranks of relatively unexamined popular authors.

In the '20s, he published short stories in British pulps like *Hutchinson's Mystery Story Magazine* and *Adventure-Story Magazine*, *The Yellow Magazine* and *The Red Magazine*, *Pearson's*, *Cassell's*, *The Windsor Magazine*, and others. Many of these were reprinted in the American pulp, *Flynn's* (1926), and *Detective Fiction Weekly* (1928-32). He had a long absence from American publications after that. From 1929-39, he appeared regularly in the British pulp, *The Thriller*. In 1939-40, he made several appearances in Thrilling pulps, *Detective Novels Magazine* and *Thrilling Detective*, reprints from *The Thriller*.

It's not clear that he wrote any of his fiction directly for the U.S. market; the vast majority, if not all, of his U.S. appearances were secondary publications of the British appearances. Story titles were often altered, though, making identification difficult without direct examination of the texts.

"The Black Spider" had near-simultaneous publication in the U.S. and England, appearing in the January 1927 *Ghost Stories* and the February 1927 *Hutchinson's Mystery Story Magazine*.

He published some two-dozen novels from 1923-50. Some of these were exotic adventures tinged with science fiction, such as *Kontrol* (1928), about medically-created supermen; *The Z-Ray* (1932), about, of course, a death ray; and *The Red Spinner* (1937), about a disintegration gas. This formula is certainly reflected in "The Black Spider," his only *Ghost Stories* appearance, which has nothing supernatural about it. A 1937 book, *The Finger of Destiny and Other Stories*, collected twelve shorts.

He was living in Worthing in Sussex from at least the early '30s until his death in the summer of 1972.

Uncanny, Spooky, Creepy Tales
Mystery—Suspense—Surprise

Ghostly mystery shrouds your life. It dogs your steps in daylight and rides upon your shoulder after dark. It governs your life—it *is* your life, for life is mystery—and death is mystery, too.

The earth upon which you ride came out of a mysterious past upon a mysterious errand into a more mysterious future.

Mystery surrounds it, permeates it, overshadows it.

The dark canons of city streets are rife with ghostly mystery. Stealthy footsteps in the dead of night—burning eyes peering out of darkness—cold, icy hands that wither what they clutch — ghastly tortured sobs piercing solid walls—and always, the silent lynx-eyed servants of the law watching, waiting, watching and preparing to spring their traps.

And in the country—the wild, weird wail of banshee and vampire — the creepy horror of the cellar of an abandoned house at midnight — the hollow, nerve-shattering clank of phantom chains — flickering firelight stirring chimneyplace wraiths to life—grotesque, dancing, shadowy shapes—ghouls sweeping about the tottering tombstones of a forsaken graveyard—mystery surrounds and exudes from them all. Ghostly fingers brush the universe with a clammy, chill, unnatural touch.

Because mystery is in your blood, ghost stories, saturated with mystery, fascinate you. That is why the tales in *Ghost Stories*—a startling, surprising magazine of thrilling interest—will stir your imagination as no other magazine ever has. You will want to read the July issue from cover to cover without letting it get from your hands for an instant. Your copy awaits you at the nearest news-stand. Get it right now.

Special Offer

You owe it to yourself to enjoy these tales of mystery. If no news-stand is convenient, you can obtain them by mail—at a saving! Use the coupon at the right.

Partial Contents
of the *JULY ISSUE* of
Ghost Stories

The Phantom of the Fifteenth Floor
The Coming of Roger Crane
In the Shadow of Voodoo
He Fell in Love with a Ghost
Superman or Clever Trickster— Which?
The Girl Who Lived with the Dead
The Transferred Ghost
Back from Beyond
Chained to a Bed of Roses
The Curse of the House of Gables
The White Seal of Avalak
$1,000.00 for a Ghost
Hands in the Dark
Convicted by a Silent Witness

On All News-stands :: :: May 23

True Detective Mysteries, June 1926

In Touch with the Unknown

By

George William Wilder

WE LIVE IN A MATERIAL WORLD. All around us are things. We rise in the morning and touch a bed-post, a dining-room table, a newspaper; we see walls, rugs, pictures—material things all.

The man is yet to be born who has penetrated the mystery of Life and Death. Where did we come from? Where are we going? No man can say. Yet there are many who claim to know that there is a life beyond the grave. There are many who claim contact with a spirit world. The experiences of such persons you will read in GHOST STORIES magazine.

During the past few years Spiritualism has numbered thousands of new believers among its followers. Who is to say that a spirit world does not exist? Voodooism is practiced in Africa, in portions of the United States, and elsewhere on the globe. Necromancy holds thousands in its weird spell. Mental telepathy is conceded to exist; practiced scientists of standing assure us that the control of thought transference is a discovery so imminent it may be made any hour of any day. Crystal gazers seem to have looked into the future and predicted events with uncanny accuracy. Many are the men and women whose lives are guided by superstitions which they dare not oppose.

From these and other departments of psychic lore we are drawing to build a magazine. What could be more fascinating than to journey into an unknown world? What more enthralling than to read the unique, spooky, creepy tales of those who have made the journey? You will make the journey with them. You will stand beyond the brink of eternity, you will tear aside the veil that shrouds the spirit world, you will be held spellbound as each new issue of GHOST STORIES reaches you. Read—and discover for yourself.

$10,000 for a Ghost

$10,000 will be paid by GHOST STORIES Magazine to the person—spiritualistic medium, student of psychic research, or layman—who will produce a bona fide materialization which, in the opinion of the Judges in charge of this award, is proven to be a materialization of a spirit from another world. Further particulars and full details will be announced later.

> The Judges in charge of this award include: Bernarr Macfadden, noted physical culturist and publisher; Fulton Oursler, celebrated novelist and playwright; Arthur Garfield Hays, distinguished counsellor at law; Howard Thurston, well known all over the world as a magician almost without a peer; Doctor Emanuel de Marnay Baruch, physician, Professor of Bacteriology and Pathology, University of the State of New York, Consulting Physician to the Hospital for Deformities and Joint Diseases and to the Philanthropic Hospital; George Sylvester Viereck, poet and novelist; and Ralph Welles Keeler, D.D., Crawford Memorial M.E. Church, New York, N.Y.

So that readers of GHOST STORIES may know of the progress of this remarkable experiment, we shall publish the true and unbiased accounts of such investigations as the committee of judges may make.

Have you ever seen a ghost? Are you in communication with the dead? Have you any justification for your claim that you can materialize a being from another world? Write the Editor of GHOST STORIES and due consideration will be given your claim. Succeed—and you acquire a fortune and live to see undying fame. You have your opportunity through

GHOST STORIES
MAGAZINE

He Fell in Love with a Ghost
As related by Arnold Fountain

The Fantastic Experience of a Master of Melody

Unhappily married, young Dick Armstrong encounters a dream girl whom he knows he loves. Married to one woman, adoring a vision, what is he to do?

WHEN I MARRIED ETTA TRENT, with her masses and coils of yellow hair, I made, I am now certain, the most damnable mistake of my youth.

With a red-haired woman as my wife, I might have developed a brilliant genius for musical composition, instead of passing my days as a dawdling dreamer, spending the fortune my father accumulated in business. Today, my sonatas might have been on the programs of Rachmaninoff; my concertos and symphonies played by all the great orchestras. As it is, my music is all unwritten; I may die with all my songs hushed in my heart. Called "master technician," I want more.

There remains with me now one strange and dazzling hope, and it is of that singularly reawakened hope that I shall tell you.

A famous physician, not many months ago, told me I should have selected a red-haired wife. He was a specialist in new form of psychology. By his peculiar methods of analysis, he insisted that he could probe the very soul of a patient. Actually he pretended to divine the suppressed desires of the heart. After hours of asking me peculiar questions, to which I returned only indifferent replies, he announced to me that I cherished a secret longing for a woman with red hair.

Blandly he suggested that I divorce my wife and try to find another with suitable tresses.

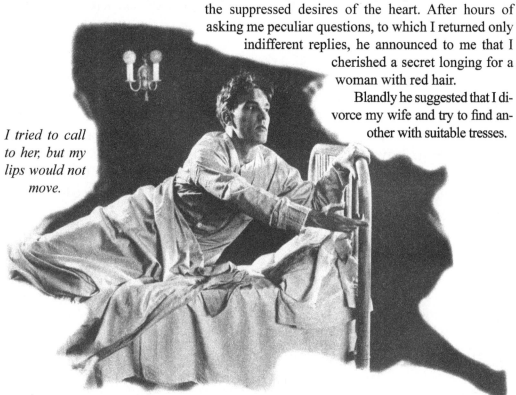

I tried to call to her, but my lips would not move.

"Go find a girl with hair like scarlet flame," he advised me, with a tempting smile. "You will follow her all the way to perdition, for with her you can be happy, even in hell."

"That does not answer my question," I persisted. "I came here for a mental examination. Good God, Doctor, am I going crazy?"

"You are perfectly sane," he assured me.

"Is there the slightest indication of madness? Have I the first symptom of being insane? That is what is highly important for me to know. No quibbling, doctor. I don't want you to be tactful. I want to know the truth."

"You are entirely normal," he assured me gravely. "You are freer of unsatisfied impulses than most people who never question their mentality. No one, sir, is entirely sane. We are all a bit crazy. But you less than most others. No! You would be happier with a red-haired girl, because you happen to want a red-haired girl. But you are sane, sir—one hundred per cent sane!"

I smiled gratefully. I paid him his fee, which was atrocious. If I ever had to begin life over again, as a poor man, I should become a specialist in psychology and get rich. I thanked him, though it was he who should have thanked me, and I departed.

But I did not take his advice.

I had not told the learned doctor the whole truth, as I intend to disclose the whole truth now. Even then I was involved in a stupendous domestic entanglement. My wife had already threatened to leave me. My purpose in going to see the man was to be sure that I was sane. He was definite in telling me that I was perfectly normal mentally, with the exception of that desire for a red-haired girl. My mind was not unbalanced. This assurance was, no doubt, worth the price he had demanded of me.

I knew also

that he had found out the truth about me.

All my life, I have admired red-haired girls. I remember the first time I ever saw one. It was at a birthday party given for my cousin, Edwin Bowers. The children were playing a game very popular in those days called "Choose!" The girls took turns in choosing the boys they wished for partners. Among all the little girls there, one drew my eyes like a magnet. She had a pale face, but piquant; dark blue eyes and hair flaming like the crimson leaves of autumn. In dumb worship of her beauty, I stared at her.

I was an extremely shy child. The other boys were boisterous in the fun of the game, calling loudly to the girls and there was scuffling and boyish riot. I retreated from their midst and stood off, in a corner, also, watching that one little girl. She felt my gaze and returned it. My heart seemed to expand when she walked up to me and kissed me.

She had chosen me.

The memory of that childhood kiss from that red-haired little girl was one of my life's most vivid experiences. I never saw her again but I have never forgotten her.

As I grew older, my musical studies completely isolated me. In the experiences which my friends and companions knew, as they came out of adolescence into manhood, I had no share. They had sweethearts and adventure. I had my piano, my melodic dreams, and the inspiration of all the great composers who had gone before me.

My relaxation was in athletics. Seemingly I cared nothing for women; that phase of manhood slumbered within me, like a drowsing giant. My friends told me I was handsome, and should find a mate—but in this they were mistaken. I was not handsome. I was—and am—of big frame, with sturdy muscles and great vitality. But my face is carved in the lines and angles which are fashioned by the impress of study and profound thought. I have not the idle regularity of features which attracts the eyes of women. In spite of this defect, however, women were kind to me. They made me feel uneasy in their presence; persistence, I suppose, of my old shyness. I shrank from their company.

Then, one evening, less than two years ago, I left Aeolian Hall after a concert, intending to hurry home and work after dinner on a little song which had greatly captured my imagination. As I reached the corner of Forty-second Street and Fifth Avenue, the lights in the traffic tower were changing. From mellow gold, their illumination blinked into bloody scarlet, and last, to envious green; a deep and gloating green, that gashed the velvet grey of twilight and beckoned the homing workers east and west across the boulevard.

I had stopped in a tobacco shop to buy a supply of evening cigars. Tucking them in my upper left vest pocket, I tossed two quarters clinkingly on the glass top of the showcase, and hurried through the door.

With detestable distinctness, the entire incident remains in my mind. I made an invariable practice of returning to my suburban boarding house on the 5:23 out of Grand Central Station. On this particular evening I was already a bit late, and I was anxious to reach the opposite corner before the signal lamps should change again and the traffic tides shift north and south.

As I scurried through the sidewalk crowds, I nearly upset a bowling cripple and his pile of evening papers. Shouting an apology over my shoulder, I was about to hasten across the avenue, when a hand seized my wrist in a detaining clasp.

I turned and saw that a woman was accosting me. My first sensation was one of annoyance, because I was being delayed. My second impression was that I ought to recognize the lady; but that I had forgotten her.

*"Good God, Doctor! Am
I going crazy?"*

She was tall,
full breasted, statu-
esque, voluptuous. Her cape-like costume of marine blue, the crimson plumage
of her hat, her golden hair, and the warm coloring of her cheeks and lips, gave her a charm of
peculiar and vivid vitality. She was the kind of a woman who leaves a trail of staring men
and envious women behind her, as she approaches a table in a restaurant.

I remember especially that I thought her hat was beautiful.

"Mr. Armstrong?" she asked eagerly. Her voice was deep and clear, and darkly colored
with vivid music.

"Yes," I admitted a bit dazedly. "Yes, I am Mr. Armstrong. And, er—"

At that instant, a bell sounded from the gaunt tower in the center of the crossings.
The giant policeman near the car tracks raised a glistening whistle to his lips and blew a
warning blast. The green light surrendered to red, and that to glowing yellow; north and
south streamed taxis, private cars, and busses of gold and green.

We were forced back on the sidewalk. The magnificent stranger still clung to my arm.

"I am Etta Trent. Have you forgotten me, Mr. Armstrong?"

Immediately I recalled her. She was the widow of one of my friends who had served with me in France. His death was extraordinary. I had always believed he committed suicide during an engagement, a few days before the armistice. He had a secret sorrow. I had called on Mrs. Trent when our company was sent home. Strange that she remembered me so well. It seemed that she was having some difficulty with the government. She wanted to bring home her husband's body. I had been his captain, and she thought my influence would help. She was overjoyed at our chance encounter. Wouldn't I assist her?

I promised, there on the sidewalk, in front of the tobacco shop, while the violet dusk darkened into the deep purple of early evening.

After that I saw Etta Trent frequently. There was a quality of bold and voluptuous appeal in her; a seductive allurement in every movement of her body. Her eyes were blue, and the vacancy of their stare impressed me as mysterious. I considered her a very remarkable woman, and I was pleased to help her.

I called at her home in the evenings to go over the details of our negotiations with Washington. The oftener I called, the less we talked of the business. We thought no more about it. My friend Lieutenant Trent still sleeps in a French grave.

One night I blurted out a proposal, and she willingly agreed to marry me. I remember a distinct and leaden sense of disappointment when for the first time I pressed my lips against her full-blown, sensuous mouth. I wondered why a long remembered, dearly treasured thrill was missing—the thrill that mesmerized my senses on the only other occasion when I had kissed a girl. That had been at a child's birthday party, years before. Then I angrily trampled down my disappointment, and fancied I had crushed it.

I should have admitted that psychic objection. At least I should have given my soul the courtesy of a hearing; of entertaining its doubts and prejudice. But my mind and body were under the spell of Etta's physical glamour.

We were married two months later.

For the first few weeks of our honeymoon, I was astonishingly pleased. New and unsuspected delights came to me like an initiation. I rejoiced as a strong man with his bride. Etta's love was supremely passionate and possessive. Utterly virtuous, she poured over me such an excess of incalescent ardor and devotion as startled and sometimes frightened me. After a few months her love had become a tyranny.

When I returned to my piano and assigned long, glad hours to my musical composition, she became fretful and impatient. If I withdrew from her a single hour, she was distressed. She was jealous of my art and drove me to neglect it with all her womanish weapons of torment, seductiveness, pouting and tears. Every hour she kept me from my music was, for her, an hour gained for love-making. She refused to let me talk to her of my ambitions and aspirations. At first she despised, then abominated my work.

Why should I be ambitious to compose new songs? Weren't there enough already? Why should I be ambitious to do anything but make her happy? These were the questions she flung at me scornfully when I pleaded my work as an excuse to be to myself.

I say excuse advisedly. It was a fact that I was losing the urge to make music. Inspiration seemed to have fled from my piano keys; no melodies danced through my heart as of old.

But I began to invent excuses, just to find a little time to myself.

And then I began deliberately to woo back my prodigal genius. A verse of something that John Burroughs had written was often in my mind, and I was seeking a melody that would translate in terms of emotion the intellectual inspiration of the old poet's words:

Serene I fold my hands and wait
    Not care for wind, nor tide, nor sea.
I fret not more 'gainst time or fate,
    For lo! My own shall come to me!

The stars come nightly to the sky,
    The tidal wave comes to the sea:
Not time nor space, nor deep nor high
    Can keep my own away from me!

If only I could string those beautiful words, like beaded gold, upon a melodic string of music! This was the preoccupation to which I set myself. From the infinite resources of my soul I must draw out the strains that would add the power of spirit to the mighty thought which the metrist had uttered.

But it seemed utterly useless.

I was a slave to the demanding love this yellow-haired Etta chained me with. Unable to elude her, I found myself breaking up spiritually; losing the capacity to conceive a dream, or compose three simple bars of music.

One by one my friends drifted away. Very plainly Etta showed them she did not welcome their visits. She refused to return calls. She was not interested in friends or relatives. All she wanted was me. She clung around me in constant embraces. She demanded thousands, thousands, thousands of kisses! I must make everlasting love to her. I must recite my devotion like a priest telling his beads. I must caress her with unflagging and unresting tenderness.

She wearied me.

Very secretly, at the very bottom of my heart, I began to detest her. Her blonde hair began to make me recall a yellow taffy which I ate when a boy; I ate too much of it, and got a pain in my stomach. Her blue eyes reminded me always of the vacancy of her intellect, which I had mistaken for mystery. She was a stupid woman, my wife, Etta. She was interested in loving me, and in nothing else in the world. If I tried to read her a beautiful book, she would tear it from my grasp and throw it out the window. Then she would purse her full, red, wet lips and croon:

"Come kiss me! Come kiss me!"

I had months of that. Months of her passionate tyranny over me. I could not dream of escaping. I was like a prisoner behind invisible bars. But the hate which began at the bottom of my heart rose like a tide and overflowed. After the first year I loathed her.

I was married to the most loving woman in the world and I did not know how to get rid of her.

Then, gradually, I found a means of escape. My own thoughts were a refuge. In them I would find solace from her eternal plaguing of me with outstretched arms and inviting lips. After she fell asleep at nights, I would commune with my own thoughts.

"She lies when she says she loves me," I would tell myself, in the loneliness of my waking hours, while she slept nearby. "She loves this big, hulking frame of mine, and to possess that she would destroy my immortal soul; crush my yearning to create; blot out my dreams."

And then I began to wonder about her first husband; my old friend Trent, who, they told me, had shot himself during a fight with the Germans. He had not been willing to wait to be killed. Why? Already rumors had come down the lines that an armistice was near. Trent had gone through battle after battle like a charmed man. Did he fear to be sent home to his wife? Was that why he had killed himself?

I turned and looked upon the prostrate form in the other bed with a shiver of suspicion.

My wife was not such a lovely object when she slept. I would look at her and shudder. Then her mouth was open, with her full lips widely parted, exposing her teeth. Her cheeks would be ruddily flushed, and her breath would make a guttural noise. I would turn away from her in repulsion, and busy my mind with beautiful images.

I loved those secret thoughts, often so near to waking dreams. It became my nightly practice to indulge in them. Memories would come to soothe my tortured mind; of valleys wrapped in misty melancholy; of quiet pools in which the bare limbs of trees would reflect against a leaden sky; of tumbling surf, crashing in boisterous play upon white and drifting sands.

A saying from a book I had been reading recently, in such spare moments as Etta permitted, recurred often during those silent meditations:

"We desire what we imagine; we will what we desire, and at last we create what we will!"

I wondered if that were possible. Desire! The trouble was my desire was only negative. That is, I was not conscious of desiring anything at all, except an escape from the intolerable requirement of making love to Etta.

Except, of course, my music!

Objectively, I mean, I had no desire. Never once had I consciously formed a desire in thought. Lying there, in the silence of my bed chamber, my eyes gloating in the darkness at the joy of simply being awake with myself while Etta was sleeping, I would let my thoughts wander as they would in aimless frolic. Sometimes I could almost fancy that Etta was away. In the joy of that little bit of freedom, I could not definitely organize a desire, even for my music.

And then, one night, an extraordinary impression came to me!

I felt as if I were not alone. I mean that I had the singular sensation of companionship, as if the darkness and the silence were shared with me by some waking consciousness.

So real was the feeling that I turned to her bed. Was Etta awake? Could she be lying there awake, without speaking? I could not believe it. She never lay awake without speaking. She is intolerably loquacious. I arose and went to her to see. She was lying with her head upon her left arm. Her hair was disarranged, and she was breathing deeply, stodgily.

It was not Etta.

Yet the impression of not being alone persisted. I felt the certain nearness of another presence in the room. Intently I listened. Was there a burglar in the house? The suspense got on my nerves. I leaped out of bed and turned on the lights.

I saw no one else in the room. Not satisfied, I made a search of the entire house. But the closest examination of the premises, in which all the servants assisted, yielded no clue. At its conclusion, my impression was stronger than ever; it had reached the proportions of a conviction!

In the light of what I know now, I realize that this precipitate search for a prowling intruder delayed for several months what eventually came to pass. This incident occurred in February, and it was not until the soft spell of April lay over the earth like perfume, that it was repeated.

When it did return, however, it was an infinitely more definite and tangible phenomenon.

Again I was lying awake. The hour was well after midnight, and our sleeping room was dark and utterly soundless, save for the sound of my wife's breathing. Of a sudden, I was conscious of a strange, warm thrill. This time I knew there was someone in the room, and the fact of knowing it affected me most oddly. In the presence of that unseen guest, a door seemed to open within me; a door, barred up and bolted, ponderously locked for so many years, swung wide open.

Feelings, sensations, delicious tremors of emotion, long imprisoned, rushed gladly out. The sense—the bewildering and intoxicating sense—of sheer beauty flooded me with pleasure. I was neither startled nor afraid. I was unreasonably and inexplicably happy!

I lay looking out into the darkness, perfectly still, my senses like an orchestra in the ecstasies of a symphony. What was about to befall me? I dared not guess. I had lost the power or capacity for thought. I merely waited.

It seemed to me that the darkness parted, like velvet curtains drawn by an invisible hand. No light came; only the shadows seemed to grow transparent. I could see without the aid of light. This is difficult to convey; the sensation was utterly unlike anything I have ever experienced. I looked through the darkness and saw clearly; I was looking at the softly draped figure of a girl with red hair!

The lovely surprise of her is beyond all words. Only music could recapture her shining beauty. In that first miraculous moment when she disclosed herself to me, an artlessly beguiling passage from a Chopin fantasy seemed to sing through all my nerves—yearning, tender, sweet.

What can it mean to eyes that have never beheld her to hear mere words that spell out lightness, the gauzy texture of a fairy's whimsy, graceful and altogether lovely? How can I tell you the divine glory of her oval face, the lambent refulgence of her smile?

For she was smiling down upon me! Smiling, while from her eyes of unfathomable blue came a steady glance of such poignant sympathy that my own eyes were wet with the tears of joy. I felt choked, delirious with her beauty and her smile.

She made a pretty gesture with her hands. They were such small hands, so unbelievably white and graceful. She seemed to be greeting me in friendly comradeship.

I tried to call to her, but my lips would not move, nor could I summon sound from my throat. Every muscle seemed unresponsive. I saw her toss her head; her red lips moved as if in utterance, and then—

She melted into the darkness and was gone!

Etta's bed was groaning beneath her weight, as she turned in her sleep. At once, with a fierce anger, I understood. A rage of rebellion swept through me. I could have shaken my wife in a frenzy of punishment. She—this gross, physical Etta, this tyrannous, soulless wife that was mine—she had stirred and threatened to awaken, and my phantom guest had fled.

The next morning I convinced myself that I had dreamed. But what a dream! The memory of it gave me recurring little thrills of ecstatic delight. I could think of nothing else, and braving all of Etta's tricks, I brooded through the day over the piano keys, now playing Chopin, now improvising lacy, delicately tinted themes and rich, rare harmonies that expressed the beauty of that wonderful girl in the night.

I was impatient for night to return; eager to dream that dream again. If only I might see that wondrous apparition once more! And when at last I lay again beneath the coverlets, staring out at the gloom which filled the room, still convinced that I had dreamed, I feverishly tried to woo sleep to my expectant eyes.

But the hours crept on, and sleep did not come. The same hour which the clock had marked when I saw the girl of my vision returned, and I was still awake.

As if the hour were a tryst, a time appointed for a sacred communion between us, she came to me again. It was not a dream! My pulses beat a thunderous challenge to my brain, pounding home the amazing proof that it was not a dream. I was awake. In the face of all that your pompous scientists may argue and declaim, I was awake! Etta was asleep; deep in her slumbers, but I was acutely awake and aware, and I saw her come to me like an angel out of a cloud.

At first she appeared just beside the bed, weaving about her rosy form a gauzy veil of soft violet grey. It clung about her like a drapery of twilight mist.

Again came that wonderful smile, so full of sympathy and understanding. I smiled up at her from my pillow. The desire to call to her had left me, replaced by a feeling of security and peace, and a strange new sense of power. Somehow I knew that she could address me, and though no sound came from her arched and tempting lips, yet I knew I could receive her thoughts.

"Madeline!" was the thought I heard. "My name is Madeline!"

"Beautiful name! Sweet name! Dear name!" I mentally exclaimed, and she smiled, her eyes dropped, and blushes tinged her cheeks. She had received my thought—a feeling of godlike power seemed to gush up within me like a fountain.

"Shall I dance?"

Her head was turned inquiringly, her hands lifted in a gesture of poised grace, as this thought impinged upon my consciousness.

"Please! Please! Please!" I cried in my mind.

Such a delicious sight my tired eyes had never before looked upon. As my answer reached her, she drew back, the darkness closing around her like an iris, until only her face was visible. I feared she was about to fade from my view. But no! It was as if she had yielded her form to the ministrations of unseen attendants. Presently she emerged into full vision once more—attired in a fashion two hundred years old.

In quick and graceful succession she danced for me the dances of many times and many places—her garments changing as the dances changed, while from very far off—an almost illimitable distance—came the soft music of muted strings.

I saw her first in a stately, old fashioned pavan, moving through its waltzing rhythm in her gown of Colonial times, shimmering with bright bits of silver. Again I beheld her in a Spanish dance, whirling and tapping her little feet imperiously in a love bolero that suddenly was transformed into an arduous saraband. Across our bedroom floor she glided, weaving vivid patterns with a trailing scarf of red and yellow, its black quivering fringes atremble with the staccato chant of distant castanets. Her pink and supple form undulated to the pulsing beat of far away drums and tambourines, and the soft, whispering tunes of plucked and amorous guitars. At last, freed from all raiment except her veil, gauzy as a spider's web, she whirled and flitted and pirouetted, rosy and ethereal. In the giddiest moment of her dance, she paused, poised on her toes and wafted me a farewell with her little hand, while a nimbus closed in about her, embracing her form until even her smile had vanished and I was alone again.

This time Etta sat up stiffly in her bed, rubbing her swollen eyes and gaping. Her voice was thick with sleep as she asked me in sodden suspicion what was wrong.

"There is nothing wrong, Etta," I answered her crossly. "Go back to sleep!"

"Kiss me!" she pouted, holding out her arms from across the room.

The next day I was forced to ponder very seriously over these clandestine experiences. For all of my artistic promptings, I am naturally a practical man. I began to cross-examine myself.

Did I actually believe that a beautiful red-haired woman came to me out of the air, at night, when Etta had gone to sleep?

Did I not realize that such a thing was completely absurd and impossible?

I did realize that such a thing was impossible. Yet I did know that the impossible had happened.

It had certainly happened, unless I was losing my sanity. I was forced to question my mental status. Was I going mad? If so, Etta had driven me mad. I was conscious of no particular symptom; I felt entirely normal, yet I did insist to myself that I had actually witnessed those two visits after midnight.

This was what sent me to the office of the famous doctor of the mind. I urged him to apply every test that he knew to determine the state and quality of my brain. He dismissed me with the blandiloquent assurance that I was one hundred per cent sane.

What, then, was the explanation?

I knew—and know—nothing of the mysteries of the soul. None of my time had ever been wasted—or ever will be wasted—in the pursuit of occultism or metaphysics. I have an inherited, a native distaste for such stuff.

But in the disturbed condition of my mind, I resolved to call upon an old friend living in Sheridan Square; a man whom I felt might help me. He is what is called a mystic, that is, he does not accept the conclusions of orthodox science, religion, or philosophy but tries to find truth on his own account. How old he is I do not know; at least he is twice my age.

After leaving the doctor, I boarded a Fifth Avenue bus and rode down to Washington Square. A few minutes' walk brought me to his door, and I was lucky enough to find him in.

Although he represses all emotions rigidly, he permitted himself the luxury of being glad to see me.

"Half an hour and you would have found me gone," he told me. "I am taking my wife and daughter to the art exhibition this afternoon. That is too important to be put off. Can you tell me your business in half an hour? I know it is important, for I get the psychic vibrations of your excitement!"

There you had the man! The kind of fellow who accepts the most impossible fancies as scientific truths. He actually believed himself when he said he could interpret my soul vibrations!

"I am very much puzzled," I confessed, "and I want you to tell me what is happening!"

Not a single detail did I omit in relating my experiences. All of it I poured into his sympathetic ear, although he betrayed not the slightest surprise at my narrative. When I had finished, he took me by the hand and said:

"The doctor you went to see had more sense than most of his brand ever reach. He was perfectly right. You are sane. And you do need a red-haired girl. I am afraid, my son, that I understand more of this queer business than I am permitted to reveal to you!"

Bah! I felt enraged! More mumbo-jumbo! That was the way with all mystics. When they couldn't explain, they talked nonsense.

Such were my thoughts.

"I am not talking nonsense," he broke in evenly, as if he had read my mind. "There may be several explanations. Perhaps—but there! The minx! Why should I try to explain what cannot be explained? Only, my son, it may be that your true mate is reaching out for you—a living woman projecting her astral body to your room. But be assured, if that is so, your own will come to you!"

An extraordinary sensation gripped me at his words. He had voiced the very spirit of the poet's lines that had formerly so impressed me! The verse for which I had sought the music so long, so vainly!

"Good-bye, my son," he said kindly. "Perhaps we shall meet again. Meanwhile—I have promised the folks that art exhibition!"

I left him, feeling better. At least, he had not derided me. And he had served me a good purpose, in the perhaps accidental choice of his language.

"Your own will come to you!"

I resolved to find the music for those words—to finish that self appointed task; to create, in spite of Etta and her love.

The remainder of the day was unpleasant. Etta was in a nasty mood. It was as if she suspected something; we quarreled bitterly, and the crushing sensation of defeat gathered in my heart. I looked forward for night to come, secure in the belief that in the dark hours my lovely vision would return.

To my blackest disappointment, she did not return. Not that night, nor the next, nor yet the next. I lay awake all night waiting, but in vain. I prayed, my heart wildly calling for the phantom that had evoked real love in my breast at last, but all to no purpose.

Of all men alive, I was then the most miserable. More than ever, I found it impossible to compose. The only satisfaction I found was in quarreling with Etta. Something cringing in me had been killed; I no longer submitted to her domineering love; I defied her and acquainted her with my aversion to her.

Months passed. They were months of increasing rancor in my household, unrelieved by a single visit from my dream girl. At last I began to fear that it was only a disordered fancy, after all. This but added to my bitterness. The inevitable clash came at last; Etta let forth a final boiling spurt of fury, and left me. A week later I was served with a notice that she was suing me for divorce, and to my ears came the scandal that she was flirting with a naval officer.

I was glad she was gone. For the first time peace came to my mind, as I trod the solitary rooms of my house. In just a few days I was measurably tranquil again. My spirit felt convalescent. I unlocked my piano and let my fingers roam idly up and down the keyboard.

She had been gone a week, when the fever of composition came back to me with redoubled emphasis, after two years of lying dormant. I got out paper and pencil, and with the sheets propped above the fallboard of the instrument, I returned again to the Burroughs verses, sure now that the elusive melody would come.

Perhaps I was a bit too eager; too impulsive; too sure. At any rate, I labored over the task, tearing up paper until it lay littered in disordered piles around the pedals, and I no nearer the music than before.

*The girl of my dreams was there, in the flesh,
before me.*

I felt defeated. All unnoticed, the hours had sped by me, and it was past midnight when I rose from the piano and staggered over to my desk. There, with the white light of a green-shaded lamp bathing my head, I bowed my face in my arms and gave up.

And then the miracle of all my days occurred. I feel the thrill of it yet.

To my wearied ears came the strains of far-off music—a familiar music that set my heart quaking in a very agony of mingled apprehension and hope. I sat bolt upright, and a sob of joy broke from me.

My own, my beloved, was there before me!

She smiled at me—the old, sweet, loving smile! This night she was unclad, save for a golden girdle about her rosy loins, and she glided before me, as if eager for something beautiful to happen.

Raising a finger to her lips, she looked away, as if bidding me to harken.

I listened.

The sweet strains of the orchestra had died away, and now I heard the solemn music of a mighty organ, its perfectly voiced reeds and pipes singing a grand hymn of exultation. It was simple and yet sublime.

And then, as she smiled at me so wisely, I received her unspoken thought. The lovely apparition fascinated me; held me so chained with adoration that at first I could barely grasp her meaning.

"Write!"

"Write!" That was it! Write down the swelling harmonies and exultant melody that pealed from the unseen organ.

This was music I could not reach; she had brought me as a gift of her love the music of the poem that promised so much to tired hearts:

> *The stars come nightly to the sky*
> *The tidal wave comes to the sea;*
> *Nor time nor space, nor deep nor high,*
> *Can keep my own away from me!*

As the last note was recorded on the paper before me, I looked up.

My darling raised her hand and touched her lips—then blew me a phantom kiss and was gone!

The next morning when I played over my notes I was absolutely certain that I was the composer, or really the transcriber, of a masterpiece of music. But I wanted another's opinion—the unprejudiced opinion of some one who knew.

With the precious manuscript tucked under my arm, I walked over to Fifth Avenue from Grand Central Terminal. I remember when I reached the corner the traffic lights were changing. It stirred old memories of a purple twilight, when I had first met Etta. Now, as I looked at them they changed again—from green, to scarlet, and then to kindly gold.

On a Fifth Avenue bus I rode down to Greenwich Village and walked hurriedly over to Sheridan Square where dwelt my friend, the mystic. Again I was lucky to find him home.

He sat down before his grand piano with my manuscripts, and easily played over the melody which had been dictated to me out of the air. At its conclusion he turned toward me, his eyes shining with fervor.

"It is beautiful! It is magnificent! It is sublime!" he cried, allowing all his emotions full play. "Wait until you hear it sung. My daughter shall sing it for you."

He got up and went to the door.

"Madeline!" he called softly.

Before I could breathe twice, he had stepped back, his face transfigured with an unearthly smile, and his daughter came into the room.

The girl of my dreams—the red-haired angel of my vision—was there, in the flesh, before me!

As I told you, I believe I could be a great composer, if I had the proper kind of wife! And, as I also told you, there remains one strangely dazzling hope.

There seems to be no doubt that Etta will get her divorce. And there seems to be little doubt in my mind that I shall have a red-haired wife!

Perhaps Rachmaninoff will yet play my sonatas, and the great orchestras of the world my symphonies?

Who knows?

The White Seal of Avalak

By Walter W. Liggett

Is it possible for an animal to be imbued with the spirit of a living, human person? If not, how do you account for the weird activities of that white seal at Avalak?

THEY SAY YOU CAN'T KILL A GHOST, but my friend Mike Dempsey—Corporal Dempsey of the Royal Canadian Mounted Police, he was then—says he saw one killed. He actually touched the blood on the ice; but maybe Dempsey was wrong, at that, for according to his own story the ghost walked again. He saw that, too.

It happened way up in Northwest Territory, at Avalak, a little Eskimo village on Coronation Gulf, a hundred miles or more north of the Arctic Circle. Dempsey was up there then, doing his bit with the Mounties. Afterwards he went prospecting for an oil company. That's why I can tell the story. There's no danger of Dempsey losing his stripes—now.

Dempsey and I were boys together on the Calgary prairies. We hunted, fished, harvested and broke broncos together. He was my best friend then and has been ever since, although I only see him about every five years. I got into the grain business—exporting—and finally came to New York. Mike joined the Mounties and drifted up north. But we always wrote to each other whenever we had time, and whenever he got a furlough he would come to New York to see me. He says he likes to take in New York from top to bottom—everything, shows, opera, cabarets and night clubs—about every so often because afterwards he's glad to get back to the Arctic. That's the kind of a fellow he is.

Mike never has

"Stop it, stop it, you fool!"

made much money, but at that I envy him at times. He's lived life. I've only read about it. He's a big, broad-shouldered, upstanding chap; tight-lipped, with clear, keen gray eyes that seem to look through you. He's had enough adventures up north to fill a dozen books. More than once he's gone out alone after some native murderer, bucking blizzards, mushing over floating ice, sleeping in the snow when it was sixty below zero, and risking a bullet in his back after he got there. He's grit all the way through; cool, matter-of-fact, even cynical. The last man in the world that you'd expect to "see things."

I've put this in so you will know what kind of man Dempsey is, and why I believe what he told me. You would believe him, too, if—well, I'll tell you the story in his own words and you can draw your own conclusions.

"It all started over a white seal," Dempsey said, beginning the tale. "A white seal isn't seen once in fifty years. I suppose they are freaks—albinos—but once in a while one does come along. The Eskimos are superstitious about them; say they are the spirits of the seal gods.

"Well, Morrison—he was the factor of the Arctic Trading Company post at Avalak— was a green man up north. He'd never heard the legend. He saw a white seal crawling on the ice, the first ever seen in that part of the Arctic since the white man came. He shot it. Then there was Hell to pay.

"Na-Kut-Tah, the shaman, or witch doctor, immediately said that Morrison had offended the seal god and that the Eskimos

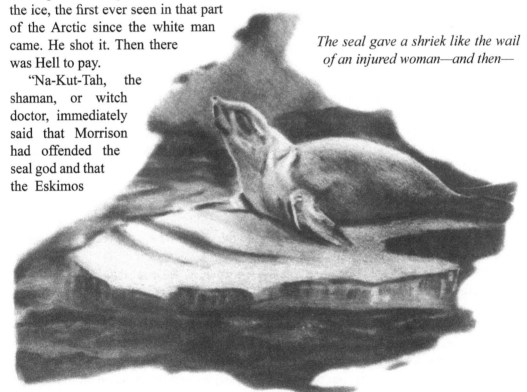

The seal gave a shriek like the wail of an injured woman—and then—

shouldn't trade with him. Na-Kut-Tah also said that the seals were angry and would go away—until he, Na-Kut-Tah, was able to propitiate them with presents. The people gave presents to Na-Kut-Tah and he was supposed to give them to the seals, but I think he cached them in his igloo. Anyway, the natives were boycotting Morrison and he sent word to me by a native.

"I was at Tree River. You know the Mounties established a post there in 1920 after two explorers and two missionaries were killed, and I was in charge of it, with two constables to help me patrol a coastline of one thousand miles. The native messenger didn't have the facts straight, but he said that Morrison had told him there was 'hi-yu trouble,' so I harnessed my dog team and hit the trail, although it was forty below zero. I made the sixty miles to the westward in two days.

"Morrison fell on my neck and almost wept when I got there. He seemed to think that I could go out and command the Eskimos to resume trading with him—I told you he was new to the Arctic—but I knew it would be nothing as simple as that. You've got to go slow when you're dealing with one of these native shamans. The witch doctors are the real rulers of the Eskimo tribes and most of them are pretty crafty old birds.

"Besides, I soon found out that another independent trader, 'Broken-Nose' Frazier we called him—though that wasn't his real name—was mixed up in the affair. It was no business of the Mounties to butt into a trade rivalry, though I didn't mind giving Morrison some good advice on the side.

"This Broken-Nose Frazier was, or had been an English remittance man in Alaska. He came from one of the oldest families in England. That's why I don't give his real name. He had been cashiered out of the British army in India and finally his family had packed him off to Alaska. He spent his remittance as fast as he got it, on booze mostly, and finally drifted up the Arctic coast. His face was badly scarred and twisted on the left side, hence his nickname, 'Broken-Nose,' though his nose wasn't really broken at all.

"No one gets quite as low as one of these aristocratic remittance men. They drop all holds when they finally let go. Frazier was living with an Eskimo 'klootch,' and peddling 'hootch' that he made in a home-made still, though we never could catch him at it. He had come to Avalak a few months before and already he and the shaman, old Na-Kut-Tah, were thick as thieves. I figured out right away that he had had something to do with the boycott, though of course Morrison had made things easy by killing that white seal. He showed me the skin. It was a beauty, but I never want to see another.

"I went to see Na-Kut-Tah. He admitted that he had declared a boycott on Morrison because he had killed the white seal. He said that all the seals were angry and had gone away—that the whole tribe would starve unless he could persuade them to come back. Well, it was true. The seals had gone away. Naturally, that made the Eskimos one hundred per cent believers in Na-Kut-Tah's magic.

"Me? Oh, I think the old bird could predict the weather. The seals always disappeared when there was an east wind. Old Na-Kut-Tah must have known the east wind was coming before he made his prediction. How? I don't know, but usually the job as shaman descends from father to son and in the course of a few hundred years they probably pick up some pretty good trade secrets.

"Anyway, the seals had gone and the tribe, as well as Morrison, would starve, unless they came back. I pointed this out to Na-Kut-Tah and he said the seals might come back if the people gave them presents. Of course, the old scamp attended to the distribution of these presents himself, and I was morally certain that he already had all the fox skins in the village—he or Frazier.

"Then I suggested that maybe it would help if Morrison gave him a present—a rich present; that maybe then he could take off the boycott. It seems funny, perhaps, to hear of a Mounted Policeman suggesting a bribe, but I knew this old bird like a book and there was no other way out of it. You see Frazier already had fixed him—the old scoundrel's breath was reeking with liquor when he talked to me—and Morrison would never handle a skin unless he got into the game and bid for the shaman's favor.

"Na-Kut-Tah leered at me and said he would consult his spirits, so I went back to report to Morrison. He went up in the air at first, swore and stamped and said he'd never pay a bribe to the shaman. He even berated me for suggesting it. But finally I calmed him down. He saw it was the only way, and I went back and told old Na-Kut-Tah that Morrison would contribute ten sacks of flour, five boxes of candles, oil, and a lot of other truck if he would bring the seals back.

"Just to bring the seals back, mind you. He hadn't agreed yet to take the curse off Morrison.

"Well, I guess Na-Kut-Tah knew the wind was due for a change—that the seals would come back anyway the next day—for he didn't hang out or haggle about the price. Instead, he called the tribe together in his igloo and prepared to 'make medicine,' or work magic to get the seals back.

"Of course no white men were supposed to sit in at that séance, but Morrison and I saw it just the same. We heated a poker and sneaked up beside the igloo and made a little hole in the snow walls with the poker. We both were nervous and excited. What terrible thing would be brought to light in that temple of ice? No man could tell.

"I tell you it was weird. The Eskimos, men, women and children, were huddled together in the middle of the igloo and Na-Kut-Tah was sitting on a little ice platform in one corner— before a curtain of skins. A stone lamp was burning at his feet and that was the only light in the igloo. We could just see pale smudges—the faces of the Eskimos—when we took turns peeping in and we couldn't understand much, either, for Na-Kut-Tah was using words of incantation that we never had heard before.

"Well, we saw enough to understand his hold over those simple, primitive, superstitious Eskimos. The lamp would burn low and then it would burn high. Once he sprinkled some powder on it and it burned green, then red and yellow. Old Na-Kut-Tah was chanting while he slowly swayed back and forth and finally he had them all swaying and chanting in rhythm. He was getting them worked up, slowly, like they do at revival meetings, and finally voices began to cry out from all corners of the igloo.

"Ventriloquism, I guess. The old boy had a pretty good bag of tricks. Finally, when they were shouting, and throwing themselves about, all half hysterical, Morrison, who was taking his turn at peering through the hole, leaped back, his face as white as a sheet.

" 'Good God, Dempsey!' he cried—they would have heard him inside if they hadn't been making such a racket themselves—'Look! Look!'

"Well, I looked, and for the moment the hair stood up on my head. Waving beside the shaman was a white form that looked for all the world like a white seal. And it was crying, low and plaintive, like a woman.

"I stared, horror stricken. Had the shaman raised a ghost, or—

"Then an Eskimo dog started barking and we stuffed up the hole with snow and got back to Morrison's cabin. We didn't want the natives to know we were listening in.

"Well, the next day the seals did come back, and once more Na-Kut-Tah was solid with the natives. He had said the seals would go away, and they did. Then he had said he would bring them back, and they were back. Seeing is believing and the natives were singing his praises and the old boy was stalking through the village with a smirk of satisfaction on his face.

" 'What's he going to do about me?' Morrison wanted to know, so once more I hunted up Na-Kut-Tah and acted as go-between.

"Na-Kut-Tah was non-committal for a time. He said it had taken big magic to bring back the seals, but that they still were offended at Morrison. If the people traded with Morrison maybe the seals would go away again. The seal spirits were very, very angry, and so forth.

"Of course I listened politely and complimented him on his magic—I did think what I had seen was pretty good—and ended up by asking him how much of a present it would require to square things for Morrison. He hesitated. I could see he was trying to figure out just how much Morrison might be made to pay. Finally he said he would go into a trance and ask the seal spirits. He said it might take days to get an answer, but that he would let me know in due time.

"Once more Morrison stormed and raged, but there was nothing to be done about it. Morrison had to wait whether he wanted to or not. I figured that I was needed there about as badly as any other place along our thousand mile patrol, so I decided to wait, too. I had a hunch that something was going to break, yet I didn't see how I could interfere any more than I had.

"The native hunters were out now, day and night, killing seal. The ice was black with carcasses, and the women were skinning them and blowing up the hides, the way the natives cure them. It was the biggest kill the tribe had made for several seasons and it was plain that some one was going to do plenty of business, but whether it would be Frazier or Morrison I couldn't tell.

"Then Frazier did a fool thing. I told you he was a 'klootch-man' didn't I? I mean he was living with an Eskimo woman. Well, he started trifling with old Na-Kut-Tah's favorite girl—these shamans in the Arctic aren't celibate by a long ways. Frazier should have known better, but Oh-It-Ok was the prettiest woman in the tribe and Frazier always had an eye for feminine beauty, even Eskimo. It was because of a woman, another officer's wife, that he had been kicked out of the British army in India. I suppose he thought he could get away with this affair without Na-Kut-Tah finding out. That's where he was foolish, for that old bird had eyes in the back of his head and when it came to collecting gossip he could beat a whole women's sewing circle in one of our Calgary villages.

"Na-Kut-Tah never let on that he knew, and he continued to drink Frazier's home-made hootch, smiling and friendly. Privately he told me that if Morrison would give him another present, a rich, very rich present—for the seal spirits, of course—he would work his most powerful magic and try to fix things so the people could trade once more with Morrison.

" 'What kind of a present do you require?' I asked him and right off the bat he said that first of all he would have to have the white seal skin, and there was plenty beside that.

"You should have heard Morrison when I told him. He fairly raved this time. He swore he'd see Na-Kut-Tah and the whole tribe to Hell before he'd part with that seal skin. It was a beauty; it must have been worth a couple of thousand dollars. Of course it was Morrison's private property for he had killed it himself and hadn't taken it in trade.

"I went back and told Na-Kut-Tah that Morrison would give him everything except the white seal skin. He insisted on that. He said he would have to work powerful magic and impart life into it; that if he could make it live again the seals would be satisfied. Otherwise the taboo would always be in force against Morrison and the whole Arctic Trading Company, too.

"Finally Morrison surrendered and I took the seal skin to Na-Kut-Tah. He grinned when

I gave it to him, then announced he would retire for a couple of days alone to try to bring back the seal to life—which sounded pretty thick when you consider that it had been killed two weeks before, and skinned on top of that. But that was his story, and he said that if he brought it back to life he would return and the white seal itself would announce its wishes to the people.

" 'He'd better not try to double cross me or I'll kill him,' Morrison declared when I told him.

" 'Then you'll go in irons to Tree River,' I promised. 'There'll be no killing, Morrison. That's why I've stayed on the job. I'm trying to straighten out your dirty squabble.' All the same, I resolved to stick pretty close to him when old Na-Kut-Tah pulled off his final demonstration, for Morrison was murdering mad over losing that white seal skin, and I didn't blame him much, at that.

"Then I went to Frazier. I had no love for the man—he was a disgrace to the white race—but at the same time I was up there to prevent crime and I knew he'd end through a hole in the ice if he kept on playing with old Na-Kut-Tah's girl.

"He was in his igloo when I found him, the place piled high with furs, and he had a drunk on. I couldn't see any evidence of the still in the igloo. He was too smart for that; he knew I'd run him in for hootch peddling if I got the chance. He laughed at me when I warned him.

"Oh, I know you're taking sides with Morrison because he represents a big corporation,' he remarked. 'You Mounties are always siding against the independent traders.'

" 'You're a damned black-hearted liar,' I told him. 'If I had my way I'd kick all you traders out of the Arctic. The Eskimos were all right until you fur hunters came. But all that aside, I'm telling you not to fool around with Oh-It-Ok. Not if you value your health. Smart as you think you are, the old shaman is smarter. Leave the girl alone, man.'

" 'Maybe there's a method in my madness,' is his hint. 'And perhaps you overrate the smartness of our friend, the witch doctor, merely because he is smarter than you and that flannel-mouthed Morrison.' Oh, he could talk like a book when he was half drunk.

" 'Wait and see whether he is smarter than I am,' he boasts. 'Tell Morrison he may have a surprise coming, when Na-Kut-Tah stages his last grand performance entitled "The Return of the White Seal." ' He grins again and I turn and go out. I was surprised that he had learned about Na-Kut-Tah's plans, until suddenly it comes to me that the girl must have told him. And then I knew what he meant about there being a method in his madness.

"Well, to make a long story short, old Na-Kut-Tah disappears for three days, and then he comes back, sends for me, and says that he has consulted the seal spirits and brought the white seal to life. At midnight, down on the beach behind the village, all the people would assemble, and the white seal would come out and make known its wishes.

" 'The white men may be there and see and hear,' he adds, and right then I knew he must be pretty sure of his magic.

"Na-Kut-Tah was sure of himself, but I was damned uneasy. Oh, I know, it sounds foolish, telling you this down here, in civilization, but that was in the Arctic, and those natives believe in witchcraft and magic. Perhaps I should have stopped it, but then Morrison would have been out of luck and I figured he was entitled to a fair break on the fur trade. After all, I was only referee, so I decided to let things slide and see what happened. That's where I made my big mistake.

"That night, an hour or so before midnight, the natives began assembling down on the beach. Na-Kut-Tah started them singing and swaying, and I tell you it sounded uncanny, with the echoes among the ice hummocks. The Northern Lights were flashing over head, every color in the rainbow, and there was so much electricity in the air that our hair was standing up straight.

"Morrison and I were standing in the shadows, about thirty feet behind the natives, and pretty soon Frazier came along and stopped ten feet to one side of me. Morrison never spoke to him, but Frazier grins at me and nods. It was plain enough that he was confident of the result of the show and I commenced to think that I'd be a referee in real earnest if the shaman double-crossed Morrison.

"After about an hour of the chanting—by this time the natives were worked up to a frenzy—Na-Kut-Tah steps behind an ice hummock that ran right down to the beach. Beyond it there was a patch of clear ice, about a hundred yards wide, and black open water beyond that. That old boy was a showman; he certainly had an eye to stage effects. The ice was the stage and the hummock was the wings, where he was doing his stuff. A narrow water strip divided us from the stage.

"We could hear him singing. Suddenly there was a flare of light from behind the hummock; that died down and then Morrison grabbed my arm.

" 'Look! Look!' he whispered, and sure enough, as I followed his finger, I could see something white creeping out on the ice.

"It was a seal, all right, a white seal, or if it wasn't you couldn't tell it from one.

"The Eskimos raised a wail and for all that I knew it was some kind of a fake. I could feel the shivers running up my back and Morrison's fingers were digging into my arm.

"The seal was out of the shadow of the hummock now, sliding and flipping across the glare of ice, and you could see it plainly in the flare of the Northern Lights. I would have gone into court and sworn it was a seal and nothing else. It kept moving straight out towards the open water and when it was about two yards from the water it turned and swayed just as any seal, black or white, does; and then it stopped, and raised its head, and barked—and still I would have sworn it was a seal.

"Then it spoke, and I felt like giving a guffah of laughter, for it was Na-Kut-Tah's voice. He had a husky, deep, throaty voice, one that you couldn't mistake. I knew that he had sewed himself up in Morrison's white seal skin and was staging this performance. Morrison knew, too, and so did Frazier, for all of us drew closer to hear his words. But I doubt if the Eskimos knew—they were still too much under the spell, too willing to believe in his magic.

"I couldn't distinguish the first words. Probably they were more of his magic ritual that we didn't know. But suddenly that seal began to use trader's terms that we all knew—and that started all the trouble.

" 'Morrison good man,' it croaked, still in Na-Kut-Tah's voice. 'He sorry he kill seal. People can trade with him. It is Broken-Nose who made bad medicine against seals and people.'

" 'He delivered the goods,' Morrison whispered in my ear and moved away. There was the roar of a rifle and as I jumped and looked around, I saw Frazier, dropped on one knee, pumping his 30-30 as fast as he could work it at the seal. The Eskimos were watching, faces blank; Morrison was staring, as though struck dumb.

" 'Stop it! Stop it, you fool!' I shouted and I was on him in two jumps.

"Before I reached him the seal gave a shriek—it was a seal's cry all right this time—like the wail of an injured woman, and then, as I wrestled with Frazier for the gun I saw the seal roll off the ice, into the open water, and the tide dragged it under an ice floe.

"I cracked Frazier in the jaw. He was crazy—half drunk, too—and for all I knew he might have a knife or a pistol, and use it on me. He went down, and just as he did, old Na-Kut-Tah, rubbing his hands and grinning, stepped around the ice hummock and came towards us.

"Morrison started to run—he won't deny it—and I almost fell over on top of Frazier. I would have sworn that Na-Kut-Tah was in that seal skin. I could have testified in any court to his voice. But here he was, asking what the row was about.

"Well, I had the devil's own time in calming the Eskimos down and getting Frazier back to the trading post alive. But I did it, and Na-Kut-Tah helped me. He didn't want any run in with the police. That wasn't his method.

"Of course you've guessed the answer. It was the girl Oh-It-Ok who was sewed up in that skin. No, I couldn't swear to it. There was blood on the ice, but it might have been seal blood. Na-Kut-Tah solemnly insisted it was a seal we saw, but I knew a damned sight better, because the girl was missing.

"Na-Kut-Tah said he had seen her last with Frazier and suggested maybe Broken-Nose had pushed her through the ice. Again I knew better, Frazier had sent her through the ice, all right, but not deliberately. He thought he was killing Na-Kut-Tah, and take it from me, that old bird knew in advance just what was going to happen, and was morally certain that Frazier would be so enraged that he would shoot.

"What did I do? Put Frazier under arrest, of course. But what case did I have against him? Morrison and I would both have to swear we thought it was a seal, at first. Frazier could swear anything he pleased. The Eskimos all would swear it was a seal, if their testimony was taken. That voice? Ventriloquism, of course. Na-Kut-Tah was behind the hummock all the time.

"The more I thought about it the more I was convinced that Morrison and Frazier and I would all end up in New Westminster (the Dominion insane asylum) if any sane jury heard our testimony.

"Well, luckily we didn't have to give any testimony. Oh, yes, there's a sequel, and it happened the same night, or rather the same morning.

"Na-Kut-Tah had come to me after the shooting.

" 'Will Big White Father make Broken-Nose dance on the air?' he asked. He meant, would he be hanged.

" 'The Great White Father ought to make you dance on the air,' I answered angrily. 'You make much bad magic.'

"He grunted and walked away, but he had learned what he wanted to know. If I had told him we did intend to hang Frazier, it probably would have saved his life. But how could I guess what the old scoundrel was planning?

"Morrison and I were down on the ice where the seal—the girl, I mean—had gone through. We were trying to find the body, for of course there could be no case at all against Frazier without a corpus delicti. Frazier was with us, handcuffed, of course. Believe me, he was sober now. He had been pretty drunk when he did the shooting, but he had come to realize that Na-Kut-Tah had tricked him into shooting the girl and I never heard such cursing. I don't think he was worrying much about our finding the body, for the Arctic ocean never gives up its dead. The water is too cold; bodies never rise.

"It was morning, as I told you, but, of course, up there in the Arctic—in the winter, I mean—the days are darker than the nights. And it was blacker than a black hat this morning. I hadn't any hope of finding the body myself, but of course I had to make an effort for form's sake. Mostly I was trying to dope out what I would do with Frazier. I didn't like the looks of the whole thing and I knew it would mean a black mark on my record.

"Suddenly, out of the darkness, came the cry of a seal, a whimpering that somehow made my blood run cold. It kept coming nearer and nearer, still whimpering, though we couldn't see a thing. Then I saw. By God, it was a white seal! And walking—yes, walking towards us.

"My hand was fumbling for my service revolver, but my fingers were numb with the cold and I couldn't seem to unclasp the holster. Morrison saw my motion.

" 'My God, do you see it, too?' he cried, catching my arm again.

"Then the damned thing spoke—yes, spoke, in a woman's voice—and it was crying out like it was accusing somebody of something. It was in Eskimo, but I couldn't make out the words.

"I guess Frazier could, though, and I guess he thought it was the girl, Oh-It-Ok, reproaching him, for I heard him give a sort of sobbing groan and then he cried out, 'Keep away! Keep away, damn you!'

"I tell you, Tom, it wasn't fifteen feet away, and I could see it as clear as I see you now. It was a white seal—walking, mind you—and its eyes gleamed like flame.

"Some trick of the shaman's? Maybe—but if you'd been there with us that day you'd have been as scared as we were, and I'll admit I was damned scared. Besides, our nerves were jumpy over that other killing, and remember Frazier had been soaked with rotten home-made booze for weeks on end.

"The thing kept coming, and I edged over to one side, still fumbling for my revolver. Morrison was behind me, hanging on for dear life.

"It sheered off from us and started towards Frazier, still whimpering and crying like a lost soul. I tell you my blood was colder than ice water and I could feel my hair stiffen inside my fur parka hood.

" 'Keep off! Keep off!' Frazier was hollering, his manacled hands held before his face.

"But it didn't keep off. It kept right for him, and suddenly, with a wild cry, he (Frazier, I mean) backing up all the time, slipped on the edge of the ice and toppled over backwards into the water. He tried to catch himself, but remembered he was handcuffed.

"And that damned white seal, or ghost, or Na-Kut-Tah, or whatever it was, dived in after him, head first, as slick as a whistle.

"Ghost or no ghost, I was going to save my prisoner. Besides I'd finally got my gun out, so I ran to the edge of the ice as fast as I could, with Morrison still clinging to me.

"He never came to the surface—Frazier, I mean. The tide was running and there was floating ice in all directions. And the seal, or whatever it was, didn't show up, either.

"Sure, I reported it as an accidental drowning. We Mounties don't always tell all we know.

"Some damned queer things happen in the Arctic and when you see the Northern Lights swishing across the sky, so close to earth you can hear them, green, yellow, red, casting dancing shadows on the snow; when the ice floes are grinding, the seals crying like lost souls, and the Eskimos swaying and chanting, you're about half ready to believe that those simple, primitive natives may know some things that we civilized people have forgotten."

The Ha'nts of Amelia Island
By T. Howard Kelly

**Ghost-guarded gold drew him into the blackness of the jungle—
and he paid for his greed with a terrible reckoning.**

SINCE THE BEGINNING, AMELIA, WHICH THE INDIANS CALLED GUALE, has been lying in shark water off the northeastern coast of Florida—a little green and white island eternally pounded by booming surf.

I drifted down there last winter intending to loiter only a few days. But some places cast a spell that is inescapable for a man who seeks romance and adventure. The lonely sweeps of white curving beaches were seductive in the flaming sunrise and the purple dusk, and the jungles that brooded mysteriously behind the sand dunes seemed places where one might drop out of life for a little while, or forever.

I stayed on, lured by the unaccountable premonition that something was going to come of those long days of sun splendor that throbbed lazily with the haunting voice of great waters, and those deep nights that seemed asleep, and yet mysteriously awake.

One night a mulatto man, digging in the yellow sand of Old Town bluff, unearthed gold coins—Spanish doubloons! About five hundred dollars' worth according to the local bank's appraisement. The chamber of commerce bought them from the mulatto man, and hung the gleaming pieces for all the island town of Fernandina and its winter visitors to see.

There is a lure about gold, old or new, that is as ancient as Man. I examined the doubloons dated 1655 and asked questions. I was told that treasure had been dug up three times before on Amelia Island. On one occasion a negro named Saunders had struck a chest said to contain thirty thousand dollars in money and gems. He reburied it, and went into the jungle looking for more. Saunders had never been heard of since.

The stories of the other two treasure discoveries ended as grimly. On one occasion the finder was found in his own bed, his throat slit. The other two men who had happened across buried booty disappeared and nothing was ever heard of either until years later. Then an old colored man named Uncle Jimmy Drummond, who continually spoke of his friendship with the "ha'nts" of Amelia Island, said he had seen the men wandering through the tangled hammock shackled to each other by ship chains. The men had no throats, according to old Jimmy, and they had brushed past him without so much as a sound or touch.

An old seafaring captain present suggested that I go to Uncle Jimmy Drummond's shack in the north jungle, and ask him about the treasure he swore was buried there, and guarded by the ghosts of the pirates Captain Kidd had murdered.

"Uncle Jimmy's over a hundred and five years old, part African and part Indian, and he swears that he, and his Indian father before him, have met people down in the hammocks there at night who used to be on this island centuries ago," the captain told me. "Indians—Spaniards—the twelve priests that were massacred in 1593—pirates—soldiers—and everybody else who met violent death have appeared to Uncle Jimmy.

"Maybe, if you don't believe that the dead haunt the places where they were killed, you won't take too much stock in Jimmy unless you go with him some night through the hammocks. I've been through 'em at night, and if there ain't any ghosts down there, I'll bet there's none anywhere else. Anyhow, if you want to hear about the buried gold and booty, you've got to catch Uncle Jimmy at night. He, and them snakes he charms, sleep all day," concluded the captain.

Pirate-haunted gold! The very idea set my pulses to pounding. I decided to visit Uncle Jimmy that night, and go treasure hunting.

It was about eleven o'clock when I left town and headed for the north hammock which lay directly behind the lonely sand dunes. The sky was overcast, and there was an ominous threat of storm in the air—a sort of warning that is really always in the wind down in those countries of the sun where squalls are continually blowing out of the Caribbean like miniature hurricanes.

The road was wide and straight. It ran between the river side of Amelia and the eastern shores that faced the open sea. A distance of a mile, perhaps, and I was on that part of the highway that splits the jungle in half. Uncle Jimmy Drummond's place was buried in the deep gloom that stretched away to the north.

Now, as I stood there, hesitating before plunging in on the path that I had been told would eventually bring me to Jimmy's shack of snakes and superstition, an ever thickening darkness shrouded all form and movement. The sky overhead had descended like a lowering canopy, and there was not one point of starlight to be seen in all of that overhanging blackness.

But the light from Amelia's light house pierced the shadows as it revolved in its tower. The war had taught me a few things about plunging into the unknown. It is always a wise thing to have something by which to guide yourself. I could climb a tree, I decided, and look for that light if I lost my sense of direction. The light blinked exactly due south of the jungle.

I pulled out the Army automatic that I had used in France. My fingers, sensitive to its every detail, ran over the weapon, and assured me it was ready for action. Of course I knew that, if there really were such things as ghosts, they would be far beyond the touch of bullets. You cannot kill a dead person. Ghosts at best, could only be the immaterial spirits of the dead—

But there were living things in the hammock that might need a bullet. It was early spring in Florida, and the deadly snakes were breaking ground. A wild cat, or one of the few panthers said to be left on the island, was not exactly the sort of an adventure I wanted to experience with my bare hands. I was ready for anything—anything human!

A last look at the green light and I struck out on the jungle path. It was down trail for over a hundred yards, and in the baffling dark, I felt as if I must be descending into some yawning black maw. Occasionally I flashed my light to be sure I was still on the vague path. Great oaks and pines, dripping with beards of gray Spanish moss and fenced by a hopeless snarl of palmettos, bush, and rope-like vines, leered down at me like brooding, prehistoric giants. The shaft of light never was able to penetrate more than a few feet of the encompassing gloom, and I really had to feel my way.

Those tangled woods throbbed with mournful sound that was like a strangely muffled funeral chant. It was the echo of the sea drumming against white shores that I felt must be miles and miles away, an echo that seemed to creep stealthily through the unmoving shadows. As I forged along I thought of the echo as a dirge for the dead of the jungle. Surely it was no hymn for the living!

At last a faint glimmer of light reached me through the dark. I was sure it was the cabin

I was seeking, and I called for Uncle Jimmy. There was no answer to my call. I pushed on until I found that faint light sputtering away in an oil lamp that hung inside the queerest old shack I'd ever been in—a shack that seemed woven into the very tangle of the hammock.

The lamp flickered out just as I reached the door. I remained stock still in the pressing dark until I sensed a movement somewhere back in the old shack. It was a smooth gliding sort of movement and made a ghostly swishing sound. It was something—yes, something without feet! I wheeled, spraying the shack with light. A soiled old piece of rag which hung from the ceiling for a curtain was fluttering faintly, as if something had passed through it.

I did not go over to that curtain immediately. I was not exactly afraid to do so, and yet I hung back, postponing advancement until I had almost convinced myself that my eyes were playing tricks.

Then I heard a sound that froze the blood in my veins. The shack was filled with a hollow ringing, as though something were rattling against something dead! If I had recognized that ringing sound I never would have summoned nerve enough to pull the curtain back—

A big rattlesnake lay coiled a few feet beyond the curtain, his rattle ringing ominously!

I jumped back, dropping the curtain as if it were flame. Backing to the door, my searchlight playing on the floor, and my gun drawn, I found myself trembling and breathing harder than I ever had when facing death in France. Somehow, I could not shake off the blood-curdling idea that the great striped and ringed reptile had trailed me. Believing that noise would frighten the snake away, if he really had followed me, I began shouting for Uncle Jimmy.

"Who's calling Uncle Jimmy?" demanded a voice that gave me a start on account of its closeness.

I was outside now, and I flashed my light in a circle to discover the owner of the voice. But the jungle gave no sign of a human presence. Well, there was nothing else to do but answer the invisible questioner. I explained my mission and the silence that immediately followed my words seemed more deathly and mysterious than ever. Then suddenly a wailing that might have been the cries of lost souls, or of abandoned babies, filled the hammock. I stood rooted to the ground, right hand on my automatic. Something brushed against my shoulder. Panic swept through my blood. I wheeled about, nerves on edge.

My light revealed a picturesque old man with the glow of a fanatic burning in his beady eyes. He saw my pistol and waved at it with a long curious-looking stick which I learned later was his so-called "cha'm stick" with which he charmed snakes.

"You ain't got no need for that weapon now, suh. I'm Uncle Jimmy Drummond, and I'll tell you what you want to know. Come into my house. You needn't be afraid of Gonga, my snake. I was right nearby when you went in to look around. If you'd meant any harm Gonga'd struck you, suh. He's my guard— There goes that wild cat's ghost again! That fellow's been crying down there like the devils had him for the past few nights. Hear him?"

I didn't have to make an effort at listening. The wail of that cat was something a deaf man would have heard. "You say it's a wild cat's ghost, Uncle Jimmy?" I asked, following him to the house hesitantly. I did not like the idea of entering the place where a poisonous reptile was at large: for I did not have any positive reason to know old Jimmy had real power over crawling things.

"Yassuh, that's the speerit of that cat Cap't Kidd and his men tormented to death the night they buried the treasure down thar in the hammock."

"Then the jungle—hammock as you call it—has buried treasure in it?"

"Yassuh, it's full of it all right. Gold! Silver! An' all sortsa sparkling booty. Chests, an' pots, an' barrels of it!" he answered, rubbing his gnarled old hands.

"Doesn't anybody know where some of it is buried, Uncle Jimmy?"

The old man who boasted that he was the last of his father's race upon the island—a Cherokee admitting a half strain of negro blood in his veins—gave me a quick look. At that moment I became forebodingly aware of swishy, gliding movement in the room.

"It's Gonga. If you'll feel better I'll send him back," he said, his eyes more beady than ever.

"I'm not any too crazy about his company."

Words, or rather sounds that I cannot describe, came from the old fellow and I heard the snake retreating.

"Gonga always gets nervous and excited when he hears folks asking me about that thar pirate treasure. Sometimes I almost figures he's one of them hants in snake skin. But, course he ain't. 'Cause it's like my father often told me. Hants ain't things like people and snakes. They's something a lot more powerful. But you asked me if anybody knows where that thar treasure's buried. Yassuh, somebody knows just where it's buried right now. Course, not all of it. But, all them thar chests, an' pots, an' barrels Cap'n Kidd buried—"

"Who's this somebody, Uncle Jimmy?" I asked, pretty certain of his answer. I was sure he knew things no white man on Amelia Island could tell me.

"Uncle Jimmy, suh. I knows where all Kidd's treasure's buried," he said, "an' I reckon I'm the only human that does."

"Then why haven't you dug up all that money and bought yourself a new house, and an automobile—"

"A man dasn't touch that treasure, suh. It's hanted, every drap of it!"

"Haunted?" I interrupted him. "That's interesting. You say you know where all the gold is but the—er—hants won't let you touch it?"

"That's it, suh. Them pirates' speerits ain't letting nobody take their plunder. It's buried about two miles from here under a big tree that's got an anchor chain nailed to it—"

"How did you find this out?" I asked.

"The hants told me all about it when I was a boy roaming through the hammock one night. They's been friendly with us Drummonds a mighty long time. I never walks through the hammock but I meets up with some of 'em—thar's two down there at the end of my path now—"

"Who were these hants when they were alive?"

"The hants? Oh! they were the pirates what hid the treasure under the big oak tree with the chain, and then had their throats split by Cap'n Kidd." Uncle Jimmy's voice dropped as if he feared some invisible presence was listening to his words. "Old Kidd was a stingy devil. He wanted all the booty himself. He murdered 'em in cold blood so's nobody but him would know where it was.

"But you can't get the best of speerits. When a man dies he gets new power. Them pirates got it, time they was murdered. They've been guarding their treasure ever since that night in 1799, the same night Kidd tormented that wild cat to death on a pole. If Cap'n Kidd had ever tried to come back after his treasure they'd have got him just as sure as they'd get me if I tried to take them thar chests an' pots, an' barrels."

"Have they ever 'got' anybody for tampering with the treasure, Jimmy? I heard you'd seen two men walking through the hammocks one night with chains on, and no throats?" I said.

"Them fellows was Means and Smith what dug up some treasure, and disappeared mysterious-like on the island. Course the hants got 'em."

"Then you wouldn't advise me to look for that treasure?"

"No suh, not if you values your life. It's terrible the way things happen down thar by that tree. Sometimes they don't know it's me coming, and the goings-on is enough to scare even me to death, and I've seen and heard more hants than any living man on Amelia. Why, I seen Lafitte, Morgan, and even old Blackbeard himself in this here hammock, and all of 'em had blood dripping from their hands!"

Jimmy Drummond had a long tongue for the subject of dead men who come back to haunt the living. He told me how in 1799 Kidd had crossed Cumberland Bar, his ship's hold loaded with precious booty. That night Kidd ordered nearly every man on board to carry ashore all he could lift of the treasure. He left a half-witted cabin-boy, and a black cook ironed in the brig, and went ashore after his pirates. Finding a place in the hammock under a great oak tree to bury the chests, he snared a wild cat, and tied it to the end of a long pole and hoisted above the branches of the jungle trees. His men on the beach saw the green cat eyes shining through the dark and heard it squalling, and were thus piloted to the tree. Uncle Jimmy's eyes were snapping with excitement as he got to this part of his story.

"After each pirate buried his pot of treasure, the old devil led him away, and with that poor cat wailing and crying its head off atop that pole, Kidd slit the pirate's throat," he went on. "When they was all killed, and the treasure buried, the Cap'n nailed an anchor chain to the oak, and leaving the wild cat still screeching on the pole, sailed away in fear of an English man-o-war. Them pirate hants told me all this the first night I met 'em."

"How did you come to meet them?"

The lamp Jimmy had re-lighted suddenly went out before he could answer. I could have sworn that some unseen person or thing had blown a heavy breath through the shack. The darkness of the hammock rushed in upon us like a black shadowy sea. I tried to flash my searchlight, but it refused to work for the moment.

"Light up again, Jimmy," I said, more afraid of Gonga, the snake, than whoever, or whatever, had blown out the lamp. My voice did not sound natural in the inky darkness, and the old man's seemed thinner and reedier as he answered.

"I dasn't. They'd only blow it out again—"

"They? What do you mean?" I asked, getting up uneasily.

"Them two hants what followed me here. They're warning me. They do it every time I talk about their treasure. Wait here," was his command. "I got to go out thar and tell 'em we ain't figuring on touching them chests and things."

I could not see him moving, nor could I hear him, but he touched me as he passed out of the shack, and the contact made me tremble as if I had been brushed by a phantom. No sound reached me from beyond the shack except the voice of the sea. I never would have known Jimmy was back if fingers had not gripped my hands. The fingers were clammy with the coldness of death, and at first I was so startled I could not be sure they belonged to the old man. It was his voice that made me certain finally.

"You can't fool them hants, suh. They know you came down here to try and find their gold. That's why they followed me home. They knew you were coming—they told me what you aim to do—"

Jimmy's words made me feel shivery. I decided it would be best not to admit that I was determined to hunt for the gold. Because in that case he wouldn't give me any more information. I got my flash to working and turned it on.

The old man went on, terror in his voice: "You asked me how I met them hants the first time. Well, I was coming through the hammock, and I heerd the most awful cat cries I ever heerd. Sounded like a baby howling and yelling and dying. Next thing I knew two green eyes was blazing at me from a tree. I jerked my shot gun up and shot at them eyes, believing they belonged to a live varmint. But voices spoke to me and told me not to waste my shells. It was the pirate hants. They said them green eyes belonged to the ghost of the wild cat old Kidd left on the pole to die—"

A sound that brought cold sweat to my brow suddenly interrupted Jimmy. Instinctively my hand went to my automatic, but clammy fingers prevented me from drawing it.

"I told you that pistol ain't going to do you no good against things that're dead. Didn't them hants tell me not to waste shells on that wild cat's ghost? Well, that's the cat's hant carrying on down there now. Listen to it!"

"God! It's the most horrible noise I've ever heard," I exclaimed, unnerved by the thing. If you've ever heard a wild cat sending its feline wail through the night you'll understand how that crying curdled my blood. And yet I could not bring myself to believe that what Jimmy declared to be the case was an actual fact. I was not willing to admit that animals possessed souls. Ghosts were either the souls of departed humans, or they were the work of vivid, or unstrung imaginations."

"You'll hear worse, suh, if you try to find that thar treasure, and move it."

"I'll give you one hundred dollars to take me to that tree with the anchor chain, and then you can go back," I said, suddenly determined to test old Jimmy.

But Jimmy believed too strongly in the power of the dead to revenge themselves upon the living who are false to them. He said they would get him quicker than he could say "Jack Robinson." When I realized he could not be tempted to guide me, I concluded not to waste any more time.

"I've got to be going then, Uncle Jimmy," I said.

"I know what's in your mind. You're bent on tampering with them hants' treasure. You don't believe them speerits are down thar in the hammock—"

"Good-bye, and thanks for telling me everything." I shoved a bill into his clammy hands, and turned away. Several uncanny experiences in France had served to make me somewhat tolerant of the idea that the departed spirits could influence us, but I couldn't believe, as Uncle Jimmy did, that they could actually harm us physically. I was determined to find that treasure.

"Good-bye, suh—and don't stir them ghosts' anger." His voice was sepulchral as it drifted after me, filling the dark with uncanny vibration. As he spoke my flash flickered and died.

Something began sucking at my legs as I dived deeper into the jungle. Step by step the going became harder. The black force—whatever it was—seemed to gather strength. The suction that I felt became more and more like hands holding me back. Repeatedly I bent down, breathing laboriously, to pry away what I thought were shackles. Remembering

*"I know what's in your mind. You're bent on
tampering with them ha'nts' treasure!"*

what old Uncle Jimmy had told me about seeing two men wandering through the hammock
in chains and without any throats, I half-expected to find that phantom chains had been
mysteriously woven around my legs. But upon each investigation I discovered nothing of
the sort. The only material impediment to progress was the ever-thickening undergrowth.
Still, the sensation that I was being strangely held back became more and more inescapable
with every new step.

Imagination? Possibly—after all I had been told about the supernatural activities in the
beach hammock. But I stood six feet high, and tipped the scales at one hundred and ninety-
five pounds. It takes more than mere imagination to invest a man of those proportions with
the sensation that some force is sucking his legs from under him.

If the path had not ended abruptly in a maze of Spanish Bayonets, and tropical growth,

I'm sure I would have lost my nerve and turned back to the main road beyond the hammocks. Uncle Jimmy had said the pirate haunts followed him to the end of his path—and, strive as I would, I could not shake off the uncanny feeling that I was not alone in the forbidding dark. Over and over again I told myself that I heard the sound of breathing—and it was not my own. I tried to ridicule the idea. I told myself that the dead do not breathe.

But—something was near me! Nothing that I could see or touch—if it had been visible, or tangible, something I could have measured with my eyes or struck with my fists—I would not have minded so much. But to be there, swallowed by an impenetrable gloom, and know that Something was heeling me proved more than I could stand. I began to call for Uncle Jimmy.

No answer came except a mocking echo. I fired my Colt twice. Still there was no sign that the old man had heard anything, and the staccato reports were swiftly swallowed by the brooding menace that pressed down upon me. Feeling about carefully, I selected a tree, and began to climb into its hidden branches. It was high time for me to get my bearings if I ever expected to leave that fatal jungle.

The green eye of the lighthouse blinked at me—but not from the direction I had expected. I had been completely turned around. I made my way to the ground, and began crashing through the jungle in the direction which I thought would get me back to Uncle Jimmy's path, and then to the road.

As I struggled through the hammock I knew I was being followed. This knowledge was not born of imagination. In self-defense I had forced myself to belittle the sensations of supernatural phenomena that I was experiencing. But I could not fight down the same kind of feeling that had warned me of Gonga's presence in Uncle Jimmy's shack when I first entered it. There was movement—hidden, menacing motion in the jungle—and when I stopped, it stopped!

The chant for the dead that had been drifting through the woods from the nearby sea began to throb with a note that I cannot describe. And yet it was only rain, beating steadily, heavily, against the leafy roof of the jungle.

Drip! Drip! Drip!

I tried to shut that sound out of my ears. The attempt ended in desperate failure. And then—suddenly, out of the night, figures commenced to dance like yellow veils around me! Horrible figures—mystic, full of terror—

I fired a whole chamber of shells at these veils. The answer to my volley was a blood-curdling cry that made me think of the wailing of lost souls screaming in eternal torment. I began to lash at the foliage and bushes as a man will lash at whatever is near him when panic sweeps through his blood—

There was a noise as though the heavens and earth were being rent and I felt myself being driven into the brambles and ground as this deafening sound surged over me. It was a force more inescapable than the power that had been sucking at my legs ever since I left Jimmy's shack.

What rain that was able to seep down through the foliage pattered against my face and hands, increasing the clammy sensation that had assailed me from the moment I realized I was being followed. The lightning was flame weaving through the gloom, and the pealing of the storm-frenzied heavens smote my ears with a din of war, while the blood-curdling screams of that wild cat added the last touch to my terror.

Closer and closer came the cries of that cat. I was approaching nearer and nearer to the very Thing I sought to escape! Approaching against my own will, drawn on and on by an invisible force that I could not fight because I could not touch it.

I tried to change my route a full dozen times, but always with the same result. I kept drawing closer and closer to the cat voice whose wailing had my hair standing on end.

Suddenly the cries seemed to fling free of the storm thunder, the drip of rain, and the chant of the sea. They pierced down into my very soul. I began screaming as a man may scream when unknown terror grips him. When balls of green fire flashed at me then I almost lost my reason. A man's mind can stand only so much horror—

I whipped out my automatic and pumped the lightning-ripped dark with lead, aiming directly for those balls of blazing green. If there had been a human being or an animal there, one of those bullets fired at such close range would certainly have reached the mark. But there was no let up of that horrible crying; no cessation of the mad, whirling dance of those balls of green fire.

I had suddenly run afoul of something stronger than human power, and my flesh cowered before this knowledge as I stood there banging away at those phantom balls. I emptied my revolver, and turned to flee, but the hammock seemed to rush at me, and beat me down. Or, was it some ruthless supernatural power that struck me to the ground? To this day I cannot be sure what felled me, but, I did go down—under vicious blows.

I did not lose consciousness. I wish I had! I saw—yes, I swear I saw—them! Things crowded me down and down into the wet earth as I tried to rise. At first great eyes spun around me, then long, unsheathed feline claws and red hands that gripped knives whirled over me, threatening me with destruction that never came. I raved, struggled to my feet, and plunged headlong toward the things. I expected to feel my body cruelly ripped but instead cold—yes, freezing—yellow flames enveloped me, and lighted the hammock with a ghastly glow. In a frenzy, I beheld an oak tree with a chain hanging from a limb.

Then the flame that had wrapped me for a fleeting moment died down and the jungle went black again. Out of those surging shadows something damp and furry brushed past me, filling my nostrils with wild scent that cleared my mind for a moment. A live wild cat!

The chain on that old oak was clanking and rattling as if trying to escape from some horrible torture! Frenzy again became fever in my blood—the desperate fever of panic! I rushed toward the tree and chain. I had to stop that awful clanking sound or else go totally mad.

The chain moved like a wet clammy snake of steel in my grasp. It writhed as if possessed of the strength of the living, plus the power of the dead. I clung to it desperately. When it seemed that I would lose my hold, I flung myself around it, and dragged downward with all the strength I owned.

There was an excruciating pain in my head. Then I pitched forward with a moan. Down— down—down—I hurtled through interminable depths of shadows that swirled with balls of green fire; writhing, clanking chains; red hands that gripped knives; and rough, swarthy men whose throats were nothing more than crimson smears!

At last I began to rise upward through those depths of swirling shadows. Pain tortured me as I reeled to unsteady feet. But pain did not blind my eyes to the vision of two men whose hands were wrapped in chains, and who were throatless. They swept past me; brushed me in doing so. I tried to cry out, but my tongue only labored in my constricted throat.

I stumbled after those throatless men who floated through the blackness as if it were empty of trees and tangled brush. Limbs and brambles struck me like fists, and tore me like claws.

Suddenly the throatless men became only vague mists. Then they faded into the dark. I put my hands to my head where the pain was sharpest. My whole body seemed shot with jagged spears and arrows. My knees bent under me. I fainted!

A shadow was bending over me when I awakened. Immediately I threw my aching arms up over my eyes. I did not dare look upon that shadow. It had the outlines of a man, but my disordered mind would not accept it as such.

"It's Uncle Jimmy," said a voice.

My mind struggled feebly with memories—I could not place that voice until I dared to take my arms away and look at the shadow. It was the pair of black hands dangling

Things crowded me down and down into the wet earth. . . . Great eyes spun round and round me.

over me that started my mind functioning again. If they had been white hands I would have screamed at the thought that they belonged to those two throatless men I had trailed through the hammock—

"You're Uncle Jimmy," I began, my voice uncertain.

"Yassuh, I'm Uncle Jimmy all right," he said, "and I figured I find you down here somewhere—especially after them two hants, Smith and Means, come to my cabin just before daybreak. Course they couldn't say nothing, being throatless. But, they give me signs and I knew they meant something about you. Well, suh, you brought it on yourself. A man ain't got no business rushing afoul of hants—"

"Jimmy, how far is that tree with the anchor chain from here?" I asked, still trembling.

"Not far, suh. But you'll never find it again. Them pirate ghosts told me long ago they never lets a human being find it twice. Maybe you ain't satisfied yet as to what kind of Power laid you out last night. Maybe you think just because a real live wild cat crossed you, and because there was a storm, that the hants ain't to blame—"

"I know I did pull that chain down, and it's quite possible the old limb came with it, and gave me this nasty blow over the head—"

"And, suh, if you'll pardon me for saying so, and I've been in these here hammocks over one hundred years, it's just as possible that one of them pirate hants struck you over the head!"

"But, how do you account for the live wild cat?"

"She's dead now. Fetched up in front of my cabin! She dragged herself that far after you put a ball through her. Wild cats got a way of answering each other's calls. That old hant cat's always luring other varmints down there where she guards that gold with them thar pirate hants," he answered, his beady old eyes glowing with a fanatical light.

Jimmy helped me to the road. I was picked up by an automobile and went to town. The confused state of my mind kept me from coherent thinking for days, but, finally, in company with another visitor in Fernandina, I went back to look for that tree and anchor chain. We searched for it by day for a long time, but we never located it again.

I may go back some day, but I shall steer clear of those pirate ha'nts.

TRUE GHOST EXPERIENCES

Have you ever seen a ghost? Have you ever had a message from the dead?

Nearly every person in the world has had some experience which could be classed as psychic. Not everyone would recognize a ghost, or would understand a message or warning that purports to come from another world—but most people have had at least one thing happen to them which could not be explained logically.

This department is for the readers of GHOST STORIES magazine who believe they have had some contact with the spirit world, and they are urged to send in accounts of such experiences. As many as possible of the letters will be published; and if any of the letters call for an explanation, perhaps some of our readers will be glad to write that also to this department. Some of these letters are printed below—and readers are urged to send in their answers. It must be made clear that we will not consider dreams.

GHOST STORIES wants the account of your experience. Send letters to True Ghost Experiences Editor, GHOST STORIES magazine, 1926 Broadway, New York, N.Y.

The Beheaded Bride

MINE HAS ALWAYS BEEN KNOWN AS A PSYCHIC PERSONALITY, altho' I lean more towards art. Last summer I rented a small, somewhat isolated, furnished cottage, solely for the purposes of sketching the charming rural scenes that abound in the quaint little village of Whitman, Massachusetts.

The cottage had been vacant for some time; the real-estate man from whom I hired the place told me so somewhat reluctantly, when I commented upon the thin layer of dust over the furniture. He volunteered no reason for its remaining empty so long.

I had not been there an hour, before I realized vaguely, that something was wrong with the place. For some unknown reason, it was shunned like the plague by the neighboring cottagers. Even the milkman that I hailed, seemed loath to bring me my milk, standing on the bottom step and waiting for me to come after it. But the first real clue I had, was when a fruit peddler of that vicinity refused point-blank to step foot into the yard.

"That place is haunted," he shouted at me, from the gate. "Not for me!"

I laughed at what I termed the childish superstitions of the villagers, and retired that night without a qualm. However, along about midnight I found myself suddenly wide awake, and listening. It seemed to me that a shriek had sounded through the quiet house. I put on a light pair of slippers and lighting a candle, for the electricity had not yet been connected, I made my way softly downstairs. All seemed right in front of the house. Without a fear, I made my way kitchenwards. How I would laugh at myself in the morning!

Then, as I approached the kitchen, such a strange, musty odor filled my nostrils that involuntarily I shrank back. Then, suddenly, my candle was extinguished as if by a gust of wind, although I was positive I had closed every window before retiring. By the light of the moon which shone in at the uncurtained windows, I beheld a fearsome sight.

There, lying in the shadows by the sink, I could plainly discern the huddled form of a woman. Her head lolled horribly sideways, and I could see that it had been nearly severed from her body. Those glazed, dead eyes seemed staring at something that filled her soul with horror.

Then a brilliant shaft of moonlight illumined the scene, and there on the sink-shelf I discerned a butcher's cleaver, stained with blood. There on the floor was a pool of bright red, where the blood had dripped!

Horrified beyond words, I stood there stupefied, rooted to the awful scene. Then the woman's pallid lips moved, and the one word, "Bill," came from them, clear and distinct.

Even as I looked, the scene faded away into nothingness.

Fumbling for matches, I relighted my candle, and crept up the stairs to my bedroom with trembling knees, bolting the door behind me with shaking fingers. I felt half paralyzed with shock.

Next morning, bright and early, I packed my suit-case, returned the key to the real-estate dealer without a word of explanation (although he looked at me askance, as if he knew my reason for departing so hastily), and made my way to the station.

But before leaving the scene of that hideous experience, I "quizzed" the grizzly-bearded old station master a bit, asking him in a round-about way if he knew the details of the murder in Thurman's Lane.

"Sure," he replied, garrulously. "Everyone in Whitman knows about that. Bill Gentry, the butcher, killed his bride of three weeks there with his butcher's cleaver. He was stark crazy. She must have known it before she married him. He always did have queer spells, and being gassed in the World War just about finished him. They didn't hang him. They confined him in the State Insane Asylum for the rest of his life."

I was glad when the train pulled out of the station, leaving the scene of that ghastly, gruesome scene far, far behind me!

MURIEL E. EDDY,
39 Pennsylvania Avenue,
Providence, R.I.

Marked with the Curse of Obi

Woe to him who gives offense to the great god Obi! Hugh Purcell lived to regret the day he censured a West Indian maid.

By Hugh Docre Purcell
Told by W. Adolphe Roberts

OF RECENT YEARS, THE WEST INDIAN NEGRO HAS BEEN COMING TO NEW YORK in ever increasing numbers. The men seem to specialize in running elevators, while the women go out as domestic servants. They are queer negroes, decidedly more primitive than the blacks born in this country, yet apt to be sharper-witted and more aggressive. Doubtless the political liberty they have enjoyed in Haiti and the British island colonies has stimulated them, though it has not altered the fact that they are close to the jungle type. They bring north with them a somber faith in voodooism and other black magic, a terror of ghosts, and all sorts of bloodthirsty practices.

I got up against West Indian deviltry the other day. This is what happened to me:

Needing a woman to come in twice a week and do chores around my flat in Brooklyn, I phoned an employment agency and a young colored woman was sent over. She was pleasant looking and soft spoken. She told me that she was a native of the island of Jamaica.

It seemed for a while that I had found a treasure among cleaning women. But one day I missed a spoon from an old set of silver I had inherited from my grandparents and which I greatly valued. I could not help suspecting the colored girl. Instead of accusing her, I kept my eyes open and finally laid a trap for her. I started away from home, but returned almost at once and let myself in noiselessly. From the living room I could see Cora rummaging in my bureau drawer. She came upon a marked dollar bill I had planted there, and promptly pocketed it.

When I flung the charge of theft at her, she paled to a strange ashen-gray. I thought she was merely frightened. But suddenly her eyes blazed, and to my astonishment she struck me across the face. I seized both her arms above the elbows and pinned her against the wall. I was pretty mad, I guess, and hurt the girl, for she started to whimper. Then I took the dollar bill away from her and threw her out. She denied having stolen the spoon, of course. It seemed useless to try to recover it. I was willing to be quit of Cora at the price.

A week later, I noticed a fuzzy object on the outside door of my flat. I glanced hastily around. What was the meaning of the thing? It looked something like a shuttlecock, the feathered "ball" used in the ancient and obsolete game of battledore and shuttlecock. I dislodged it and was much interested to discover that it was really a small bone to which three colored feathers from a rooster's neck had been tied with a strip of dried skin.

Most persons would have figured it to be a freakish toy made by a child. But I knew better. My study of the occult and of primitive superstitions caused me to see the hand of Africa in the business. The object was a witchdoctor's charm, devised to bring down evil upon the dweller in the house—myself. The voodoo priests of Haiti use contraptions of the sort, as do the obeah-men of the English-speaking West Indian islands. Obeah, I may say, is a form of voodoo. It stops short of human sacrifices and of cannibalism, but it is governed by the same theory of magic, and the rites resemble those of voodoo. The deity worshipped

Who could have put that feather and bone on my apartment door? What did it mean?

is Obi, the snake-god, and if his blood-lust is satisfied with a goat or a rooster, it is simply because Anglo-Saxon laws against murder are harder to evade than those in Haiti. Obeah is regularly practised in the islands from Trinidad to Jamaica, and it is occasionally heard of in Louisiana.

I thought immediately of Cora, the Jamaican negress, and the grudge she doubtless bore me. I had twisted her arms. Possibly she feared I intended to have her arrested in connection with the spoon.

The incident amused me a whole lot. It was fantastic to think of jungle witchcraft being invoked against an everyday citizen of New York. Why, there must be an obeah-man right here in some colored tenement! Charms, such as I had found, are not believed to be potent unless manufactured by a "priest."

I placed the absurd little package of bone, feathers and skin in my desk, and felt rather pleased to own it as a curio. It never entered my head that I might be monkeying with supernatural dynamite.

Four days had passed when I realized that the palms of both my hands had begun to itch in a peculiar way. Small blisters had appeared, but the main symptom consisted of reddish circles about the size of a half-dollar piece, which enclosed the blisters, and which tingled unpleasantly. Fearing I had picked up the malady known as ring-worm, I rushed to see a doctor. But he declared flatly that I had not got ring-worm. The latter often appears on the back of the hand, and almost never in the palm. The medical man was provokingly enthusiastic about my itch. It was something quite new to him. He called in a skin specialist, and they gloated over it in the hope of getting a line on a hitherto unrecorded disease. However, they ended by saying that it did not appear to be a serious matter. They painted the rings with a liquid that I suspect was merely iodine, and told me to report if the trouble grew any worse.

I did not grow worse. But the marks stubbornly refused to disappear, and I was bothered at my work, which is that of assistant to a Wall Street broker, by an irritating sensation in my hands. I was still far from imagining the cause.

I had engaged a new negro maid-of-all-work, also a West Indian. She saw me examining my discolored palms several times, but made no comment. Then, one day, she started to clean my desk, and out of a pigeon-hole fell the obeah-charm. She leaped back as if it had been a serpent. She stifled a shriek, and her eyes became enormous. Her body shook with an ague of fear.

"Mis—Missa Purcell, what's dat t'ing doing in your house?" She babbled the words, her voice breaking.

"I found it—" I started to say, but she interrupted me wildly.

"Your hands! Your hands!" she screamed. "Dere's a curse been put on you."

And she dashed madly out of the place, without even claiming her half-day's pay.

I'll admit that my nerves were considerably shaken for the moment. It surprised me that I had not thought of this obeah stuff before, in connection with my itch. The theory was familiar to me. Of course, I didn't believe that magic could be practiced upon me by a half-savage witch doctor, and perhaps that was why my mind had remained closed to the tie-up. But there were grave material perils conceivably lurking in that bunch of feathers and other trash. I didn't like the appearance of the strip of skin that had been used as binding cord. It was scaly, foul-looking. It might have been smeared with poison.

My first move was to return to my doctor and ask him whether he thought it possible I had contracted an obscure tropical disease through handling what I told him were natural history specimens. I had taken the obeah charm apart, and I submitted to him the objects that had composed it. He was vastly intrigued. Later in the day, he reported that the bone was the finger joint of a monkey and the piece of skin had once been worn by a boa constrictor, the largest of snakes. They were in as wholesome a condition, however, as such relics could be expected to be, and he was sure I had not been poisoned by them. The rings on my palms, he added, had not changed for the better or the worse. He slapped some more iodine on them.

I then took a subway train and rode to Harlem. The girl, Cora, had lived there, and fortunately, I remembered her address. I needed it for the investigation I proposed to make, though I had no intention of visiting her personally.

I sought out the Captain of the neighborhood police station and questioned him about the superstitions of the West Indian negroes with whom he had to deal. My interest was due to the fact that I was writing an article on the subject, I said. What he did not know about voodoo and obeah was a pity. He simply had never heard of such things. He classified the whole business as "fortune telling," but as far as he was able, he was quite helpful.

"The Jamaicans pull off the most marvelous stunts of all," I said. "I'm anxious to get hold of a practitioner from that island. Do you happen to know of some very old man with a woolly beard, who lives by himself, keeps his room in half-darkness, and won't allow more than one person to visit him at a time?"

The Captain stared at me in amazement. "Say, you're kidding me along!" he exclaimed. "There's only one Jamaican fortune teller in Harlem, and you've described him. If you've got all the dope on him already, why come to me?"

Actually, I had not been "kidding" the Captain. Books on negro witchcraft had taught me how to visualize obeah-men. They are not held in much honor until they are old, and they always wear beards as badges of their trade. The rest was easy. I explained this in a casual way, and I was given the aged sorcerer's name and address without having aroused undue suspicions. Police interest in my affair would have made a laughing stock of me, if it had gotten into the newspapers.

The obeah-man was called Tom Cudjo. To assure myself that he was the one who had been employed to injure me, I played the following trick:

I manufactured my own charm, with a bone from a pig's knuckle, a bit of fur, and the withered claw of a chicken. This looked like very powerful medicine. I wrapped it in a dirty piece of paper, addressed it to Cora, and hung it over the letter box bearing her name, in the vestibule of the tenement where she lived. I knew that this would drive her crazy with fear, and that she would rush to seek a spell to counteract it.

Then I went and posted myself to wait for her, outside the obeah-man's house, a still more squalid building on 136th Street near the Harlem River.

If the reader asks why I did not shadow her, I can only reply that I am not a detective. I doubted my ability to keep on her trail without being conspicuous. It would have spoiled my whole scheme if she had recognized me. So I had to take the longer chance, wait for her and hope that I had figured correctly.

My hunch proved to be an excellent one, all right. About eight in the evening, as I stood with my hat pulled down over my eyes, Cora darted past me. Her body was shaking visibly and she jabbed at Tom Cudjo's bell until the door was clicked open for her. I needed no more to convince me that he was the obeah-man with whom she was in the habit of dealing, and I strolled on home.

My next step in this peculiar business was taken after much hesitation. Apart from satisfying my curiosity as to his methods, I could have only one reason for interviewing the obeah-man: to get him to cure my hands. Frankly, I hated to admit that he might possess the power. Then, the rings on my palms suddenly became a good deal worse, and I decided to act.

I made no theatrical attempts to disguise myself, but I did slip an automatic revolver into my back trousers pocket. Outwardly as cool as a cucumber, I went on a Saturday evening to 136th Street and climbed four flights of stairs to Cudjo's door. The wrinkled, white-bearded face of an incredibly old negro, warned by my ringing of his bell, peered at me around the edge of the half-opened door. I spoke his name firmly, and he nodded.

"What you want to see me about, white man?" he asked. (It is better to make no attempt to reproduce his quaint broken English.)

"I have need of your wisdom," I answered. It was a stock phrase, understood by magicians all over the world as an appeal for professional aid.

He shook his head. "The white man is making fun of Cudjo."

I stepped closer and stared hard into his eyes. At the same time, I drew out my pocketbook and showed him a twenty-dollar bill. "Your time won't be wasted," I said.

Whether he was shrewd enough to size me up correctly as not being from the police, or whether his cupidity got the better of him, I don't know. Anyway, he stepped aside, let me enter, and immediately double-locked the door. I didn't like that last detail too well.

I was in a room lighted only by an old-fashioned kerosene oil lamp, turned very low. A faint noxious odor, as of moldy bones, pervaded it. My eyes growing accustomed to the gloom, I made out the skulls of various animals suspended from nails, as well as a number of nondescript packages which somehow succeeded in giving a perfectly appalling impression. They might have been bundles of dried snakes, or monstrous tropical vegetables, or God knew what. In front of a dilapidated chair stood a small table on which there were cups and glasses containing murky-looking liquids. The uncarpeted floor was littered with odds and ends, which got in the way of one's feet disconcertingly.

The obeah-man sat down, after he had drawn up for me a straight-backed kitchen chair. He waited craftily for me to speak.

I felt like an utter fool. Yet I stretched out my hands to him, with the palms upward. "What is the matter with them?" I demanded.

"How can I tell? You should see a doctor," he replied.

"I have seen one. He can do nothing to cure these rings, for he does not understand them. They were perhaps caused by obeah."

The old rascal fingered his beard. "You believe in obeah?" he asked.

"No, but I do not deny that anything may be possible. I am willing to have you try to cure me, and to pay you for it." I thought it best to avoid even a hint that I suspected him of having manufactured the charm I had found above my door.

"You are asking for very great magic. It will cost you fifty dollars. It is harder to remove a curse than to put one upon a person."

My blood boiled at the extortion, and I vowed silently to go ahead with the thing in order to collect evidence that would send Cudjo to jail. To my amazement, he seemed to read my thoughts.

"It will only harm the white man if he hates me," he said coolly.

Without waiting for me to reply, he arose and went behind a curtain. Startling sounds came to my ears. A creaking metal object was dragged along the floor, and rusty chains rattled. A chicken squawked. The footsteps were decidedly those of more than one person.

In about ten minutes, the curtain was pulled aside, revealing an alcove room lighted by a gas jet which appeared brilliant compared to the dim oil lamp in the room where I was sitting. Fantastic, horrifying preparations had been made. On a round, cast-iron table a huge white rooster lay bound. He was really secured with string, but a chain lay across his body for dramatic effect. Two young negro men, stripped to the waist and armed with knives, stood on either side of the rooster. A pot bubbled upon an alcohol stove to the right of the group.

I did not see Cudjo at first. Then he came out of a dark corner, carrying a knife in one hand and waving the other in a series of queer gestures.

"We must sacrifice the white bird to the God, Obi," he said, his voice droning. "You shall plunge your hands in its blood."

"This is the sort of evil mummery that goes on in the Congo," I told myself. "There can be nothing to it. I'll not lend myself to such horrors."

I glanced about me, figuring on a way to escape. If I pulled my gun, could I scare them into opening the door? I was quite willing to shoot my way out of the place, if necessary. I half rose to my feet, but as I did so the gas was turned out, and guttural snarls menaced me from the dark. Plainly, I was trapped. I'd be able to accomplish little against three negroes with knives. Yet I couldn't afford meekly to allow the obeah-man to practise his deviltries upon me. It was possible that his game might be to inoculate me with a deadly poison, to destroy me because I knew too much about him.

My brain functioned with lightning speed. A project suggested itself. I rejected it in one breath, and turned back to it in the next. It offered a gambler's chance of getting myself out of a dangerous mess.

Lolling in my chair, I placed my hands on the table in front of me and stared arrogantly into the gloom.

"I know a lot about magic myself, so you'd better not try to play any tricks on me,

"You see, I am a medicine man myself," I told the black. Tipping that table was my only defense.

Cudjo," I said, in a stern, level voice. "My kind of magic is not your kind. It's ten times as strong. God help you, if you make me angry."

"You say you have power, white man?" he asked.

"Certainly. Shall I prove it to you?"

He nodded.

"Sit down opposite me and rest the tips of your fingers upon the table," I directed him.

I am strongly mediumistic, and if at least one other person is present to complete the circuit I can nearly always bring about that simplest of all phenomena—table tipping.

We had been "sitting in" for less than a minute when a preliminary tremor through the wood assured me that the break was going to be good. The table hesitated, then tilted up onto two legs, while the eyes of Cudjo bulged. A heavy rapping followed. I brought a more intense concentration to bear, and the table rose clear of the floor. It hung suspended, then crashed, as the obeah-man let out a shriek and jumped away.

I yawned deliberately. "Have I proved that I have power?" I asked.

He came crawling back to me. "You are the stronger," he answered, whimpering.

"Open that door," I ordered him.

He started to obey, but interrupted himself.

"So you will not be Cudjo's enemy, I take the obeah off your hands. Your magic not good for that," he said.

I raised no objection, for I felt sure he would not dare to harm me now. Ignoring the flub-dubbery of the rooster and the boiling pot, he took a jar from a shelf, dipped his finger into an ointment it contained, and smeared the rings upon my palms. A moment afterwards, he had let me out of the flat.

Believe it or not, I was cured within twenty-four hours. I earnestly suspect that the charm I had found above my door conveyed some unknown tropical poison to my skin, and that Cudjo merely applied the proper antidote.

I lost no time in tipping off the police to Cudjo's outrageous violation of the laws of the state. But when they raided his flat, they found the bird had flown, taking all his truck with him. Doubtless, somewhere in the heart of Twentieth Century New York, he is still pursuing his weird and evil trade.

Creepy, Spooky, Cryptic Tales of the Black, Uncanny Night

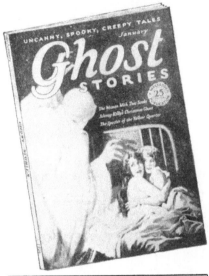

PHANTOMS—ghosts—weird messages from past the grave—dread spells and mordant curses—uncanny happenings in the dead black hours—these are the stuff of ghost stories. For ghost stories are spun of mystery—that same inscrutable mystery which shrouds the shadowy universe about you—which clothes a mystic company from whose unearthly companionship you can't escape. From birth through death eternal mystery is at your shoulder always.

In the funeral wail of a moaning Banshee shrieking its morbid course about a rural chimney-top—in the dank terror of the cellar of an abandoned house at midnight—in the vigil of vultures winging watchfully above a place where, yet, there is no death—in the ghastly swirl of vampire ghouls sweeping about their horrid work in the tangle of a forsaken graveyard—mystery pervades the countryside.

Nor can you escape it in the city. For the deep chasms of the silent streets become a labyrinth of mystery in their darkness—the murky shadows scarcely hide faint, furtive forms which scurry stealthily about their secret errands—a frightful feeling of the touch of things unseen hastens the progress of a lone pedestrian and sends his footfalls echoing down deserted streets until a phantom regiment of threatening shapes keeps pace behind him, step for step—gaunt, hopeless, desperate faces leer evilly from atop grim skeletons still half alive—unanswered mystery is everywhere.

And ghost stories—tales of these obscure things—stories which cause exquisite thrills of icy fear to catapult along your spinal chord —strange tales which never fail to stir you to the very depths—the mystery of the world is in their hearts just as it is in yours.

Collected in print at last, with illustrations so astutely done that you can not explain them, these mystic tales of the borderland of the unknown await you in *Ghost Stories*—a magazine you will take straight to your heart.

Partial Contents
of the *JANUARY ISSUE* of
Ghost Stories

Special Offer

You owe it to yourself to enjoy these tales of mystery. If no news-stand is convenient, you can obtain them by mail—at a saving! Use the coupon at the left.

STORIES

February Issue Out Dec. 23rd

Dream World, July 1926

The Black Spider
By Edmund Snell

Kamaga the Jap thought he could improve on the laws of God and Nature. He paid a terrible price before he learned the truth.

THE FURY OF THE STORM HAD DIED DOWN. But the *Batilcoa* still dipped and rolled to the tune of an enraged sea-god whose anger was gradually diminishing. There was a suggestion of dampness in the corridors and a constant rattling and shifting of heavy weights overhead that was eloquent of the thoroughness with which the original labor of screwing, lashing, and stowing, had been undone.

Of the two hundred or so first-class passengers only two could muster sufficient courage to face breakfast in the saloon. One was a thin, dapper Englishman with a good humored, weather-beaten countenance. The other was a tall, slim girl.

The man—whose age might have been anything between forty and fifty sat at a small table at the starboard side, his table-napkin across his knees, studying the menu. He glanced up presently and caught the girl in the act of looking at him.

Two forlorn people in a forest of white tables! It seemed absurd.

"Why don't you come across here, Miss Seldon? I hate eating alone."

Bianca Seldon flushed and smiled.

"So do I. My companion—Mrs. Parrett, you know—is completely knocked out. I'd rather you come over here, if you don't mind, Doctor. I don't think one notices the movement so much nearer the middle, do you?"

"Keep as far away as you can. It may start roving in search of food—and some of these things have poisonous bites."

Andrew Langley crossed over.

"It was a wild night," he said. "Did you sleep?"

She shook her head.

"Not much." A sudden thought made her smile. "I suppose one oughtn't to laugh. But it really is too funny. Poor Mrs. Parrett was supposed to look after me—and I've been doing nothing but look after her ever since we left Southampton."

"Not a good sailor?"

"By no means. She was ill in the train before we embarked. Dr. Langley, I suppose that really was a storm last night?"

He raised his brows.

"I should imagine so. What did you think it was?"

"A really bad one, I mean?"

Langley rubbed a spot on his chin that his razor had somehow missed.

"The worst I ever remember—and I've done a few trips. Why?"

"I'm glad to hear you say that, because the second officer spoke of it as a *squall*."

Her companion laughed.

"One of the first duties of an officer on a passenger ship is to keep up the courage of the passengers. As a matter of fact, he's not the only one aboard who's heartily glad we pulled through with as few casualties as we did."

Bianca's dark eyes opened wide.

"Casualties! You mean people were injured?" Langley looked at his hands.

"Er—yes. Just one or two, you know."

"But not passengers?"

"Good heavens, no. Lascars, principally. It's these risks that inspire people to take up the sea as a profession. By the way, I shouldn't say anything to Mrs. Parrett. It might frighten her. What are you eating?"

"Anything!"

The doctor found a pair of glasses in his top pocket, rubbed them carefully, and perched them on the bridge of his nose.

"You mean that?"

"Why certainly. I'm not feeling the least bit ill, if that's what you think, only I do like to have my meals on as firm a floor as possible. The purser tells me you're from Borneo. Perhaps you've met my brother?"

Langley started.

"Not Barry Seldon?"

"That's right. He manages an estate near Mirabalu. I'm going to join him there."

The man leaned back in his chair, staring at her incredulously.

"Barry Seldon! Of course! You couldn't be anybody else's sister."

"Couldn't I?"

"Not very well. You're extraordinarily like him, you know. Can't think why it didn't occur to me before. I imagine it's because he's known all over the island as Barry and nobody thinks of him as Seldon at all. So you're going to Mirabalu? We shall be quite near neighbors."

Bianca's eyes sparkled.

"Now isn't that just too delightful! Mrs. Parrett's going on to Foochow and I shall have to find my way from Singapore without her. I wonder if you're willing to undertake a fearful responsibility?"

Langley was engaged in smothering his grape-fruit with castor sugar.

" 'Fearful responsibility'? Just what do you mean?"

"Taking charge of me from Singapore to Mirabalu."

The doctor relinquished his spoon and sat up.

"I shall be delighted, of course."

"Then that's settled. What an idiot Barry was not to tell me you were coming by this boat. It would have saved such a lot of trouble."

"Barry didn't know. I was due back a month ago, but managed to get my leave extended." He surveyed her doubtfully. "I don't know that you're going to be altogether satisfied with this arrangement. I have no small talk and my dancing is execrable."

"You can tell me all about Mirabalu," suggested Bianca hopefully.

"In about half-a-dozen sentences. Mirabalu is a wilderness populated by half-baked niggers and Chinese coolies, with about seven white men to look after them. There's not another white woman for fifteen miles."

The girl laughed.

"What a charming description! If it's really as bad as you try to make out, why does anybody live there at all?"

"That is a question which invariably crops up at about the fourth whisky. The queer thing is that nobody's ever been able to answer it. Whenever a chap goes on leave he takes a fond and final farewell of his friends, murmurs something vague about influence and a comfortable job at home—and drifts back to the same old area as soon as ever his time is up."

Bianca frowned.

"Then it can't be such a desperately bad place after all," she declared. "Would you like to live in England?"

The doctor shuddered.

"Not on your life. D'you know, Miss Seldon, I believe there were only nine days in the entire seven months when it didn't rain."

"There you are," cried Bianca triumphantly; "you men are all the same. You drink more than is good for you, develop liver trouble, and distort your outlook on life. Really and truly, I expect Mirabalu is a delightful spot, with glorious views and any amount of amusement to be had if one only takes the trouble to look for it."

Langley smiled.

"You'll find out soon enough."

"I suppose I shall. Anyhow I've fully made up my mind to enjoy myself."

"You'll be bitten to death," said the doctor.

"I don't care. Barry says you get over that."

"You'll be eternally pestered by a mob of disorderly young ruffians, each with a proposal of marriage in the back of his mind."

"I shall like that."

"And you'll be very unwise if you accept any of 'em, because your brother's bungalow is the very best in the neighborhood; the only one, in fact, with glass windows." He chuckled to himself and moved to one side to allow the steward to take his plate. "You'll like Mirabalu, the life, the views, everything. Presently you'll be bored to extinction and then you'll like it so much that you won't want to leave it at all. Mirabalu's an acquired taste, but once acquired it sticks to you like a leech until—"

"I see," said Bianca thoughtfully; "but you didn't want to let me down too lightly at first. I suppose that's the line you take in your profession. You swoop down upon your unfortunate patient, send him to bed, terrify him with an endless list of probable complications, until the poor wretch feels so utterly grateful to you for saving him from such terrors that he cheerfully sends an enormous cheque by return mail!"

The purser's steward, entering suddenly, stared around the saloon until his eye fell upon Langley. He came across to the table.

"Excuse me, sir, but Dr. Murphy sends his compliments and would like to see you in the cabin."

The doctor glanced up sharply.

"Oh?—what's the trouble?"

"I don't know exactly, sir. I think he's got his hands pretty full."

"Wants help, eh?"

"That's my opinion, sir."

Bianca, who had been trying to see out of a port-hole, touched Langley's arm.

"I believe we've stopped," she declared.

"Been stopped this half-hour, miss," said the steward. "Our wireless carried away in the storm last night and we haven't been able to pick up calls. They've just brought aboard a fellow who was tied to some boards. The chief steward thinks he's Japanese, possibly washed overboard from the ship we passed yesterday afternoon. He was fully dressed, with a small box strapped to his waist. I saw him when they got him up."

"Is he still alive?" interposed the doctor.

"I believe so, sir; but he's in a bad way. Must have been in the water for hours."

"Very well. I'll come along now. You'll excuse me, Miss Seldon, won't you?"

"Why, of course. Isn't there some way in which I could help?"

Langley shook his head.

"There are plenty of stewardesses," he reminded her; "besides, you may have to look after your friend."

"No," said Bianca; "they won't let me. Do send for me if you're short-handed."

"We're short-handed right enough," put in the steward. "All the staff that aren't sick themselves are up to their eyes in it. There's hardly a bit of china left in the kitchens—and how we're going to serve dinner tonight I don't know."

"We'll be in Colombo tomorrow," said the doctor grimly, "and nobody's likely to want much dinner before then! Let's see—which way do we go?"

As he made his way down the corridor at the steward's heels, it occurred to him that Bianca Seldon was going to be something in the nature of a disturbing influence in Mirabalu. For one thing, she displayed an enormous amount of character for a girl of her age; and for another, she was a great deal too good-looking. For all his morbid description of the place where he lived and worked, he knew Mirabalu as a colony that was essentially masculine—masculine in its outlook, its amusements, and its excesses.

There was not a more amiable group of men to be found anywhere, and why Barry Seldon had been such an unmitigated ass as to bring his sister out there, Langley didn't know. He wasn't in the least sorry for Bianca, for she could look after herself and was bound in any case to have a tolerably good time—but he was mortally sorry for Mirabalu. For some reason or other he was feeling depressed that morning and was prone to regard Bianca in Mirabalu, and a bottle of fire-water in a camp of Indians, as one and the same thing. They had been perfectly all right up to now. But—when she arrived—

He found the ship's doctor in his shirt-sleeves. He was a fat, broad-featured man, with a Belfast accent, and dark lines under his eyes which betrayed that he had been up all night.

"I hate to trouble you again, Doctor—" he began; but Langley cut him short.

"Trouble be damned, Murphy! If you had had the nerve to attempt to carry on without me I should have been mortally offended. What do you want me to do?"

"Have you had breakfast?"

"I've had enough to carry me along, thanks. I don't mind betting you haven't had a bite yourself!"

"Right—but I'm going to now. I wish you'd take that poor devil of a Jap off my hands for a bit. The steward here will show you where he is. I tell you, Doctor, I never want another night like this. I've had eight more fresh cases through my hands since you turned in and I don't think one of 'em will live."

Langley dropped a hand lightly on Murphy's shoulder.

"Get some food into you and try and close your eyes for a spell."

A patch of green water obscured the port-hole and receded again, revealing a stretch of blue sky.

"We're getting into clear weather again," said Murphy.

"That's something to be thankful for. Well, cheerio! I'll be getting along to see my man."

He found his patient in a spare, second-class cabin. A man in a white coat rose as he came in.

"Did Dr. Murphy put you here?" Langley asked.

"Yes, sir."

The man moved aside so as to allow Langley to come close to the berth.

"How is he?"

"Pretty queer, sir. He's in a high fever now, and keeps talking, first in Japanese and then in English."

The doctor bent down.

"It'd be a pity to let him slip through our fingers—after all he's gone through." He glanced at a chart, fixed to the wall by a couple of pins. "You've been up all night, too, I suppose?"

"Yes, sir."

"Anybody about who can relieve you?"

"No, sir. Dr. Murphy told me I'd have to hang on for a bit longer."

"Ah! Well, we'll see what we can do."

He drew a card from a silver case and bit the end of his pencil thoughtfully. He wrote something and handed it to the man.

"Take this along to the dispenser."

"Anything else, sir?"

"Yes. I want you to go to the first-class saloon and find Miss Seldon. If she's not there, the purser will tell you where she is. Ask her if she'd mind coming to see me here as soon as possible. You can turn in after that. I shall want you back at one o'clock."

"Very good, sir." At the door he paused and looked back. "Er—I suppose Dr. Murphy will understand? You see, he told me—"

Langley took him by both shoulders and pushed him out of the room.

"I'll make it all right with Dr. Murphy," he assured him and went back to his patient.

The Japanese was moving restlessly and a crimson spot burned at each cheek-bone. He seemed to be gabbling something that Langley could not catch, clutching all the while at the white coverlet with fingers like yellow claws. Suddenly he sat bolt upright, a gaunt fragile figure in a borrowed pajama-coat that was four sizes too large.

"The box," he said in English, staring before him with glazed eyes, "—they must not take that! They will forget to feed it . . . the thing will die. I want it to grow. . . ."

The doctor forced him gently back and covered him.

"Your box is here all right," he muttered, rather for something to say than having the least hope he would be understood.

The man struggled feebly for a few minutes, then relapsed into the vague, restless state in which Langley had found him.

There was a box in the corner, a square box of painted wood with a double row of perforations round the top. It measured approximately a foot square.

Langley picked it up and, holding it to the light, tried to see in. He was about to put it down when he became aware that something was moving about inside.

He whistled softly to himself.

"Good Lord! This then, whatever it is, is alive too."

He set the box on the closed top of the washing cabinet and stood looking at it, his hands deep in his trouser pockets. He had the usual scruples concerning prying into other people's property, but he was equally prepared to set such scruples aside when it was a question of an animal requiring sustenance. He could not make up his mind as to the nature of the beast. The movements had been queer—similar in some respects to those of a bird. And yet, he did not think it was a bird. He brought his head closer. There was a peculiar, unpleasant odor about the box that both puzzled him, and—was very nauseating.

He glanced at his patient through the mirror, then withdrew a kind of skewer with a polished knob that appeared to secure the drawer. It had occurred to him that this drawer might contain a supply of the particular type of food that the creature required. But to his amazement he found nothing but minute metal cylinders, securely corked and labeled in Japanese characters, and a hypodermic syringe!

He closed it again and replaced the fastening.

He remained for some seconds, gazing at his own reflection in the glass, then deliberately withdrew a second rod and threw open the lid.

He dropped the skewer and sprang back a yard, nearly falling over the foot of the bunk. At the same moment, the door behind him opened softly.

Queer, hairy claws appeared over the edge of the box, waving suspiciously. The box tilted, then fell on its side and there emerged—an enormous spider, its body as big as his two fists. The thing was black and, hardened as he was to jungle phenomena, Langley thought he had never seen anything quite so loathsome in his life. A second later it had disappeared and then he saw it racing up the white-painted wall with a glistening strand waving behind it that might have been a rope. It sought refuge in a corner of the ceiling.

He heard Bianca's little, gasping cry behind him.

"Dr. Langley, what is it? Oh, isn't it horrible!"

He backed towards her, his eye still riveted on the monster.

"It's a spider," he said calmly. "Our friend here brought it on board with him in that box. I'm afraid I let it out, and our problem of the moment is how to get it back again. Don't stay here if you're frightened."

He reached over and pressed the bell.

"I am frightened," said Bianca; "but I'm going to stay."

"Splendid! Well, keep as far away as you can. It may start roving in search of food—and some of these things have poisonous bites."

"But I've never heard of a spider as big as that."

"Nor have I. As a general rule I prefer them about an inch long. The Japanese gentleman on the bed, however, isn't satisfied yet. He wants it to grow!"

The girl stared at the yellow face with its two crimson spots.

"Do you mean to say he keeps that thing as a pet?"

Langley nodded.

"He's been babbling about it a good deal in his delirium. He seems to have it on his mind."

"I'm not in the least surprised," said Bianca.

A steward knocked on the door in response to the doctor's summons.

"Don't come in," said Langley. "Find me the biggest jar you can—one with a large opening—and bring it here at once."

Ten minutes later the knock came again and Langley put his head round the door.

"That's not large enough," she heard him say. Then: "That's better. I think we might manage with that."

She saw him cross the floor, armed with a large receptacle that might have been used for salt. He placed a camp-stool on the floor, under where the spider was crouching, and mounted it gingerly.

A feeling of nausea swept over her and she shut her eyes.

Minutes passed and suddenly she realized that he was bending over the washing cabinet, doing something with a towel.

"Get me a piece of string, Miss Seldon, if you don't mind. I've got him inside."

She returned presently and watched him pass the cord several times round the mouth of the jar. He swore softly to himself as the knot slipped. The second time, she bit her lip, then went over to him and put her finger on the cord, to hold it for him.

He dumped the imprisoned insect in the cupboard and shut the door.

"Thanks awfully. You didn't like doing that, eh, Miss Seldon?"

"No, I didn't. I hated it. But I like to make myself do the things I hate. It wasn't really very difficult, once I'd assured my weaker self that the creature was safely inside and couldn't possibly hurt me. It was nothing to what you did."

"No," smiled Langley. "But I'm a—a doctor—and have to do a whole lot of unpleasant things."

"You were going to say 'a man,'" she challenged him. "I don't see why you didn't. Why do men hate referring to themselves as men? Women aren't ashamed of their sex."

"That's possibly because they've nothing to be ashamed of."

She moved forward impulsively.

"I'm glad you consented to look after me. I know I'm in good hands. I think you're a *super-man*."

They met that evening at dinner.

The band was playing and there were perhaps a score of people scattered among the tables.

"Tired?" asked Langley.

"Not in the least, thank you. I think our patient is better already, don't you?"

The doctor pursed his lips.

"He has a grip on life that is positively uncanny," he said. "We're going to pull him through, you know. I understand the spider has found a new keeper?"

"Yes. Hales—and isn't he a most peculiar looking man?" commented the girl, with a shudder. "I'm told he pushes lumps of meat under the towel and the brute stands up on its hind legs and asks for more. Do you believe that?"

"No," said Langley firmly, "—I don't. But the fact that it eats meat doesn't altogether surprise me. There are such things as bird-catching spiders, you know. We've discovered our friend's name, by the by. It's Kamaga."

"That's interesting. I hate to have to refer to a human-being as 'him' or 'it.' Spelt with a K?"

Langley nodded.

"Spelt with a K. Has he disclosed anything more about the spider?"

"Oh, yes—whole strings of it. It's perfectly weird at times. You'd think he knew you were there and was propounding his theories. He talked this afternoon about Japanese gardens and the infinite pains taken to dwarf things. Then he spoke of himself. It's awfully difficult to get a connected story, because he has a disconcerting habit of reverting suddenly to his own language. At least, I suppose it's his own."

"What did you gather?"

She held her head on one side and screwed up her eyes.

"Oh, that he's a sort of scientist. He aims at increasing the size of things—everything. That's his main theme. He hammers away at that for hours."

The doctor looked up from the wine-list.

"Increasing the size of things, eh? You don't suppose he was responsible for the exaggerated growth of that confounded insect?"

She uttered a little cry.

"You mean that he—"

"I mean that a creature like that would command a high price at a zoo or a freak show. I don't believe a spider of that size exists under normal conditions. There was a drawer under the box which contained drugs, and a syringe. God! I wonder if he's doping that thing with something he's discovered?" He shuddered. "Let's forget about it and have some dinner."

"It didn't look very dopey," insisted Bianca. "It went up the wall like a streak of lightning."

"You saw that?"

"Of course, I was at the door. Don't you remember?"

"I do," said Langley. "But I'd like to forget it. If I really thought there were insects like that in the tropics, I'd never place any confidence in a mosquito-net again!"

" 'Bigger and bigger and bigger,' he keeps saying," pursued the girl, with evident relish. "If he really goes on as he's started, it ought to add a new zest to big-game hunting."

"We'll drop it," said the doctor coldly, "—if you don't mind."

They were on the point of disembarking at Singapore when Kamaga joined them at the taffrail. He had borrowed a suit of clothes that almost fitted, and presented the appearance of a sleek, good-looking boy.

"Good-bye, Miss Seldon," he said. "I shall never forget what you have done for me."

Bianca crimsoned and clung tightly to the doctor's arm.

"Really, Mr. Kamaga, I had little or nothing to do with your case. If you wish to thank anybody, you should thank Dr. Langley. It was he who pulled you through."

Langley turned.

"Oh, it's you, Kamaga. Glad to see you're better. You're lucky to be here at all. You've the finest constitution of any man I've ever come across. Come along, Miss Seldon. I'm going to take you to the hotel—without further delay."

They moved a few paces nearer the head of the gangway, and still Kamaga followed.

"I am coming to Borneo very soon," he enlightened Bianca. "I shall be seeing you again."

"Oh, yes, Mr. Kamaga? Er—goodbye."

"Good-bye," said Kamaga, a shade of wistfulness in his voice.

She lost sight of him in the crowd, but felt somehow that he was staring after her until the rickshaw had whirled them out of sight—into the atmosphere of Singapore's dust and intense heat.

"Infernal cheek!" said Langley. "What did I tell you?"

"I don't suppose he meant any harm," returned Bianca.

"Harm!" snorted the doctor. "He means nothing but harm. Cultivates spiders as big as footballs, and means no harm? Damn him!"

The girl was drinking in the sights and Kamaga was already a back number in her memory.

"I don't see that it's anything to get huffy about. It's a hundred to one we sha'n't see him again. Aren't those black kiddies just sweet! I'd like to take one home with me."

"You wouldn't," declared the doctor. "They're like lambs; they grow up! I can imagine nothing more unpleasant than a sheep about the house!"

Dr. Andrew Langley was dining with Stewart—magistrate at Mirabalu—on a high veranda with an oil-lamp above and a pall of blackness all round.

It was ten months since he had left the *Batilcoa* at Singapore, and he was beginning to forget that he had ever had a vacation at all.

Langley rested both elbows on the rail and peered into the darkness.

He nipped the end from a cigar, lit it carefully, and threw the match into the night.

"Barry can be mighty hot-tempered at times," he remarked suddenly.

Stewart was pouring out liquor from a long earthenware bottle with a Dutch label.

"I know," he replied, without looking up. "It takes a good deal to rouse him, but when he's really thoroughly incensed—then look out! But what made you say that?"

"Something that occurred on his estate the other day. Jimmy, has anyone complained to you lately about Barry Seldon?"

The magistrate shook his head. He was a long, lean man with straight, clean-cut features, and eyes that were particularly blue.

"Don't think so. Has he been knocking his coolies about or something?"

The doctor emptied his glass.

"Not exactly. He kicked a stranger off the plantation last Thursday—kicked him pretty thoroughly, as a matter of fact. The fellow went away swearing blue murder. I thought you'd have heard of it by now."

Stewart grinned.

"Oh? What sort of stranger?"

"A yellow-skinned blighter of some education who met Bianca on the boat coming out—and tried to renew the acquaintance. Barry warned him once before."

The D.O. came slowly forward, his face flushed, his fists clenched at his sides.

"I don't think I quite understand you, Doc. A Chinaman—and Bianca!"

Langley glanced from the end of his cigar to his friend.

"There's nothing to get excited about. The fellow was washed past us in a storm and one of our boats picked him up. He was unconscious, of course, and Bianca volunteered to nurse him until one of the staff could be spared to take her place. We hoped to have seen the last of him at Singapore—but, unfortunately she rolled up here three months ago. He's Japanese."

Stewart started.

"Not Kamaga?"

"Yes. That's his name. You know him?"

"By sight only. He's taken over a few odd acres that were not the remotest use to anybody and put up some ghastly looking buildings. I was away when he came, but Brown saw him. Nobody raised any objection to his being there—so we let him stop." He clenched his teeth. "Some of these chaps have the cheek of the devil! If I hear the suspicion of a complaint against him, I'll have him deported."

The doctor nodded sympathetically.

"My sole regret is that I was the person who was instrumental in saving his wretched life. If you've got a couple of decent packs of cards in the house, I'll play you *Canfield*, for cents."

It was close on midnight when a man rode furiously into the clearing that surrounded the bungalow and called to the magistrate from the saddle.

"Stewart!—are you up there?"

The D.O. looked over.

"Hullo, Wright! You look hot. Come up and have a *peg*. The doc's here."

The newcomer slung his reins to an orderly and came up the steps, three at a time.

"I can't stop a minute," he panted. "Miss Seldon's up there alone."

He grabbed at the glass Stewart held out to him and drained it at a gulp. It was at that moment the magistrate noticed that Wright was white to the lips.

"Alone? Where's Barry?"

The planter caught at Stewart's arm.

"God—it's awful! We were up there—the three of us. The others had gone, and Miss Seldon had just come out in her dressing-gown to persuade Barry to go to bed. She was frightened at something, I think, and didn't want to admit it before me. I had picked up my hat and was making for the dining room door when a ghastly thing happened— Something black squeezed its way through the open window and dropped to the floor in front of us."

He paused for breath.

"Well?" ejaculated the D.O. impatiently. "What was it?"

Wright stared wildly, and swallowed hard.

"You'll think I'm mad, or drunk or something. It was a thing like a spider, only a million times bigger than any I've ever seen."

The doctor glanced up sharply.

"It was black, you say? About how big?"

Wright stared vaguely around the veranda as if seeking some object with which to compare it.

"It was tremendous. The body must have been nearly a yard long. For a matter of seconds we all stood there, paralyzed. Then I pushed Miss Seldon behind me and Barry pulled open the drawer in which he kept his pistol. The next thing I knew, the brute had sprung upon Barry and bitten him. . . ."

"*Bitten him*?"

The magistrate's face wore a puzzled expression.

"Yes! It all happened so quickly He staggered backwards with an ugly, gaping wound in his neck. The entire drawer came away with his hand and somehow or other I managed to get hold of that automatic.

"I fired at the thing, of course, and I suppose I hit it. Anyhow, one of my shots found the lamp-glass and blew it to atoms. That was when the creature was crossing the table, and I aimed a bit too high. The lamp flared up and smoked like blazes, and through the fog that descended upon the room like a pall, I caught sight of a shadowy horror clawing itself out by the way it had come.

"When I had adjusted the wick, and got back to Barry—*he was dead?*"

Stewart took him by both shoulders and shook him violently.

"Dead! Are you quite sure?"

"As certain as I stand here. The thing's bite had poisoned him. I got Miss Seldon to her bed, sent in the black girl who looks after her, and dispatched a runner to the doctor's place. Then I reconnoitered the ground all round the house, but could find nothing. I had another look at Miss Seldon, found Barry's pony—and came across."

Dr. Langley reached for his hat.

"The *black spider!*" he muttered, staring straight before him.

A moment later all three men were in the clearing.

They reached the veranda together.

Stewart threw open the dining room door and went in, the doctor following at his heels.

A cloth had been hastily thrown over the body. Langley removed it.

"Well?" asked the magistrate presently, a lump in his throat.

"Dead," said the doctor and put back the covering. He rose to his feet and glanced round the room. "I must see Bianca."

Suddenly Wright—who was in the doorway—raised a warning finger.

"Keep quiet a minute. What was that?"

Above the chirping of the crickets, the ceaseless hum of insect creation, there floated to their ears the sound of a woman screaming.

Stewart clutched Langley's arm.

"Bianca!"

The other faced him squarely.

"Rubbish," he insisted. "It's more likely some native girl in the Kampon, on the other side. The sound came from a good way off."

He crossed the floor, and, gaining the passage, knocked loudly on the door. There was no response. He tapped again. The others, listening in silence, heard the handle turn.

"Jimmy! Wright! Come here, both of you!"

The room was in darkness and the doctor was striking matches, feverishly looking for the lamp.

"Stop just where you are for a moment!"

A light flickered and presently the apartment was dimly illuminated. They saw an empty bed, an overturned chair and the figure of a black woman lying in the middle of the floor.

The doctor turned her over.

"She's had a deuce of a knock from behind, but she's still breathing. We must send somebody to her." He looked up. "Are all you fellows armed?"

Stewart tapped his pocket significantly. He was unusually pale and beads of perspiration stood out on his forehead.

"Then it was Bianca we heard! That spider has been back again." He turned fiercely on the planter. "You ought never to have left the place."

Wright spread out his hands, babbling incoherently.

"I? What on earth was I to do? I had to find you! I had nobody to send. . . . I hit the thing, I tell you . . . how was I to know . . .?"

"The spider has not been back," said Langley calmly.

"But man alive!" shouted the D.O. "Bianca's gone. Don't you understand that? She was taken from here."

"I know, but not by the black spider. The spider's master is the perpetrator of this fresh outrage."

Both men stared at him incredulously.

"The spider's master! What in the name of heaven—"

"I haven't time to explain it all to you now. We've got to find our mounts and ride like the devil. Wright, you'd better round up the estate watchmen and a couple of dozen reliable coolies and bring them across after us. Then send for Stewart's men. I want you fellows to be prepared to fire the scrub. Do you understand?"

The planter nodded grimly.

"I'll fix that all right. Where are they to go?"

"To Kamaga's place. I want them to surround it and await instructions."

The magistrate's fingers were moving nervously and his forehead was deeply furrowed.

"Kamaga's place! What on earth has that blighter to do with black spiders?"

"Everything," said Langley. "He breeds 'em. Poor old Barry has been the victim of one of his ghastly experiments. No, I'm not mad, old man. I know what I'm talking about. Come on."

They rode into the night, taking an easterly direction through the rubber trees.

A pale moon bathed the hillside in yellow light. A fresh breeze from the sea rustled the leafy branches overhead and from the strip of jungle at the foot of the slope a hornbill shrieked.

"A whole regiment to tackle one Jap," shouted Stewart suddenly.

"I'm not afraid of Kamaga," returned the doctor. "If he was all we had to contend with, I shouldn't worry."

They galloped down a steep incline and onto the flat land again. The doctor ducked to avoid a branch and swung himself to the ground.

"There's a fence of some sort here. I noticed it when I came past last week."

The magistrate, joining him, flashed an electric torch on a high wall of painted stakes, set closely together.

"He didn't mean anybody to get in here!"

"Or out!" added Langley, as he moved off to the right.

"There's a light up there," said the D.O. peering through.

"And a gate here. It's padlocked on the inside. We shall have to break it down."

They had found a stake and were wrenching off palings when Stewart turned and looked back.

His eyes had long grown accustomed to the darkness of this lone glade where even the moon's rays scarcely penetrated.

What he saw there behind him froze the blood in his veins. He dropped to his knees, pulling his companion after him, as a black horror—crawling painfully on five of its eight legs—crept from the trees and scaled the fence barely ten feet from them. They heard it drop on the other side.

"God!" exclaimed Stewart. "It's incredible!"

Langley had picked up the pole again.

"It's interesting to know that spiders have a homing instinct," he muttered. "Kamaga must have taken it there in some way—and let it loose. We can get through here."

They clambered through on foot, leaving their mounts tethered by the trees.

There was a broad, moss-covered track on the far side. Negotiating this, they made for a solitary light that showed ahead, then slowed down to a brisk walking pace as the first belt of outbuildings emerged from the shadows.

Stewart went first up the crazy ladder and pushed the door wide open. There was a strip of matting across the floor, a Japanese stool and a piece of low furniture, like a desk without legs.

As the Englishmen entered, Kamaga—clad in a white kimono that was guiltless of embroidery—came softly through a curtained aperture and stood before them.

Langley had him covered.

"The game's up, Kamaga," he jerked out. "Put up your hands. Do you hear me?"

The Japanese raised his arms slowly.

"Good evening, gentlemen," he said quietly. "You have doubtless good reason for breaking your way into my home. I shall be interested to learn your motive."

"Kamaga," interposed the doctor, "I saved your life on the *Batilcoa*. We want you to tell us where you have taken Miss Seldon."

Stewart's finger, hooked round the trigger of his automatic, restrained itself with difficulty.

Kamaga blinked.

"The lady has disappeared?"

The magistrate's anger boiled over.

"I can't stand this! Keep this blackguard here, Doc. I'm going to search this place!"

"Be careful."

"Oh, I'll look out for myself."

He plunged through the curtains.

Langley opened his case with one hand, struck a vesta on his shoe and lit a cigarette.

"It's no use beating about the bush, Kamaga," he told his prisoner. "I know everything."

The man's face betrayed no sign of emotion.

"Indeed?"

"I am referring to the black spider. You spoke of it in your delirium. You wanted it to grow—and grow—and grow. We know now, Kamaga, that it *has grown*. Keep your hands above your head, you yellow devil!"

A cry came from within.

"Doctor!"

"Hullo?"

"Bring Kamaga here. Make him walk in front of you and don't take your eyes off him for a second."

Langley pointed to the curtains.

"Get a move on," he said curtly. Kamaga obeyed.

He was on the point of passing through when the doctor caught the curtains up and ripped the material from the rod that held it suspended. He was taking no chances.

He found himself in a long, narrow apartment stocked with appliances and glass jars. Stewart had his back to them, gazing down a broad passageway to a room beyond, the door of which stood open. There was an oil lamp in a bracket and its light was sufficient to reveal to the doctor's horrified gaze a menagerie of the most revolting specimens that it had ever been his fortune to encounter.

He saw tier upon tier of little square cages, each numbered and ticketed and containing specimens of insects of every sort and description, greatly magnified. A blue fly, as big as his hand—a centipede like a serpent, that kept up a ceaseless race to the roof of its prison, only to drop to the floor and begin again—a moth, with closed wings which, when opened, must have covered a couple of feet from tip to tip—giant ants—beetles—gnats . . .

At the far side of the room beyond, there was a bed, completely screened by mosquito-curtains, hung from a wooden ring fixed to the ceiling.

"I want Kamaga to tell me who is sleeping in that bed," said the magistrate.

The Japanese did not reply.

"Why don't you go and see for yourself," asked Langley.

For answer, the D.O. stepped aside, revealing the form of a second enormous spider—a quarter of the size of the one that had poisoned Barry—crouching on the inner side of the opening, a metal collar round its middle and a long chain stretching from it to a staple in the wall. The creature had four eyes with great hairy flaps over them like lids, that kept lifting.

"Shove Kamaga in here," suggested Stewart. "It may help him to find his tongue."

He caught one of the uplifted arms and began pulling the Japanese towards the doorway. On the very threshold Kamaga gave an unearthly scream.

"Oh, no! It will kill me! I am not ready. . . ."

His gaze shot to the ceiling and, following it, the magistrate saw an enormous metal syringe hanging in a sort of cradle over a zinc tank.

"We don't want you to be ready, Kamaga," he said. "Mr. Seldon wasn't ready when you let your vile creation loose on him. Come on, my friend. In you go!"

The man had struggled to his knees and hung limply, like a sack.

"Stop," he screamed. "I will tell you. I will tell you everything. The English lady is in there. She is tied, but I have not harmed her. No closer . . . oh, no closer . . . it can reach . . ."

Stewart threw him back towards the doctor and hooked down the syringe. He gave it an experimental pump up and down, then dipped its nozzle in the fluid in the tank and drew out the handle until it appeared to be full.

"What's that?" demanded Langley suspiciously.

"Don't know," said the other. "Dope for the spider, I fancy. Isn't it, Kamaga?"

Kamaga inclined his head.

He squirted a steady shower of drops at the brute's head.

Presently, as he watched it anxiously, the flaps drooped and did not come up again—

the legs drew gradually closer to the body, and, before the doctor could intervene, the magistrate had passed it on his way to the bed.

Langley's eyes were turned from the Japanese for the fraction of a second, but in that short space Kamaga found time to act. . . . A cloth—snatched from the top of a case—fell over the doctor's head, completely enveloping him. He threw it off after a brief struggle to find the tank overturned, flooding the passage with a sickly, sweet-smelling fluid. Every cage was open, and Kamaga was disappearing through the farthest doorway.

The shot he fired after him must have missed by a hair's breadth—and Kamaga was gone.

The doctor was left amid a host of crawling, buzzing, fluttering horrors, with Stewart— unconscious of anything except that he held Bianca in his arms—coming towards him.

"It's all right, Doc. I've got her."

Langley brought his boot down heavily on something and yelled at the top of his voice.

"Is there a way out through that room?"

"No, it's a *cul-de-sac*."

"Then run for it, for all you're worth. Kamaga's slipped me and his entire menagerie's loose!"

By a miracle they got through. Langley declared afterwards that they owed their escape in this instance to the fumes of the chemical Kamaga had overturned, to prevent them from employing it.

They were in the open again with the door of the house shut securely behind them.

"We must go warily," said the doctor. "I've an idea at the back of my head that we haven't finished with Kamaga."

Bianca blinked up at Stewart and smiled faintly.

"May I try and walk please?"

The sound of her voice sent a pleasurable thrill coursing through Stewart's being. He lowered her feet gently to the ground, but still held her supported.

"You feel all night now?"

"Oh, yes, I think so. I'm stiff, of course, but that's all." She rubbed her eyes. "What a horrible nightmare! It seems to have been going on for years. I can't imagine how you found me. Did you hear me scream or did the doctor guess?"

"Both," said Langley. "Try and walk a few steps. That's splendid. Now try again. Keep moving your legs as if you were marking time." He pointed suddenly towards the huts. "Look, Jimmy! There he goes. He's making for the path."

"I can't see anything. Who was it?"

"Kamaga! He's thrown open the doors. Heaven knows what's hidden behind them. Bianca, we've got to run for it. You'd better hang on to both of us. If you find yourself falling, yell out—and we'll carry you."

They had gone twenty yards when Bianca screamed.

"Look! Look! Can't you see them in that patch of moonlight? Spiders! Spiders! Hundreds of them!"

Both men glanced back. The entire place seemed alive with them. Stewart swept the girl from her feet and they raced headlong for the gate.

Kamaga was out of pistol-shot, but they appeared to be gaining on him, his white kimono clearly visible among the trees. Suddenly he halted, stared round him in bewilderment, and began coming back towards them.

A voice from the direction of the fence indicated clearly why he had turned.

"Stewart! Are you up there? Stewart!"

The magistrate paused and bellowed back.

"We're coming now. Tell them to fire the forest. Look out for Miss Seldon. I'm sending her on ahead." He released the girl again. "Bianca," he told her, "the gate is immediately in front of you and Wright's waiting for you down there. I want you to go there—alone. Are you afraid?"

She looked straight up at him.

"I am afraid, Jimmy," she whispered, "—but I'm going."

He found time for a single sentence more.

"I'm glad it was I who found you—and not the others. I'll tell you why—some day."

"I'm glad it was you, Jimmy," she said—and was gone.

"She's a wonderful little woman, Jimmy. What are we going to do now?"

The magistrate started moving off at a brisk pace through the trees.

"Try and secure Kamaga—dead or alive—before the fire gets a good hold. Can you see which way he's taken?"

"Yes. He's over there to the left. We'd better split up and endeavor to corner him."

It was ten minutes before Stewart had his quarry in range, and he fired wide to make him aware of the fact. Langley appeared on the other side.

The Japanese faced them placidly, a knife balanced on the tips of his fingers. He allowed them to approach within a few feet of him, then touched the naked blade with his lips.

"You will allow me the privilege of an honorable death, gentlemen?"

"Honorable be damned!" said Stewart.

Langley touched his sleeve.

"He means *hari-kari*. Better let him do it. It'll save a lot of trouble."

And then a peculiar thing happened.

A black mass dropped suddenly from the tree above them, smothering Kamaga with its enormous bulk.

Both men started backward.

"The *black spider!*" gasped the D.O.

They fled down the slope, with Kamaga's unearthly cry ringing in their ears and a belt of flame threatening to encircle them—and not once did they look back.

"You can't marry Nadia. She's already married to Ashley" . . . "Carramba!"

Talking Glass

Ashley, the vaudeville hypnotist and crystal gazer, used his showmanship to a sacred end. But no one, not even his closest friend, could foresee the frightful result of his experiment.

By Fred Collins
Told by John Miller Gregory

MAYBE YOU THINK THAT ALL A FELLOW'S GOT TO DO IN VAUDEVILLE THESE DAYS is to get a big act, give a yearning agent a try-out, and then sit back for four or five years on the big time, with rolls of soft money making life easy.

If you think it's like that, don't bet any money on it until you've tried it out, for the best you get out of the big acts don't pay you for the worry and anguish they bring you sometimes. That's why I'm off 'em for life.

For instance, there's the "hyps."

"Hyps" is my name for the mind-reading, hypnotizing acts that used to be so popular in the two-a-day. In former times, all you had to have was some kind of an Oriental set and a guy dressed in colored pajamas and a turban. If it was a hypnotizing act, you could carry along a lot of phonies, and when the town guys couldn't or wouldn't be hypnotized, you could put your own men through a lot of foolish stunts and have your audience screaming with laughter.

But it ain't nothing like that today. Not by a jug-full! If a guy does hypnotizing, he's got to hypnotize Monday afternoon at the matinee, or that night he'll find somebody else occupying his place on the bill, and he'll be outside in the alley collecting his props.

And that's no bunk, either, as I found out when I tried to run in a fake hypnotizing act on Solly Kern, the booking agent.

You know Kern, maybe?

He's that round guy with a paunch as big as a baby balloon and a face like a piece of smeared bologna. He comes into the house where we was giving a try-out and waddles down the aisle to the front row. He sets there heaving and puffing as my man comes out, in a cheap, black calico set, and starts his routine. As soon as Solly saw what he was doing, he gets up and yawns loudly, then walks out of the theater, right in the middle of the act. The next day, when I goes to his office, he sends out word he'd give me just two minutes to make it to the elevator, otherwise he'd show me a new parachute leap, without the parachute, from his eleventh-story window—me being the leaper.

Well, me and my pal had to have some money, so we takes the rattler and they throw us off in a little town in Connecticut. I puts up a proposition to a motion picture man whose business ain't been so good, and he tries us out. But of all the razzes! What we got sounded like a flock of angry bees looking for the guy that stole their honey. So they rang down on us.

"If this is a New York act, I'm the Shah of Persia," said the manager, as he gave us the gate. "Why there's a man in this town who'll make the bimbo you've got look like a skinned eel. Take my advice and go to some big town where they fall for stuff like yours."

I was for trying it, but my pal was sore. He climbed aboard the first freight that came through, and I went back to the hotel to think matters over.

I was sitting in the lobby wondering how to stall my bill, when a queer looking guy comes up. He wanted to know if I was Fred Collins. He was tall and lean, almost to emaciation, and was dressed in a long, black coat with a black bow tie. His hands were white and tapering, like a musician's. His face was as pale as a sheet of book paper, and his dead eyes, set back under black eyebrows, seemed to be trembling. They had a peculiar effect on me. My backbone quivered as if someone had put a cold sword along it.

"I saw your act at the Nicko," he began, but I interrupted him.

"Well, don't blame me, I needed the money. But I'm off vaudeville for good," I hastened to add, "and my partner's on his way back to the street cleaning department where he belongs."

"Perhaps you would like to see me work," he suggested, a hopeful look in his eyes.

"Are you a 'hyp'?" I asks. "If you are, you're talking against the north wind."

"I'm a hypnotist and a clairvoyant," he replied with dignity. "I want to go into vaudeville, and perhaps we can come to a satisfactory arrangement if you like what I do. But you must understand that I am not a professional. I am a scientist, and I'm taking this means to find a certain person among the public who may help me in my work. Of course, I must have a manager."

I looked up to see if he was kidding me, but his face was still serious, and his eyes had begun to burn like a fanatic's. "All right," I replied, thinking of my board bill, "if you're any good, you've got one."

With that, he turns suddenly and walks away, stalking across the floor with great dignity, and I followed him down the street to where he lived.

It was a dark, rambling old house set back among some great overhanging trees, and looked as if it hadn't been occupied for years. The steps had fallen in and the porch was rotted and decayed. But if it was spooky outside, the inside, as he closed and locked the door, was about as light and cheerful as the interior of a tomb.

He turned up an old-fashioned kerosene lamp with a blackened chimney, and led the way down the hall to a closed door. The house smelled musty, like the dead odor of smoked opium struggling with cheap incense.

The odd-looking man opened the door, and almost immediately came the tinkling of small bells and a tall, hard-faced man, with swarthy skin and a curious nervous movement of the body, slid forward into the yellow light which came from a flickering candle.

I ain't claiming to be no character reader nor nothing like that, because my education ain't what it should ought to have been. But I do know men when I see them, and this guy, squinting his black eyes through the dim light, was a crook if I ever had seen one. I could feel it in his beady orbs set close together, his long beak of a nose jutting between them, but especially in his cruel mouth. If Nero fiddled while Rome was burning, this guy would have been out robbing the corpses. That's the way I put him down.

Evidently he had expected the tall fellow to bring me, because he muttered something about "Collins, Sahib," whatever that means, and pulls a chair in the center of the room for me to be seated.

He was dressed up like something in a long, black coat, buttoned up tight, with his white collar showing at the throat. Around his waist was a red satin sash, and a black silk turban rested on his head, with a sheaf of dark green and black feathers sticking up in front, fastened with an imitation pearl ornament.

Right away I saw if there were any brains in this combination, the big fellow had them. The other man was a dreamer. This one was all action. And they had as clever a stage set in that old room as I ever saw in my life.

"I assume that Mr. Ashley told you what we wanted," the man in the turban said. His voice was low and insinuating, and he hissed his s's in a way to give you the willies, like a snake was hissing at you.

He lit another candle near a small, low table, covered with a black velvet cloth, before which Ashley stood, and for the next half-hour I saw the most wonderful spiritualist act I'd ever seen. Ghostly arms came out of the shadows. Banjos played. Cold hands were laid on mine. Faces appeared in clouds of white smoke. Forms materialized. And then, to cap it all, Ashley told me what I was thinking about. And listen! I'm telling you, he knew.

Right away I saw I had the greatest vaudeville act the world had ever seen, if these bozos had the money to dress it up right. But I wasn't going to let them know it until I had my share signed and subscribed to on the dotted line. So when the act was over and the lights on again, I lay back in my chair and heaved a sigh like Solly Kern's.

"You've got a pretty fair act, brother. Spend a little dough on it, and I might frame it for the big time."

The swarthy-faced man answered. "That's what we want, Sahib."

Right away I shot at him: "Are you an Indian?"

"No, but I spent years in British India. I am simply playing a part. Many of the things you saw done here today I learned in India." He hesitated for a moment. "It is my pleasure to help Mr. Ashley in his scientific efforts."

"I get you," I replied.

He nodded toward his partner, who was sunk back in his chair, his eyes closed in weariness. "This gentleman is Mr. Herbert Ashley, who is greatly interested in psychical research. He is a born medium and clairvoyant. My name is Boto."

"Italian?"

"Spanish ancestry," he replied, shortly, as if not caring to enter into that. Then hurried on:

"For many years Mr. Ashley has been studying animism—"

"Ani—what?" I interrupted.

"Animism—the study of the soul. As I was saying, he and his aunt spent many years studying animism and black magic. She was very famous before she died. Now I have persuaded Mr. Ashley that he can better extend the propagation of his work by public appearances. Unfortunately I am a foreigner and not equipped to manage a large vaudeville act. Therefore we are forced to call on someone else. You should make a great deal of money out of it."

"Brother," I broke in, "you said that like a regular showman."

"I know something of vaudeville," replied Boto, coldly. "I was connected with a similar act abroad many years ago."

"The only one I ever heard of over there was Yanhiti, the English medium, who died under mysterious circumstances." The sensational story as I read it in the vaudeville papers came back to me. "Did you ever hear of her?"

The black eyes of the big fellow bored through me. "No," he replied, "I never heard of her."

I knew he was lying. I could see it in the twitching of his face; in his half-closed eyes, and I resolved, if I signed up with them, to keep my eye on him.

But you know how it is. When you become closely connected with a man, even though you know he's a crook, you overlook. And that's what I did with Boto. I hate to think of the result. It ended in a tragedy—and what I'll believe to my dying day was a murder. Perhaps two of them.

Anyway, the tall guy went on, his words hissing out: "Now, Sahib, can we come together?"

"Cut out the 'Sahib' stuff and talk business with me in United States," I ordered. "We can agree on my terms. I want to be manager with one-third the profits. You two will work on the stage, and I'll put a girl with you, a swell looker, to make a flash. Then I want the swellest stage-set in the business. You've got the coin to do that, haven't you?"

Ashley aroused and leaned forward. "Oh, yes," he spoke, for the first time. "My aunt left me a great deal of property. We spent many years studying together, and her passing was a loss to me that can never be remedied. However, it may be for the best, for my sole object is to find a person—"

He stopped suddenly at a cough from Boto, and his pale face flushed.

"Go on," I prompted.

"It's quite all right," he said wearily. "You need have no fear about what you want."

"Right," I put in quickly, and drew out a couple of blank sheets of note paper from my pocket on which I scribbled an agreement. I thought it best to get it all down in writing before somebody else got hold of them. The act looked good to me.

Ashley signed the paper without reading what I'd written, but Boto scanned the words carefully before affixing his signature. Then with the contract in my pocket, I took the train for New York and Solly Kern.

I'm not going to ask you if you've ever seen Zeno, the Indian mystic, because everyone who goes to vaudeville in this country has seen our act—or tried to. There never was a better ballyhoo than I gave Ashley, who on the stage was known as Zeno, and the houses were always sold out where we played.

Talk about your mind-reading and hypnotism stunts! Why that red-headed, pale-faced, spiritual-looking young fellow of ours did things that even made *me* creep. Of course he was under the influence of Boto. That cold-eyed Spaniard molded him like a piece of clay and I knew it. But what could I do? He never did anything to hurt Ashley at first, so far as I could see. But I ain't exactly dumb. I couldn't prove anything, but to me it was as plain as day that Ashley was under some kind of hypnotic influence.

Do I believe that's possible? Sure, I know it is, and I'll tell you why, after a while. Anyway, when you're with an act like ours, you get to believe a lot of things you never believed before. It's like smelling hop smoke. After a while, you want to try it yourself.

Well, we hadn't been going long when the psychical research sharks began to investigate us. Of course that was pie for publicity and just what Ashley wanted. He was analyzed from abnormal psychology to practical psychomancy, whatever that means. Then, one day, someone asked if he had any experience in scrying.

That gave me the brilliant idea. Why not have Ashley gaze into a crystal ball, if he could do it, and read the fortunes of people in the audience? It had never been done before on the stage, and I thought it ought to be a wow. So I put it in the act, and we became the greatest sensation that vaudeville has seen in many years.

It used to get me creepy hearing Ashley telling in a faraway voice what he saw in that crystal globe, which he looked into with dreamy eyes in the dim light of the stage.

"Listen," I said to him one day, "is this crystal-gazing the bunk? Do you see anything there, or is it all a fake?"

"I'll show you tonight," he replied, his eyes going sad at what he considered my ignorance. And he did it. He told me things about myself and my family he couldn't possibly have known if he hadn't seen them in the globe.

Well, that satisfied me. Everything was jake—except Boto. But even he didn't worry me much. He went about his duties silent and suspicious, watching every turn and move Ashley made. It makes me shiver when I think about him. I got to hate his soft tread and his sibilant words like poison.

But the crystal-gazing act was a tremendous sensation. We put it on with a plain background, Ashley standing in the center behind a small, low table covered with black velvet.

At a soft sound from a deep-toned gong, a curtain set overhead would part slowly, and a spot-light blazed on a silver frame in which stood a girl, dressed in solid white velvet, bearing a silver platter in her hand on which was the huge crystal globe. I'll tell you more about the girl later, because it was she who brought to its climax all the evil in the heart of that devil Boto. It sent her to the hospital, with her mind verging on insanity from its attempt to reach for things I'm claiming we ain't got no right to inquire into.

However, with the spot-light on her, the girl would come down the long flight of steps bearing her globe, and kneeling, place it on Ashley's table. In the meantime Boto would light two candles in the back, and in this weird light, Ashley would peer into the globe. In a few minutes he would start to talk, and you could hear the quick in-drawing of breaths in the audience. I'm telling you it was devilish, all right, when he spoke.

"I see a hand coming out of the rushing clouds. Slowly it closes and disappears. The clouds are growing thicker. They rush by as if blown by a mighty wind. There's a ray of light which grows larger. It turns to pink, and in its center is a lotus flower. It has five points and the inside is hollow. I see a face in it—a woman strained with worry. She has large, brown eyes and pale skin, and the black clouds are hovering over her. She is beset with torment. Now—the name! Alice! Is Alice in the house?"

Quickly the girl would step to one side of the stage, and Boto to the other, and their voices would go out over the gasping audience.

"Alice! Alice! Are you here, Alice? Speak up, please."

I'm telling you, it was great. I've seen women straining back in their seats pale and shaking, and men fighting mad. Many a time we have had to stop the act and put up the lights. We always carried a bunch of "plants" in the audience to quiet people who got hysterical. And I'm telling you that they did—lots of 'em.

Did Ashley see things in that globe? As I've told you, there ain't a doubt in my mind that he did, because I found out there wasn't nothing new in seeing things in a glass. I asked one of those four-eyed scientists, who used to come to see the act, about it. He told me about the accumulation of lunar magnetism and magnetic rapport between the ball and the cerebellum of the gazer—all of which didn't mean nothing to me. But what I really got was that it's been done for centuries. The old birds, back before the time of Christ, looked into a pool of black shiny stuff like ink. Others saw images in mirrors. Even the savages looked into human blood to see things.

There ain't never been a doubt in my mind that Ashley saw things in that globe, and Boto believed it too, because if the Spaniard didn't believe it, he couldn't have pulled off his stunt which broke up the act and sent the little girl raving to the hospital. Boto knew he saw them.

It didn't take me long to find out what Boto was actually trying to get from Ashley. The hard-faced guy was a crook all right, and, of course, he realized how easy it would be to get money from the public in private séances—thousands—hundreds of thousands, if he worked it right. One day I heard him trying to persuade Ashley to do this, and the way he did it proved conclusively to me that he had the young fellow under some kind of control.

"I'm not after money," Ashley replied to him, with dignity. "I told you in the first place that I would only go into this public appearance because it might enable us to reach new depths of psychical knowledge. Before my aunt died she promised to come back to me in her disembodied spirit and tell me facts that have been denied us. Somewhere—somehow—I believe I shall find a medium in the audience through whom my aunt may speak."

"You don't mean you'll chuck the game if you do find her?" demanded Boto.

"I shall follow the advice of my aunt, whatever it may be," said Ashley.

I was standing behind a piece of scenery and despite myself I couldn't resist the temptation to stay and listen to them. Anyway I had my own interests to look out for.

Suddenly the Spaniard spoke up, quick and sharp. "Ashley—look at me!"

I strained through the dim light to see the young man's face, but once again came Boto's words, domineering and commanding.

"Ashley—look at me! Look into my eyes!

I saw Ashley struggling to keep his gaze from the beady eyes of Boto, but finally the Spaniard conquered.

"You'll do what I tell you," ordered Boto. "You'll take your orders from me and no one else. Do you understand?"

"I'll take my orders from you—" repeated Ashley, his voice weary, "in all things except—"

"In all things," insisted Boto.

"In all things—except—"

"Damn you," hissed the Spaniard, "you'll do what I tell you, or I'll kill you!"

"In all things—except—" But suddenly Ashley's head went up and his eyes cleared. Then he walked slowly away as if tired, his shoulders hanging wearily.

That night one of those four-eyed professors came to the show. The house manager pointed him out to me, and I introduced myself. He was Professor Reinhardt, the great writer on psychical subjects, and the leader in the little group which has shown up a number of fake mediums.

I shot my question at him. "Professor, is it possible to keep a man under the influence of hypnotism for any length of time without him knowing it?"

"Do you mean if the subject is quiescent?" asked the professor.

"Oh, no. Going along doing his regular work and not knowing he was hypnotized."

"Yes," replied the professor, promptly. "But I'd prefer to call that a state of 'constant suggestion' rather than hypnotism." He smiled a little. "I believe Trilby was under such an influence, wasn't she?"

"Sure she was," I stated, because I'd read the novel to get some material to use in the press work for the act, and I remembered well the great singer whom Svengali, the hypnotist, had made out of an amateur. "But I want to know," I went on, "when a man's in this state, can he refuse to do what the hypnotist wants him to do?"

"Undoubtedly," stated the professor positively. "He can do that even if he were under complete hypnosis. We call it auto-suggestion. If a hypnotized person, for example, is not a murderer at heart, it would be impossible to make him commit murder."

"You mean his own fixed ideas are stronger than any the hypnotist might suggest?"

"Exactly," smiled the professor. "You spoke that like a savant."

"Well, sir, I don't know what that is," I explained, "but I'm thinking that this Zeno is going nutty with that glass ball—and maybe something else," I added, thinking of Boto.

The professor looked serious. "Scrying or crystal-gazing, like all other psychical phenomena, may be productive of great disorders," he replied, slowly. "I have no doubt that a man who spends his life doing what Ashley does, day after day, and night after night, might be so influenced by his emotional impressions that his entire life would be clouded by the mysteries of his profession. What have you noticed?" he added, with interest.

But I didn't want to go into that—not just then. "Oh, nothing, except that Ashley is getting kind of nutty. But if he's under what you call 'constant suggestion,' he still is holding onto one thing, and as long as he holds on to that, he ain't exactly crazy, is he?"

"No, I think not," said the professor.

That night I put it up to Ashley. "See here," I said, "how long have you known Boto?"

"Only for a short time," he replied, frankly. "He spent much time in India and does many odd things which intrigued me when he lectured in my home town. When he heard I was interested in psychical subjects, he consented to work with me, so we got together."

"What sort of things does he do?"

"Well," remarked Ashley, as if forcing out the words, "he can hold a thick book between his hand and mine in a still room, and I can feel a cold blast of air rushing on me."

"Gee, whiz," I exclaimed, "what else?"

"He can make his pulse and the circulation of his blood stop, and he claims he can make his heart stop also, but I wouldn't let him try that." Ashley rose as if to end the interview. "You mustn't ask me about him," he stated. "He doesn't want anyone to know. Besides, it will all be over soon."

"What do you mean by that?" I asked, quickly.

He smiled patiently. "I mean that I have found my medium—the one through whom my aunt is going to speak. Not in the audience, however, but among ourselves. She is Nadia."

Nadia was the girl who assisted Ashley in the act. She was a beautiful creature, with great wistful, brown eyes and long, black hair. She was slim and spiritual looking and her face was emotional and sensitive. On the stage, in a white dress, she looked about what you would imagine an angel would look like, and since she had been with us, she seemed to have taken on a more unearthly appearance. Her cheeks were colorless, her lips pale, and she spoke in a thin, velvety voice.

She moved like a cloud and showed but little animation except when Ashley was near. She called him "Master," and whenever she approached him her face would turn pink and her hands tremble. She spoke to him as if she were uttering a prayer, and when she brought the great crystal globe and knelt by the table, the face she raised to his was rapt with adoration.

Don't tell me this was healthy. Of course it wasn't. But it just crept into the act because the act itself was unhealthy. I never thought that the girl would fall in love with Ashley, and yet there wasn't any reason why she shouldn't. But I was a showman, and most of my thoughts were spent on filling the house. Now, as the whole thing burst on me, I tell you it knocked me to the ropes groggy and gasping for air.

"Do you mean Nadia's seeing things in the globe, too?" I asked.

"Oh, no. But my aunt speaks through her voice. She has told me many things. One of these days she will manifest herself through Nadia."

My anger flamed out at him. "Listen Ashley, forget this stuff. She's nothing but a kid, and I won't have you filling her mind with all your crazy notions. The first thing you know, you're going to crab the finest vaudeville act in the world."

"I'm not thinking of the act," he maintained.

"The hell you ain't? Well, I am. And I'm darned if you're going to throw away the work I've put in on it. If that little gal don't get hep to herself, she'll be looking for another job."

"She is my wife," said Ashley, and floored me again. "We were wed two weeks ago in the flesh, and when we are wed in the spirit, my aunt will speak to me through her."

"Say!" I shouted, "where do you get all this dope?"

"My aunt has told me," he responded, quietly. "I've heard her voice."

Well, that settled that. Grumbling, I stuck on my hat and went out for a walk to clear my brain. At the stage door, I met Boto.

"Were you talking with Ashley?" he asked.

"Why?" I temporized.

"I was passing his dressing room and I heard you say you were going to let Nadia out."

"Well, what of it?" I demanded.

"Nothing, except if she goes, I go, and Ashley, too," he said, his thin lips parting over a row of white teeth. "You see, I'm going to ask her to marry me."

I looked at him over my shoulder, and smiled. "That'll do you a lot of good, Boto. You can't marry Nadia. She's already married to Ashley."

I swung around at the black look of hatred that rushed into his face. He hissed, like a snake. "Are you sure?"

"Of course. He just told me."

"Carramba!" He rushed headlong toward Ashley's dressing-room.

Events after that moved rapidly toward their tragic culmination, because Boto made no effort to hide his love for the little assistant. But there was a difference between the two men, that must have been apparent to Nadia, even if she had not already chosen Ashley.

Boto was harsh and crude, although he tried to hide his coarseness with a polish of courtesy. His dark skin and eyes gave him a sneering, loathsome look, and dissipation had drawn great lines in his face with their ineradicable marks of evil.

On the other hand Ashley was a mystic. His pale face shone at times with an inner light and made him almost beautiful. His inspirations might have come from a disarranged mentality, but they gave him the face of a saint and reflected the spiritual thoughts with which his mind was filled. To Nadia, I soon saw, Ashley was almost a god. She worshipped him with the undeviating loyalty of a pagan devotee. If he had told her to sacrifice herself for him, I have no doubt but she would have done so.

Boto could never understand the thoughts which animated her, irregular and morbid as they were. He appealed to her with material objects. He tried to hypnotize her; but the professor had been right, and she laughed at his efforts. Finally, when he told her he would put her in Ashley's place at a tremendous salary in their own act, if she would leave the mystic and go with him, she told me about it.

The proposition brought matters to a climax, so I hurried to Ashley and put the whole thing before him. For weeks Ashley had been going around as if in a dream, his black eyes wide and staring, and talking to himself. He let me finish what I had to say, then smiled wanly.

Don't worry, Collins," he said to me. "Pretty soon it will all be over, because I am not going to be here."

"What do you mean by that talk? Where are you going?"

He shrugged his shoulders. "How should I know? My body will he here, but I shall be out there where our souls go when we are free."

What did the man mean?

"Say, I'm getting tired of this," I exclaimed, jumping up. I was fighting mad. "What's ailing you, anyway? What you want to do is to get down to earth."

"Lights! House lights!" I called.

"On the contrary," he replied, "I want to get off the earth. You see, I've been warned."

"Warned? Who's handing you stuff like that—Boto?"

"Oh, no. I've heard my aunt's voice," said Ashley. "She's coming for me soon, as you shall see."

Was the man crazy? I backed away from him. I tell you I was scared, he looked so queer staring up over my head with glazed eyes, just as I'd seen him stare into the globe. I wanted to get away from him. That "voice" thing got me all wet, for hearing voices ain't nothing new either. It's as old as crystal-gazing, one of them four-eyes told me. He said some scientists really believed that mediums heard voices. But whether Ashley did or not, didn't make any difference. He had the idea in his head, and that's the same thing.

"You're going crazy," I said.

He smiled sadly. "Oh, no. I know my aunt's voice. Sometimes she speaks as if far away. Again, her voice seems to come from my own chest. Then it sounds in the air above me."

I'm telling you it made my flesh rise, he seemed so cock-sure, and I knew I could have talked myself hoarse without effect on him. I was pretty near to the point where I was willing to smash the act myself, if I could only get away from those morbid thoughts that seemed crashing in on us from all sides.

The big blow-off, as they say in the show business, came the following week. We were playing the Memorial Theater, which is a tremendously large vaudeville house. The place was packed until the people were almost hanging out the windows. I had taken matters in my own hands, and for the past week stood in the wings, when the act was on, to see that nothing went wrong.

That night it went all right until the time came for the crystal-gazing. The routine of the act was as previously described—Ashley in a silver costume standing with arms folded across his chest, when the spot-light went on showing Nadia in the big frame. He was there when the white light blazed, but his arms were upraised and his face was rapt as if by the

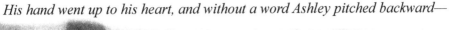

His hand went up to his heart, and without a word Ashley pitched backward—

sight of someone in the air in front of him. And when Nadia came down with the globe and placed it on the table, *I heard a voice.*

It sounded as if it came from far away, and the words made me cold all over. A woman was speaking. "Herbert—the time is here. See—I come to you through the globe."

As if in a trance he stared into the crystal ball. I heard him speak.

"You are going to tell me—now?"

In some way the audience felt that something extraordinary was happening. You could have heard a pin drop, so still was it, and the vast crowd leaned forward in its seats breathless in expectancy. Standing at one side of the table was Nadia, her pale face showing in the light, like a ghost. Her head was out-stretched, her hands clasped on her breast. Then Ashley began to speak.

"I see white clouds." I could hardly hear his voice, but as he went on, it became more audible. "I see many white clouds banking together. Now they are changing to red and yellow, which means that trouble is coming to someone—perhaps death."

He stopped in the tense silence, and a stage hand at my side said "God!" and tiptoed away. Then he went on again.

"Now I see my own eye. It is very large and there is a brilliant line down one side of it. It's fading now, and I see sands—miles and miles of sands, as far as the eye can reach—and a palm tree. There's a woman and she is weeping. Now she has gone."

Once more he fell silent, and somewhere in the audience I heard a whimper, as of a child crying. Then again his voice.

"I see the sky at night, and millions of stars. They are covered by smoke, which blows in a great wind from unseen flames. There's a sudden burst of red light." His voice rose sharply. "Now—flashes of red light! Orange and red! Yellow flames! Everywhere—rushing together—burning—burning. They are bursting apart, and a woman's face comes through."

Then a scream and a frightened voice. "Aunt Ellen! Aunt Ellen! Here—here—come to me!"

All at once I saw something I had never seen before, for the globe itself was lighted as if by colored rays coming from beneath it. I took a step forward, but the voice of Ashley stopped me.

"Aunt Ellen—I've been waiting so long for you to come. There's blood all around you. Now—you are coming through. Oh—how lovely you are! Speak to me. Tell me about—that other life. Speak!"

Then, from right there in front of him, I heard the woman again. It filled me with fright. "Herbert," she was saying. "I can't tell you, I can't tell you. You must come to me. Herbert—Herbert— Come!"

With a curious gurgle in his throat he sank to his knees. His eyes stared at the globe. Then his hand went up to his heart and without a word Ashley pitched backward to the floor.

"Lights! House lights!" I called. "Put down that curtain. Quick! Somebody get out there and quiet that crowd!"

With a swish the great curtain came down, and muffled through its velvet folds I heard the sounds of the orchestra. In a second I was over to Ashley, but Nadia had his head in her lap. She raised a white face.

"It's too late," she said, "he is dead. Oh, why didn't he take me with him? I loved him so."

Then she started to laugh, and screaming and laughing, they led her away.

"Get the doctor," I shouted to a stage-hand, but I knew that it was too late for Ashley at least; for his heart was still, even as we raised him, and carried him to his dressing-room.

I rushed to find Boto, but as I came to the stage, he ran past me, carrying a box under his arm. I made for him, but he sprang down the stairs toward the furnace room. My foot caught in a coil of rope and I went down, but when I scrambled up and followed, I found him in front of the furnace pulling open the door which closed on the flaming coals. The next instant the box went whirling into the flames. Only a string of film rolled from it, and that was gone in a second, like a writhing scarlet snake on the floor, as a red flash licked it up.

I grasped Boto by the coat and pulled him back. "You'll stay where you are until the cops come," I gasped. "You killed him—somehow, you devil!"

"That's a lie!"

The next instant I felt a blow between the eyes, and Boto sprang from me and up the stairs. Groping and half groggy I followed, but he had vanished like an evil black wraith through the stage-entrance.

We waited until Nadia was taken to the hospital raving in her delirium, then the house manager and I went to Boto's room and opened his trunk. In it we found some old newspaper clippings, and among them the stories about the mysterious death of Yanhiti, the English medium. But the ones which gripped our attention told of her assistant being arrested and questioned. He was described as a tall, swarthy-skinned, black-eyed Spaniard whose name was Cartez, and who also did an act by himself as a ventriloquist and hypnotist.

"The voice came from him—from Boto, who used to be Cartez," I said. "That's plain enough, but what lit up the globe?"

"I can tell you about that," said a new voice, and a young man in overalls pushed his way through the gaping crowd at the door. "I'm the assistant electrician, and I connected a projector under the table which held the crystal ball. The Spaniard told me he had to have it for the act, and I didn't think nothing of it, because you can throw pictures on a glass ball just the same as you can on a mirror screen. Lord, I never thought anything like this would happen."

"That's why Boto was anxious to burn up the projector and the film," I put in. "He wanted to destroy the evidence."

But at that I doubt that he would have gone to the chair for murdering Ashley. The doctor said he died of heart-failure brought on by sudden excitement. But I know better than that. He died because he lost hold of the one thing that prevented Boto from getting him under complete hypnotic control, just as the old scientist said.

Of course there's still Nadia. I'm praying she'll pull through, and there's a bare chance. But if she doesn't, Boto ought to go to the chair for what he did to her. It seems to me it's just as much a crime to kill someone's mind as it is to kill his body. And Ashley's death did that to her.

Anyway, as I said before, I'm off the "hyp" acts for life.

He Refused to Stay Dead*
By Eric Marston and Nictzin Dyalhis

Are innocent babes born into the world, imbued with the spirit of some restless ghoul come back to earth to fulfill its destiny? Eric Marston thought so, when—

GHOSTS? WE THINK OF THEM AS PALE, FAINTLY LUMINOUS DOUBLES or counterparts of people who have departed from this life. But are these the only true ghosts? Isn't it possible that ghosts of the dead sometimes evade the powers that watch over them? May not phantom wraiths sometimes slip stealthily into the bodies of new-born infants?—to take up again some love or hate not consummated?

Was I myself such an infant so chosen to fulfill the destiny of some dissatisfied ghoul? At times I doubt it. Comforting thoughts come, and I deem it all my imagination. Yet, at other times I feel positive that such a one I surely am! For I have, at intervals, remembrances of that which I dare not admit, even to myself.

My hair is white, my face is lined with the deep furrows due to shock; my eyes reflect within their staring depths something of that awful terror which has made of me an old man long before my time. For as years are counted, I am still fairly young, being on the near side of forty; yet I look and conduct myself more like a man over sixty.

My experience has been terrific. But let the facts speak for themselves:

During the World War, I was with Allenby's forces in the Mesopotamia campaign, and I saw things then which I do not like to think about. Yet when I returned to England I was in no wise altered in appearance, save that I had been considerably browned by exposure to sun and weather. I took up the threads of civilian life precisely where I had dropped them, and was, as life goes, a contented and happy man. And why not? I was my own master once again. Furthermore, I was engaged to a most charming girl, even before the War, and she waited for me faithfully with that same sweet, half-shy graciousness.

She was dark haired, dark eyed, exquisitely formed; her face one of that rarely-seen but never-to-be-forgotten type which artists and others romantically inclined describe as "Oriental," perhaps because of the combination of dark eyes and hair, and slightly olive-tinted complexion.

Edwina was quite the antithesis of myself; for I, Eric Marston of Falconwold, English born and English bred, am typically English in appearance. I stood, before I acquired this feeble stoop, nearly six feet in height, was rather bony in structure, florid featured, gray eyed, and with light, almost yellowish-brown hair.

Was it memory on my loved one's part that, even as a child, she would have none of the good old English name of "Maud" bestowed upon her by her lady-mother—insisting that, instead, her name was Edwina? I am sure of it now. She was, as I have just implied, a trifle peculiar, given to reading odd books, studying forgotten languages, positively reveling in folklore, in tales of witchcraft, and in legends of the various historical places near by.

She questioned me eagerly regarding the scenes and traditions of the country through which I had passed with Allenby's forces. Naturally, I could tell her but little. A trooper on active service has small time to post himself on such topics. Foreseeing this, however, I had

---
* Announced in the previous issue as "My Encounter With Osric, The Troll."

brought back with me such few mementoes as could with ease be transported.

An old Arab, dying, gave me as a last token of esteem, a small stone amulet, which he assured me solemnly was a very potent talisman. Both sides of the little octagonal tablet were intricately carved with queer characters. I call them "queer" advisedly, for a very distinguished savant assured me that they were in no known language, ancient or modern, of which he had ever heard.

But Edwina, the instant I showed her the talisman, gasped, murmured a strangely

musical phrase, and went off into a dead faint.

Naturally I was appalled, horror-stricken. Had this occurred before the War, I doubtless would have resorted to the usual methods of lovers, and taken her into my arms, covered her face with kisses, murmuring fond and foolish endearments.

But my late experiences had taught me the value of practical methods. Despite my perturbation, I promptly brought her out of her swoon. And as soon as she came to herself she demanded the talisman. I was not overly pleased at the idea of her having anything more to do with the confounded thing, and expressed myself plainly, telling her out-and-out that if I'd known the effect it was to have upon her, I'd never have brought the amulet from the Near East.

She smiled all that away, as she did my request that she translate for me the phrase she'd uttered before she fainted. All in all, I was a badly puzzled man, and a somewhat angry one as well, when I took my leave shortly after.

But from then on, Edwina wore that talisman as a thing sacred.

"It helps me to know myself, for I lost that charm ages ago," she would state with a look in her eyes I did not at all admire. It was as though she gazed into infinity and saw something which, while it evidently pleased her, left me completely out of her calculations and out of her life.

"She'll get over her notions, once we're married," I'd assure myself. But at times I'd wonder if she would. "And if she didn't get over her notions?" "Oh, well, I'll make allowances!" Every lover has indulged in the same sophistry.

I was a proud and a happy man when I took her, as my wife, over my ancestral home, the gray old castle of Falconwold—from then on, to be her home likewise. Romantically inclined as she was, there was enough romantic history attached to the place to satisfy even her seemingly insatiable nature. And as for legends, both historic and supernatural, there was goodly supply of both.

Although Falconwold had a ghost, there was but little known about it. Once only had it ever manifested itself, and that was many, many years ago, away back in the time of King Charles the First. An event that occurred during that period gave rise to the belief that "our" ghost dated back to at least the time of the First Crusade.

There were two brothers of the house of Falconer, according to the story told me. Hotheads, both, given to dicing, gaming, carousing, and all the follies of that period. Touchy, too, upon points that pertained to their "honor."

Filled with wine and self-esteem, these two brothers—and to make a black matter even blacker, be it said that they were twins—came to words late one night over a notorious beauty of the court.

To such hotheads there was but one course open. In less than no time the center of the floor was cleared, swords were out, and with but a valet each for seconds, the madcap brothers started to finish each other off as deliberately as Cain slew Abel.

Their slim rapiers had no more than touched when, without sound or warning, there appeared suddenly a mighty arm with broad bands of gold gleaming around it, and in its mighty hand was an enormous sword—such a blade as those two foolish brothers could scarcely have lifted, together.

In sheer mockery that terrific, spectral long-sword played between the would-be fratricides; played around them and about them, brandished lightly as a feather in that huge hand. Gleaming and flashing with a lurid flicker, it swept in dazzling arcs until the brothers, appalled, dropped their silly splinters of rapiers to the floor and clung to each other in their mutual fear. At which, in final, supreme mockery, the great blade saluted them in different fashion than that in vogue at their period. A deep, bellowing gust of derisive laughter pealed in their aghast faces—and the apparition vanished as abruptly as it had materialized. So the story ends.

Needless to say, Edwina was gifted with a considerable share of that strange spiritual faculty called "intuition." I related the tale of our family ghost to her, and asked her what she thought about it. Her reply rather surprised me.

"Surely," she exclaimed, "that was no Crusader's ghost! The spectral long-sword apparently gave birth to that idea. But the Crusaders wore armor, and that spectral arm was bare, with great torques of gold gleaming about it. And that seems more like one of the ancient Northmen. I think, Eric, that the ghost of Falconwold dates far back beyond the First Crusade."

But her mind refused to stop at that point. Would that it had! Her next question came direct.

"How long has this castle stood as it is? And when was it commenced?"

"Allowing for additions and renovations, it was first begun by a Saxon Thane in the time of Alfred, which would be about the year 890 or 900 A.D.," I replied. Then, struck by a sudden thought, I added: "Incidentally, there are old monkish scrolls in the library, hand-written, in black-letter—"

After that chat, whenever Edwina was missing from the usual living-rooms, I knew exactly where to locate her. She became a veritable bookworm, seemingly engrossed in her researches amongst the musty old parchments in the somber library of Falconwold castle.

There came a day when I glanced up from my desk, where I was going over certain rentals and other business accounts, to see Edwina standing before me, a strangely exultant look in her dark eyes.

"Oh, Eric!" she exclaimed, all excitement. "The most wonderful, amazing discovery—"

In her hands she held an old, yellowish-stained scroll of parchment which she opened and spread before me on the desk. It was in black letters, which I could not read. To her it was as plain as everyday print, and she proceeded to render its bad Latin into good modern English for my benefit.

It would take too long to give it in detail, and would seem too prolix, for those old monks were not sparing of their words—but briefly, the scroll revealed to us an heretofore unknown page of the history of Falconwold. Allowing for brevity, I give it almost literally:

> I, Rolf the friar, who am Chaplain to Count Hamo Falconer in this his castle of Falconwold, have, by virtue of the power vested in me as an humble servant of our Lord, this day placed upon the oaken door which closes the burial mound of the Norse Viking, Thorulf Sword-Hand, that symbol which all such as he—Trolls, ghosts, vampyrs, witches, warlocks, and their ilk—fear and avoid.

> With proper exorcisms, with bell, book, and candle, and with earnest prayers, I affixed the charm, carved upon a silver plate to the door, so that that evil being should be thereby bound, obliged to await in his own proper grave-mound the coming of that final great Day when all bonds shall be sundered.

> But until that time, no more shall the revengeful ghost of Thorulf the Viking be reunited to his unhallowed body to the sore travail of the countryside, for I affixed the silver seal, the symbol of power, at a time when his ghost wandered in the castle, leaving his Troll's body still seated at the table within the barrow-mound.

> Let no mortal hand disturb the Silver Seal that holds him fast, lest that be liberated which may not again be restrained—

From that point onwards, the scroll told that Thorulf the Viking was buried somewhere on the lands of Falconwold; that he had landed on our coast with a strong following of

Northmen at his back and had promptly attacked the castle, some ninety years before the scroll had been written. After a bloody resistance, the garrison had been conquered. Thorulf with his own long-sword had slain the Saxon Thane Eric, and had taken Eric's beauteous wife for his—Thorulf's—leman.

So, with his Northmen Thorulf had held Falconwold, terrorizing the country-side with sudden, fierce raids. But Eric left a son, which boy Thorulf had spared at his mother's pleading. This son, coming to man's estate, fled the castle. He, Harold, son of Eric, in his turn gathered to him a great force of Saxons, stormed the castle, and in the fierce affray which followed Thorulf Sword-Hand was slain by Harold.

But Harold seems to have been a merciful man, according to those wild times, for he forbore to slay all the Northmen. Instead, he suffered those who had survived the actual fighting to inter Thorulf after their wild, heathen Norse fashion, and had then allowed them to sail away wherever it might please them; only, he exacted from them first a solemn oath that never again would one of them set foot on English soil.

Thereafter, Edwina never rested content until she located the exact place where Thorulf had been buried. It proved to be a low hillock which I had always supposed to be natural; and located only about a thousand yards from the castle. And that added fresh fuel to Edwina's enthusiasm.

She coaxed so earnestly that I detailed a small party of workmen to start excavating. They had better success than I had anticipated, for in a couple of days John, the head gardener, came to me late one afternoon reporting:

"We've uncovered what looks to be a door of some most mighty hard wood with stone doorposts and lintel. Door's got a queer plate of some black metal fixed on't, and a lot of odd letters burnt into the wood above the plate and on each side and below, too. Will you come and inspect it, sir—or shall us break in the door first? Although"—he added dubiously—"it's going to be none so easy a job, breaking in that door. That wood do be as hard as iron, a'most."

"Leave things as they are," I replied after a moment's consideration. "Send the men about other matters until I tell you to resume work there. Get them all away from that vicinity. Do you understand?"

He departed reluctantly, obviously consumed by curiosity, but I gave him no explanation. I meant that Edwina and myself should be the first ones to see what lay hidden within that burial mound. And if any breaking in was to be done, I considered my own muscles fully adequate to the task in hand.

It was late in the afternoon, as I have said, and for once Edwina was reasonable, agreeing with me that it would be better to wait until morning before commencing on that door. But she was in a high state of excitement, as I was myself, for we both realized what a wonderful thing was this finding the actual tomb of one of those daring Northmen who in their time had so thoroughly stamped their seal of terror upon the little island Kingdoms of the Angles.

That night I dreamed a strange dream, if indeed it was a dream. Rather I should say that the gates of the past had opened and allowed me to know somewhat of a former life, wherein I had sown causes that were soon to bear strange fruits for Edwina, for myself, and for another. . . .

I saw myself, clad in much different garb than that of this present time. I knew that I was I, yet also I knew that I was that same Eric the Falcon, that Saxon Thane who had builded him the strong, fortified castle of Falconwold as a defense against forays of the wild, Northern sea-thieves.

In the dream-vision I sat in my great hall. Outside a tremendous tempest was raging. Presently there rushed in a shock-headed serf. His hair was dripping, his jerkin was saturated, but his manner betokened wild delight.

"A foreign ship—such as never before saw I the like of—in distress!" he panted. "She will strike the rocks—soon! Rare pickings—from the—sea! In such storm she—will—surely—strike."

I came to my feet in wrath, cursing him for his impudence. Thanes were no lily-fingered, mealy-mouthed gentry in that far-off time. I knocked him asprawl with a hearty buffet from my fist.

"Thou dog," I roared, enraged. "Since when has Eric the Falcon been named a scavenger-bird? There is a foreign ship in distress—and will surely strike, eh? Then will her people be in sore need of help! Get thee to thy feet, oaf, and summon thy fellows—"

A well-planted kick did the rest, and he scrambled up from among the rushes strewing the floor and left the hall much more rapidly than he had entered. I heard his voice raised against the tumult of wind and rain. To enforce his summons, I seized a great war-horn and blew blast after blast upon it. Then I tore out of the building and raced down to the beach where presently I was joined by my men, serfs and freedmen together.

Black squalls and a torrential downpour of rain made sight a difficult matter, but dimly through the murk we could at intervals catch glimpses of the doomed stranger. A long, low ship she was, slender, evidently built for speed. She showed the ragged stumps of two masts. Her prow bore no effigy of dragon nor of serpent, which fact we all noted with relief. At least, she was not a long-ship of the dread Northmen.

In that frightful gale time seemed to stand still. I had no idea how long we watched that doomed ship striving to claw off-shore and win its way back to open sea again, but suddenly the end came. A black squall, worse than any so far, rushed landward—there was an interval during which the keenest eyes lost all sight of her—then as the light, feeble enough at best of times, grew a trifle brighter—behold! there was no ship struggling upon the tumultuous waters.

Some of my followers cursed bitterly because the sea-demons had robbed them of all hopes of flotsam and jetsam; but I cursed them in turn for their heartlessness. But in the midst of it all, I saw a gleam of white flesh, an arm, momentarily revealed in the surf.

"One lives," I shouted, and dashed into the boiling, roaring waves that thundered on our rocky strand. To his credit be it said, that same serf who had brought me the tidings of the wreck about to take place, and whom I had stricken to the floor, took to the water only a pace behind me. Later, I remember, I rewarded him for that bit of loyal service by giving him his freedom, and a hide of land to boot.

Had it not been for his help, I would never have won to the kindly land again. Undertows dragged at me, sand and pebbles slipped and rolled beneath my feet, foam and spray stung my eyes, blinding me; yet somehow I managed to grasp that which I knew by sense of touch alone to be a woman—a woman, and still alive, although well-nigh sped.

Hardly had I seized her when two great hands clamped fast hold upon me, and that shock-head serf bawled in my ear:

"There be no more—back to land, Master!"

He spoke truly enough. No other body, living nor dead, came ashore, then or later. Nor was any wreckage ever picked up from that lost ship, although I sent men up and down the coast for half a day's journey, searching.

In my arms I bore her to the great hall, where I laid her down upon the wide bench before the bright fire in the broad, deep hearth-place. Then, and only then, did I observe that she was young, also very fair to look upon, despite the cruel buffeting she had endured from storm and wind and wave.

I called the women of the household to attend to her needs and comfort. Late that night one of them reported to me that the stranger-woman slept, but had first spoken, briefly, in a language none of the women could understand.

For that matter, neither then nor ever could any be found who could understand her musical speech, which sounded to our ears more like singing. But, she, being quicker of wit than we dull Saxons, gradually mastered our rough tongue. "Edwina," she named herself; daughter of an Arab *rais*, or ship-captain. And many were the strange tales she told—tales of her own land, and of other lands and of races of men about whom not I nor any I knew, ever had heard. . . .

Then my dream changed.

I was conscious that a considerable lapse of time had transpired. The sea-waif, Edwina, had grown more beautiful with returned health and strength. She was given to practices that had already caused the members of my household to murmur that she was a witch. Much she consorted with an old woman, one Elfgiva, who was, all knew, still a worshipper of the old gods—and from that same Elfgiva, most assuredly, Edwina learned nothing good.

Yet, in my dream, I loved that dark-eyed maiden from the seas; and, although by our Saxon law, what I had torn from the sea was mine, I would in no wise constrain her. Wherefore, instead, I wooed her and, later, wed her. The clergyman who wed us bestowed upon her by my wish and her consent the good old Saxon name of Alrica, which name had been well and honorably borne by my mother in her time. . . .

So my dream ended.

At breakfast the morning following my glimpse into my forgotten past, I greeted my wife half seriously, half jestingly with:

"Edwina—Alrica—which are you? Are you Arab—or Saxon—or English?"

She stared at me, amazement writ plainly on her flawless features, and in her darkly luminous eyes a look of dawning comprehension.

"So, you know! What do you know?" she queried earnestly.

In detail I related my dream, and she followed me attentively.

"It makes me very happy—that you do know," she stated gravely. "All this I have known for a long while; even before we were married—in the Twentieth Century. But, oddly enough, just as I ceased being Edwina and became Alrica, there my knowledge ends; nor can I remember what came after—"

"Unless the record of Rolf the friar is at fault or misstates," I said, "we know fairly well what came after. You were kidnapped by this Thorulf the Sword-Hand and—"

"B-r-r-r!" she retorted. "I am glad I cannot remember, if that's the case. Let us forget that part, Eric. Let the dead past remain buried!"

It would have been well for us both had we done that very thing, literally! But curiosity, that fatal curse of mankind, drove us on; and—as I now think—something else, a terrible mind, inhuman, outside the pale of kindly humanity, was working on our minds for purposes unholy—evil purposes that had held to one fixed course throughout a thousand years and more. The demoniac mind of that fierce Northman, Thorulf Sword-Hand, who, according to the scroll of the chaplain, Rolf, had become a Troll—and who, slain, had refused to stay dead, but whose unhallowed body could in no manner pass the magic symbol that held him prisoner; while at the same time, his revengeful ghost could not get back to its material frame—

It all sounds mad enough, I know, but—let the ensuing events tell their own story:

That door was, as John the gardener had stated, almost as hard as iron. The wood, buried and sealed from air throughout all the long centuries, had slowly seasoned instead of rotting. Furthermore, it was built of thick, square-hewn beams fully nine inches through. In its center was a plate of blackened silver which I rubbed with dirt until it shone a trifle brighter. Edwina scrutinized it closely.

"Oh, look, Eric!" she exclaimed. "The old monk was no mere dabbler in magic! It is the seal of Suleiman the Wise—that same seal with which the great King of old bound the races of the Djinns."

And a moment later:

"Oh, bother! That silver plate is fastened squarely over a lot of the words branded on the door. Eric, those characters are Norse runes; the old, old magic letters and words. I cannot read them all, but I can read enough . . . I wish that plate did not cover so many of them."

To please her, before she was aware of my intention, I drove the sharp edge of a spade under one corner of the square silver plate, and wrenched. It came partially loose and sagged askew, held by one spike only. I grasped it and tore it completely free. Edwina emitted a warning cry.

"Stop! It is the Seal of Sulieman! It may not be tampered with, lightly. You are too bold, Eric."

"Nonsense!" I smiled. "What do you suppose I care about a few queer triangles engraved on a silver plate—if its removal pleasures you?"

But the smile died out on my lips, even as I spoke. A ghastly chill pervaded the air. Even though the sun shone so brightly a moment before, somehow the light had become awesomely dulled, as when an eclipse occurs. A feeling of such horror as never until then had I known, not in all my war experience, surged through me; and, to crown that horror—through the great oaken door I thought there came the sound of low, rumbling, mocking laughter. We stood appalled, staring at each other. Then with an effort I regained my self-control.

"Clever grave-robbers we are," I jeered, humorously. "This is the Twentieth Century, the era of materialism, and in broad daylight—"

I swung up a sharp, heavy axe and attacked that massive door at one edge. Where, as we both noted, was something very like a great lock of greenish metal that was unquestionably formed of hammered bronze. I was no weakling, yet before I had chopped all around that lock it was growing dusk. And I had started on it considerably before noon. I suppose I should have become exhausted by my exertions long before I finished the job, but instead, a strength almost superhuman seemed to possess me. It was precisely as if I were anxious to get within for some motive far above that of mere curiosity—almost as though I had an appointment with that which dwelt within.

Edwina suggested that I stop, and resume once again the next day, but that suggestion I flatly vetoed.

"By no means will I stop now!" I exclaimed emphatically. "It will be dark inside there at any time of day or night. We'll go and refresh ourselves with supper, get flashlights, and I at least will come back. I've just gotten fairly started, and things will become interesting from now on."

But after all, it was nearly midnight before the last barrier was down and our way cleared. Edwina had asserted that she would stay with me to the end of the adventure, and I had not the heart to make her return to the castle. So, together, each holding a flashlight, we entered, and looked about us cautiously.

In a way, it was an impressive sight we gazed upon. Or, rather, it must have been so when first that Norse sea-thief was walled within the tomb.

Picture to yourself a thick oak table some nine feet long and over four feet broad. At the head of the table, facing the doorway, was placed a great chair, also of hewn oak, and seated therein—

He had been a veritable giant in his day, and seemed but little shrunken, despite the ages since he had departed this life. On his head was a helm of metal, from the sides of which, just above his temples, there curved upwards like a crescent moon, two horns, and from the dull yellow gleams they gave off, they were wrought from gold.

In his left hand he held an enormous drinking cup of gold, gem-encrusted; but in his right hand he grasped the thick handle of a huge long-sword that lay extended on the table, point toward the door.

His shoulders and his torso were covered with chain mail; but then, as we first viewed him, seated, we could not see his body at all. A bristling, matted beard, covered most of his face.

"Was he embalmed, then? And if not, why has he not crumbled to dust long ago?" I said, breaking the dead silence in which Edwina and I had been staring at this strange and awful relic of a long-forgotten age.

She shuddered. "I do not think the Northmen understood the art of embalming. Oh, Eric, it's too terrible! Let us go, quickly. I am afraid. It kept itself—in preservation—for a time at least— Rolf the friar did well to warn— *That* is why he made exorcisms and placed the seal of the Wise King— Oh, come away, Eric, before it is too late! Oh, Eric, Eric—*it—is—too late—now!*"

Her voice rose gradually to a horrified shriek; she ended on a gurgling, choked note, sighed, and, smitten into merciful coma by sheer terror, Edwina crumpled in a tumbled heap to the floor.

I well nigh joined her! Man though I was, soldier though I had been, materialist as I had always held myself, I, too, very nearly screamed at what followed. The closed eyes had slowly opened. The wide, ugly mouth opened cavernously in an amazing yawn, disclosing blackened tushes more like those of a wild boar than anything resembling human teeth.

A low chuckle sounded through the charnel-chamber. Then, haltingly, as one renewing acquaintance with a long-disused tongue, the hideous Troll-thing spoke in a voice whose every tone sounded in my ears precisely as if filtering through glue or slimy ooze.

"What? After all these ages? It is Eric the Falcon—the Bright Falcon of those accursed dogs of Saxons—come again to earth? Eric—whom long ago I slew, taking his lands and his very beautiful wife for my own! And now Eric came again, and opened for my spirit the way back to my body— Ho! a rare jest, Saxon dog! Thine was the hand that pulled away that silver plate I dared not pass! Great haste was thine, fool, to enter my barrow and bring back to me that same fair woman—

"Why, Saxon, it is kind of thee! Long have I waited. Yet thou hast come—even as that Devil-goddess I visited in Hela's Halls swore to my raging soul—she swore, too, that if I would yield her reverence and service I should await thy coming throughout the ages, still in mine own body. Saxon, I claim my bride! Get thee hence, swineherd!"

Oh, now I knew why I had been so determined to cut through that door. That *I* which is greater than I, knew that the Troll-thing dwelt therein, and had a heavy score to settle. . . . I heard my own voice, hoarse with wrath, speaking in frenzied words that came from I knew not where.

"Thorulf Sword-hand! Sea-thief, murderer, ravisher in life! And in death, Troll, Vampyr—I, Eric of Falconwold, name thee *Niddering*—"

But at that word, the worst that could possibly be applied to a Northman, the Troll, who had risen, slowly, lumberingly, from his great chair and taken his first stride towards me, stopped short.

"*Niddering? A coward? I?*" His gluey tones held a note of unbelief, incredulity, as though he could no longer trust his hearing.

"Aye, Niddering! *Thorulf Niddering*," I cried ferociously, almost into his matted beard. "Niddering—and worse! Art armed, hast a long-sword, and I am empty-handed! Art clad in armor, and I in cloth, yet thou dost threaten, bid me hence! Thou, Thorulf Niddering, dare not fight me, whom once thou didst slay, with weapons! Had I but a knife, I'd send thee yelling with fear, back to that Devil-goddess who rules in Hela's Halls with a fine tale—"

He heard me out, standing motionless, his ugly head nodding reflectively; while in his vampyr eyes the hell-lights flickered and flared.

"Behind my chair—a battle-axe," he growled. "It is a good axe. Long ago I took it from a Christ's-man. I will not touch it—but thou—get it, Saxon! I will fight thee once again— for her," and he pointed, leering evilly, at Edwina, lying there so still and white.

For a single second I mistrusted—and why not? It was no man, but a demon I stood facing. That great brand, his long-sword! But as if reading my thought, he lowered the point to the floor and folded his huge hands on the ball-shaped pommel. I knew I must chance it—for Edwina's sake.

In a single bound I was past him, had grasped the axe from where it leaned against his chair. I whirled about, leapt between him and my unconscious woman.

"Now—Sea-thief, Troll, Vampyr," I shouted, defiant.

"Harsh names, Saxon," he grumbled, "after I gave thee a good axe!"

My flashlight I had placed on the table, so its rays would be cast on us as we stood. Edwina's had slipped beneath her when she fell. There was a gruesome, greenish-blue half-light that pervaded all the charnel-chamber; I know not whence it sprang. But in that weird light I could see the Troll-thing's eyes shine lurid as he lashed out at me with his ponderous brand. I parried it easily with the axe-head, for as yet Thorulf's arms were awkward and stiff, as well they might be.

Then began, full-swing, one of the strangest battles ever fought—a battle between man the soul-bearer, and that which had lost its soul's heritage, becoming one of the horrible Un-dead—one who, slain, had sold his right to dwell in Valhalla for revenge and a life that was not life! And the prize of that fierce conflict between us twain was the body, and soul, of her who lay there so motionless, so waxy-white that I surely deemed her dead, and silently thanked God that such was the case. For *it* could then possess only the inanimate

"Behind my chair—a battle-axe. Get it, Saxon! I will fight thee once again—for her."

body—yet from that horror, too, I must save her!

Once that thick voice rumbled *"Thor Hulf!"* The old, wild, Northman battle-cry! And I retorted "God's Help!" Then jeered the Thing with biting scorn.

"Thor will never heed thee, Troll," I mocked. "Thor sits in Valhalla with the honorable brave, and holds no traffic with Hela's brood!" And thereafter we fought in a grim silence.

Quicker of foot I was, but the Troll had advantage of reach both of arm and with weapon. Wherefore he did most of the attacking, while I could but parry the sweeps of the enormous long-sword, dodge and swerve, and, at rare intervals, swing a futile blow at his arm with the heavy, double-bladed axe.

Where the thought came from, I have no means of knowing, but into my mind leaped, full-born, the certitude that could I once get the Thing out of his burial-mound and into the open, where was greater room, I might yet have a chance.

To that end I used all the craftiness I could command. Feinting, swerving, leaping backward and ever sidewise, I worked toward the entrance. Somehow, as by mutual consent, unspoken but understood, we both avoided trampling on Edwina as we fought past where she lay. . . .

We were outside! A thunderstorm was raging, and in my soul I thanked Heaven for it. The rain refreshed me, and I had the kindly lightning to see by. It was Nature's own light, and not that greenish-blue hell-light that shone, unnatural, within the charnel-chamber.

My foot struck against something! I staggered. The battle-axe flew from my grasp as I strove wildly to regain my balance. The Troll's great sword, swinging, barely brushed my shoulder with its flat—well for me it was not the edge! But lightly as it touched, it was enough to finish my stability. I went asprawl!

The Demon-Thing strode heavily forward, grinning hideous joy, intending to make an end! My hand touched something hard and smooth. In desperation I clutched it, swung back my arm, and flung whatever it was I had picked up fairly into the middle of that triumphant leering abhorrence of a face—

God's mercy—and His help!

A wailing yell that turned me sick to hear—and the Troll threw wide its arms, crashed backward, lay prone and forever still! I scrambled to my feet, seized the axe I had let fall, ran to the monster, whirled the axe aloft to behead—but there was no need.

Even as I looked, the Thing began to crumble into dust. Aye, even the bronze and leather, the great long-sword, and, likewise, the horn-hafted battle-axe I was holding, slowly but surely disintegrated! There was no longer a hell-preserved body—only a gleaming skeleton, gigantic, white in the lightning's flare. Then that, too, dissolved into a soft paste from the falling rain. I saw a shine of metal where the head had lain on the ground. I picked it up—

God's help—and His help is very potent!

Falling, I had grasped and flung at the Troll the silver plate which the monk of old, Rolf, had fastened to the door of the barrow! The dark hell-charm that had preserved that Troll-Thing throughout the ages, was not proof against the White Magic of Rolf, servant of the powers of light. His silver seal had done that which not human arm nor heavy battle-axe had availed to achieve.

I crept within that accursed charnel-house, and, weeping and wailing like a frightened child, I sought and found the still form of my beloved. Stumbling through the storm, I bore her to the castle. The dawn was breaking.

Then—I collapsed.

Edwina recovered consciousness shortly after the noon of the third day following. Her hair is as white as mine, but her beauty is unimpaired. She did not see what happened after the Thing opened those eyes of red fire.

She was badly shocked at my aspect when she beheld me, as I was also when first I looked at myself in a pier-glass, after I'd somewhat recovered from my collapse.

Only once did she seek to question me. We were idly sunning ourselves on a bench in the garden at the time, and she asked, a trifle listlessly:

"Eric, what occurred? Did Thorulf—"

But I looked her squarely in the eyes and—lied!

"Oh, Thorulf crumbled into dust shortly after you fainted. Ask no more, Edwina."

I had the burial-mound blown up with high explosives. Specialists assure me that I may eventually recover wholly from—whatever it is that has made me as I am. But they are badly puzzled by my case, for I tell them nothing.

Edwina promised to ask no more questions. She has kept her word; yet, woman-like, she has very nearly violated it.

Yesterday she slipped her hand in mine as we walked, saying:

"Eric, though my body lay in a swoon—yet I somehow know and remember all that happened! I think—Eric—that the soul—never loses—consciousness."

The Specter in Red
By Ethel Watts Mumford

When Tom Kinkaid consented to be hypnotized, he had no way of telling that he was to remain in the power of some unknown, bestial Thing that was to drive him to deeds of violence even his brain could not conceive.

"My hands are bloody. Oh God! What have I done?"

I REACHED HOME DEAD TIRED, after thirty hours of concentration and strain, exhausted but content, for my patient was out of danger. As I wearily asked the usual questions as to calls, Williams, my personal servant, hesitated. Evidently he thought I should go to bed at once. However, he handed me a list, and then, from a drawer in the hall table, produced a flat package.

"A man came at five yesterday afternoon," he explained. "He waited a long time, and when you telephoned that you would not be back, he went away, but he left this—a book, I think, for he was very insistent that you should read it, sir. He asked for pencil and paper and left this note for you." He produced it from his pocket. "He said he'd come back again today."

I took the package and the letter idly. "What name?" I inquired.

"Mr. Kinkaid, Tom Kinkaid, sir, and he looked terribly ill, if you'll pardon me for observing."

I stared. Tom Kinkaid! I had not thought to hear from him again. And Williams said he "looked ill." It was hard to imagine that giant of a man in anything but the best of health. Perhaps his malady, whatever it was, had been the cause of his dropping out of our circle so abruptly and completely. The memory of him was so vivid that I stood abstractedly holding the unopened letter and package, forgetful that it might contain the answer to my questions.

Tom Kinkaid was the most remarkable medium our Club ever developed, for I, together with Mellon, Standish, Humphries, and perhaps a half-dozen other professional men, had been bitten by the psychic bug, and had formed ourselves into a group of scientific investigators. We met at Mellon's, and I acted as hypnotist, when the medium needed the initial impetus, which had been true in his case.

The strangest thing about Kinkaid's communications was that he seemed to get in touch with a primitive spirit—a cave man; the control was so strong that it had developed impersonation. In fact, at the séance after which he disappeared, he had been seized by some obscure destructive impulse, and had wrecked the place. I had had a bad moment trying to bring him out of it. And if ever I have known physical fear, it was before that raging, primal brute.

I shuddered involuntarily and came back to the present. Dismissing Williams, I went to my room, ate the crackers and cream that he had thoughtfully provided me, and I untied the parcel. Three copy-books were revealed. I opened the note, and read:

"You will understand—you've got to understand—I must have help. I've brought my diaries because they will show you how it has come about. I have marked the margins of certain paragraphs with red ink—the Specter in Red, I call them. Only these are *my* entries. The rest, the others, God knows, *aren't* mine, though I've watched my own hand write them. They've got me—they and the other.

"Your servant says you are out on a desperate case, and won't be back for hours. What case can be as desperate as mine? I ought to have come to you before, but I couldn't trust myself. I hated you, all of you—but now there's no one else who can help me, and I must have help. I'll come tomorrow at five, and if you've read my diaries, you'll know that you've got to drop everything else and save me.

"I can handcuff myself to the bed tonight, so I'll be safe—but it can't go on. Be here when I come back—it's more than your duty. You are to blame for this. What has got me now isn't even human!"

I was dumbfounded. Why, the man must be mad! Most certainly I must see him, and have him placed under observation. Handcuffed to his bed for safety—and I to blame for his condition? These were the ravings of a maniac.

My first glance at the diaries confirmed my diagnosis. The entries were a confused scattering of broken sentences, and half-finished paragraphs in different handwritings. Here and there I saw a page of diagrams with curious sums and geometric symbols—a hodge-podge as crazy as it was peculiar.

"Red margins"—there they were, and in every case they invited attention to one handwriting, Kinkaid's own. I had seen it, and therefore recognized it at once. What were these others, "automatic," as he suggested, or just plain dementia? A paragraph caught my attention:

"They trepanned with a bronze, razor-like instrument and sewed the scalp over the orifice resulting from the extraction of the bone. Even to this day the Berbers and other North African tribes operate in much the same fashion, as the directions given in the Book of Toth would have the operation performed."

I was amazed. What could Tom Kinkaid know about the Book of Toth, and Berber surgery? That I knew the statement to be true, was not surprising. A physician may be pardoned an antiquarian interest in the beginnings of his profession. But Tom Kinkaid! That paragraph determined me. Dog tired as I was, I must read this astonishing document at once.

I found the first entry marked in red. It proved to be the date of March 16th of last year, which antedated the meeting when we had such trouble with him, and was the last he attended. On March 16th, Tom Kinkaid wrote:

"The damnedest thing has happened to me. I must be a sleep-walker, but if I am, I never knew it before. I didn't eat anything last night that could have upset me physically, and certainly the play I saw wouldn't have excited a guinea pig. I give it up, but the fact remains that sometime in the night I must have gotten up and perambulated, for I woke up on the roof! I never had such a fright in my life.

"The first thing I became conscious of, was the dreadful depths below, and height, to me, is, as the Bible puts it, a 'creature.' I have gooseflesh when I think of it. It must have been the cold that awakened me. I was freezing—had on my pajama trousers and nothing else, unless I include a large leg-of-lamb bone that I was gripping like a drum stick. And where I got that is a mystery. I backed away from the edge of the gulf, with my heart in my mouth and my stomach in rebellion. I was too scared even to realize then what an extraordinary thing I was doing, and in what an improbable place. Gosh!— Got down through the skylight. Dawn was just breaking, and I could see fairly well. But how I found my way about in the dark is the limit, but I believe sleep-walkers do that sort of thing.

"Got back into the old room at last. Never have been so glad to get anywhere in my life. Wonder if there is anything one can do to check sleep-walking? I ought to see a doctor, I suppose, and I will, if I catch myself at it again. Some stunt—whatever possessed me? It gives me the willies when I think of it."

There followed entries for several weeks, and then for pages the book was marked by red-ink margins of the entry of April 12, the date of our last séance:

"Went to Dr. Mellon's meeting—and never again! Never! I'm shaky. What is this anyway? Let me get the straight of it. Perhaps if I set it down as it happened, I'll be able to think things out. First, Langdon hypnotized me as usual. When I came out of it, I saw that

I had them all worried. Dr. Mellon, Langdon and Duffy were white and sick, and Standish looked a wreck. They all looked as if they'd had a first-class jolt. I guess they'd had it, too.

"The next thing I observed was the center table, split down the middle and laying on its side, and the back of a heavy armchair wrenched clean off. Of course I asked when the cyclone struck, and then I learned that I'd done it. I—me! I couldn't believe it then, but I do now. They explained that I'd been pulling down a control from way back in the Eocene, a cave man, a cliff dweller, or something. Lord! why didn't they tell me before? I'll never let it happen again, not for a million dollars. Right there and then I had a funk. I didn't tell 'em, of course, about my excursion on the roof and the meat bone, but I realized instantly that that all hung together, a sort of hold-over from the trance condition, that had come back on me in my sleep.

"I got out and walked home, scared half to death for fear that the thing would jump me. But nothing happened. Never again! I can always make a good-enough living, anyhow. I don't need their money. I'm off the medium stuff forever. I don't want even to see any of that crowd again. The very sight of them would set me off, now that I know. Damn Mellon and Langdon, anyhow! They got me into this. Anyway, I'm through. Tomorrow I'm going out to find a job, so help me. Something is grabbing my hand—"

The last five words were written wildly, each letter at a different angle, as if, literally, another hand strove for possession of the pen; and, following that, the writing became totally different, small, accurate, sharply slanted. It reads as follows:

"All six books are still in existence. On several occasions the papyri have actually been in the hands of savants perfectly capable of deciphering them."

Here the intruding spirit yielded to another, who covered the lower half of the page with lines of poetry in Rabelaisian French. I started. Was all this evidence of the mental condition of the writer, or were they, indeed, the messages of outside intelligences? But Kinkaid, poor devil, must have suffered atrociously. There could be no question but that his conscious mind must have been terrorized. I turned page after page where strange passages alternated, until I came once more upon the red-ink margins.

"It's happened again—only worse. I was walking—just walking. I wanted to get in touch with Gregory, and I took a chance of finding him home in the evening. I wasn't thinking about the roof or about the séance. The last thing I remember is an arc light in or near a florist shop window. That's the last . . .

"I came to. There was something rough and round under me, to which I was clinging. Above was a grey dawn sky streaked with white, and against it like a net were branches, bare branches, showing just a tinge of spring red in them. Then my eyes and my hands told me that I was lying along the branch of a tree, flat on my stomach as a panther lies. The rest of my body seemed dead. Then that, too, revived, and I felt the rough bark of the tree-branch under me.

"Presently I got the location. I was in the Park, a remote and sequestered spot. An empty green bench stood on the other side of a lawn, showing the existence of a path. I grew faint and giddy, and almost fell off my perch. I looked down, and there, just below, lay a huddled white thing, splashed with red—a lamb, a dead lamb. Its throat was torn, its small body twisted as if it had been wrung.

"There's a sheep fold not far away, where the Park Commission keeps a flock that feeds on one of the big concourses in summer time. The recollection swept over me, and the conviction that I must have gotten in there, stolen and killed that little creature. I looked at my hands; they were bloody. Sheer horror forced me backwards, down the limb, and dropped me from the trunk to the ground. I lay at the foot of the tree shaking.

"In the pocket of my coat I found my handkerchief and cleaned my face and hands as best I could. I gave one backward glance at that mangled, gutted lamb, and ran for the path that I knew would lead me out. It was so early that the mists from the lake still hung over everything. I slunk from tree to tree, cut across to the low boundary wall, climbed over, and hurried, hurried—

"I got home. I found my latch-key. Nobody saw me—nobody knows—but *I* know, and I know now that this is not sleep-walking. I was out of doors when it took me. I was moving, tramping along, feeling active, wide awake, my mind busy with what I would say to Gregory when I asked for work. I know, I'm sure, it's that medium stuff. The Cave Man has found out how to get into me, whether I'm willing or not. Thank God I know now—at last. This won't happen again. I'll set my whole will against him. I wasn't on my guard before. Who would have thought of such a thing? But now it's different. I can resist. My will is a living will; now that I know, there is no further danger.

"One hour later.

"I have had it out and I've won. I knew I could beat it when I resisted. But who could believe that the tussle could be so terrible? I'm wet with perspiration, my back aches as if I'd strained it. I'm weak, nauseated.

"It happened as I was looking over the damp, torn clothes I had worn, wondering whether they were worth sending to the tailor's. I had warned my mind to watch out, and my mind obeyed. I felt myself slipping. I got the warning in time to hang on, to fight, to steel my will. It felt as if someone had a hand inside my head, trying to get physical grip of my brain. I grabbed hold of the footboard of the bed and held on as if to a life preserver. I hung to it, straining with all my might—and it passed—it passed! I've beaten it! I'll be safer now—safe. Gad! what an experience!"

The handwriting of this entry was weak, wobbly, slanting downward. It showed the effects of the racking effort he had made.

Thereafter followed entries covering two weeks, when he seemed to have been free of the incubus. I will quote only one paragraph from this portion of his autobiography, because it gives the reason for his not having come for help to us, whom he considered the source of his trouble.

"I know I'm not mad, but if I went to a doctor he'd lock me up. I've thought of going to Mellon but I'm afraid, afraid first because the very sight of him might start this up again; and then I know Mellon. He'd be capable of holding me on the assumption that I was insane, in order to study me. Why couldn't they have let me alone? Thank goodness I've escaped from them, from the writing things, and I've beaten 'it.' I've felt sort of seedy, but getting better, and I'm going out tomorrow to get that job."

A later entry reads:

"I got my old place on the paper. Good work. Gregory awful decent to me."

It is evident he believed he had won clear. It was not fear, therefore, that brought the terror back upon him. He was unmolested, the record shows, for over a week, and then, margined in red, is the entry of—

"April 20th. What shall I do? What shall I do? I was all right, back in harness—doing good work, even Gregory said so. Then—I drew a blank!—blotted out, for two days. I swam a river—and I can't swim! I woke up on the other shore, wet, dripping, aching all over, tired. It was late afternoon, and I lay and shivered on the bank until night came. There was a tumble-down landing near, with half a dozen shabby boats hauled up, not yet in commission. I found a skiff moored at the wharf-end and a pair of oars under the platform. At dusk I shoved off and drifted down. Managed to steal a ride over the ferry—no money. I had on clothes, but not my own, and I don't recognize them, and they are odd pieces, nothing matches. How did I get them? I'm home—I'm back in my room. I am all in, but I've got to set this down and get it out of my system. There were telegrams here—messages. I find out I've been gone two days—*two days!* What did I do? Why have I got a hunted feeling? Were they chasing me when I took to the river? Then who, and why? Could I have attacked anyone?

"How can I hold on to my job if I do things like this? What can I do? How explain? I can't! God in Heaven! And I thought I licked the thing—fought it to a finish. And I can't call for help, even. I'd be taken for a lunatic. But perhaps I ought to be locked up—perhaps the right thing for me to do is to give myself up.

"Am I never to be rid of this terrible thing? I'm a coward. I can't endure the thought of confinement—I'd rather die. I ought to be watched, though, and that's a fact. I'll have to go to Mellon, damn him! or Langdon. He and his crowd have done this to me, and it's up to them to get me out of it. But they'll shut me up if I ask for help, and think they are proving something, making 'scientific observations.' They'd satisfy their curiosity, and I wouldn't have a chance. I'm so tired I can hardly write, but I must, before I try to go to sleep. I want to have the written record here. I may wake up and remember nothing—at least I'll have this. I wonder if I'm going crazy, and all this is delusion? I'm tired, I'm done. I couldn't have swum the river—I can't swim—but I did. How did I get on the other side? I'll go mad sure enough if I start arguing."

The next record is of the following day. It reads simply:

"Nothing happened, thank God!"

Several days elapse, and then:

"April 27th. I've been left in peace, not even the writing things have bothered me. Gregory came up to see me—he's a decent sort. I told him I'd had a drink of bad hooch and been knocked out, blank, for forty-eight hours. He saw how I looked, and believed me. I was in mortal terror I'd flop and do something queer right there before him. But I didn't. I told him I was all right now, and I'd come back to the paper if they'd take me. Now if I can hold onto myself—but I can, of course I can. I didn't discipline myself enough. I've got to be on the watch all the time. The seizures are getting further and further apart, anyway. It's wearing off. I'll give myself another chance before I go to see anyone about it."

For days after this the entries read: "O.K." "Back on the job."

"So far so good, only the writing things now"—which fact was evidenced by the interpolations, now and again, of scraps of the strange communications.

"Gregory liked my interview." "I got the Sunday Special."

"All's well—went to the Newspaper Men's dinner. Met the old crowd—fine."

Then the date in a shaking hand:

"May 12th. I'm sitting here at my table. I know that I'm alone in the room, but I'm scared to death. I know I'm going to have another fight for myself. It's coming, it's all around me. It's worse than fear. If I tried to get up, I know I'd keel over—'spell-bound.' Spell-bound—that's it. I'm writing with all my might. I've got to concentrate—concentrate. If I hold on to myself and keep my mind working, it can't get me. No, no, it can't, it can't."

Across the tragic page appeared a long brown smear. What follows must have been written only a few hours later:

"It can't be true—I—just now, this minute, I was hanging by my hands like an ape!—out there on the fire-escape!—like an ape. My legs were drawn up and crooked under me. I heard myself chuckling, just as I became aware of myself. The window was open. I got in somehow. I've been out there, like a great ape. My clock says that I've been gone several hours, but where have I been? What have I done?

"The floor is covered with all sorts of things I have never seen before. There is a clock, a gilt one; a hat, with feathers torn and broken. Some clothes, women's clothes. How did they get here? What have I done to get them? This isn't the Cave Man, I know it. It isn't human at all, it can't be. A beast—a beast— Where did I go? I can't remember anything, I must have made two or three trips to bring in all this stuff. Suppose some one saw me? What can I say if they come after me? Tell them the truth and be taken to the asylum!

"I wish I could murder Mellon and the lot of them for this. But I mustn't, I mustn't even think of it. The beast might come back and make me do it. I'm crying, there are tears so that I can't see what I'm putting down, but at least I know that I—I, myself, am writing this. I wonder if it's all crazy. But those clothes, that mangled hat—I must have brought them in here. Wasn't I out there on the fire-escape hanging by my hands?—I've made up my mind, I'm going to Langdon. I'm going to take him my diary. He's more human than the rest of them. I can't stand it, I must have help. Perhaps they can undo what they did. I'll make them!

"I'm innocent, innocent as a baby, I swear I am—

"I've just realized it, I did not seem to see it before. My hands are stained, my hands are bloody—I felt of my hair. It's there, too. My clothes are sticky with blood. I wasn't conscious of it till all of a sudden I saw my finger smear the page. On the buttons of my coat are long yellow hairs— Oh, God! What have I done? I must give myself up at once. I'm not safe. The beast may get me any time. But what did I do? I pray it wasn't murder!

"Those long golden hairs from a head I have never seen! I'm not to blame. I've looked back over my whole life, and I never did anybody any harm. I have a right to be free of this thing.

"I wonder who she was—the woman with yellow hair? Where did I find her? Who was she? Young, surely—such bright gold!—and there's blood on my hands, blood all over me."

The page was blistered as with tears. The brown smears marked it as with a ghastly signature.

I closed the book, as if by so doing I could shut away the picture that it evoked.

Mad? Of course. But what a horrible delusion—what hideous suffering poor Tom Kinkaid must have endured. I put away the books and the accompanying note. But sleep and I were to be strangers that night. Again and again I lit the electric lamp on the night table, and read and reread the red-margined confessions. If I had known where to reach him I would have dressed and gone at once, but I did not know where he lived, and Mellon, who, presumably, might have the address, was away and out of reach.

Dawn came at last. Feverishly I worked my way through the long, long hours of that never-ending day. I gave orders that when my visitor came he was to be conducted to me in my library, and that no patients were to be admitted.

*I got the drawer open, my hand
closed on the gun.*

   The hour approached. Bringing the diaries with me, I went
   to the library. Perhaps I ought to call Sullivan, the alienist, and
   have him overhear the conversation. Somehow I did not wish it.
I wished first to judge for myself. Sullivan is a hard-headed, unimaginative, incurious
specialist, who sees only what the commonest of common logic shows him. There could
be no question as to what his opinion would be. But to me there was a question, one that
became ever more resistant.

  I waited, pacing the room, my heart hammering, every nerve taut. I was prepared to see
a great change in Tom Kinkaid, but when at last Williams ushered him in, the sight of him
struck me like a blow. What was left of him was a great, cordy-sinewed skeleton. His eyes,
receded into their sockets, peered out with a look stunned and pitiful. His big hands were
shaking like a man palsied. I motioned him to sit down, and he collapsed into the chair
opposite. He stared at me in silence, and then great tears began to pour from those dark,
discolored eye-sockets, and follow one another down his hollow cheeks. A physician is
used to seeing the ravages of disease and anxiety, but never, in so short a time, had I seen
such a piteous disintegration.

  "You've read?" he managed to articulate.

  I nodded. Speech was impossible, my throat was constricted.

  "You're to blame," he croaked. "You did this to me!" A flare of anger leaped in his eyes.

He hunched his powerful, gorilla-like body, preparing to spring at me.

I wanted to exculpate myself, explain, deny the responsibility. But I sat still, fascinated, staring. The moments passed—there was silence. Then I saw fear visibly descend upon Tom Kinkaid—fear so overpowering that from very sight of it I was near to panic. I didn't run only because I could not. His great jaw protruded, slowly his arms dropped forward, down, down, until his huge skeleton hands with their knotted veins rested on the carpet. I could see his wrists, torn and gouged where manacles had ground into them. Slowly, horridly, the change came over him. His lips curled back, his teeth glittered. With shoulders hunched forward, he peered about with eyes that shone as if a red light burned behind them. Beneath his clothes I could see his muscles bunching, the movement an animal makes when feeling and testing his strength. His legs curled up, ape-like, with knees outbent, and as he blinked at the light his forehead and eyebrows twitched. The creature seemed to be striving to focus his surroundings. He grunted, and his whole body shook with it. It was a gorilla that crouched there before me.

This was no clever conscious or unconscious imitation. It was *possession*.

The deep little eyes suddenly caught mine. His mouth puckered out questioning, his expression one of curiosity. He hunched his powerful, gorilla-like body, preparing to spring at me. In sheer terror I pushed my chair back. This seemed to puzzle him. I knocked over an inkwell that fell to the floor with a thud, and distracted his attention. In that instant when his eyes left mine I remembered the revolver in the table drawer.

I got the drawer open, my hand closed on the gun. I raised it—I was safe. I could kill the beast or wound it, for I did not dare summon aid. He was between me and the door. Whoever should come in answer to my call, would be at his mercy. I had forgotten that this was not some wild animal who might attack me at any moment, but a man like myself. But it came over me when my finger tightened on the trigger that I couldn't kill him, I couldn't! I stood there, at the head of the table, trembling, sobbing with fright, with the weapon in my hand. But I couldn't raise the gun, I couldn't kill him.

With shambling gait he moved back and forth, his huge fingers picking at various objects.

A red brocade table-cover caught his eye. He jerked it off, throwing the electric lamp, amid a shower of magazines and knickknacks, to the floor. He grinned, patting the bright folds to his breast. Then the gilt figures on the fallen lamp attracted him. He reached for it. In some way, I don't know just how, he got a shock—perhaps he tore off the covering of the wire. Anyway, the sensation puzzled and angered him. He threw the lamp from him and jerked the cord from the socket. Then he turned, and saw me. His lips parted, he snarled, showing his teeth, and his chest seemed to widen as he breathed deep. Even then I could not aim the pistol at his breast. I stood there, more hypnotized than he had ever been. Death was in his eyes. His huge fingers clenched and unclenched. He was measuring his distance before he leaped—another moment and he would be upon me, and still I could not shoot.

Then the expression of the creature changed. The desperate face of Tom Kinkaid looked out at me. Then began the struggle of the will of the man with the will of the beast that rode him. Little by little the man's furious effort told. He straightened, his legs lost their apelike lift and outward twist. His arms ceased to hang, long and heavy. He was back in the chair now, gripping its arms as if he would crush the wood to pulp. He raised his head. The despair in his eyes changed to a look of triumph.

Then, in the twinkling of an eye, the beast was altogether gone, and Tom Kinkaid, white and shaken, sat panting and gasping before me. The look of power faded from his face. In its place dawned horror and desperate determination. He thrust himself to his feet, staggered a moment as if to get his balance, and without a word lunged to the door. He tore it open—and was gone. I heard the outer door slam as if it were being cracked from its hinges. Dazed and but half realizing all that had happened, I followed him, still clutching the revolver.

The violence with which the door had been thrown shut had jammed the lock. It took me a moment to get it open—a moment while I was conscious of cries and calls outside. I finally got it free, and reached the street. Men were running—a knot of people, growing larger from moment to moment, were gathered by a truck, skidded onto the sidewalk. A man hung over the driving wheel, sobbing hysterically—his screaming cut through the babel of excited voices.

"I tried not to hit him! I tried not to hit him!—he didn't gimme a chance! He got right under, I tell you, he got right under!"

A policeman came up, and the crowd made way for him. I didn't need to see in order to know that Tom Kinkaid had died—a man!

Mad? I wish I could think so.

That presence—surely none other than Ross' own self—still hovered over me.

Who Am I?
By Owen Bennett
As told to Lilith Shell

Owen Bennett faced the horror of knowing his personality was changing, of knowing that he was to lose his very soul.

ROSS LYONS AND I, OWEN BENNETT, HAD BEEN CHUMS SINCE OUR LITTLE BOYHOOD. Our parents lived in the same town and we two lads were born within a few blocks of each other. Ross was a little older than I, some six or eight months. I remember that he started to school before me so that I was never in his room, much to my childish regret.

Ross was brighter than I. He was born with a dominant soul. Always other children deferred to him and, most of all, I did. I remember that as a little chap I was always pleased to do his bidding—considered it a privilege. My mother used often to reprimand me for my subservience to him. There was no errand of his too laborious for me to undertake, no task set by him which I considered too difficult. He was a regular Tom Sawyer in our gang and of all the boys I was the easiest one for him to "work." For, I worshipped him as a hero.

And Ross was worth it. There was a nobility of soul about him even as a boy, a greatness—something which I cannot explain—which gave him an enviable place among people. He never needed to *gain* a place for himself; the place was there for him when he arrived. All through high school this was true—he always the leader, I his contented follower. But I need not stop longer to depict this dominant phase of Ross Lyons' character. It held all through college, increasing as he "increased in wisdom and stature and in favor with God and man."

Then came the call to war, just when we were both entering the business of life, I in my father's insurance office, he as a physician. We had been separated for three years just preceding the war call, but our touch with each other had remained unbroken. During this period, while I was in the university and he in medical school, I became engaged to Annie Griffin.

One drop of bitter in this sweet cup of mine was that Annie did not like Ross—indeed, could not tolerate him, and between the two, really, there was no love lost for neither did he like her. There seemed to be some sort of antipathy between them that neither had any will to try to overcome. So I was robbed of the pleasure of discussing either of them with the other. Annie and I would have been married before I went to France if her parents had not so opposed the idea, as did also my own, begging us to wait until my return. Which, as events turned out, was truly a God's blessing.

So together Ross and I went into training and later we crossed the big water. I need not describe our life over there. Too many times already the horror of that thing has been pictured. Let it suffice to say that Ross was a commissioned officer while I, running true to form, was a private. The old master and slave relationship still existed between us. Not, let me hasten to say, that Ross ever actually lorded it over me—that is, not willfully. I would not give you a wrong conception of him. He was nobility itself and he had a high regard for me, but it somehow expressed itself to fit in exactly with that dominant, high-powered personality of his which so completely controlled me.

Now, when I make this next statement I do not desire to take any credit to myself, but truly I say that when we went into battle, he commanding the line, I merely following that command, that my own thought was—not for myself, not for my country, not any patriotic notion of saving the world for democracy, but for him—for Ross and his safety.

There came to us, as came to all soldiers, a black period of rain and mud and hunger and uncertainty. Day followed dreary day and every hour we expected to go over the top. Just before dawn one morning came the command and over we went. Of it all I recall only my feeling of furious anger—anger at the enemy—and a feeling of infinite relief that we could at last actually go, that there was finally an end to that tedious waiting—that, and a deep concern for Ross. Not another thing do I recall of that attack.

Something happened—I'm not sure what—but the one thing I do know is that a stranger thing happened than any rain of machine-gun fire, any bursting of shells, any deadly infusion of gas. I do not attempt to account for it and I do not expect the world of sane folks to swallow it, but I started in to tell it and here it is.

Slowly, slowly, out of a great depth and out of a great blackness . . . through a vague and painful dimness, I realized that I was down—not rushing madly as I had been, but down on the muddy ground with rain pelting upon me. Out of my first dim consciousness I thought the rain was beating through an open window upon my bed and instinctively I reached to lower the window. This reaching was not such an easy matter for I found that my arm would not respond to my will. The pain which attended this effort brought with it clearer consciousness and with it some realization of my plight.

It seemed dark—dark—as black as ink around me, and with every moment of increased consciousness came increased agony. I tried reaching out with my other arm and found that I could move it. My hand fell upon another form near me, very near—nearer than the length of my arm. Moving my hand up and down upon it I soon found a face, a cold wet face, and in that very moment I knew somehow whose face it was—Ross' face.

At that same instant I felt some strange, some compelling presence at my side, upon me, hovering over me, surrounding me. What shall I say? How shall I describe it? I do not know. I tried to pull myself up on my left elbow to deal with this compelling thing, whatever it was, for it seemed to command me, to dominate my will in such a way that there was no resisting it.

The sky seemed to lighten in the next few moments as I lay there, and now I saw a form taking shape before me—not something tangible or material, not something shining or even dimly luminous as might have been expected in the eery light of early dawn, but a form, nevertheless, indefinite and obscure to be sure, but there, and very surely and unmistakably Ross' form. He was insisting upon something, what I could not make out. Guiltily I remembered that he was my superior officer and that it should require no such insistence on his part to secure my obedience to his will.

But I could not get it. Gladly, how gladly I would obey him if only I could make out what he wanted. Somehow the feeling came upon me that it was not as a commanding officer that he was thus communicating with me, but as a friend, as a pal, as we used to be before the war, as we were when we were boys—when his will was law with me. But try as I might I could not get what he wanted of me. Then suddenly came the realization that I myself was half demented and that this was only a hallucination. There came vaguely the certainty that beside me lay Ross' body—dead, as I was sure from the clammy coldness of the face I had touched. That presence—surely none other than Ross' own self still hovered over me, commanding, dominating, compelling something from me.

There came again the terrible physical pain and anguish and a deadly nausea, and then, no longer able to endure it, I fell into unconsciousness. How long I lay there I do not know—whether it was for a few hours or for many. However, there came a time when I regained consciousness. This time it was brought about by hands upon me, not such gentle hands but oh, very swift and efficient ones, lifting me up, raising my dangling right arm to a place across my chest, laying my legs in such a position that the pain was not so excruciating. And as they lifted me I opened my eyes and saw other hands lifting Ross. Then I had been right—that was Ross there beside me in that hell-hole with the rain pelting upon us both—he dead, as I had thought. There was no mistaking it now—half dead as I myself was.

But here begins one of the strangest experiences a man ever had. When I saw those hands lifting Ross' stark form up out of the mud, I had the most—what shall I say?—well, *possessive* feeling for that dead body. That is as near as I can come to it—*possessive*. Not in the sense that it was the body of my commanding officer, of my best friend. I said to myself, "*It is mine!* They are taking my own *body* away before my eyes." That was exactly my feeling. I had scarcely a moment to analyze this feeling, for, what with the emotion and with the neglected condition of *my* own lacerated body, oblivion again mercifully blotted out everything for me and when I again regained consciousness I lay in a hospital with dozens of other wounded men.

• • •

Slowly I tried to piece together the fragments of that terrible experience, but somehow it was such a jumble that I could make nothing of it. I recalled the aching misery of the long wait in the trenches, the savage fury with which I heard the command to go over the top, but right there things began to get confused. I seemed to be the commanding officer giving orders to the line of impatient men—the commanding officer, yes, but even more definitely than that I seemed to be Ross Lyons—thinking his thoughts, speaking his words, feeling his reactions.

I wish I could make it plain just how it was. I was myself—here was my body, my mangled right arm, my maimed leg. Here was I, unmistakably—but thinking Ross Lyons' thoughts. I closed my eyes and tried to quit thinking. This peculiar thing was due to my fever-disordered brain. "Who," thought I, "would not be jumbled up some after what I've gone through!" I did not know what had happened to me, nor to Ross.

So the days passed. Sometimes I was conscious for hours at a time, then lapsing into unconsciousness for other hours—but always in my lucid periods aware of the utmost confusion of ideas, the thoughts and memories of Ross Lyons imposing themselves upon my own, actually covering them up—blotting them out.

I never went back to the front, but after more than a year in the hospital and in convalescent camps—a year of the most astonishingly confused cerebration, I sailed for home. By that time I had ceased, to a certain extent, to struggle against my strange mental twist, being convinced as the doctors had told me, that the shock of that terrible day and the subsequent suffering had shattered my nerves, as well as wrecked my body, and as slowly but surely my body was recovering I was assured that these distressing mental delusions would pass away.

But they did not. Home at last for months, for almost a year, with my body again almost as good as ever—and they still persisted. They not only persisted but they became more and more intense. Indeed, I found myself completely changed; I found myself involuntarily falling into Ross' place in our home town. I found, without conscious effort, that I was actually commanding people of whom before I had felt a great awe. And added to this I realized that I was neglecting my work at my desk in my father's office, grossly neglecting it, and this because of an overwhelming desire to be a physician.

I talked this over with my father. He, I knew, considered me mentally unbalanced. Pity sat upon his countenance—a great and perfectly heart-breaking pity—as he gave his consent to my leaving his business and going into medical school. As well, as if he had uttered them I understood the thoughts that were passing through his mind.

"Useless," he was thinking, "but he made the supreme sacrifice—even greater than death itself."

So I went to medical school, to the one from which Ross had graduated. I worked in his class rooms, with the equipment which he had used, tried the experiments he had tried and with his teachers.

But before I go on with that, I must stop for a moment to recount two significant details of my life upon my return from the war. First there was the incident of my meeting with Ross' mother. Of course I went to see her as soon as possible and, I can never explain the feeling which swept over me as I saw her drawn, white face. Without realizing what I was doing I had her in my arms, covering her face with kisses, weeping and uttering every endearment my tongue could command. And she was responding. There was no need for explanations—nothing. A great and sweet content settled down upon her harrowed soul and a year later she died in the rich and full assurance that her boy had come back to her. "Crazy," people said. "Lost her mind from grief. Just another war casualty."

The other incident was my relation with Annie Griffin, my fiancée. Before I returned home I began to notice a difference in her letters—a certain coldness. Something indefinite at first, but disturbing—very. Later, however, I found that I did not mind this; it did not trouble me in the least. By the time I actually reached home Annie was ready to break our engagement and, since truth must be told, so was I. We scarcely saw each other after my return.

Now to go back to medical school. Here I found easy sailing. Nothing seemed new to me; everything somehow was extraordinarily familiar. Even old Doctor Monteith, with whom Ross had been a favorite, and to whom I had heard him refer many a time, did not seem unknown to me. Immediately upon my arrival he evinced the most lively interest in me and I liked him at once. Time and time again I found his eyes upon me, regarding me with a puzzled and curious look.

"And Ross Lyons was your friend?" he said to me once.

"Yes, my dearest friend," I answered.

"And he died in France," he went on in a sort of musing way. Then rather sharply he turned again to me. "Did you see him die?" he asked.

"Well, no," I said; "not exactly, for I was little better than dead myself. But he died beside me."

Here he questioned me minutely about that time, about my boyhood with Ross, about our youth, about his influence over me, about our relative positions in the army—everything—bringing out of me information about the two of us which I never knew I possessed. Then one night, sometime later, in answer to a line of most pointed questions I told him of that strange, dominating presence which had hovered over me there on that wet battlefield that night, that presence which seemed to be demanding something of me which I could not grant because I could not understand it.

The old doctor listened gravely to this. Then, "But you did grant it," he said.

"What?" I cried. "I granted what? What do you mean?"

"Have you yet no inkling?" he asked, and upon my astonished negative he went on.

"That presence was Ross Lyons, as you knew then, subconsciously, if not otherwise. He was demanding that you relinquish your ego, your personality, the *you* of you, your soul, whatever you have a mind to call it," he said, "and that you give his own soul living space in your 'house of clay.' He was not ready to pass into oblivion and he knew his power over you." Here he stopped, looked at me keenly with a wry smile upon his face. Then suddenly springing from his chair and squarely confronting me he cried sharply:

"Ross!"

With that cry the doubt and uncertainty, the confusion and mental distress which had so harassed me up to this time, vanished like a fog, leaving a clear and radiant understanding of my position. This wise old man knew, and by his knowledge led me to know the truth. Out with Ross' dead body went my ego—my soul—commanded out of me by that dominating presence there on that battlefield that night we both lay more dead than alive and into my 'house of clay' as old Doctor Monteith called it, came Ross' stronger ego, his greater soul, to dwell. All this time I had been fighting it, unable to understand the strange delusions, the mental twists, what you will—that had actuated my body, my brain.

Now I began to understand the attitude of Ross' mother and my own feeling for her, of my sweetheart, Annie Griffin, of my father. The words of this wise old doctor, Ross' friend, had revealed this thing to me. Now that his hand had pulled back the veil which had been intervening between my senses and the truth, I accepted it and acted upon it.

But, since Ross' personality now dwelt within me—where was mine? Gone—gone somewhere. "Returned to God who gave it," I have heard somewhere. Since, I say, his soul now had possession of my frame, I determined to allow his ego, without let or hindrance, to control my body.

In accord with this decision and after numerous intimate and revealing discussions of the subject with Doctor Monteith, I finished my medical course, following as exactly as possible the line Ross had followed. Then coming to this distant city, thousands of miles from the place that had known us as boys, I have established my practice under the name of Ross Lyons. I have his character, his dominant spirit, his commanding presence and I am succeeding as Ross Lyons in a way Owen Bennett could never have done.

Yet I am living in Owen Bennett's body, and the question often recurs to me, "Who am I?"—and it probably will always dog my thoughts. I think it is a question of my subconscious self, to remain a mystery.

The Ghost Light
By C.B. Bigelow

**The three mad scientists should never have brought their dreams
to the house on the hill. A greater sorcerer than they had made it a
place of awful menace.**

MY GUIDE, VALMONT, AND I, HAVING RESTED OURSELVES SUFFICIENTLY, continued our journey
through the ancient New England graveyard. A long tramp through the woods had tired us
greatly, and so we were taking a short cut home. As we neared a crumbled gravestone my
guide stopped, and, pointing to it, said:

"That, sir, is the grave of an Italian doctor. If you will look straight up between those
trees on top of that mountain, you may see his house. If it were dark, you would notice a
light in the window. Believe me, the doctor has now been dead nearly two hundred and fifty
years, but every night, as far as I can remember—and
the history of our people says that every night
since the doctor died—there has been a
light there. No one since his death
has dared go near the house, for in
the year 1680 he was burned
for a sorcerer. It was said
that from chemicals he
could manufacture
living things."

I listened

*The armless hand had seized Van Kesner's
razor and was lifting it towards his throat.*

attentively to the old man's story. When, at his last remark, I smiled and said that it was nothing but one of the impossible notions of the witch-fearing times, and that the light was caused by some reflection of the moon and stars, he became quite angry. He thought a minute, then turned on his heel and started to walk toward the town.

I followed after and hastened to make peace with him, for I was fond of the old man and was sorry to have hurt his feelings. By the time we had arrived home he had apparently quite forgotten our quarrel, but during the process of frying eggs and bacon he turned abruptly to where I was sitting: "The moon and stars do not shine every night," he said, "but that cursed light is always there."

Some weeks later at the general store, a man who by his dress and manner I knew could not be a native addressed me: "You are MacNarland, I believe."

"Yes."

"You are not in the least superstitious, of course?"

"Why, no."

"Thank you." He turned and started toward the door, then apparently on second thought: "My name is Jamison, Doctor Jamison. I am very glad to have had the pleasure of meeting you. Good day."

The man was uncanny, not only in his strange conversation but in his general appearance. His face, what could be seen of it (the greater part being covered by a long reddish-gray beard), was horribly scarred and wrinkled. The fingers of his left hand, if they had not too much resembled claws, would have been almost artistic. The fingers of his right hand, however, were chopped off at the first joint, with the exception of the thumb. When he had left, I turned to the store-keeper and asked him if he happened to know the man.

"Ah, my friend, I'm not exactly sure," he answered, "but I think he is one of those scientists. There are two other gentlemen with him. They are going to live in the old haunted house on the hill. I wouldn't live there for the world."

When I told old Valmont that his haunted house was about to be inhabited he ceased his tobacco chewing for a moment. "That's very interesting," he muttered.

"But I thought you said it was full of ghosts."

"Sure. It is."

That year I did not leave when the summer was over. I was so fascinated by the place that I determined to stay as long as I could.

Unlike most New England villages, Charlesville was not periodically turned into a summer resort. The three scientists and myself were the only transients. Its location made it inaccessible and added to its charm. Set down in the center of four ranges of mountains, it was completely isolated, the nearest village being twenty miles away. The great distance had, before the invention of the automobile, made it necessary for the inhabitants to raise or manufacture practically all the necessities of life.

Even now Charlesville was untouched by the flurry of the modern world. Its houses were on an ancient model. Not one of them was less than a century and a half old.

To the amazement of the community, the three scientists seemed to remain undisturbed in the haunted house. They were sullen, however, and had little to say to the villagers. They came down to Charlesville only when they needed to lay in a stock of provisions.

As the autumn passed they were seen less and less frequently, and finally it was said in the village that no one had seen them for weeks. People began to feel alarmed, but no one would take the risk of visiting the house.

At the end of another week I determined to call upon my strange neighbors. I urged old Valmont to go with me, but nothing could tempt him to venture within half a mile of the place.

When I started my walk up the mountain, a cold breeze was blowing. It was well on toward the middle of November, and in New Hampshire winter comes quickly; we had already had snow. The gray, unpleasant afternoon was wearing to a close.

Having reached the summit, I stopped to examine the decaying structure before me. It was large, and had it not been of wood, it might have been taken for a medieval castle. I walked over to the entrance and knocked. There was no answer. After knocking and calling for nearly half an hour and getting no response, I decided that the best course was to turn and go home. The tenants had probably left without word, I thought.

I had, in fact, turned to go when an overwhelming desire to see just what was inside of this legendary haunted house took possession of me. I pushed heavily upon the door; it opened. Within, the odor of decaying wood was very apparent. I found myself in a large room, in the center of which was a staircase. Finding no sign of life on the first floor, I began the ascent of the stairs. There seemed to be few windows upstairs—the hall was in semi-darkness.

I had searched what I thought to be the entire second floor without success, when, on opening a small door on the left of the stairway, I stumbled over an object lying across the threshold. The room was very dark, making it necessary for me to light a match. I glanced down and saw to my horror that I had tripped over the body of Jamison, the weird little scientist. There was no mark on him, but his face was distorted in an expression of unspeakable horror. Close by him was a lantern. Finding it in perfect condition, I lit it.

The room was in great confusion; everything was turned upside down. There were papers scattered about. Leaf by leaf I picked up the following note. It seemed to have been written by Jamison:

"To occupy my troubled mind and to use these strange facts in further research work, if I ever return to civilization, I have decided to keep a diary.

"*November 5*—The sun is just setting behind the trees. As I watch it, terror fills my heart at the thought of what may happen after darkness has taken possession of the world.

"There were three of us, students of the horrible, multiform and intricate workings of the disordered mind; we came far away from civilization that we might pursue our studies undisturbed. We have been making our abode in an old mansion apparently forgotten years ago, as there are only parts of it habitable. The greater part of the huge, grotesque wooden structure has fallen or rotted into ruins. The three of us were Van Kesner, a scientist of note; Ivan Stowskey—I always thought him mad, and now more than ever—and myself.

"Now there are only two. Van Kesner was murdered, perhaps by—but let me give a full account of his death.

"I was standing at a short distance from Van Kesner, and for some reason fear and agony were depicted on his face. He was staring at something with horror. Was it at me? Then he seemed to shift his gaze to the table, where there were lying a razor and shaving mug. I saw a hand reach upward—just a hand—no arm, no body. The man sat motionless, apparently unable to move. The armless hand had seized Van Kesner's razor and was lifting it towards his throat. A second later, it had inflicted a deep slash. Van Kesner rolled to the floor without uttering a sound. Then the hand put the razor back on the table and pointed to a bench not far from where Van Kesner lay, and with a great effort my wounded friend half dragged, half pushed himself upon it.

"Then it was that I seemed to come out of a mist, and there before me on the bench lay Van Kesner, his throat cut. Why was it that I had not helped him? Was it that, in my horror at seeing the hand, the full realization of what was happening did not occur to me? Or was it, as the half mad Stowskey said, 'my own hand.'

"But no, it was not my hand. I see it again. It is coming toward me.

"At the second appearance of the hand I must have fainted. I am unable to sleep, so I will continue my narrative. I awoke with a bottle of brandy held to my lips; I looked up and saw Stowskey. He put down the bottle and walked over to an armchair, where he sat watching me. For some unknown reason, the sight of the man filled me with horror. I had noticed a peculiar change in him in the past week; when he spoke, his voice came as from far away and for a whole week he had not, to my knowledge, touched a drop to eat or drink. Suddenly he arose and came over to me.

"By this time I had got to my feet. He put his hand on my shoulder. I involuntarily shrank from him, for even through the heavy coat I swore his touch seemed cold and clammy, not like a hand, but like some leaden mist.

"Then he spoke in the same far-away voice, a voice that seemed not to come from him, but from the air above his head. 'Jamison,' he said, pointing to a small door on the other side of the room, 'as you value your life do not enter that room. I think Van Kesner tried to enter there when he died.'

"*November 6*—There is a terrible blizzard raging, a blizzard more severe than I have ever seen; an owl is hooting dismally. Occasionally a tree falls, with a terrifying crash, and the wind whistles through the eaves of this old structure, like the moans and screams of the damned.

"*November 7*—In three days from now I must go for more provisions. I am afraid to leave or stay, even to think. Today the storm has greatly subsided; our fire is getting low. Stowskey has just suggested that we go out for more wood.

"*Later*—To my horror, on our way to the pile of firewood I happened to look down at the snow, and saw that although Stowskey's legs disappeared in the snow up to his knees, I was the only one who left footprints.

"My curiosity as to what lies behind the door grows and grows.

"*November 8*—I just tried to run my fingers through my hair—it has completely fallen out. Last night when I thought Stowskey to be asleep in his chair, where he always sleeps, I arose and crept stealthily to the door. I put my hand against it and pushed softly. Suddenly I was violently hurled across the room by some unseen force. I jumped back on the bed and lay there sleeplessly until dawn. Stowskey had not moved through the whole proceeding. In the morning I told him my story. 'You are mad,' he said. However, this afternoon I shall again look.

"*Later*—I have now lost all confidence in my sanity. I opened the door, and found the body of Stowskey, rotted horribly. The features, however, were still intact. Stowskey had been dead three weeks, but that was not all. Standing above the figure of Stowskey was his exact likeness, and suddenly the likeness dispersed into a mist, and from the mist condensed again into the Hand.

"*Still Later*—The horror of what I saw will surely drive me mad, if I am not already mad. The Hand—the Hand again; but no, it clears away, there is no hand. My mind clears. Great Heavens, it all comes to me! It was my hand that murdered first Stowskey and then Van Kesner. No, no, it was not I—something no worse really, but more horrible. It is coming, writhing, crawling toward me. It is—"

At this point the writing became completely illegible. Although it ran on for several more pages, I could not, as hard as I tried, decipher a word.

At first I thought the man had been insane—as I now believe he was partly, although he may have been reduced to that state in a few hours' time. Surely there had been no blizzard such as he had mentioned. We had had a few inches of snow, that was all.

I leaned over to examine the body of Jamison more closely. He could not have been dead more than three days at most. Then I found, in a chink of the wall, what at first I thought to be another leaf of the note Jamison had written. However, when I touched it to remove it from its hiding place, I found it to be a sheet of very ancient bleached leather. I am at a loss for an explanation of why Jamison or the others failed to observe it, for it was in plain view. However, this is the decipherable part of the inscription on the parchment:

"*—Knowledge of Chemicals—such per cent of each make up the human body—succeeded—life—will live forever unless destroyed—under my control—kept in cage—if he ever escapes—ruin—at the end—will myself—*"

I had by this time righted the table. Wanting to save the lantern as much as possible in case of emergency, I extinguished it and lit a table lamp, the chimney of which had been broken. The flame flickered slightly, and gave weird, fantastical shapes to the different objects in the room.

Terror now seized me. I was about to flee when a great gust of wind came from the hallway, extinguishing my lamp. From the door there came a sound of labored breathing, followed by a barely perceptible creaking. I turned and saw a figure that was neither ape nor man. In the dim light, it resembled an octopus, with a grotesquely misshapen head stuck on top and disproportionately thin arms and legs. I thought of the lantern at my feet. Gropingly my hand closed upon it, and while I lit it I kept my eyes riveted on the approaching Thing.

I thought: "This then is what Valmont meant by saying that the sorcerer of the old days could manufacture living creatures by means of chemicals."

The Thing was, yet it was not. It was indescribably animate and inanimate at one and the same time. I noticed that on the Thing's head there was a lusterless mass resembling hair.

It came creeping slowly toward me, and then with amazing quickness it closed in. We grappled. The lamp was overturned, the house caught fire. I jerked away from the monster, and fled toward the door. My enemy followed and overtook me. I tried to find its throat, and strangle it. There was no throat. Then, as a last resort, I caught in both hands the hair of its head, and by some miracle, managed to hurl the body into the flames. As soon as it struck the fire there was a sizzling, as of burning chemicals.

From that time on, I remembered nothing, until I found myself by a little brook at the foot of the mountain.

Nothing remained of the house but a thin wisp of smoke ascending slowly toward a darkly clouded sky. Then I noticed, clutched tightly in my left hand, a lock of the horrible, the lusterless, hair.

Sardonic Laughter
By Will Winship Arnold
As told to Harvey S. Cottrell

Will Arnold and his wife ventured into the haunted cellars of the madman's house—and before they left the place, they wished that they had never been born.

For Sale—The material used in building the mansion near Hamilton, Connecticut, of the late Richard Guthrie. Buyer must agree to raze the mansion and remove the building stones and other material from the premises. For further information address Hamilton Realty Company, Hamilton, Connecticut.

When that advertisement caught my eye, I proposed to Vivian, my wife, that we visit the place. I made the suggestion partly because of the enjoyment we got out of hiking in the country, and partly because I wanted to see the great dam and water project under construction near Hamilton. Viv was delighted with the idea. Consequently we boarded a train on the first afternoon I could get away from business, and eventually we alighted at Hamilton station with a four-mile jaunt ahead of us.

It was a glorious autumn day. Amber sunshine filtered through the leaves, beautiful in their fall colors, and the air had the tonic of sparkling wine. The blood raced in our veins. We were in love and ready for adventure together.

But hardly for such an adventure as lay before us.

We came suddenly upon Guthrie's castle—the Madman's Folly, as the natives called it—at the end of a woods road. There it stood above us, set partly into the hollow between two shoulders of the hills and nearly hidden by trees. As we approached, its close-shuttered windows gazed down at us like blank eyes in a skull. It was of English Gothic design and its prison-like walls were of somber gray, hewn from the granite of the hillside on which it squatted.

I had heard the legend of the place. Old Guthrie had built it in that isolated spot, intending to bring a young wife there to live. But he had reckoned without the spirit of youth. The girl took one look at it and then returned to her parents. The marriage never was performed.

Following that, Guthrie secluded himself in that drab old pile and lived the life of a hermit.

The natives met him roaming about the hills, eternally searching, they said. Often he returned with great armfuls of herbs.

"Crazy ez a loon," they decided, and went on with their labors.

Then gradually it dawned upon them that Guthrie had disappeared, that they hadn't seen him for days. They made a desultory search and concluded he had fallen into some crevice in the rocks. His body never was found. Nor did any relatives ever make inquiry. The old house stood as he had left it, the front door swinging eerily in the wind, the interior stained by storms and decaying under the hand of time.

"What a spooky-looking place," Viv exclaimed. Her eyes were alight with anticipation. "Let's explore it. Huh! Maybe we'll find Guthrie's ghost."

*She clung to me as we peered into
the haunted darkness.*

As we climbed the steps and entered the house, the dull roar of dynamite, where workmen were blasting away a saddle of rock nearby, echoed in the dim cavern of the front hall and the jar of the explosion raised the dust about us. For an instant I thought I saw a shadowy figure that whisked away around a corner of the corridor. I shook myself. It was only a cloud of dust driven by the wind, I told myself.

But even then I would have turned back—so formidable, so fraught with menace was the atmosphere of the place—had not Viv, the adventuress, been intent on exploration.

Once inside, the evidence of luxurious furnishing was everywhere, though time and the elements had set their mark of decay upon it all. Rich hangings were discolored with mildew and in tatters. Wood rodents had made their nests in silken covers. Despite the dust and decay, however, everything was in dignified and formal array, and an air of expectancy hovered over the place as though it was about to be peopled with figures or Things that lurked somewhere in the dim shadows, waiting for us to go that they might gather in ghostly conclave.

Even in the room intended for the bride, such intimate articles as a hand-mirror, a comb, and a brush, discolored and rotting, were laid out meticulously on the dresser.

A vague feeling that we were being watched by unseen eyes crept upon me. I found myself turning about, anticipating that the chairs were occupied and that I would find someone or something in each.

I shuddered.

"Come on, Viv," I urged. "Come out of this tomb—into the sunshine and fresh air."

"But the cellars," she cried; "we haven't seen the cellars yet."

I was about to remonstrate. The damp mustiness of the place, the horrible weirdness of the gloom, the moaning of the wind in the throat of the fireplace, oppressed me, set the shivers coursing up and down my spine. Again I imagined that flicker of a presence just disappearing in the hall.

Viv dashed away. I had to follow. We found the cellar stairs in the rear of the house.

Dust upon them was broken only by the tracks of small animals. Cobwebs from which dangled vicious spiders, hung in ghostly festoons. The walls were damp and slimy and, as we felt our way along, the stairs disappeared into a cavernous darkness.

"Let's get out of here, Viv," I pleaded. "If we don't break our necks, we'll be lucky."

"Oh, this is fun," Viv said lightly. "Don't be a killjoy, dear."

We went on. As we penetrated deeper into the gloom, I lighted matches. The flickering points of flame hardly made an impression in the thick blackness except to set up dancing shadows that sprang at us and receded again. The musty odor became more and more stifling until a headache set upon me. Under our feet somewhere we could hear water splashing in a pool whose wavelets broke against the stone foundations.

"Look!" Viv exclaimed suddenly. "There's a cat with one eye."

She clung to me as we peered into the haunted darkness. In the puny flare of another match I saw the eye, glaring balefully at us. It was close to the floor.

"Come, puss, puss," Vivian called; "come, kitty, kitty."

She stepped swiftly towards it.

"It isn't a cat at all," she said. "It's a tiny stone like a gem set in the wall. Oh, look; it presses."

Hardly had she spoken when there was a creaking groan, a grating sound, and before I could spring to her side, Viv, with a cry, disappeared.

I leaped to the spot in a frenzy, dire thoughts of disaster crashing through my mind.

The door stood partly open, and I found her just beyond it. She was huddled in a mass on some sort of stone platform. I stooped to pick her up, and was relieved as she leaped to her feet.

"Just a bruised knee," she said, with a laugh. "But wasn't that scary? And look, here's another flight of stairs. This is great—a moving door in the wall operated by a cat's eye. I wonder what's down below."

"For God's sake, let's get out of this place," I stormed. "Don't be silly. Let's go while we can."

"Now, don't be an old grouch, dear," was all she said as she prepared to descend the second stairway.

The sound of the splashing water came to us more clearly now. In that dank dungeon its sound raised a melancholy plaint. Again I shuddered. I thought of ghouls that rob the dead. I thought of bony fingers reaching out of the shadows at me. I could not throw off my depression.

Viv had gone ahead. Soon we both stood at the foot of the staircase and found ourselves in a vast chamber. The light came from behind a mass of rock at the far side of the room. I could not determine its source. The chamber was so large it must have underlain most of the hill on the side of which the castle had been built, and it was evident the place was some sort of natural cavern that Guthrie had discovered. Wavelets in a pool made by the brook, which the madman had diverted from its course, lapped at one side. How large the pool was, I do not know; but it extended far into the shadows beyond our vision.

Suddenly there came a rasping sound above us, followed by a dull boom. My heart skipped a beat. I had the sickening realization that the door in the wall had closed, locking us in.

Up the stairway I sprang and with searching fingers tried to find the mechanism that operated it. It was of no avail. Except for a tiny crack in which I broke my knife blade, the wall was a complete blank. We were prisoners in that underground chamber—buried alive, perhaps. I wondered if our bodies, distorted by a horrible death, would ever be recovered or if, instead, our dust would mingle with the other dust, through eternity, to the end of time.

As if in answer to my thoughts, there came a sound that turned my blood to ice. Reverberating in that chamber—flung from wall to wall like a shuttlecock and tossed back from the darkness beyond the pool—came a horrible, menacing, mocking laugh.

Viv threw her arms about me, clinging to me. Her breath came in a sob. Such fiendish laughter, cruel, unearthly, evil! It came from nowhere in particular. It was everywhere. The damnable echoes chortled here and there and all around us. I backed to the wall, staring about me, sheltering Vivian in my arms.

The echoes grew fainter, more distant, subsiding at last out beyond the pool. My mind worked quickly. There must be a way out of this hellish place if I only could find it. How did the brook run in? There might be an exit that way.

Half carrying, half dragging Vivian, I started towards the pool. Suddenly the dim light behind the pillar of rock grew brighter. It had no radiance. Rather, it was a greenish-yellow glow, like an emanation from some long-dead thing that had become phosphorized in a charnel-house.

And in that gruesome light there appeared, rising from behind the rock, a figure that I pray God I may never see again.

It was the figure of an aged man. His body was frail and wasted. His hair was long and hung about his shoulders like the stalks of old plants, blowing sear in a winter's blast. His eyes were alight with a strange, fanatical fire. They were unseeing, else he would have beheld us there. He advanced to the center of the chamber and raised his arms above his head.

With that I pressed Vivian's face into the lapels of my coat, for, as the man stood there with uplifted arms, his features contracted into the most unholy, godless grin that fiend of hell ever designed, and from his lips there issued again that mirthless, ghoulish laughter—mocking, sardonic. It echoed in that cavern like whited bones clashing upon each other. It was vile.

Vivian clung to me despairingly, and hid her face deeper in my breast. I dared not move, waiting for what the figure would do next. Had we really discovered the ghost of Guthrie, I wondered, or was this another madman, doomed by some strange fate forever to inhabit the bowels of the earth? Was Guthrie really lost in the hills, or did he die in this cavern in some ungodly way? Was this his soul, unshriven in death, standing before us in that attitude of adulation?

These questions went unanswered. In an instant the figure had dropped soundlessly to its knees. Then the man—if man he was—did a most strange thing. Thrice he raised his hands above his head and brought them flat down upon the stone floor. Each time his face contorted into that horrible grin, and each time there sprang from his lips that crazy, hideous laughter.

Upon salaaming the third time, he paused expectantly. I followed his gaze. A vague mist was forming in the shadows at the edge of the pool. Soon it resolved itself into a misshapen sphere. At first it was a shadowy, intangible thing, with a nebulous glow about it, but it grew denser and brighter.

It was about as high as a man, but it had neither form nor face. It moved as fog might be blown across a marsh. Gradually it filled the cavern with a more ghastly light than the pale radiance we first had observed.

An overwhelming fear seized me. I shook as with an ague. Vivian, her head buried in my breast, sobbed piteously.

The Thing moved half across the cavern and for a moment lingered before the prostrate old man. With fascinated gaze I watched it. Usually I am as brave as the average person. But at that moment I could not control myself. I was sick with fright. Physical waves of fear swept down my back and into my shaking legs. My scalp seemed lifted from my head.

The Thing now moved to a table of rock near the opposite wall, and stopped. There followed a ghostly ritual between those two there, as strange and horrid and fantastical as ever mortal eye looked upon.

Guthrie, for I felt sure the first figure was the ghost of that unfortunate man, remained prostrate until the nebulous cloud had come to rest upon a sort of rude throne behind the table of stone. In the silence that ensued, there now arose a shrill moaning, an eerie shrieking, as though souls forever damned were voicing a chant of the dead. For an eternity this continued.

I wanted to curse aloud. I wanted to shout at those figures there. I wanted to fight them with my hands.

But my tongue refused to utter a sound. My voice had gone. I was unable to move!

At last the moaning subsided and for a brief space there was silence again. Then I became aware of a measured, rhythmical tapping. Tap—tap—tap. Its beat began to tear at my taut nerves. Tap—tap—tap. Still and small at first, its rhythm finally filled the chamber and beat upon my temples until I felt they would burst. I was becoming desperate. That mocking laughter! Those menacing figures!

Frantic to be out of that foul hole, away from those terrifying Things in the ghastly light of that underground vault, I would have hurled myself insanely against the unyielding door of that cavern. But Vivian, unconscious at last, had slipped from my nerveless grasp to the floor.

Her body quivered slightly. Her fingers were clenched. I stooped down to lift her up again, and then I saw.

A strange, ecstatic look was on her face. Her eyes, wide open now, were sightless and staring. Slowly she unclenched her fingers and, like a worshipper before a shrine, she stretched her hands towards that figure upon the dais, offering herself!

Across her face there came an expression that was revolting, obscene.

I could not believe my senses. This lovely girl, this girl so sweet and pure—a Jezebel at my feet.

Some spell was upon her. In my rage I straightened and, glaring at those figures, I tried to shout:

"You hounds of hell, release her from your power."

My voice made no sound in that horrible cavern. It was as though I had never spoken.

Then the thick silence was broken by a voice—a deep, booming voice that filled the vault, sonorous and slow. I felt, rather than knew, that the voice came from that horrible figure on the throne.

"O man of Earth who has died a thousand deaths," said the Voice, "whom dost thou worship?"

The ghost of Guthrie raised itself from the floor, with arms falling to its sides. A lesser luminosity sprang from its figure.

"Thou, great god Sardis," said the ghost, "and I bring to thine altar the sacred herb."

The ghost moved silently across the floor of the chamber towards the table of stone.

"Since it is of the earth earthy," said the Voice, "and therefore unpresentable, what must be accomplished to make it fit?"

"A sacrifice, O great god Sardis," answered the ghost. "A sacrifice upon the altar."

"Hast thou then a sacrifice?"

"Yea, I have. I bring thee a creature of the earth that mortals call a dog. But Ammon-Ra declared it sacred. This I have brought thee."

Suddenly that awful laughter, this time more horrible, more terrifying, filled the vault so that the very stones of the earth seemed to quiver with its vile mockery.

"Unfaithful servant," said the Voice, thundering menacingly, "lo, beside thee stand two mortals doomed to dust even as thou wert. A dog? Behold, thou deservedst naught of the sacred herb."

"No, no, great god Sardis, not that," wailed the voice of Guthrie, growing higher and thinner in its intensity. "Not that, great god Sardis. Let me, I pray thee, partake."

"Then the sacrifice," said the Voice.

Humbly the ghost bowed itself to the floor. Three times that mocking laughter issued from its foul lips. Then arising, it turned away from the altar, and with arms straight out before it, it proceeded in measured strides towards us. Halfway it stopped. I looked about for some weapon. There was none. Vivian's hands still were outstretched.

The apparition advanced, and a convulsive shudder passed through Vivian's body. Sickness came over me as I saw that the girl was eager to go to him.

Now the ghost was near to me. Now I set my feet, preparing to strike with all my strength at that vile thing. I drew back my right arm. The apparition stopped.

Once more that mocking laugh echoed through the vaulted chamber. The face before me was contorted into that awful, horrible grin, like a death's-head limned with a phosphorescent glow. And instantly I found myself paralyzed on my feet. I could not move. I hardly seemed to breathe. I was like an image of stone—yet an image that could think and could know the pain of mortal thoughts when danger encompasses a loved one, and you are unable to help.

Nearer and nearer came the ghost. A cold breath blew upon me as I stood stricken. A foul odor assailed my nostrils as though a tomb had been opened and the cloistered breath of close-confined ages had been let free.

Wizened and old though the ghost appeared, hardly with an effort it lifted the unresisting form of Vivian and with measured tread carried her across the chamber. It stopped before the Thing upon the dais.

"Thy will?" asked the ghost.

"That this mortal be placed upon the altar," came the booming Voice. "There her blood shall mingle with the leaves of the sacred herb and make it fit for our use."

Altar! Then was Vivian truly to become a sacrifice in some loathsome supernatural rite? Was she to meet an untimely end—this girl I loved—while I stood helpless to prevent this awful tragedy before my very eyes? You scarce can imagine the thoughts that swept my mind, the mental agony that held me, the absolute torture of the situation. Strive as I might, I could not compel my body to function. My mind was fully alert, but my arms and legs refused to do its bidding.

Upon that table of rock the ghost of Guthrie placed Vivian. Her eyes were closed; her face had become as wax. To all intents she already was dead, forestalling whatever vicious ceremony was about to be performed.

From behind a rock Guthrie's ghost produced a great armful of dried leaves. He strewed them carefully along Vivian's body, covering her to the waist. His ghostly hands were offensive, hideous, as they loosed the clothing about her throat. He was like an unearthly vulture about to feed upon a human corpse.

Again I strained at those insuperable bonds that held me. My throat became constricted; the blood pounded in my ears, answering that strange tapping that began again like the beating of a metallic tom-tom sounding faintly in the chamber. But I could not waken my dormant physical strength. I was in a catalytic state of body, held by an insidious, unseen force that either the ghost or the figure upon the throne had sent to pinion me.

His mysterious preparations completed, the ghost of Guthrie moved back from the altar and raised his arms. Again came that rumbling, inanimate Voice:

"Whom dost thou worship, O man of Earth that was?"

"Thou, great god Sardis," came the answer from the ghost.

"How shall the sacred herb be consecrated?"

"By mingling it with the blood of woman, mortal of earth, whose soul alike is thus consecrated. Then shall it wander until again a mortal sacrifice is consummated."

The lights faded. The dagger moved . . . nearer and nearer to Vivian's breast.

"Thou hast spoken well," came the rumbling Voice with a note of finality.

The misty figure gathered itself into the semblance of a human form. From the crude throne of rock it moved as slowly as a cloud is blown across a darkening sky. Close to the altar upon which Vivian lay insensible and deathlike, it paused.

Again I struggled to free myself from that insidious spell. But the struggle went no farther than my mind, for my muscles would not respond. Bands of steel could not have held me more closely.

Suddenly, a great light sprang from the muffled figure. In its hand appeared a dagger—transparent, alight, glowing with a ghastly radiance. The unearthly weapon was poised above Vivian's body. From the muffled figure came a mocking laugh, more terrifying, more inhuman, more awful, than that which had gone before.

Once more I exerted my will to loose me from my unseen fetters. With all the effort I could concentrate, I struggled against those bonds. And quickly, like a mantle falling from me, I found myself free and dashing across that vault to rescue Vivian or to die with her. I did not care which. I loved her.

The lights faded. The dagger moved. Slowly it descended. Its point drew nearer and nearer to Vivian's breast. Perhaps it was a fraction of a second that it took me to cross that space to the altar. It seemed hours. Panting, wild-eyed, straining, I threw myself against the stone and grasped for that fearsome weapon. I had no thought of what its stinging touch might hold for me. I wanted to clutch it, to turn its point, to tear it away. My hand almost had reached it—

There came a blinding flash. The earth and the heavens seemed to meet. The sky was filled with a million fiery star points. A crash like the end of doom crushed me, stunned me, hurled me backward, down. As swift as an arrow's flight I sank miles deep into enveloping blackness and unconsciousness. The world had fallen and I was snuffed out into nothingness.

I became aware that someone was moving near me. Mentally groping for order in my senses, I at last awakened, opening my eyes. I lay on a mossy bank amid the autumn leaves that covered the ground. I looked about me. Close by was the body of Vivian—dead, I supposed.

I wished I were dead also—though I knew I was not, for beyond the veil of death, I told myself, there were no such tangible things as moss, and a running brook, and autumn leaves. I stirred and found that my body seemed without hurt. I raised myself on one elbow.

Then I discovered a strange person gazing speculatively at me. He wore corduroy trousers and shoes that laced to the knee. A khaki shirt covered his broad body and a battered soft felt hat was perched rakishly above a kindly, smiling face.

He emptied his mouth of a very material squirt of brown juice before he spoke.

"Young feller," he began, "you're damn lucky to be alive. We didn't know you and the girl were in that hole. We didn't even know there was a sub-cellar to the old place. We've been drilling there for an hour—I should have thought you would hear us.

"We put a shot of dynamite into that drill hole that would move the Rock of Gibraltar, and it seems the hole was within two inches of where you were. I told the foreman to let 'er go. He did. Raised hell, I should say."

"You—you don't know how true you're speaking," I said, as I thought of the events that had taken place in the cavern.

"I'll say so," he ejaculated. "You and the girl came floating out when the water basin ripped open, and nearly scared my men to death. You're lucky, I'll tell the world, that you're alive!"

"But Vivian," I exclaimed, "is she—is she dead?"

"Dead, no," said the man. "She's all right. Mebbe need some powder on her nose after a while. But she's all right. Great little girl."

I beheld Vivian gazing at me, somewhat pale, much disheveled, her eyes still holding a trace of fear but newly alight with amusement. I wanted to reach over and spank her for the minx she was. I never will fathom that daredevil spirit that possesses her.

We arose to our feet, and, after an examination, found that except for a few bruises and a few torn places in our clothing we were sound and hale. With the aid of pins and a dab of powder here and there as the man had said, Vivian was presentable quickly enough.

Our new acquaintance, who said he was the superintendent of construction on the new reservoir, eyed us from time to time and shook his head, muttering, "Pretty lucky."

Above us rose the remains of Guthrie's castle. One end had caved in and the rooms of the upper stories had broken open. A feeling of repugnance overwhelmed me as I looked upon that house. I wanted to get away from it all, to take Vivian with me and to forget forever, if I could, the unearthly experience through which we had passed in those few hours.

"Yes," said the man, "the water in the reservoir will back away up here when the dam is completed. That blast we put in, sure wrecked the old house. I bet the realty company that offered it for sale will be peevish. But we didn't know the cave was there. Queer old place—"

Suddenly, high overhead, somewhere in the hills that surrounded us, came horrible, mocking laughter. Vivian clutched frantically at me and the three of us turned in the direction from which we thought it came.

"Like spooks," said the man shortly. "We've heard it many times while we've been working here. Unholy sort of noise. College professor, up here the other day, said he thought it was wind fluttering in a crevice of the rocks. But after I heard it once, I seen the figure of an old man up there, bowing three times to the earth. When I looked again, he was gone.

"I dunno—" He shook his head dubiously.

We just made the 5:52 train for home.

That evening, in the coziness and safety of my library, I pondered upon the strange things that had occurred to us that afternoon. And pondering, I took down an encyclopedia and turned the pages until I came to this:

> *Sardonic laughter*: An old medical term for a spasm of the muscles of the face, causing the appearance of a grin or laughter. It was formerly believed that a certain plant which grew on the island of Sardinia, if eaten, would cause this laughter which would result in death, and that even after death the contorted condition of the facial muscles would remain.

I closed the book and sat for a long time deep in thought.

Jimmy suddenly drew in his breath, his wind-tanned face went white.

Jimmy Kenyon, Yankee ace, risked his life a hundred times in the World War—but the battle of his career was fought with a phantom plane in peaceful America.

As THE SIRENS SHRIEKED THEIR DEVILISH WARNING, Paris looked skyward and saw three black insects hovering well above the white puffs of the "archy" shells. And, as Frenchmen learned to do early in the war, the people of Paris shrugged, all but those who heard the sudden, ripping explosion of a bomb in their vicinity. These scudded to the comparative safety of the cellars to thumb their noses heavenward and mouth crackling French curses at the German airmen.

A Ghost from the Flying Circus
By Guy Fowler

*His chief stared curiously
at him.*

Then, quickly, there was but one small speck up there alone, and, droning towards it at a sharp angle from three sides, a trio of French Spads climbed at amazing speed. The lone German dived and looped like an elusive gadfly while his companions sped back over the lines towards Germany.

"It must be Von Essel," agreed the sage observers below. "None but him would be so foolish. He wants to die."

At the stick of the first Spad to rise above the German, Jimmy Kenyon maneuvered warily in hopes of holding his position. At what he estimated was the right altitude, Jimmy raised the tail of his plane and nose-dived, his machine-gun spitting a tattoo of steel.

"Damn," he muttered, as the German flopped over into "a falling leaf," then straightened, and came swooping up in his speedier plane. They passed within a hundred feet of one another and Jimmy stared from his cockpit, still scarcely believing that the other had escaped unhit. He could see the enemy pilot clearly, and in the brief instant of their passing he recognized Von Essel.

The German waved airily and grinned, his blond hair blowing in the wind. Jimmy waved back and laughed despite his chagrin, then reached for the stick and went into a loop. This time, he thought, it was Von Essel's turn. But even as his plane righted itself, he heard the crackling of machine-guns and his companions from the Escadrille were rushing up. Their trick failed, for Von Essel had gone into a side-slip, and when he caught himself up he shot off into the east and was lost to sight almost immediately.

Back at the hangars on their return, Jimmy and his flying mates regretfully made their report.

"You've got to hand it to him," Jimmy told the youthful major, with a camaraderie that existed only among the men of the flying forces. "He's always the first to attack and the last to run."

"Ever hear the story about him?" asked Rogers.

"Which one? I've heard a dozen."

"Why, he wants to get bumped off in the air, you know. He's got tuberculosis, poor devil. But he's too game to lose a fight intentionally."

"Somebody's going to oblige him one of these days," was Jimmy's rueful comment, and the others laughed.

"It'll have to be a good man, then," said Rogers. "God knows, enough of us have tried it. We figure Von Essel's sent about fifty down so far, and he's still going good."

"How did you get the story about him—that he wants to pass out?"

"A German lieutenant we brought down in our lines told us that. And I believe it. You see, he knows it's got to be a fall—or T.B. in a hospital. I've never seen Von Essel run, unless it was the only sensible thing to do. As long as he's got the ghost of a chance, he'll fight. He seems to thrive on it."

"He does," Jimmy admitted, again rousing a laugh.

"This lieutenant told us," resumed the major, "that Von Essel told his friends in the German circus he'd never die on the ground. And what's more, he said he didn't care a damn if he got it in the air, but he'd take somebody with him."

"Humph, he didn't act so bloodthirsty," said Jimmy. "He waved at me as though we were going to have tea together."

"Um-um, he always does that—always debonair—laughing at you. He laughs when he gets over you, too, with that damned gun of his pumping merry hell into your fuselage."

"Yeah," drawled Jimmy. "I noticed that, too."

When later, in his quarters, Jimmy discussed the day's event with his roommate, big John Bates, of Yale, he talked about his disappointment more freely.

"I'll meet that bird again, John," he promised. "He can gentle a ship better'n any man I ever watched. It's a pleasure just to get over him once. Do you know what I think? The only way to get him is to be just as crazy as he is—"

Bates interrupted him.

"Maybe," he conceded, "but others have tried it that way, too. And so far, old timer, they're down and he's up. How do you figure that out?"

"I don't know. But I do know that Von Essel's got my goat, and I'm going to get it back."

Bates smiled. "Well, here's luck. I hope you do—or somebody does, before he cleans us all out."

But many months were to pass before Jimmy Kenyon realized his ambition to meet the German ace; the French were to be driven back until Paris itself was threatened, and the British on the western front were fighting in stubborn despair; America was to enter the big show and now, instead of flying the colors of France, Jimmy's plane bore the familiar insignia of the U.S.A. and he reported to American officers instead of the veterans of the Escadrille.

His chance came when he least expected it. He had taken off at dawn and for nearly an hour played above the clouds over Apremont, with Saint-Mihiel only three miles in the distance, waiting for the sight of a German below him. Almost before he realized it, Jimmy was pitching down in a side-slip, with the whining of steel slugs cutting among his struts. His maneuver was instinctive. As he flattened out, he pointed skyward and climbed, looking over his shoulder at the plane he had so narrowly escaped.

At the moment, Jimmy was intent only on the essential business of getting altitude and getting there rapidly. But this also was the aim of his enemy and it became a matter of skill and speed. Once over the German, Jimmy turned and opened his gun in bursts. Peering down to watch the effect of his fire, he saw again that familiar blond face, and again Von Essel grinned as he waved.

The plane below passed directly under him and so out of his range, whereupon Jimmy nose-dived, zooming for speed with which to climb when the German would turn on him. As he came up, the slim wasp-like ship darted from a cloud bank and plunged straight at him.

"God, he's going to ram me!" Jim spoke aloud and banked over in a desperate attempt to elude the oncoming plane. Another burst of fire rattled into his plane as the German passed, and Jimmy wondered if his tank had been hit. He could see gaping holes in the wings, and there was the uncanny song of loosened wires straining in the wind.

"It's now or—" Jimmy climbed sharply, and taking a final chance, turned over like a leaf caught in the breeze. As he gathered momentum on the downward plunge, he found the German once more in range. This time Jimmy turned loose a fury of bullets and saw Von Essel fling up a hand as his plane slackened and began to fall in great, awkward loops on its side.

"Got him!" shouted Jimmy, exultantly, following down, watching for the flame to burst from the enemy's fuselage.

But Von Essel straightened after dropping a thousand feet, and, again taking that graceful, sweeping plunge which carried him away at tremendous speed, waved back over the gunwale of his cockpit. Jimmy shot down after him, giving his motor every ounce of power it could take. The German, though, was faster.

Suddenly, when Von Essel's plane was just discernible against the rise of the hills below, Jimmy saw what he had been looking for. From the fuselage of the wasp that carried Von Essel there spurted a tongue of flame and a discharge of thick black smoke. The ship seemed to pause in the air, then slipped down, spinning gradually. It fell beyond the lines, but high overhead a tiny "chaser" hovered—then, turning, sped back towards the Allied territory, descending swiftly as it progressed.

At a limping gait indicating to the watchers below that he had not brought Von Essel down without injury to his own plane, Kenyon headed back for the hangars, idling his engine so as to lessen the strain on the ripped wings. The observer soared above him in a wide circle, then turned his nose down and dived, righted himself at a thousand feet, and swooped to a finished landing right in front of the hangars.

When Jimmy bounded across the field, he found the observer pilot, Terry Lawrence, waiting for him.

"You hit him, Jimmy"—Lawrence ran up beside the ship—"but the son-of-a-gun was diving to keep the fire behind his tank. He made a perfect landing behind that hill, and hopped out. Good work, old man, just the same—"

"The Dutchman's got a rabbit's foot," replied Jimmy, grinning in spite of his disappointment. "But for that matter, so have I. Look!" He pointed to the gaping wounds in the wing surface.

Lawrence nodded gravely. "You were lucky," he agreed.

The bleeding months dragged on, taking their hideous toll from both sides, and each month recorded some new miracle in the troubled air, with Von Essel always the central figure. Jimmy Kenyon met him no more in single combat, try though he did, but a dozen times they were aligned against each other in group formation, and a dozen times Jimmy saw Von Essel's superior gesture of contempt as he swept off into space.

"It seems almost supernatural," he told Rogers one night when the artillery was boring a way for the infantry to advance at dawn. "I know that Von Essel's plane was hit today—we sprayed it, sir. And not one of the bullets got him in a vital spot. I can't account for it."

The major nodded understandingly. "He can't keep it up forever."

But eighteen months passed into tragic history, and the Armistice came. And on that eventful morning at eleven o'clock, Jimmy Kenyon was ripping clouds apart as he roared above the hysterical lines in a final flight as a bird of war. Out from the mist above him a Fokker burst in full descent, dropping like a bird that has been shot and will fly no more.

Instinctively, Jimmy manipulated the stick and fell into a side-slip, then righted himself in time to glimpse once more the saturnine smile of Von Essel just above him. This time the German might have turned his gun upon him and scored, perhaps, but, instead, he suddenly began to climb and disappeared in the golden glow of a sun-swept cloud.

And that was the memory of Von Essel which Jimmy carried back to the United States with him, a memory of mingled emotions, admiration and respect set against natural rivalry, with perhaps even a tinge of hatred. Above all, he felt a great disappointment that he had not been able to finish it out with Von Essel alone—just the two of them up there in the clean sunshine, each with an equal chance.

As naturally as an eagle soars to the crags, Jimmy Kenyon applied for service in the newly-established air mail service, and with his record, of course, he succeeded. That was in the early days of the service when it extended only between New York and Washington.

"It's straight flying," he explained to his friends. "There isn't any action to it, but it's flying. And that's what I want. I simply couldn't quit aviation now."

Through the trying period of experimentation, before night flying was sanctioned—even before the transcontinental lines were established—he made the lonely flights day after day—happiest when aloft, and a very taciturn man when on the ground. Then came the memorable decision to launch coast-to-coast service, and with it, Jimmy's appointment as a cross-country pilot.

"This is going to be the real thing," Jimmy said hopefully to the little group of flying men with whom he spent most of his time off duty. "Here's a route two thousand, six hundred miles to cover. They're allowing us thirty-four hours and twenty minutes for the west-bound schedule; twenty-nine hours and fifteen minutes east. That'll be flying."

"Won't it be pretty dull, Jimmy—for you? Just straight flying, day after day?"

"It would be," he admitted, whimsically, "if it weren't for the ship—"

He flushed and smiled at their laughter.

"You know what I mean," he tried to explain. "You don't think of being lonely when you're flying—you birds all know that."

In the group at the moment was Terry Lawrence, who had observed Jimmy's fight with Von Essel and had watched the German drop behind the lines in a flaming plane.

"When are you going to start night flying, Jimmy?" he asked.

"I don't know," was the reply. "It'll come some time though. There's nothing against it that I can see, except the fears of people who don't understand flying."

"Would you go in for it?"

Kenyon looked at the questioner and nodded. "Why, certainly," he replied. "Why not?"

"Oh, I don't know, except—well, it just seems that some pilots wouldn't exactly relish it."

Jimmy shrugged expressively, indicating that flying was all one to him, night or day, clear weather or fog. And that, as his companions were aware, was exactly his view-point.

That was in 1924, before the farmers accustomed themselves to the sound of a droning motor winging over them each morning and another speeding eastward, with mail from the Pacific. Soon Jimmy became as familiar with his route as the rural free delivery carrier bumping along the roads beneath him in a rusty flivver.

On the eve of his first night trip, Jimmy was seated in the office on the landing-field with a little group of pilots and mechanics.

"Did you ever hear what happened to Von Essel?" inquired Lawrence during a lull in the conversation. "I'd give a night's sleep to know what has become of him."

"No," replied Jimmy, "but I'd like to know about him myself. The last I heard of him, he was in Berlin—sick from T.B. He surely could fly, eh, Terry?"

Lawrence nodded his quick agreement. "There was something uncanny about that fellow," he went on, reminiscently. "I never saw a man so set on dying who failed to do it. The chances he took—" He ended his remark with a soft whistle.

"We'll hear of him some time," Jimmy predicted. "A man of his sort doesn't stay put."

Jimmy glanced at his watch as the sound of a motor tuning up roared from the field beyond.

"Well, my truck'll be along directly. Got to load up. So long, boys."

"So long, Jimmy—keep out of 'archy' range," said Lawrence, laughingly.

Far down the field two mechanics were working on his plane, and Kenyon trudged slowly towards them, listening to the song of his motor with practiced ear.

The mail truck came rumbling on to the field as he reached the plane. Two guards loaded the sacks, and Jimmy signed their receipt. As he climbed into the cockpit, his comrades back in the office emerged to bid him a hearty farewell. He leaned out and waved, and as he did it, a thought of Von Essel flashed into his brain—and a vision of the blond German, when he, too, waved in that familiar gesture.

"Contact!" he called to the mechanic.

"Contact," came the echo, and the man spun the propeller, then leaped back.

Jimmy opened the gas, toyed with it, and rejoiced at the rhythmic roar of the motor, hitting perfectly on every cylinder. Then, with a final toss of his hand, he moved swiftly out across the field and began to rise. Making a wide circle to gain altitude, he set her nose into the west and presently the little group below could no longer see him, even though the sound of his motor still returned to them in a faint, staccato drum-fire.

Over his stern Jimmy saw a sky unclouded, darkening as it rounded to the horizon like the inverted bowl of a deep blue saucer. Ahead, the sky was orange and red, and the dying sun sent gilded rays into a warm haze that shielded the far horizon. Of rain and its discomforts he had no thought, nor did he concern himself seriously about wind. But there were two obstacles set by nature which Jimmy, like any other pilot, disliked whole-heartedly. These were fog and sleet.

However, as he scanned the universe and studied his instruments, he found no indications of these arch-enemies, and with a sigh of contentment he stretched his legs and made himself comfortable for the flight.

"I'll have to watch her over the mountains, though," he considered. But that was a later consideration and for the time he forgot everything but the joy of the flight.

Between New York and Cleveland there was but a single stretch that air-men sometimes feared, and that was over the Allegheny Mountains beyond Bellefonte. Cleveland lay but a hop away, once they passed through the bumpy lanes where cross-currents and pockets were plentiful. By night the passage was more difficult, and Jimmy climbed long before he felt the first uneasy swaying of the ship.

There was a curling fog about him, and even had the air been clear, there were no lights below, no guiding marks by which he might make certain of his course. But he had flown by dead reckoning a thousand times, and this was no new experience. Then, too, his instruments were trustworthy, for, even as he looked, the barometer gave its silent warning.

"We'll just skim this smoke." He spoke half aloud to his plane, as a rider speaks to his horse, or as a seaman might do on the lonely deck of his ship.

"It ought to be fine up there in the moonlight," he added, watching the gray mist whirl as the propeller shattered it viciously.

But as the plane rose at a sharp angle, lurching heavily when it careened into an air-pocket, Jimmy realized that he would see no moon that night, nor any light at all except the dim bulb before him on the instrument-board. Above and below was thick fog, ominous and damp, like a breath from some subterranean vault.

He thrust his face out beyond the windshield, and fine particles of ice drove him back with the breath halting in his throat.

"Hell," he muttered, "now we'll have to go down."

For sleet will collect on the surface on a plane until its weight becomes too great for the motor to sustain. Nor is it a lengthy process. Accordingly, Kenyon lost no time. It was a choice between the driving sleet above and the rough passage, with its attendant dangers, at a lower altitude.

He hoped that in the lower and warmer atmosphere the sleet would have dissolved, but again he was to be disappointed. As low as he dared descend in the mountainous region, the sleet pelted down, although here he found it in smaller particles, rapidly melting into rain.

"It can't last forever," he decided, and fed more gas until the speedometer showed that he was crashing through the night at a hundred miles an hour. At best, he reflected, there would be ten or twenty miles more.

Crouched low in the cockpit, with his eyes on the instrument-board, his ears strained for the least change in the hum of the motor, Jimmy lost himself in thought. At first, his mind held close to the situation of the moment.

"If she'll hang together," he considered, "we'll get out of this in thirty minutes or less . . . have to hold her up . . . can't land in these mountains . . . nothing to do but go on . . . go on . . . like Von Essel did . . . remember Von Essel? . . . He'd be keen for this sort of thing . . . bucking the night . . . God, what a devil that fellow was in the air! Remember the night—"

A fog bank ahead of him split apart like a wave that is hit by the prow of a giant liner, and Jimmy's wandering mind snapped sharply as he straightened and braced himself. In the fleeting second that he glimpsed the rift in the troubled mist, a weird sight seared into his brain—a fragmentary, but appalling spectacle that sent chill draughts to his spine that were like spasmodic electric shocks.

Another plane was somewhere there beyond him in the fog. A slim, black ship it was, that had been diving, for it had straightened and swung upward in a swiftly beautiful arc as he sighted it. With an instinctive gesture Jimmy reached for the stick to dive. His flying sense warned him that the other had climbed, and this was the way to avoid a meeting that would send them—locked, wing to wing—in a long plunge to the rocks.

At a thousand feet he righted himself and swept on, still driving through fog. Knowing that it was futile, he still listened for the faint drumming of the other plane's motor, and equally certain that it was useless, he tried to penetrate the thick gloom for another sight of the plunging ship.

"What fool could be flying this route on such a night?" he questioned himself. "Not even the wildest barn-stormer would do it unless he had to."

The ship lurched in the hollow of a pocket, and he gripped the controls to right it.

"Here, this won't do." Jimmy speculated for an instant, then shot up to greater altitude.

"Better to hit this bird than hit the mountain," he decided grimly. "And there's a lot of air to choose from, up here," he added, whimsically.

But he cut down the speed and even dared to idle the motor in momentary bursts, hoping against hope to catch a foreign sound from the nothingness about him.

Then, when he had concluded that the mysterious pilot was far on his flight, Jimmy saw the thing above him, hovering like a great, black bird. And from the cockpit he saw the face of the pilot, gray and indistinct in the fog. But it was the face of Von Essel! If he doubted it for one hellish instant, there was the familiar wave of a hand as the black ship plunged down at him.

Without any hesitation Jimmy turned over and began to descend in the slow, awkward maneuver that the Escadrille had dubbed a barrel loop. It was instinct, motivated by experience over in France. As he fell, Jimmy found himself wondering why Von Essel had not turned loose his devilish gun. Or, he asked himself crazily, was the German following him down to pour steel into his tank when it was too late to climb again, or even straighten for a landing?

Twisting about in his narrow seat, Jimmy saw that his last thought was obviously the correct one. The black plane was diving, a little on his right. The fellow seemed to have no thought for himself—only a fiendish desire to drive the mail plane down.

Jimmy straightened, and sent his ship off to the left on a bank that dropped one wing almost at right angles beneath him and sent the other thrusting upward, perpendicularly. It was a mad maneuver, but it worked. As the shadowy wasp-like plane careened past him, Jimmy leveled his automatic at the dim figure in the cockpit and fired.

Almost instantly, the plane was lost to sight in the darkness below, but before it disappeared, he saw the pilot throw back his hand and laugh, and a slim white hand waved playfully in the mist.

"Missed!" Jimmy barked aloud, and fired again into space, as his plane lifted at a sharp angle and climbed. Recklessly, he idled the motor and soared blindly, listening for the sound of the other engine, but it did not come. Instead, out of the drab gray above him, the weird plane darted like a hawk in pursuit of a swallow.

This time, Jimmy pulled up with a suddenness that jarred his plane, and the ship sat back on its tail like a dog begging for food. In that frantic instant Death was close upon him. The plane seemed to hang there for a long moment, then dropped, and the black shape sped past harmlessly, but unbelievably close.

"God, I can't keep this up," thought Jimmy, despairingly. "How does he find me—every time? My ship can't stand this—she's not made for it."

Nevertheless, he gave his motor all the fuel it would take, and shot off into the brooding fog at a tangent, hoping that in this ghastly game of hare and hound he might elude his mad pursuer for once and all time. A minute passed, and his hopes began to rise with his plane, as he sought altitude.

"I'll go up over this damned fog," he determined. "It's got to have a top somewhere. I haven't got a chance with this maniac here. He can find me—every damned time."

A sob choked in his throat, not so much of fear as of bewilderment.

Steadily the plane climbed, and Jimmy now leaned close over the instrument-board, for he had switched off even the dull glow of the bulb. But again, this time behind him and overhead, the black plane cut out of the fog and pointed down upon him with its menacing bow. Leaning out of the cockpit, Von Essel disregarded the terrific battering of sleet and wind as he peered down. Even then, Jimmy saw that the man was smiling.

"Damn you," shrieked Jimmy, growing wild in his terror. "I'll meet you that way—if you want it."

He knew as he spoke, of course, that the other could not hear him. Yet Von Essel nodded and waved, as he sent his ship straight after the fleeing mail plane.

Jimmy turned in a dangerous bank, and now they were on a level, with perhaps a hundred yards between them. No longer conscious of himself, all caution thrown away, Jimmy roared ahead straight for the black ship that was speeding upon him.

As the German loomed just over his propeller, Jimmy closed his eyes. Involuntarily, his body stiffened as the nerves telegraphed to his brain in preparation for the shock.

An instant passed and registered in his brain like a lifetime. He opened his eyes and was staring wildly into the fog. The black plane had disappeared. All about him the mist was whirling and eddying in terrific agitation. His plane was bucking like a crazy thing, and the motor was pounding heavily.

"Great God," cried Jimmy, "I couldn't have missed him."

Yet there had been no concussion beyond the bumping passage of the ship through the air-pockets.

Jimmy rubbed his dazed eyes and reached for the controls mechanically. He noted dully that the sleet had ceased, and as he climbed, he came suddenly out into a universe of silver and indigo blue. A great moon hung in the heavens and the sky was studded with brilliant stars. Below, the clouds were rolling in soft, restless mounds, bathed in the silver glow.

He tried to fathom what had happened.

"He must have banked just when I got ready for the crash—probably missed me by inches. But there was no sound. I could have heard his motor—unless—unless he had it shut off, unless he was coasting down. My God, maybe it was—suicide—"

He sat upright and forced himself to conscious thinking, concentrated on his instruments and found that he was off his course by ten miles.

Shaken and half sick from the strain of the night, he nevertheless circled over the Cleveland landing-field only fifteen minutes behind schedule. He saw a crowd waiting there to greet him, and determined to say nothing of the experience until he could make his official report.

Mechanically, he took the field beneath him in a swinging circle and dropped lightly to the ground, bumping across the turf.

"Good stuff," shouted a pilot, seizing his hand, before he could climb down from the cockpit. "You're all in, old man. It was a rotten night. Better get some grub, and sleep all day."

Others surrounded him, half pushing, half carrying him across the field to the hangars. Someone brought steaming coffee and sandwiches. He would wait, he decided, until he was alone with his chief later in the day. In his present condition they would attribute his story to a mind haunted by fog wraiths. After he had slept, and had dressed himself again in his flight togs, Kenyon sought the district chief, who had been a colonel in army aviation.

"Pretty tough sailing, wasn't it, Kenyon?"

"A little bumpy, sir—over the Alleghenies. Some fog and sleet, too. That bothered me."

"Well, you proved that it could be done," continued the other. "The air mail is established now—night and day, by the lord Harry! Look at the paper—they're giving us the glad hand in great shape."

He thrust a Cleveland afternoon newspaper across the desk. Jimmy took it and glanced at the head-line announcing his flight. Then his eye roved down the column. Jimmy suddenly drew in his breath. His wind-tanned face went white. His chief stared curiously at him.

"What—what the devil do you see, man?" the latter asked.

But Jimmy did not hear him. He was reading a paragraph beneath his own story:

GERMAN ACE DIES
(BY SPECIAL CABLE)

BERLIN—Baron Ludwig Von Essel, famous German war ace, died here early today from the ravages of tuberculosis, acquired in the aviation service during the World War. Von Essel was noted as one of the most daring fliers in the German 'circus,' and it was current knowledge that he had hoped to die in the air rather than surrender to the disease. The funeral will be conducted with full military honors.

Jimmy pushed the paper back to his superior. His voice sounded thin and far away.

"Did you read that?" he asked, dully. "Von Essel—the bird who was always chasing me in France—"

The chief seized the paper.

"Curious, isn't it?" he mused, looking across the table. "He tempted death in every way he could, that fellow—and couldn't beat the game."

After all, Kenyon decided, why try to explain anything? Early morning in Germany—midnight over the Alleghenies. What explanation could there be? Closing his eyes wearily, Jimmy concluded that the world was not yet ready for an expose of the fourth dimension. Von Essel's ghost had sought peace in the death the man had courted. It could rest now—in another world.

Dead Man's Vengeance
By George Malherbe

A long, air-tight sea-chest may have a purpose so sinister as to confound the human mind—as the Old Man knew, and the parrot also.

THIS IS THE STORY OF A STRANGE CASE IN LIVERPOOL STREET. In the police records it is dismissed by the curt word "unsolved"—but Johnny Kehoe, the longshoreman, knows better than that, and so does Inspector Perch. Johnny, himself, who saw more of those weird doings on the water-front than any other living man, told the tale to me substantially as it is written.

Ever since the Old Man died, shrieking in his sleep, the house at 310 Liverpool Street had had a bad name. The Old Man had come to the house from his ship,

Harrigan truthfully thought that Perch was another of those cranks from Headquarters.

the *Surinam*, bringing with him a salt-crusted sea-chest, and a pea-green parrot that screamed and screamed, hours on end. The *Surinam* was a smutty tramp, with a reputation as questionable as the coast is long. The Old Man's reputation was more obscure, more sinister. Rogue, rascal, rum runner, "black-birder," pirate, were the words borne on the whispering winds along the wharves. But none knew for sure—none but Captain Greer, creaking the minutes away in a twisted rocking-chair on the second floor of the house where the Old Man had guttered out in a frenzy of delirium.

Captain Greer kept silence, a silence that snarled when it was questioned. He had come into the house two days before the Old Man died, and sat rocking there still as sole possessor—rocking and staring at neither street nor roofs, but only empty air, as the parrot screamed from its perch.

It was on the day of the first snow that the Captain's silence, his smooth routine of rocking to and fro, were shattered into bits. Down Liverpool Street he came just before dusk, swaying like a drunken man, his armless

"Ever think, Harrigan, that the only witness to this weird business was that bird over there?" the Inspector said crisply.

sleeve lifting in the little wind, his huge body all a-lurch on frozen sidewalks.

But it was not at these things that Liverpool Street stared; it was the stark fear flaming from his eyes.

He swayed into the little café on the corner, and dropped into a chair. His huge bulk quivered. He huddled in his seat as if terror's hand was upon him. His bluish fingers drummed on the table, and he called hoarsely for whisky.

His voice was a harsh mutter as questioners crowded round him. "He walks . . . the Old Man walks . . . up and down, like he did on the quarter-deck. And at the turn, you can hear his pipe clink as he taps it out, like he always did. And you open the door, and there's no one there! No one in the hall . . . no one in the house, savin' that brimstone bird a-squallin'. I can't stand it . . . I can't. . . ."

The Captain's face went waxen white, and Johnny Kehoe, the longshoreman, sitting in a dusky corner, turned to shrug his shoulders. "He's loony," he whispered—"clean barmy in the head."

"And there's no one there, you say?" asked one of the group about the Captain's chair.

"No one—no one livin'!" said the Captain, and gulped his whisky down. "Nights, you're settin' there, an' the door swings open like a hand was on it. Not like the wind done it, but slow . . . slow like an old man was comin' in. Then, sometimes, there's the three raps. . . ."

"Huh!" said Johnny, and turned his head.

"Raps?" asked a curious one.

"Cap'n's call," said Greer, and stared at space, his chin sagging. "Three raps, two quick together, then a minute, then the last. The Old Man called his cabin-boy that way on the *Surinam* . . . called him by poundin' with the cane he allus carried. And the Chink Number One Boy would skip into the cabin, and then come out like a bat from hell. Only on'ct he didn't come out—not till dark, when they chucked him overboard to the sharks. Dead—he was stone-dead, and not a mark on him to show how 'twas done." He stopped to gulp down another glass of whisky. "Las' night and the night afore that, come the three raps in that pitch-dark house, an' not a livin' soul to make 'em."

His audience shifted uneasily, shrinking instinctively from the shadowy dusk that was settling down on ships and docks and houses along Liverpool Street, and one of the men said in a shrill, piping voice: "The Old Man died pretty soon arter you come to take care of him, Cap'n? I remember well the last time he come down the street, the black patch over one eye, and his cane a-swingin'."

"He died two days after I got here," said the Captain, and his fingers twisted nervously on the stem of his glass. "Two days, an' he out of his head and screamin' most o' the time! Came to, on'ct, long enough to write me a paper leavin' the house to me, providin' I took care o' the parrot. If it warn't for that, I'd have twisted the bird's neck afore now. Sixty years old, maybe seventy, the thing is, and it's seen plenty in its time."

He got to his feet unsteadily, and stood, a gigantic shadow in the flickering light. "Alive or dead," he muttered thickly, "it ain't healthy to monkey with such as the Old Man. Tonight's the last night I spend in that hellish house. Tomorrow, I'm gone for good."

Afterward, there were many to recollect his words, and, even at the moment, all of the loungers were seized with strange, uncanny panic, as they stepped out into the snow to watch the Captain lurch down the street, scrape a foot on his clean-swept doorstep, and click his key in the lock.

Even Johnny Kehoe, who sniffed at the supernatural, was a little less sneering as he stood with the little crowd in the snow outside the house, watching the Captain's hulking shadow on the window shade as a wick turned up and a red lamp began to glow.

The Captain's story must have seared into Johnny's brain, for, ordinarily, he says, he sleeps like a log. That night, it was different. Sleepless in his bed across the narrow street, he alone heard and saw the strange sequel.

He was wakeful, stirring uneasily—on the alert for strange sounds, though he cursed himself for a superstitious fool. He kept his eyes on the lighted window of Captain Greer's bedroom, and occasionally saw the man's figure silhouetted on the window shade. For a time, he thought he could hear the Captain's rumbling voice; probably, he was speaking to the parrot; perhaps, he was feeding it, for it squalled no more.

Captain Greer then seemed to be busying himself in the rear of the room; at least, he never came near the window, and, as a siren roared down the bay, Johnny had a premonition of evil that set him shivering all over.

A minute past midnight, Johnny says, and the lamp in Captain Greer's room went out as if in a gust of wind. There was silence, a thin, half-throttled scream, and then the piercing shriek of the parrot. That was all.

It was enough to send Johnny whispering at street corners when daylight came; it was enough to make a knot of hardy spirits go knock on Captain Greer's door, when the bright light of morning made weird tales seem a mere absurdity.

They knocked, and nobody came, and there was no noise at all save for the steady shrilling of the parrot. So at last they became bold enough to break down the door—and grim death awaited them!

What they found there, sent Johnny Kehoe racing down the street to the station-house, as fast as his feet would carry him. The sergeant at the desk sent down Barney Phelan, the patrolman, in the police flivver, with Detective Harrigan sitting by his side.

Captain Greer was dead as a stone; dead with the turned-out lamp above him; dead on the floor with one hand stretched out as if to grasp something. His face was not pleasant to see, Johnny says. It was a glaring mask of horror, staring dully at a pea-green parrot that sat preening itself in it's cage.

The Captain's cap was on the floor; his pipe, shattered into bits, lay beside the sea-chest. Within the chest, which was half empty, a pair of dungarees had been tossed so carelessly that you could almost see the huge, hulking man himself, stooping down, his good arm reaching out to rearrange the contents of the long, narrow, salt-stained box, his empty sleeve pinned across his chest.

"And as he stooped," said Harrigan to himself, "somethin' happened to him. But what? There's not a mark on the body!"

He went through the chest, but found nothing significant—an old sextant, an oilcloth slicker, a few shabby trinkets from the Orient, and clothes such as sailors wear. He searched the house. There was not a single clue to the murderer of Captain Greer!

"Somethin' came for him . . . somethin' that warn't human," whispered Johnny Kehoe to the little group outside. "When the light went out an' I heard that scream, I says, 'The Cap'n's done for!' an' he was! A ghost killed him. You can't tell me no different."

"Bah!" said the patrolman. "We'll get the guy quick enough. Out o' the way, there! Here comes the Medical Examiner."

All day long a crowd of varying size stood outside the house, and, in the afternoon,

Inspector Perch came down from Headquarters. His stooped, rather shabby figure almost deferentially squeezed its way past reporters and curious hangers-on.

He wore blue glasses, and had an habitually sleepy and apologetic air. Harrigan began a blustering explanation of his failure, but stopped abruptly when the man spoke.

"Has anything been moved?" said Inspector Perch, and his tones cut like a knife.

"Nothing except the body, sir."

"Anybody been in the house except the Medical Examiner's men and yourself?"

"A crowd broke in and found the body, but I put everybody out as soon as I got here. Phelan's been guarding the door."

"Hum!" said Inspector Perch and went up the rickety stairs and into the room where the Old Man had died, screaming, and the Captain had been murdered. Harrigan followed him.

Captain Greer's body had been taken away by the Medical Examiner, but the place where it had lain was outlined in glaring white chalk: the head here, the legs there, the dead man spread out—so.

Harrigan squatted by the sea-chest, ready to explain things, but the Inspector paid no attention to him and gave only a passing glance at the chalk-marks. Instead, he went over and poked a finger at the parrot, which screeched angrily.

"Harrigan," said he, "send out a man to get some feed for the bird—crackers and probably a bit of raw meat."

Harrigan truthfully thought that Perch was another of those cranks from Headquarters. But he went to the window and called out some orders to the patrolman. Then he sank back into his place by the chest.

"Ever think, Harrigan, that the only witness to this weird business was that bird over there?" the Inspector said crisply.

Harrigan had not, and he wondered still more when the Inspector strode over to the sea-chest, examined it, and then entered something in his note-book.

"What'd the Medical Examiner say killed him, Chief?" asked Harrigan.

"Tell you later," snapped the Inspector, and stepped back to survey the long, salt-crusted box. "Ever think, Harrigan," he asked suddenly, "that the chest's as long as a coffin—long enough, say, to hold the body of a man?"

Harrigan started. The business was beginning to prey a little on his nerves. "Can't say as I did," he muttered. "Look, Inspector, we found somethin' queer on this table. You'd better have a look at it."

It was a ragged sheet of ordinary white paper, scrawled upon with a soft pencil. "One . . . two . . . three . . . four . . . Dead Man's Button. . . . One . . ." The scrawl ended abruptly with the faint semblance of a "t" as if the man's writing hand had been snatched aside.

"H'm," said the Inspector, pursing his lips. "Well, Harrigan?"

"Can't make nothin' of it," said the detective, shaking his head. "That's the Cap'n's fist, though. We had him up at the station a couple o' years ago. Drunk and disorderly."

"For one thing," said Inspector Perch, "the Captain wasn't bending over that sea-chest when he was killed. He was writing at this table. Yet—"

Again he stepped over to examine the chest. He flung down its lid and there was a faint click. Again he entered something in his note-book. "This chest," he said, "has a spring lock. Put down the lid, and it locks. Yet there's no lock or keyhole visible. Peculiar, Harrigan!"

"One . . . two . . . three . . . four . . . Dead Man's Button," said a husky voice behind them, and Harrigan spun on a heel, his hair on end.

It was only the parrot, preening itself in its cage.

"My God!" said Harrigan, and the parrot squawked, "One . . . two . . ." and stopped.

"H'm!" said Inspector Perch, shutting his note-book with a snap. "What d'you make of that, Harrigan?"

The detective's mouth had fallen open, and he said, with a distinct effort, "Those were the words that—"

"That Captain Greer was writing down on the piece of paper, as he listened to the parrot," finished Inspector Perch. "You stay here for a while, Harrigan, and see if the bird talks again. If it says anything at all, note it down. Have the parrot fed. Keep a man outside the door of this room. Tell Phelan to stay at his post, and place another man at the back of the house. Meet me at the station at five this afternoon."

Harrigan shook his head slowly as the door closed behind the Inspector. The whole affair was too much for him, and he shuddered in spite of himself.

At five, he went down to the station-house, where Inspector Perch was already sitting, his note-book open before him.

"Did the parrot talk again?" he asked.

"No, sir."

"It will," said the Inspector placidly, "and meanwhile the whole case is beginning to be clear in my mind. We already know how Captain Greer was killed, and why."

Harrigan scratched his head. "You may, Chief, but—"

"Simple!" snapped the Inspector. "The Captain died from suffocation. Someone seized him when he was writing down the parrot's message, stuffed him into that sea-chest, and slammed down the lid. It locks automatically: it is air-tight. It was built for the purpose of sheer, stark murder. Captain Greer was talking of the mysterious death of a Chinese cabin-boy, just before he was murdered. The cabin-boy was killed in that chest by our mysterious friend, the Old Man."

Harrigan gasped. "But why—"

"The motive? That's as simple. Somewhere there's an atoll or an island called The Dead Man's Button. It's probably so small that it's not even charted. On that island there's something men will do murder for—treasure, no doubt. The Old Man knew of it; he undoubtedly had a map of it, with the treasure-spot marked. 'One—two—three—four' may be four steps, four paces, four rods. There's no way of telling till we find that chart. And the chart, my dear Harrigan, is somewhere in the murder room. Cap'n Greer was looking for it last night; the Chinese cabin-boy was killed because he knew something about it. Possibly he helped the Old Man hide it, and that was the cause of his murder. Dead men tell no tales, you know."

"Ugh!" said Harrigan, shivering. "It's a nasty business, Chief. What I want to know is how Cap'n Greer's murderer got into that house, and then got out again. Johnny Kehoe was watching at the front; there's a night watchman in the factory behind the place. Neither of 'em saw anybody come in or go out. And why did the murderer take the Cap'n's body out of the chest after he'd killed him?"

"The last," said the Inspector, rising and snapping his note-book shut, "is easy. To conceal the manner of the killing, or—as a warning, Harrigan. Other people about here may suspect the existence of that chart. After one look at the Captain's face, which was fairly contorted by fear and horror, no one's going to risk such a death by searching that room for a treasure-chart. No one, Harrigan, except you and me. We'd better start now."

They went down Liverpool Street, with a light flutter of snow following them, and the first twilight was already faintly purple over wharves and ships and houses.

At last, they came to the Old Man's house, the house with a bad name, where Captain Greer had been killed, as he wrote down gibberish that a pea-green parrot squawked. Outside, there was no one in sight, save a police officer on the corner, and Johnny Kehoe, all a-shiver with the cold. The Inspector looked about, angrily, for Phelan.

He and Harrigan stopped near Johnny, and they stood silent for a moment, listening to the parrot's steady screaming inside the house. Suddenly it stopped midway of a high-pitched, almost human scream, and the street was still with an uncanny stillness.

"Look!" shrieked Johnny Kehoe, pointing up at the window of the death-room.

Even through the dim, smoky twilight, they could see the horrible Thing. . . . A man . . . a malevolent old man . . . yet too shadowy for a man. A black patch over one eye . . . a cane in one hand . . . on its face, a hideous, twisted smile of triumph. . . . Then, suddenly, there was nothing at all at the window, but they heard the cane tap three times.

"God!" screeched Johnny Kehoe. "*It's the Old Man!*"

Inspector Perch hurled open the door, and sprinted up the stairs.

A burly policeman was guarding the death-room, and Perch cried out, in the thin, high voice of hysteria: "Anybody been in or out of the room?"

"No, sir. The parrot's quit screamin', though, an' there was three knocks, just now. Sounded sort o' funny."

The ray from Perch's flashlight fell upon a grotesque bundle of feathers that lay on the floor. It was the parrot, dead, with a twisted neck.

As Harrigan gasped, the flashlight's beam found the bird's cage. It, too, lay on the floor, and its metal bottom was split apart.

Beside it was a strip of old, yellowed parchment. The Inspector's hands shook as he picked it up, and held it to the light.

It was a chart, the chart of an island, but barely discernible. Something had blurred its outlines, reduced what had once been thin, precise writing to a hopeless smudge. The chart was ruined, useless. The treasure would never be found.

Johnny Kehoe can finish the story best.

"Right there," says he, "the police dropped the case. Dead or alive, the Old Man guarded his secret. Alive, he killed the cabin-boy who knew it. Dead, he killed Cap'n Greer who guessed it. Dead, he twisted the parrot's neck so it could never tell. Me, I moved out o' that neighborhood fast as I could go. Down there, they say, on a foggy night, you can still hear a parrot screamin'—screamin' almost like a human!"

A Ferryman of Souls
By Constance Bross Eckley

"Crazy Tom" brought drowned folks to shore. In his cabin, they walked and talked, and—

JOHN ROCHESTER GAVE UP HOPE AND RESIGNED HIMSELF TO WAIT FOR DEATH. He wrapped his great waterproof coat about him and sat down on the highest point of the rock, still out of reach of the turbulent waters of the Pacific that were creeping slowly higher and higher about him.

"Then, you are—dead?" he asked.

He had gone out there at dusk to fish, when the tide was low. He had lost track of time in his absorption, and noted suddenly that the waves were breaking on all sides of the rock on which he sat. He had snatched up his belongings to make a dash for shore, but the sea had come foaming in between him and the main rock, which was itself far out from the shoreline. A seething whirlpool of water, with tremendous waves rushing in from both sides of the rock on which he was trapped, promised a death even more horrible than that of waiting where he was. Should a miracle permit him to reach the main rock through the desperate intervening sea, John Rochester knew that he could never get a foothold on the other rock, to climb up to safety.

"I'm a goner this time, all right," he muttered as he prepared to wait. With hands clasped about his knees, he stared gloomily out across the water. It was dark now, but he could see the white foam that rode in on the crests of the mighty breakers, and the volcanic spurts of spray as they crashed on the rocks.

John Rochester considered, with an air of detachment, how strange it was that out of all the gay and dangerous places he had been, he should come to his death like this, alone, in a primitive village on the coast of Washington. Doctor Borus had sent him here and there to watering places all over Europe and America, but that hadn't helped much. His nerves were still all shot to pieces. Then Doctor Borus had discovered this village almost shut off from the world, where he could have a perfect rest, and where nothing would remind him of Lillian.

It was funny about Lillian, Rochester mused. For the millionth time, perhaps, he asked himself what had become of her. She had left him a note, saying she was going to abandon him and join Martin in Alaska. But when he went after her in a frenzy of rage, he found that she had never reached her destination. Martin admitted that she had arranged to come, but when he went to meet the boat on which she had said she would arrive, she wasn't on board, nor was her name on the passenger list.

Truly alarmed, the outraged husband and his wife's lover tried every means to find out what had become of her. Every attempt failed. Then Martin married, and Rochester grew interested in other things. It was only lately that he'd begun to brood about Lillian. He had a feeling that something was wrong with her, that she needed him. He pictured all sorts of horrible things happening to her.

In the midst of his pondering, Rochester suddenly heard a shout. With profound relief, he turned toward shore where he saw a lantern waving at him from the main rock.

"Come on across," a cheerful voice shouted. "Hurry up! You'll be swept off any minute."

Rochester looked down at the churning sea that stretched between him and his rescuer. His relief settled again into despair.

"Hurry!" the man shouted. "Hang on to the life-line—the lifeline!"

Rochester looked, as well as he could on all sides of him, but saw nothing that would aid him.

"Those wooden blocks, to your left—they're on a life-line. Hang on tight and you can make it."

Rochester found the line then, and cursed himself soundly for not having seen it before. He tore off his coat and slid into the foaming sea, one hand clutching the life-line. Several times he thought he was gone, as he made that perilous journey. With the waves dashing and receding over his head, he tugged at the rope and reached the main rock at last. His rescuer pulled him up with another rope.

"Thank God, that's over with," gasped Rochester when he was once more standing on safe rock. He turned to thank his companion, noting that the man was stocky and bearded, a queer primitive-looking man, who seemed somehow not to be in the best of health.

"How on earth did you have the strength to pull me up?" he asked.

"Oh, that!" laughed the other. "It's because I am crazy. They call me 'Crazy Tom' down in the village. I'm not so used to pulling in live people, though. I live here in a cabin on the rocks, and many's the corpse I've fished out of Dead Man's Hollow. It's to the left of these rocks, you know. All you have to do is to wait, and anyone who's been drowned around here will come floating in, some calm night at high tide."

Rochester was shivering with cold as the night breezes whipped his drenched clothing.

"Come up to the cabin with me and warm up," Tom urged.

Rochester saw a light from the window of a small cottage alone up there on the barren rocks.

"Funny," he muttered to himself, "I never noticed that house before."

They reached the cabin, and Tom threw open the door with the cordiality of a prodigal host.

"Step in," he urged cheerily, "and have a bite to eat."

Rochester stood stock still in the doorway, as though frozen to the spot. In the bright kitchen before him, four skeletons, fully clothed, were seated around a table set for a meal. Rochester passed his hands across his eyes.

"If you have something to drink," he mumbled, "I—I might feel better."

Tom gave him a little shove inside and shut the door behind him.

"These are my folks," he explained happily, with a comprehensive gesture at the extraordinary supper table. "They don't look much now, but then it's only a little after midnight. Sit down by the stove. I'll get you a drink."

Rochester did not look again at the supper table until he felt the warmth of the fire and of the whisky seeping through him. His head cleared.

"Supper's ready, supper's ready," called Tom from his cooking at another stove. "Come on and join us."

Rochester rose and braced himself to look again at the table. A pleasant young matron smiled at him and three children beat their knives and forks upon the table.

"Food!" they cried in unison.

"Hush!" the mother said. "Remember we have company."

Rochester moistened his lips.

"God, what a horrible hallucination I had!" he thought. "I must tell Doctor Borus."

The meal was a hilarious affair. The family grew more and more excited until they verged on hysteria. Tom stopped eating several times and walked about the room, rubbing his hands.

"Half-past twelve!" he shouted at length triumphantly. "Look, Rochester—a surprise for you!"

Rochester turned toward the doorway to which Tom pointed. He rose violently from his chair, sending his napkin and fork flying. He clutched the back of the chair to keep himself steady.

"I'm crazy as a loon," he muttered. "It couldn't possibly be Lillian."

But the smiling young woman came on toward him.

"Why, Jack," she said, "don't you know me? See, Jack, I'm just as I was when we first met—at Carmel in California. Just as I was the first two years of our marriage—before we grew rich and I met Martin. I've waited so long for you to come. Tom and I have tried every way to call you, but it took so long."

Rochester looked furtively at the others, to see if they saw and heard what he did. Tom spoke up impatiently.

"Of course it's Lillian, your wife," he insisted. "She'll only be able to stay a little while, so don't waste any time. She's brought you from the other end of the world to talk to you."

Rochester stared fixedly at the woman beside him.

"If you are Lillian," he said, "for God's sake tell me where you have been all this time. I've tried every means to find you."

"I know all that," she said. "You see, I did board the boat for Alaska, but under an assumed name. I hadn't gone very far when I changed my mind. I seemed to see all at once what an awful thing I was doing. You and I had grown so far apart those last few years, but when I got out there by myself on the ocean, away from my old environment and associates, I seemed to become myself once more. I knew that in my heart I loved you just as I had when we first met.

"I bribed one of the stewards to signal a fishing boat, and I got aboard that to be taken to shore. It was almost directly out from these rocks."

"But why all this long silence? Were you afraid I wouldn't take you back? What happened after that? Why didn't you let me know before?" Rochester asked.

"I did try—over and over. So many times, I almost got you. That night at Monte Carlo— you remember? You heard me call you, I know, but you said it was the wind. Then at Miami—it was after that that you first consulted Doctor Borus. I only succeeded in bringing you here now through the minds of others. I couldn't seem to reach you otherwise."

"Are you crazy?" demanded Rochester. "Why didn't you do something sensible, instead of all this silly telepathic stuff?"

Lillian looked at Crazy Tom, and Tom shook his head despairingly.

"You're thicker than I thought," he remarked. "She was drowned off that fishing boat on the way in. They ran into a storm, and the bodies of the men and Lillian all drifted in eventually to Dead Man's Hollow. The dead always speak, but most of the living will not listen."

Rochester gazed at the tousle-headed little blonde with forget-me-not eyes whom he had married years before.

"Then, you are—dead?" he asked.

Lillian laughed and shrugged her shoulders.

"Call it what you like," she said. "I had to get you out here, because the dead can be seen most clearly at that spot on earth where the last bit of life went from them. I couldn't rest until I had told you that I turned back of my own accord from that last fatal trip. I wanted you to know that although I left the note, I couldn't see the thing through, and went to my death still faithful to you and loving you."

Lillian turned away quickly then.

"My time is up," she said. "I must go now. I won't come again, Tom. I am very tired. I want to rest. I'll see you again, Jack, when you come to this side of the line. You can go your way in peace, now. I won't trouble you again."

She went out through the door she had entered. Rochester dropped into his chair and sat very still, staring at his plate.

"Whatever it is that's happening," he kept repeating, "I've got to keep a grip on myself."

When he looked up, he saw to his astonishment that in place of the happy family gathered about the table, were the four skeletons he had seen upon his entrance to the cabin. He thought his mind had broken completely.

Crazy Tom was walking around in great agitation, wringing his hands.

"You'd better get ready to go," he said to Rochester. "It'll be a quarter of one soon, and you can't possibly stay here a minute after one o'clock. I'm sorry you have to see my family in this condition. It's my fault. I didn't know they could come back like they do, or I wouldn't have kept their bones all these years. They were all drowned, you see—oh, ever so many years ago—when the *Point Roma* was wrecked on these rocks and every man and woman aboard her drowned.

"They were coming down from Alaska to join me in Portland, Oregon. When I got the news, waiting there to welcome them after a two years' separation, I came right down here to the scene of the wreck. I heard about the Hollow, and I built the cabin here and waited for their bodies. It wasn't until I'd lived here quite a while that I knew they'd come back. They all come back—like Lillian—and I help them find their people when I can.

"But it's nearly one o'clock," Tom fairly shrieked. He pushed Rochester to the door and ushered him unceremoniously out. "Hurry! Hurry!" he cried.

Rochester ran blindly along the high rocks toward the shore. When he reached the beach, he saw a group of men with lanterns, coming toward him.

The leader of the men said that they had missed Rochester at the Inn, and organized a searching party.

"We wouldn't have butted in, of course," he explained, "if they hadn't said you'd gone fishing. Newcomers around here don't know all the tricks of the tide, and when you didn't come back we got scared. A city fellow got drowned off Death Rock, just last summer. But I see you had sense enough to stay back on the regular rocks."

"No," said Rochester. "I was out on the farthest point."

The man looked at him suspiciously. He put a hand on Rochester's clothing, to see if he was wet.

"How'd you get back in?" he asked belligerently.

"Why—why, by the life-line."

The man threw back his head and laughed.

"That's a good one," he chuckled. "You seemed so serious-like, I didn't catch on at first that you were kidding. I thought you were just a plain liar. It's been a long time since we got a good laugh out of Crazy Tom's life-line. I'd almost forgotten. The poor nut spent years trying to fix one up out there."

"And wasn't he successful?"

"Of course not. Use your bean, man. God Almighty himself couldn't keep a life-line between two slippery rocks in that hell-hole out there."

Rochester moistened his lips again.

"Who is this Crazy Tom?" he asked.

"Oh, a nut who used to live up in a cabin on the rocks! He used to watch for the bodies that came in from wrecks, and lived mostly off things he salvaged out of Dead Man's

Hollow. He'd hoist up a black flag when he'd found a body, and someone would call for it. They say he used to be real smart, but went off his bean when his family was lost at sea. Folks said he kept a bunch of bones that he found around the Hollow and fixed them into skeletons that he talked to like dolls.

"He was afraid someone would take him away from the rocks. He got crippled up a little, some years before, bringing in a woman's body; but he had some crazy idea he ought to die right there where his family were drowned. So one day he hoisted up the old black flag and then went out and jumped into the sea."

They walked on toward the Inn in silence for some time. Rochester decided that, after all, perhaps he had better not tell Doctor Borus.

Then he noticed that his great waterproof coat still flapped about him. His face broke into a broad grin of amusement.

"I remember now," he laughed to himself. "I must have fallen asleep, and never left the main rock after all."

The grin slowly faded, and he moistened his lips once more. The dream did not explain everything. Not Crazy Tom, of whom he had never heard before he fell asleep, not—

"Funny thing about that woman," his companion mused, half to Rochester, half to himself. "That was the last body Crazy Tom fished in. He got a terrible banging up on the rocks. But, do you know, they never did find out who she was. The only wreck anywhere around these parts at the time was a fishing boat, full of men, but nobody figured how a neatly dressed woman like that would have been with them."

The Wolf Man
By Mont Hurst

She poked fun at him, and said she would never marry him.

The young beauty of the woods little dreamed how deadly it was to reject her mad adorer.

LAST YEAR I WAS DOWN IN LOUISIANA in my capacity as scout for an oil company. My duty was to make reports on locations; wells, leases, and drilling operations. I secured board and room with a "Cajun" family by the name of Benoit in the village of Fleurville. The little town had a population of about five hundred persons. It had originally been settled by the French, and the families were descendants of the earliest settlers.

That section of the state is sparsely settled; and a heavily wooded tract, called Bisnau Forest, covers hundreds of square miles of the territory and includes many alligator-infested bayous within its limits. One would hardly believe that such a wild region existed in these United States. I was told that there existed sections of the woods that had never been seen by white men.

The Benoit family consisted of Mr. and Mrs. Benoit, and six grown children. One of them, Peter, was demented. They told me that, several years before, he had fallen madly in love with a "Cajun" girl who lived on the banks of Bayou Chalique in the adjoining parish. The bayou was on the other side of the small neck where Bisnau Woods began. The girl did not return Peter's love with the fervor he demanded. She poked fun at him, and said she would never marry him. He brooded over it for four years and finally made up his mind that no one else would ever possess her. One night, about six months before I came to Fleurville, the girl disappeared from her home, and the whole citizenship of the parish turned out to search for her. A weird feeling of horror prevailed.

Peter stayed at home, a sinister smile playing upon his lips as he heard the excited trappers and farmers discussing the strange disappearance of the girl. She was never found.

During the time that I was staying in the Benoit home, Peter frequently made long trips into the woods and always came back smiling. It was said that he knew the forest as no other man did.

One morning he returned to the house with blood stains on his gnarled hands. He was laughing hysterically and talked like a madman. We were aroused over this. When his family asked me my opinion of his strange actions, I advised them to notify the sheriff of the parish. They did this at once.

Mr. Benoit and I met the officer, and we decided to try to trace Peter's movements the night before. We picked up the trail by means of bloodhounds. Dark stains of dried blood were found, as we penetrated into the dense forest.

The hounds stopped on the banks of a large bayou. We could see a small island in the middle, and so we made a crude raft and crossed over, to investigate. On the island was a little stone hut, hidden by brush and trees. Inside, we discovered some bits of clothing that belonged to the girl who had disappeared, and later we found her comb, a brush, and her sunbonnet. The hut had two small windows that were barred with iron taken from an old harrow. A small pantry was filled with food. We knew at once that the girl had been held prisoner there.

We searched all over that section of the forest but found no further clue. When we returned to the village after dark, I went directly to the Benoit home.

Peter was under the care of a physician. He was nothing but a gibbering maniac, and the doctor said that he would be even more violent by morning. The air was rent with his cries, which resembled the screaming of a panther on the mountainside. I felt sorry for the poor fellow.

After the doctor had gone home, I stood in the doorway of Peter's room and saw him thrashing about in the bed in which they had tied him. Outside, a storm had begun. Suddenly he began to laugh fiendishly; then he started baying like a timber wolf. He kept this up until I could stand it no longer. I found Mrs. Benoit and told her that I was going to spend the night somewhere else.

After a few moments' thought, I decided to go over to the home of the Boissoins, who lived near Bayou Chalique. I looked at my watch, got my revolver, and left the house. Making my way to the edge of the forest, I plunged into the dense brush.

I managed to keep on the right trail by means of the flashes of lightning, but in less than a half-hour the storm subsided and then I had much difficulty in finding my way through the complete darkness. I floundered around, trying to get my bearings, and I must have wandered in circles for a considerable time. Then, suddenly, my attention was arrested by something that passed a few feet in front of me. I stood still, my eyes straining through the blackness.

Jerking out my revolver, I held it ready for any emergency that might arise. Something was directly in front of me, about twenty feet away, but I could not make out just what it was. Then I picked up a club, and threw it in the direction of the thing.

It sprang at me—and I fired as it did! The animal fell at my feet.

I stepped back, waiting to see if any signs of life remained. It moved only once or twice. I crept up to where the thing lay crumpled in a heap. Striking a match, I saw that I had killed a big timber wolf. It was the largest one I had ever seen. By a lucky shot, I had hit the ugly animal directly between the eyes. I had fired only once.

After looking at it for a few minutes, I went on through the forest and eventually found my way out. I reached the Boissoin home after midnight, and spent the remainder of the night there. At the breakfast table next morning, I told them of my experience. Steve Boissoin said he would go back with me to get the hide of the huge wolf. I wanted the thing mounted as a testimonial to my lucky bit of shooting.

When we arrived at the spot where I had killed the animal, it was not to be seen! However, there was a big pool of blood there. I was positive I had killed the wolf because I had kicked it around and no sign of life had remained. Steve kidded me a little, but the dried-up blood was evidence of the fact that I had, at least, shot something. We searched all through the woods for an hour but found no trace of the dead animal. Steve went home and I walked on to the Benoit home.

When I arrived at the house, I was met by Mrs. Benoit. She was in tears. She told me that they had found Peter dead in his bed that morning. There was something strange about it because he had been tied in the bed—but he was found with a bullet hole between his eyes! Furthermore, he had apparently escaped from his room an hour after I left the house the night before, but they had found him back in bed—and tied—a few minutes later! It was uncanny, and I wondered whether I was dreaming or not.

I went into his room and looked at the body of the dead maniac, with weird thoughts racing through my mind. I recalled the stories of the werewolves that I had heard on my trip to Silesia. Myths, they were—*or were they*?

Peter's sightless eyes were staring at the ceiling and his mouth was wide open. The bullet hole was squarely between his eyes! He was tied in the bed just as he had been when his family had last seen him alive.

But they said he had been missing from his bed for a short time. Who had untied him? Or had he really been missing? I did not know what to think.

The physician had removed the bullet from his skull—and I learned that it was the same caliber as those in my revolver! I began to feel dizzy. They told me that nobody in the house had heard the shot, and Mrs. Benoit had made two trips into the room during the night. Each time he seemed to be quietly sleeping, and so she went away, without disturbing him.

In answer to my questions, I learned that the doctor believed the maniac had been dead since eleven o'clock the night before! That was about the time I was lost in the woods! Cold perspiration stood out on my brow, and I felt nauseated.

Things seemed to whirl before me. The doctor also stated that Peter had died of heart-failure; that the bullet had pierced the brain some time after the man had died; and that rigor mortis had set in before the bullet had been fired into Peter's head!

I stumbled out of the room, in a daze. I went down to the village and wired the home office of my company that I was coming in, and that I'd had enough of that section. Next day I made my departure.

While oh the train, I took out the little dictionary I carry in my brief-case and found the word "werewolf" defined thus:

> A person changed into a wolf, or able to assume the form of a wolf at will, and in that form practicing cannibalism.

There must be some basis for the existence of that word! I realized that Peter, the maniac, was nothing save a werewolf after he died of heart-failure. But the bullet hole in his head? The strange disappearance of the dead wolf? The short absence of Peter from his bed?

Who can prophesy a soul's journey?

Important!

Change

in

Ghost Stories!

NEW
CONVENIENT
SIZE

Next Month!

BEGINNING with the August issue, GHOST STORIES will appear in a new, slightly smaller size designed to give greater convenience in handling and reading.

There will be no deviation from the standard and type of stories which have made the magazine unique from the moment the first issue appeared on the newsstands two years ago.

In its new, handy form GHOST STORIES will be slightly smaller, 7 by 10 inches outside measurements. We are sure you will welcome the altered size—it will be so easy to carry and to hold.

You will recognize it as usual by the same attractive cover designs which have always identified it among other newsstand periodicals.

Don't Be Misled!

Watch for the
New Size

Ghost Stories

NEXT MONTH

July 1928

Sweetheart of the Snows
By Alan Forsyth

Baldur was in love with a phantom. His wife and his best friend battled for him, but—

TWO FEET DEEP ALONG THE HILLS LAY THE WHITE, SILENT SNOW; six feet deep it would drift in gullies and gorges, dry and crystalline. I think I never saw an afternoon so unearthly still as this one, when the least little breath of wind would have whipped up fantastic shapes of snow, geysers of white glittering dust, and yet not a breath blew. The second-growth pines and hickories—good-sized trees by now, forty years after the last timber cut—held their black branches toward the sky in attitudes of frozen prayer. And the sky was a low inverted basin of gray lead, heavy with dull menace, that stared back and seemed a blank face stricken with cadaverous indifference, the indifference of the eternal to the supplications of any snow-bound forest.

And then as I walked, my boots creaking on the trampled snow of the lonely lane, the first flakes came fluttering from that gray sky. They were huge flakes, big as squirrels' paws, floating slowly down through the silence, as if the silence had mingled into the atmosphere and given it a new density on which the snow lay buoyant. But the wind was coming now, a sough went rustling through the trees; and the snow fell more and more thickly, and now a whole troop of gusty winds chased each other through groves which left off prayer and groaned as they writhed.

I bent my head into the winds and the snow, and made haste. I could feel the flakes gather on my brows and lids, and melt in sweet cool trickles on my cheeks, and moisten my lips with an exquisite flavor of woods and moss and gray snow-water, delicate and fugitive as—as a phantom kiss, I mused, the romancer in me getting the better for a moment of the practical man on a serious mission, who must needs reach his destination before the threat of a blizzard was fulfilled in reality.

Cool as a phantom kiss, I mused. And almost as if in answer to my thought, I heard a sound which brought me up in amazement, and I lifted my head out of the furry collar of my sheepskin and looked around startled, and even a little frightened. It might have been a whistle of wind. It might have been one of those voices of bare branches rubbing together which teases the imaginations of old woodsmen into thinking up tales of such spirits as the lumber jack's "tree-squeak." But it was neither of these.

It was a girl's laugh, blithe, and seductive, and mocking. And as I gazed bewildered about me a scurry of snow swept coiling past me, huffing and whirling . . . and I saw an incredible thing. I saw a figure naked as the trees within that flurry of snow, gathering the very snow itself about hips and bosom like a diaphanous gossamer shift, glancing back over one smooth shoulder at me with a pucker of taunting lips. In the brief instant of that glance, the face impressed itself on my memory so that today I see it as plainly as then: eyes that were green as lichen on an old stump, green-gray with one fleck of strange and subtle vermilion in them; and lips gray as the eyes; and a flowing wealth of hair, finespun and young and sweet, and gray as the lips. . . . Then the snow scattered, the vision was gone, and I sighed and buckled once more into my tramp.

Two minutes later I laughed at myself, for having been deluded by as wild a fancy

as a healthy mind ever conceived. I had been brooding too much, I reflected, over the strange invitation which had called me from my office in lower Broadway, hissing with comfortable steam, to northern New England wrapped in snow and isolation to visit Baldur Blake and his wife Agatha. Agatha, whom I loved, and Baldur, my dear old friend!

Four months before, they had fled New York and I had not had a word from them until this recent letter. In my melancholy understanding of the passionate love that united them, I understood why they didn't write me.

It was I who had brought them together, when Agatha was my betrothed and all the desire of my heart, five years ago. I introduced them, and they loved each other in spite of their efforts not to and their confessions to me; and I had given them my blessing, finally. Agatha kissed me good-by, and I could not bear to be at their quiet wedding. Since then naturally, although we played at being the same good friends—and were indeed, at heart!—there was a strain about our relationship. Perhaps it was my fault, being unable to dissemble the sorrow that the sight of their happiness would give me. We came finally to see each other only at long intervals. They were wonderfully in love! At last Baldur had realized a little money and had taken his bride into the north country. And then, like a wail of terror from a clear sky, came this letter to me.

It was a letter from Baldur, in his own finely wrought handwriting. When I got to the perusal of it, I found it a strange enough missive:

> I haven't done any work for a month. (Baldur was a playwright, and I knew that he had a great theme that he wanted to work out this winter up in the woods.) Perhaps I'm sick. Have you ever heard of any sort of fever that comes with snow, like malaria in the tropics? There ought to be one. I don't know. But how beautiful the snow is, and how very tender! I put my face into it and . . . Last week I went to sleep, something like that, out in the woods; and if Agatha hadn't found me I would have frozen, sure as you're born. Perhaps you'd better come up. Or . . . never mind. Anyway, if you would like a wild week-end in the woods, come on up sometime. No, don't go gawping with any damn fool doctor, I'm not sick. Just . . . like the snow, that's all. . . . BALDUR.

Yes, as I say, when I came to the letter it was a strange enough missive, rambling and incoherent and seemingly hesitant. But I had not opened the envelope for some time. On the outside, scrawled in the handwriting of Agatha but nervously hurried, was another message: *Alan, for my sake, come. I'm afraid. A.*

So I had come. Half an hour before, I got off the train at the little hamlet with its lovely Indian name, Onekama. No one was there to meet me. The ticket-taker seemed to have little hope that I could get a conveyance, but he knew where Baldur's cabin was. It was a three-mile walk; but I'm a good walker, and the directions were simple enough: "Follow the road through the woods."

The old fellow looked into the sky and sniffed. "Feels like a blow comin'," he remarked. "If you wait till mornin' you might get a ride, but then again you mightn't be able to get there. Be a blow most likely before mornin'."

So I left my bag at the station, changing my overcoat for the sheepskin that I had brought, and pulling my heavy oiled boots on in place of my Manhattan oxfords and spats. And I set out alone, too anxious to wait. That Baldur or Agatha had failed to meet me I found not very surprising; perhaps they had not yet got my letter telling of my coming; the mail can be slower than thaw, in the woods country. But Agatha was afraid, and Baldur—was he raving?

Thus I meditated, stumbling on through the flurry with my head into the wind, and trying hard to laugh aside the vision of that mocking glance and laughter which had so startled me. But this was not the final blizzard; it was only a preliminary flurry, and it stopped as suddenly as it began. It vanished into the gray sky and left the world once again silent, hushed, foreboding. I mopped my face with my handkerchief. Topping a rise I looked ahead up the lonely road, and there I saw a figure striding idly toward me. It was Baldur, and apparently he saw me at the same time, for he lifted his hand in a hearty hail.

In a moment he was pumping my hand.

"Will you ever forgive me? There isn't any excuse at all. I just got mixed up with my dreams and walked on and on and forgot that the finest chap in the world might be waiting for me. With"—and his eyes twinkled—"a bottle of gin, maybe. Did you bring a bottle?"

"I did; but it serves you right, I left it in my bag at the station," I said. Baldur's blue eyes twinkled, his cheeks were full and red, his grip was firm and his step resilient. I studied him curiously, but tried not to let him see how curious I was.

And I decided I must not mention Agatha's hurried appeal to me; if he knew about it, he would speak, and if he didn't know, I would wait for Agatha's own explanation.

So, chatting as if nothing in the world were strange about my hasty coming to Onekama, we continued on together. He laughed about his work.

"I'm getting so damned lazy I'm good for nothing at all," he said. "But you know, Alan, this snow fascinates me."

Agatha was well enough but a little lonely, perhaps; my coming would do her a lot of good; it had been wrong of him to drag her away from the excitement of New York. He was forcing himself to speak casually.

Now and then, as Baldur talked, I caught a sly glance out of his eye, and I knew that he was appraising me. For the first time in all the years of our friendship, I began to feel a wall of concealment between Baldur and myself. And the impression grew and grew, until I felt an impulse to shake him by the shoulder and tell him to out with his trouble. But we turned at last out of the road and up a path that crossed a frozen brook and went under a thicket of leaning birches; and there was the cabin, and at the door—my darling, my lost beloved, every year more the lodestar of my dreams!—stood Agatha.

As I kissed her forehead in a big-brotherly fashion, the wind once more went soughing through the birch thicket, and two great lazy flakes settled on her dusky hair.

Could there have been, in the greeting between Agatha and me, cool as hers was and cold as I tried to make mine, some revelation to Baldur that between us was a deeper understanding of what had been going on all winter up in this lonely snow-fast wilderness, than he had known? I cannot say. But from the moment the door swung fast on the three of us, and we stood together in the great low living room where a genial fire roared on the hearth, there was no more concealment. I don't mean that all was explained there at once. But the fact that trouble of some profound and mysterious kind had fallen upon that household was obvious.

Agatha went back to the kitchen to finish preparing dinner. It had been impossible for them to induce a servant to go with them into the wilds, she explained; and she tried to laugh, insisting that she liked to cook, and that her only sorrow was that Baldur brought home no bears for the oven. But her mirth was forced and artificial.

Baldur took me to my room. Upstairs under the eaves of the old farmhouse, it looked out southward and westward on the woods and snowy hills. The gray sky seemed to have wrapped itself even more tightly about the frozen earth. But its grayness was flecked and mottled now with the snow-fall, and the wind drove scuds of white cloud under the trees and over the ridges. A fretful, cramped nervousness came over Baldur. Restlessly he went from chair to window, and window to fireplace, and fireplace to window again. His blue Swedish eyes, as he stood there at the pane looking out, seemed to fill up with the grayness. His mouth would twitch and he puffed furiously at his cigarette. He answered any question I put, in a curt monosyllable, and offered no information of his own, as I washed and made the best of my appearance.

We dined in a feverish mood of distraction, trying to appear at ease, and glad to be together, and light-hearted. Outside, the blizzard howled now, frantically. The drifting of clouds of harried snow against the panes made a soft brushing sound, and the old house creaked in all its beams beneath the wind, and the fire on the hearth leaped and sputtered, blown back now and then by a breath down the chimney which sent puffs of smoke out into the room.

Was it my imagination? I cannot say, but in Baldur's eyes the blue seemed dimming into a cloudy gray, streaked with a wild fire. Long minutes he would brood over his plate, when it would seem I could almost hear him *listening*, for something that was outside, out there in the whirling blizzard. I was not surprised, when I stepped out of the room for a few minutes, to find on my return that he had gone.

"But where?" I asked.

"Outdoors, and God knows where after that!" Agatha paced the room in an anguish of anxiety. "Sit down, Alan. Oh, I'm so glad you've come! I was going mad! And let me try to tell you why—

"You know a great deal about Baldur. I wonder if you knew about his father and his mother? His father, Blake, was the descendant of an Alabama family, a lazy good-for-nothing with some money. How he met and won Baldur's mother, when he was on a trip in Sweden, doesn't matter. He took her, a yellow-haired, outdoors, hyperborean creature, back to Alabama with him. And there she wilted away, neglected by her husband who soon tired of her, drained and enervated by the heat and the indolence of their life. She died, shortly after giving birth to their son.

"So I think perhaps Baldur's love of the northland, his longing for snows and forests long before he ever saw a good deep snow, was born in him out of his mother's longing and spiritual starvation.

"You remember how, in New York, the least scatter of snow in the wind would send him out like a drunken man, to roam on hour after hour along the slushy pavements, with his face lifted to the snow? He used to tell me he liked to feel it blow down his throat. He wanted to feel it on his skin, to go out and run naked in the cold wind.

"And then last fall, when he sold his play and found himself at last with enough money to quit Broadway for a year, he decided to come north.

"Alan, from the first snow last autumn, Baldur has been a different man. I can't explain it. He will get up in the morning with the announcement that he is going to work. For half an hour after breakfast I'll hear him at his typewriter. Then he'll jump up and swing off into the woods with hardly a word of goodbye to me, and perhaps he won't be back until evening. And in the evening he'll sit down to read, and for an hour a book will seem to hold his attention; and then all at once he's off again, and sometimes isn't home before morning.

"I watch him at night, now. It fascinates me, and fills me with terror. He will sit there and stare at one page minute after minute, so that you know he isn't reading. You will notice his hand on the arm of his chair, gripping it so hard that the knuckles stand out bluish white, like ice. And now and then, as he goes, he'll look at me so queerly!"

Agatha dropped wearily into a chair, so pale that I thought for a minute that she would faint.

"But Agatha!" I exclaimed. "He shouldn't leave you alone here at night! I can hardly believe it! He loves you so!"

She looked at me with eyes red-lidded from weeping. How it stabbed me to see her so wretched! Oh, but what a brute Baldur had become in his madness, to subject her to such loneliness and terror! And now, in answer to my exclamation, she shook her head.

"No, Alan, he doesn't love me. Not any more. He—"

Agatha faltered and her eyes dropped. "Yes, you had better tell me, dear!" I insisted; and I drew my chair close to hers and took her hand in mine. "Tell me! I came here to help you, in any way I could. Tell me everything!"

"He— Oh, Alan, I'm afraid of him! He hates me! The way he looks at me when he goes out, there is murder in his eyes! And once I woke up in the middle of the night, and he was bending over me, with—with a knife in his hand!" Blurting out her confession, she burst into a paroxysm of tears; and if I took her head on my shoulder then to comfort her, it was without any feeling of treason to her husband, my friend.

"Dear, my poor dear, my darling!" I murmured. "You can't stay here. Baldur is mad! I must take you away with me, at once!"

Agatha dried her eyes and braced herself, and got to her feet again. "No, no, I can't go!" she murmured.

"Agatha, you must! I understand! You love him, but—"

She tried to smile, my brave sweet girl! "You don't understand, Alan," she said, quietly.

"I don't love Baldur. How can I love him? I love what he was, but what he is I don't love. Love isn't that kind of thing."

"You don't love him!" I cried. And now indeed there was hope in my bosom, for something I had long since given up hoping for. Agatha would be free! Then might she not grow to love me?

"No, I don't love him; he has killed my love. But, you see, I am still his wife. My place is with him, so long as I am that. I must see him through this madness." She thought a moment, and then drew herself up proudly. "If it isn't madness, I could leave; the only thing I could do, and keep my self-respect, is that. But if it is madness, if he is just sick, I must help him."

Rebuked by her fine loyalty, I hung my head. Presently I managed to speak in a voice as cool as hers. "Forgive me, Agatha. I do understand, now. What do you want me to do?"

"Stay here."

"Stay? But I can't leave my office for very long!"

Now Agatha drew her chair to mine, vehement with earnestness. "You must stay, and help me watch him, to see that he doesn't—doesn't come to some horrible, tragic end. If he would come with us I would be glad to go, away from this terrible solitude. But he won't, and I must stay. It is almost spring; in two or three weeks now, the thaw may come. Then the danger will be over. Oh, Alan, you are so good! Won't you stay with me?"

At that moment the great door swung open; a howl of wind rushed in, sweeping a magazine from the table, blowing the curtains out straight before it, whipping the flames on the hearth to a frenzy, scattering snow clear across the room to where we sat, so that I felt the sting of it on my cheeks. Baldur stood in the door, his heavy sheepskin open and his head bare, his yellow hair disheveled and filled with snow, his naked hands raw-red and dripping from cold and wet.

Blank as the face of a man just coming out of a trance were his wet, chapped cheeks, and his eyes were glazed. "I don't know, I—don't know—" he muttered aimlessly; and I saw him sway slightly, as if on the point of collapsing. Then he turned and lurched away through the hall which connected the big living room with the downstairs bedrooms occupied by Agatha and Baldur. I heard the heavy fall of a body on a bed.

. . . "Yes, Agatha, my dear," I whispered. "I love you, and I love, too, what Baldur was; and I'll stay."

So, with trumped up explanations by wire to explain my indefinite absence from lower Broadway, I began my vigil with Agatha over the madman. Or was he mad? There were moments when, although he never got so far as confession or apology, he seemed in his manner to be trying to convey to me the secret of a fascination which was beyond his power to break: the lure that took him plunging out into the blizzard by night or by day, to rove bareheaded through the drifted vales and climb the frozen hills. He made me feel that he was suffering a terrible anguish of body and soul, mingled at times with a joy of body and soul that was no less terrible. He made me feel now and then that he wanted to speak and tell me what afflicted him, but that he dared not.

And Agatha and I kept vigil, praying for spring and thaw and the end of the white madness that haunted us all.

For five days the blizzard continued, until the valleys were deep seas of white, dusty snow—as if the blizzard were trying to drown us in our little shelter. Yes, strange as it may seem, the feeling of a presence in that snow, a snowy spirit who had no love for me or for Agatha, and that was luring Baldur, crept more and more upon me until at last I would have sworn that it was true. At night a man would say, sitting by the leaping hearthfire, that the blizzard wailed and screamed at our door and huffed against the windows. But I knew it was not the blizzard only! It was no voice of any mere wind; it was a woman's wail, a call, a cry of despair, a cry of fierce mockery.

Stepping outdoors one night on some errand, I was met three rods into the night by a whirl of wind and snow so wild that it took my breath away. It seemed to lay cold hands on me and try to throw me down in the drifts; and though I braced myself with legs apart and lowered my head bull-like into the gust, I swayed and bent and nearly fell. And in the middle of this queer encounter with a flurry of snow I felt—I am sure that I felt—icy fingers close savagely on my wrist. What else could it have been that wrenched my arm around behind me so that, unless I had yielded suddenly to the tug—an old wrestler's trick—it would have thrown me over? The darkness and the snow blinded me, I was fighting for every breath, and I could not see. But a wild cry sounded in my ears. Panic seized me. Slipping, sliding, lurching from side to side of the path while the gust fought bitterly against me, I struggled desperately back toward the cabin.

I knew beyond a doubt that if I fell, I would never rise again. Oh, the terrible vindictive hate that I felt in the wind and the snow that night! Those deathly fingers of ice would be at my throat, they would cram my mouth with snow until it froze in my gullet and stifled me; they would bury me in a minute beneath a drift of the snow that surged and sprayed in the wind like billows in a storm at sea.

Beating them back from my face, I blundered at last to the door, and there I slipped. Now it seemed that with a scream of unearthly, murderous joy the snow and the wind pounced upon me. But Agatha, sitting inside by the ingleside, heard the thud of my shoulder against the door as I fell and came to get me, and dragged me in, more dead than alive.

In the depth of my daze, I heard her exclamation: "Alan! Alan! Your head! Look what you have done to your brow! You must have hit it on something!"

Across my brow, when I pulled myself still gasping to my feet and looked in the mirror, was a long, bleeding scratch, from the left temple across and downward, just missing my right eye, clear to my ear. But I had not hit my head! And that was not a bruise! It was a jagged tear, and the thought came to me that one claw—*one sharp finger-nail*—would have left just such a wound as that.

And then I remembered. I knew that the lure which called Baldur out for his crazy wandering all night long, or all day long, the menace which wailed in the heart of the blizzard at our window and which had lain in wait for me that night—all this was in some way connected with the vision I had seen on the lonely road, the day I came to Onekama. I remembered the queer death's-light in those gray eyes shot with dull red; I remembered the mockery of the laugh, as that creature brushed by me, veiling her naked loveliness with a shift of snow. And I shuddered with a new terror, as I pondered.

From far in memory came a name and a verse from one of Lew Sarett's poems of the north country: Kee-way-din, the "ghost of frozen death." But what might that other name, the name of this very haunted solitude—Onekama—mean? Three days later, when the blizzard had abated and I could make my way back to town for my bags, I inquired. I found that

Onekama was the name given by the Indians to a spirit *living in the snow*. A beautiful and fatal woman's body she had, and all who loved her she tempted out into the blizzard, and they were never seen again.

But I remembered more than that. I remembered how the ancient occultists declare that there are spirits, half-heavenly and half-earthly, inhabiting the various elements. The sylph is the spirit of the air, and the salamander the spirit of fire; the gnome of the subterranean grottos, and the undine of the green waves. Then why not a spirit of the snow? The Indians had seen her and had given her a name.

Yes; an *elemental* dwelling in the snow, as did her sister in the pure flame. Around her bare bosom she would wrap the gossamer scarf of the snow, as her sister wrapped the flames around her fiery bosom. In the wail of the blizzard she would scream, and in its gusts she blinded the belated traveler through the wastes, until he stumbled from his path and slipped into the snow; and then—her fingers at his throat!

And it was she who sought Baldur, and whom, in his moments of weakness, he desired to follow. Then for God's sake why didn't he go, I thought; go off and join his glacial beloved, yield himself into the embrace of her gray, deathly sweet arms? Agatha would remain, my Agatha, my beloved! But I put the thought from me, and when I got home from the village that afternoon I greeted Agatha coolly as a distant acquaintance; and I said nothing to her about the undine of the blizzard, the lady of frozen death. I thought it best not to tell her of that.

And what did we do, as the days lengthened and added themselves together, and the gray sky hung lowering over the hills, or the snow-storm went howling up the gullies, to help Baldur? I did a great deal. I saved his life a hundred times. For over Baldur Blake I exercised a strange and compelling influence.

Never once did he confess his anxieties to me, nor did I question or advise him. But I represented to him sanity. I, in my city clothes—heavy, but citified enough for Broadway—represented to him all the normal, healthy world of business and work and achievement. I represented to him too, I think, the love of Agatha. He knew I loved her. He knew that she had been engaged to me, and that my devotion had never wavered. When a man is confronted by someone who loves and treasures one of his possessions, he begins to love and treasure it anew.

So it was enough, when Baldur came creeping out of his room at night, to see me sitting, apparently deep in a book, beside the fire, to bring him to his senses. With some muttered explanation that he couldn't sleep, to which I would reply in kind, neither of us deceiving the other, he would sit down with me. The wild glitter would fade out of his eyes, and presently they would be a drowsy blue filled with weariness; and now and then, his tension broken, he would drop off into a labored sleep there by the fire.

So I lived a night-time existence, leaving Agatha to keep watch by day, except when she needed and called me.

But would the snow never end? It was the middle of March, and still the roads were well nigh impassable with bottomless drifts. For two days it would be quiet, even the sun would shine for a few hours at a time and the surface snow would get soft. But then a new gale would whip out of the west, a weird blindness of snow would fall out of the overcast sky, as if the chill of the uttermost spaces were congealed in those drifting white crystals, falling on the earth. And the old madness would return to Baldur, and he would be gone—if

I was not there to halt him.

I lived by night, sitting alone at the fire. From time to time I would read. From time to time, for hours on end, I would listen, frozen with terror, to the wail of the wind, the *whushing* of the snow across the roof, the heaving of it at the windows; and then I would not have stepped out of doors, into the power of the malevolent, beautiful spirit of that snow, for all that a man could offer! I would not have gone outdoors for anyone in all the world—except for Agatha.

Yes; sometimes when it was quiet outdoors I would sit hours on end in front of the fire and dream of her, and long for the tenderness of her bosom. I knew that Baldur loved her no more as he had loved her at first, with the joy of the bridegroom. I knew that she loved him no more; this was merely her duty as she saw it that she was doing. I knew, I knew by the intuition which tells every lover when he may take his mistress' hand, I knew she loved me. And I loved her.

Then I would shake from my reverie, with a curse at my own falsity. "Dear God, give us spring!" I would cry in my heart. "Melt away this snow and this terror and the wailing of this murderous, cruel, deathly blizzard! Give us thaw and sunshine, and then once more Baldur will be sane; and then . . . ah, then we shall see!"

But one night I could not rouse from my reverie.

Easter was coming, and this was the first day of spring by the astronomer's calculations; yet it might as well have been mid-January so far as one could see. The snow lay so deep that the lower boughs of the great spruce trees would be buried in it. All day the sky hung, ashen-gray and heavy with the menace of even more snow, low over the trees. In the afternoon the blizzard began, and on and on late into the night it raged. It shook the whole house in its fury until the windows rattled and the very beams creaked, and you could feel the sway of the floor as you walked. Then toward midnight suddenly it ceased. I went to the window and looked out. The clouds withdrawing were far in the east. Immediately over us was a full moon, so burningly bright that not a star could be seen until, staring fixedly into the swirl of moonlight, you discerned at last a few faint pins of light. All silver, and the hill beneath deep, deep in silent snow.

I went back to my chair and sat down. After the torment, the silence left me with nerves utterly shaken, so that my hands shook like poplar leaves. And the thought came into my mind, *What if spring never comes?* What if spring delays, held back by the malign spirit of the beautiful and deathly wraith of the snow, until at last I am caught some night when I can't fight back to the door, or Baldur goes to his death, or *Agatha* goes and never returns. The idea struck me rigid with horror. It was unconscionable for me to allow her to stay here any longer, always under the shadow of hovering death; oh, it was all right to think of Baldur; he had been fine, he might be fine again some day when the spell was broken, the spell of this frozen solitude! But it was not all right to sacrifice Agatha to that chance! Agatha was fine, *now*. She must come with me, away, to safety!

From under the door of her chamber, which in that old farmhouse opened directly off the great living room where I sat in helpless longing, I saw a light. She was awake!

Impelled by a desire I could no longer control, I tiptoed to her door and softly, very softly, I knocked. I could hear her slippered feet scurry across the carpet. She hesitated a moment, and then the door opened. In a deep red padded-silk dressing gown she stood, her black hair falling in rich braids over her shoulders. She had been crying; her sweet eyes were moist with tears. I opened my arms and she came to me, her whole body clinging to mine with a fierce and despairing eagerness. I bent my face to kiss her, and at that gesture, very gently, she drew away.

"No," she whispered. "No, my darling, not now! We can't, now!"

I followed her, and without the least fear or surprise she shut her door behind us. We were alone in her chamber.

Then I fell on my knees and all my thoughts, my fears and my desires, poured out of me in a torrent as I knelt before her, clasping her, her sweet hand on my brow and her fine eyes gazing at me tenderly.

"Agatha, Agatha, I love you!" I said. "I worship you! Come with me! I'm afraid for you here in the madness of this lonely place. There is, I know it now, there is a malevolent phantom out there in the snow, and she will kill you if she can. Once she tried to kill me, and without your aid she would have succeeded. Come with me! We have some right to happiness in life, and life is so terribly short! And this is a region of horror and death. I can't let you stay! Come with me!"

She drew me to my feet, and through her tears she smiled. "Tomorrow, I will go with you," she whispered, "if Baldur will come. But you mustn't lose heart! Happiness that is built on deceit and treason will never last. We must be brave, and keep on fighting."

"But spring will never come!" I cried. "This is no natural winter; it is all a trance, an ugly dream, a witchcraft, the work of a malign spirit!"

She rebuked me gently with a glance. "Yes, spring will come. I'm praying for it. There may be evil in the world, but there is also God."

"Oh, but I love you!"

She put her hands on my shoulders and let me fold her once more in my arms. "I love you too, Alan," she murmured. "I will tell you that. But you must not forsake me. And now—you must go."

My heart bounding so that I could not think, I let myself out of that chaste and passionate boudoir. How long I stood on the other side, by myself in the great living room, I don't know; it could only have been a minute. Then I leaped across the room, for the outside door stood open! Someone had opened it while I was with Agatha! Baldur had escaped me!

What I saw as I reached it, I can never find words to describe, for all the eerie cold magic of it, the beauty, and the horror! In the full, chill light of the moon two figures were running down the hill, over the snow, toward the woods, both naked and unashamed. One of them was a girl's; her smooth young body seemed to be all a soft jade-green in the moonlight, and the long wild locks of hair that streamed across her bare shoulders as she ran were of a cool, delicate, luminous gray. She looked back over her shoulder, with a smile on her strange face that for one moment transfixed my heart with utter desire. And the other figure, running stumblingly after her, knee-deep sometimes in the snow, with both hands held out beseechingly, was a man's. It was Baldur Blake.

They were a hundred yards away already, going downhill toward the blue fringe of the woods. As I looked, I saw Baldur stumble and fall in the deep snow. But with a gesture of sudden sweetness the girl's form paused, and she leaned down, reaching forth her hand; and I saw Baldur seize it, press it to his lips madly, and get to his feet. Together now they ran, they seemed to be dancing, with lifted knees. Before I could gather wit enough to cry out, they were gone.

There was no second to lose. Stark mad, perhaps, Baldur had gone!

At any rate, he was naked; he would perish out there. For one moment the impulse seized me to let him go and be done with all my agony. Agatha would be mine! But I fought down the temptation and, crying aloud to warn her, I hastily pulled on my sheepskin and fur cap.

Clear in the snow were the footprints of one running figure—*only one*. Yes, I had seen truly; there were two shapes in the moonlight over the snow, but only one of them with heavy mortal feet had trod it down. Terror gripped my heart, and yet I must continue. The pistol that I carried in my sheepskin pocket would do me no good in a case like this. What spirit would fear a pistol? Yet I held fast to it, for the mere comfort that the feeling of the smooth butt in my fingers gave me. A hundred yards I went. There was no sight or sound now of my quarry; I must follow the tracks. But they were clear enough, in the bright moon!

Until, suddenly, they ceased! The snow here had been tossed and threshed; this must have been where Baldur fell. But he arose and went on with her! I had seen that! Then why were there no tracks?

Stupidly in my bewilderment I ran around in circles there for a few minutes. I called: "Baldur! Baldur!"

There was no answer. A crazy presentiment seized me, and I hurried madly back to that trampled place where he had fallen; and reaching into the snow I felt—his body!

It had been only dusted over with the fine, white, deathly flakes. It lay there, dead. On the face was a smile.

Spring came to Onekama the next morning, a burst of spring that seemed as if pent and at last loosed by the soft word of a chaste prayer. In a day the snow was gone, the mountain streams were torrents of sparkling, singing water. Birds showed up from nowhere.

"See," cried Agatha, calling me to the door, "there is a robin!"

And there he was, jocund red-breast, flitting his wings and hopping industriously about in search of dinner after his long flight.

And the day that Agatha and I—our trunks sent on ahead of us—strolled down the road toward town, we found both crocuses and violets. She found them. I put them in her hair. And we said one prayer for Baldur, and one for us.

Painted Upside Down

By Mark Shadow
As told to Robert W. Sneddon

The great ghost detective solves a mystery far stranger than a crime.

IT NEVER TAKES ME LONG TO MAKE UP MY MIND. To this I attribute such success as has been mine in the profession which has more or less been forced upon me—that of psychic investigator.

I pressed the button on the desk in the front room of my little house, looking out into Eleventh Street, New York City, and Maurice showed up immediately.

"Maurice," I said, "there's a girl walking up and down on the opposite side of the street, looking over at this house as if she wanted to come across, but hadn't the nerve to. Suppose you go to the door and look out as if you wanted to call a taxi. If the girl comes over and asks for me, bring her right in. Her behavior suggests a mystery."

Maurice never questions me. He is the perfection of servants, a Frenchman who has become an admirable citizen without losing his distinctive birth marks.

I watched out of the window, and I was not disappointed. The girl hesitated and came across. In a minute she was in my room. Tall, slender, dark. I had a renewal of the impression that I had seen her before.

"I can recommend this chair," I said.

"Oh, Mr. Shadow, I really didn't mean to—" she broke off and tugged at her gloves.

"Well, what does it matter what you meant?" I said cheerfully. "Here you are, and no one comes to see me—outside of my close friends—who hasn't a purpose."

"You don't know my name," she said, as if surprised, "but I know yours. You bought one of my pictures at the Independents this year. My name is Margaret Hawthorne."

"Oh, yes! 'Sand Dunes'—of course. A very distinctive piece of work. You see how nicely I have hung it over there. Delighted to meet you, Miss Hawthorne."

"Perhaps I shouldn't tell you, Mr. Shadow—it's not very tactful—but until you bought my picture, I didn't know who Mark Shadow was."

"I can't hold that against you," I said smiling. There was something adorably naive in her manner.

"But now," she continued, "I've heard of so many people you've helped—people who didn't understand things, and got frightened."

"Are you frightened?"

"Terribly," she answered with direct sincerity. "There was no one I could confide in. I had to come to you. You liked my work, and I thought you might understand."

"That was right, Miss Hawthorne."

Now that she had come to the point, the whole atmosphere of the room was charged. I could feel the tension of her anxiety.

"I made up my mind to come to you, but when I got out there, my courage gave out and—"

I did not tell her that I had seen her from my window, and had caught her mental signal of distress.

"Now you are here," I reassured her. "Nothing could be luckier. I haven't a thing on my mind at present. Suppose you start your story at the beginning."

"Perhaps you'll think me silly," she began. "If you do, stop me. When my people died, I thought I had a lot of money, so I came to New York, to the Village here, and I took a studio that was too expensive for me. I was living on capital, but I thought before long I'd be making money hand over fist—the dream all artists have. I ought to have taken a job as a commercial artist, and painted in any spare time I had, but it's too late to think of that. Well, last month, I came to my senses, and figured things out. I had a hundred and eighty dollars, my studio furniture and a pile of canvases. I couldn't go on, that was plain. I knew just one thing to do. I own an old house on the shore of the Sound, miles from anywhere. It's been in the family for nearly two hundred years, and came to me from an uncle—Father's brother. I packed up, sold my furniture, and got the landlord to let me go. I settled myself in the old house."

"Alone?" I asked.

She hesitated.

"Yes—I—why yes, there's nobody living with me, but—"

"I understand," I said gently. "You feel you are not quite so alone as you seem to be."

She nodded, and all at once she broke down.

"Oh, Mr. Shadow. What am I to do? I simply have to live there till I get going, but it's getting on my nerves—the horrible whispers—it's as though the whole house kept whispering in a weird, uncanny way."

"Quite so," I said calmly. "That's nothing unusual. There's an explanation of that somewhere. And what do the whispers say?"

"That's the horrible part of it. I lie awake at night, straining my ears, listening so fearfully. Perhaps if I could make out what the whispers said, I wouldn't mind it so much, but it's not knowing that is so dreadful."

"Anything else out of the ordinary?"

She hesitated.

"It's ever so strange, but something is happening to my work. I'll start to paint the rocks and the water, and then I'll suddenly find myself doing something else."

"What, for instance?"

"Painting some other subject. So far, it hasn't taken form or shape—just daubs—yet there's a vague suggestion of dark human shapes. I can't explain it—only it makes me shudder as though it were something nasty—unclean."

I looked at my engagement book.

"I'd like to see this whispering house of yours," I said.

"Oh, would you?" she asked eagerly, and then her face fell.

"And if I do anything to help you, you'll give me another canvas just as good as 'Sand Dunes.' Is that a bargain?"

A look of relief leapt into her face.

"Oh, but your time—it's not right!"

"I'm really interested," I said. "Don't worry about my not being repaid. I may be paid very well. When can we go?"

"We? Must I go, too?" she asked.

"Absolutely. I must find out—you'll forgive me saying this—if you are in any way responsible for the phenomenon. Whether it is produced through you as a medium."

"Oh, but how could I? I hear the whispering, and it makes me afraid."

"Quite so, but there are instances where people hear knockings, and these knockings stop when they leave the scene. It has been proved that they are the wholly unconscious mediums for the production of these noises. Do you know anyone who would go with you?"

She thought for a minute.

"I think I can get Janet Dunlop. She's a good sport."

"Right! I'll bring Maurice whom you just saw at the door. He'll attend to the food part of the picnic."

"Picnic!" she echoed. "So you don't think there's anything to be alarmed at?"

"Not if we keep our heads," I told her, but perhaps I might have done better to warn her of the dangers ahead. After all, when one opens a door by accident into the dark past, and some vile aspect peeps out, it is well to be armed at all points. Here was a house venerable with age, impregnated with the record of deeds, good and evil. What its history held, I had no idea; but that it was black, I already had a shrewd suspicion. I made up my mind to guard against all risks.

As the "Whispering House" has within the past few weeks changed hands, Miss Hawthorne having found a purchaser for it, I do not feel at liberty to state its exact location. One must be careful to steer clear of the laws of libel, and not state a house to be what is usually called "haunted."

The house is visible, however, to passengers on ships traversing the Sound. Perched on a promontory of rock, its clapboards are gray and silvered with age, fretted with the sand blasts of many a gale. It is three stories in height, built on a substantial base, with deep cellar. A hexagonal look-out room rises a floor higher. Built of massive timbers, its framework is as perfect as the day it was erected. There is at least one paneled room which I would like to have, but to tear it from its setting would be vandalism.

Behind the house is a barn, and there are several sheds attached. A few trees stand in the midst of a stony pasture.

I drove Miss Hawthorne, her somewhat silent girl friend, and Maurice to the house, two days after our interview. It was a cool drive on this April day, and inwardly I wondered what sort of cold cheer I was letting myself in for.

I ran the car into the barn and we went on to the house. As we stepped inside, I shivered involuntarily with the chill of the place.

"This will never do," I said, "I suppose there's some way to heat the house."

There was a furnace, and Maurice disappeared down the steps to the cellar. We heard him raking the bars vigorously. Meanwhile, I got a blaze going in what was the principal living room, and the two girls set the table, and then went up to the bedroom overhead. I planned that Maurice and I should sleep in the living room. A knock on the floor would rouse us in case of need.

I started a fire in the kitchen stove and set a kettle of water on it, and while waiting for it to boil I climbed upstairs. I looked into each empty room, and very musty and chill they all were. I saw nothing out of the ordinary, nor did I have any warning of anything unseen.

On the top floor, I came to the ladder up into the look-out room, and climbing it I was taken with a faint dizziness, a most unusual thing for me. For a moment, I clung to the ladder with both hands. The vertigo passed. It was quite unaccountable, and it puzzled me, especially as I felt myself without reason stooping my head as if afraid it might strike upon something overhead where obviously there was nothing.

I stood for a moment in the look-out room with its windows on all six sides. There was a seat all round it, and a table with a telescope. Over the table was a heavy iron hook screwed into a beam, from which probably a lantern had been suspended. The dust was thick here. Nobody had been up for ages.

I came down, and as I set foot on the dusty floor I paused abruptly. I could see my own footprints plainly, but beside them were others—newly made—the unmistakable marks of a naked foot. The prints stopped at the foot of the ladder. I traced them to the landing, and there they ended. They had not been there when I crossed the floor, and yet I had heard no sound. I examined the prints. Each toe mark was widely separated, as though the person were given to going without shoes. I stood for a little, startled, as was Crusoe when he saw a savage footprint on the shore of his desert island. Whatever inhabited the house had not been long in showing it meant to attach itself to me.

"Mr. Shadow! Oh, Mr. Shadow!" Miss Hawthorne's voice recalled me to pleasanter thoughts, and I came down. I saw the question in her eyes, as I entered the living room, and I shook my head.

"Not a thing," I said lightly. "I don't suppose you ever saw anything strange."

"If I did, I'd jump out of my skin, I think," she said.

"Does Miss Dunlop know what's on?" I asked.

"I told her about the whispering, that's all. She's dying to hear it."

"Wonderful timber in the house," I commented. "These beams in the ceiling. They look like ship's timber."

"They are. You see my people were ship owners in the old days."

"Whalers?"

"No. I don't think so. They traded with Africa principally."

There was a question on my lips, but I kept it for another time.

We gathered about a comparative cozy supper table. There was a fair heat coming up from the furnace, and Maurice had prepared us a remarkable meal in the circumstances.

I noticed Miss Dunlop looking expectantly at the kitchen door, and finally she turned to Miss Hawthorne:

"What does your old woman do, Margaret? Doesn't she wait on the table?"

"What old woman, Janet?"

"The one who opened the bedroom door after you went downstairs. I was fussing with my hair at the mirror, and all at once I saw the door open and an old woman peer in. When she saw me, she shut the door again."

"Why, Janet. You must have been dreaming. There's no old woman in the house," said Miss Hawthorne in amazed tones.

"I couldn't see her face—she had on a sort of funny old hood or cap, and—goodness!—did you say there was no old woman?" She stopped and stared at us with a horrified expression. "What is it? Don't tell me I've seen a ghost. I am scared to death."

She began to shiver.

"Drink some hot coffee this minute," I said sharply. "Now, let us get this straight. You didn't actually see her. You only saw a reflection in the mirror."

"I certainly saw the door open, and then this—this thing looked in—I saw her hand on the door. You don't suppose, Mr. Shadow, she's the one who's doing the whispering?"

"I can hardly answer that. The main thing is, not to be afraid. You know any apparition—and I don't say definitely that your old woman was one—gets the power to appear, pretty much from the waves of fear you throw out. You become a sort of electrical apparatus, which creates the usual ghost. Not always, however; I won't say that. So don't be afraid. Courage is a strong armor against such intruders."

I did not add—there was no need to alarm these young ladies any more than could be helped—that in many cases of hauntings, the most brave and fearless are as helpless as children against the attack of the evil creatures which materialize out of the atmosphere, the ghouls, the vampires, the shapeless monsters of the borderland.

Nothing of an alarming nature happened during this first night under the roof of the old house, though at some hour of the morning I was awakened by a faint sound as of someone whispering; but, with the consciousness of the sound, the noise stopped instantly. I thought I must have been dreaming, and dozed off to sleep again. No one was disturbed in the night, and we met at breakfast cheerfully.

I spent the morning prowling about the house. Somewhere in it was secreted the moving force of whatever haunted it, the focus point of evil. There was a fair-sized library of old books, and I went through them carefully but without finding a clue. Much may be gleaned from a local history, or personal writing such as a diary, but there was nothing of the kind here.

Miss Hawthorne showed me one of her spoiled paintings, as she called them, and I studied it for a time.

"Do you mind if I turn it upside down?" I asked. "Now, does that suggest anything to you?"

She looked at it puzzled, gasped slightly, and said:

"Why, it looks like an African scene—or what I imagine an African scene must look like—and there are figures—and this circle certainly looks like a drum—there's a man with a drum, I'm sure—how amazing!"

"They are celebrating some heathen rite, round an idol. This hideous shape might be an idol. You've heard of spirit writing? Well, this might be spirit painting, Miss Hawthorne. You said your ancestors knew Africa?"

"Yes, but I've never been there. I don't know the first thing about it—about the coloring."

"I have seen some sketches of the West Coast, and I must say this is suggestive of them. Whoever is at your elbow prompting you, or working through you, knows Africa. You might call this an African primitive—it might be done by a native with a smattering of art as we know it. There is no doubt this is a picture of a ceremony. It grows on you as you look at it."

"It does," said Miss Dunlop. "I can see exactly what you mean. There is action in it. It's really a very vivid picture, Margaret."

"But why should I paint it upside down?" asked the artist. "No wonder I couldn't make out what it was."

"Some people do mirror-writing automatically; that is, writing which has to be held up to a mirror before it can be read. This, no doubt, is something of the kind."

"Well, I don't like it," she said decidedly, "and I won't be happy till we find out what is wrong with this old house."

I sent the two girls out with Maurice in the car, in the afternoon. No sooner were they gone than I went up to the look-out room. That peculiar sensitiveness to occult trouble which has assisted me in other cases had warned me that the room would bear further investigation. I was not mistaken. I was quite prepared for a repetition of that faint dizziness which had overtaken me on my first visit, but not for the experience which for a moment checked the beating of my heart.

As I took my foot from the topmost step of the ladder, about to step into the hexagonal chamber, my ankle was gripped in a grasp of steel. An unseen bony hand had encircled my ankle. I could almost feel the individual pressure of fingers and thumb. Powerless to move my leg, I tottered uncertainly. Then I toppled forward, luckily for me, not backward. Had I fallen backward, I would have gone down the trap and broken my neck, or at least some of my bones, on the floor below.

As I went forward, I thought my ankle would snap, and then the pressure was gone as mysteriously as it had come. I peered down. Of course, there was no one there. I turned down my sock and looked at the angry red ring on my ankle. It was only by good luck that it was neither sprained nor broken.

Things were growing warmer now. Whatever was in command of the house was not going to stop at harmless pranks. Violence was in the air. This was no playful poltergeist moving furniture and throwing pots and pans about, but a dangerous entity, animated with murderous malice. I had received definite warning to mind my own business.

But this was not the first time I had received such a message, and I was not to be moved from my purpose by it. From this moment onward, however, I could not afford for a second to relax my vigilance. At any instant, the forces of evil now spread throughout the house might gather to one point and strike—even with death.

Something had happened in the past in this very look-out room which was being mirrored in my experience. I must find out if possible, and be ready to avert another tragedy of a like nature.

I came down that ladder very warily but composedly, and back to the living room. As I entered it, I could have sworn someone went out of the room and into the kitchen adjoining. There is a certain movement of atmospheric particles which signals that someone has been in a room, and besides, the door to the kitchen, a swing one, was vibrating slightly.

I darted forward and into the kitchen. There was a faint sound of lightly slippered feet slipping down the stone stairs to the cellar, and I followed. There was nothing visible when I reached the stone-paved floor—the place was dim and I had no light—and I was just turning away when I heard a faint whisper at my ear. I turned my head sharply. Within a couple of feet of me I saw a little old woman—or something which resembled the shape of one—and with a prickling of my scalp I saw that where there should have been a face was nothing—a white smooth surface without features, encircled by a hood.

I did not hesitate, but shot out my hand. I touched nothing but the wall, or rather the end of a beam projecting from the wall. I recoiled and scuttled upstairs, as startled as any amateur ghost hunter. There had been something especially repulsive about this white mask, as though it cloaked a horror too grim for human eyes.

But I did not escape scot free. Close to me up the cellar stairs followed this whispering—irritating as the dripping of a tap—which became a torture almost as unbearable as must have been, the single drop-drop of water upon the shaven skull of a prisoner of the Inquisition. As it continued without cessation, the ear strained to catch the inaudible syllables, till the nerves provoked by impatient curiosity were raw and tingling.

The others, when they came home for supper, heard the whispering the moment they entered the house.

"Now you know," said Miss Hawthorne. "I used to lie awake waiting till I could make out what was being said, but I never learned. It wasn't like one person whispering; it was as though the whole house, every plank and beam in it, were trying to convey a message to me—only I couldn't tell whether for good or for bad."

"I can stand most things," said Miss Dunlop, after we had eaten supper to the accompaniment of the infernal whispering. "That old woman didn't really scare me until I knew she was not supposed to be there, but this ceaseless whispering gets me. It's too uncanny for words. If only we could find out what was being said!"

"We may—at any time," I answered, "and when we do, the trouble will be very nearly over. It is the pent-up desires and unfulfilled purposes of those who have gone which lie at the root of all troubles of this kind. A man going upon some desperate errand who is killed in an accident, is likely to linger close to earth—to be earthbound by his anxiety until the burden of care is lifted from the person concerned. You know how unsettled you are yourself until you have carried out something you've planned to do. If you die before you have a chance to put it across, you may not do so your own self after death, but that desire may be transmitted to another. Only—here is the danger: your desire may be captured on the way by some soulless thing waiting for such a chance to gain a spark of ghostly life, and used by it to wreck and not to benefit human life. Therein lies the danger. But this is dull stuff, isn't it? What about a game of bridge?"

After our game, we settled round the fire.

"Now, Miss Hawthorne," I said quietly, as I saw that the cards had played their part in quieting her nerves, "I want you to think back. Tell me what you can about your ancestors. Tell me the history connected with them and this house."

"I am ashamed to know so little, but I'll do my best," she volunteered.

• • •

There was nothing about her father and mother, good people as they must have been, except that they died at a too early age of influenza, nor of her grandparents; but when we came to the period of Amos Hawthorne, her great-grandfather, I felt sure I was on the track.

Amos had made a comfortable fortune in a way considered quite reputable in his day. He had shipped hogsheads of rum, bales of cloth and cheap muskets to the Guinea coast, bringing back ivory, white and black. He had made a number of voyages, each time carrying a cargo to Newport or Charleston of hundreds of unfortunate blacks, packed between decks like herrings. Retribution must have struck him suddenly, for he was found hanging in the look-out room where he spent much of his time when ashore.

"There's a horrid hook up there yet," added Miss Hawthorne. "I wouldn't go up to that room at night for worlds. One of the house slaves found him. They say he cut the tongue out of one of his slaves, but whether this was the one, or whether the story was just hearsay, I don't know. You know how these tales get twisted as they come down, and of course they were only whispered in the family. There's no doubt Great-grandfather Amos was a brutal old man—and what he must have been when he was younger and on his own poop deck, heaven only knows! They say my great-grandmother was scared to death of him. Once in a fit of fury he caught her by the throat and nearly strangled her. He injured her so, she never could raise her voice above a whisper."

"Oh, my God!" cried Miss Dunlop, jumping up to her feet and looking over her shoulder. "Then it's she who's doing the whispering—she must be in this room with us. She's the old woman I saw, don't you think, Margaret? Oh, why can't she tell us what she wants and be done with it?"

As we sat there in the fire-lit room with its shadowy corners, in the silence which had fallen upon us all after this suggestion of the identity of the whisperer, the sound seemed to grow in intensity, pleading, pulling at us. But now there was added to it another sound, like the subdued and stifled growl of some savage animal.

Maurice raised his head suddenly, and the cigarette dropped from his fingers.

"Hush!" he said softly, leaning forward. "A drum—I hear a drum—far away, surely. What—"

I looked at him in surprise. I heard no such sound, and all at once I came to my senses. The power beyond had nearly managed to divert my attention. I turned to look at Miss Hawthorne. She had risen to her feet and was almost at the door. Something in the rigidity of her body startled me into action. I leaped to my feet and set myself in her path.

"You must not leave the room. Return to the fire. Now! At once. Obey me. Now!"

I summoned all my will power to enforce my repeated command.

She appeared to shake herself free from something drawing her forward—in no other way can I express her action—and looked at me with amazed eyes.

"Why! What did you say? I forget what I was going upstairs for. How silly of me."

"Don't bother just now," I said, with a warning glance at the others. "Put some more wood on, Maurice. And what about some coffee?"

He went out, and I heard him stirring in the kitchen.

We talked spasmodically for a little, and then I called out:

"How about that coffee, Maurice? Isn't it ready yet?"

There was no reply, and urged by sudden alarm, I signed to the girls to stay where they were and went hastily into the kitchen. There was no sign of Maurice, and then I discovered him. He was struggling to close the back door, feet firmly planted on the floor, his back bent like a bow with the strain. He knew I had come in, and over his shoulder he managed to squeeze out a muffled, "Help!"

I threw my weight against the door. For a moment, I felt its stubborn resistance, then it closed quite easily.

"What's the matter?" I asked, as Maurice straightened up, puffing.

"Matter! I was by the sink here, and I looked up—and *voilà*—through the window against the glass, like in the morgue, a negro with a knife through the throat here—and such eyes. I rush to the door which is open, and just as I begin to close, I feel him push—and such a push! But, sir, it is a dead man who push. I have seen many dead—I help bury them in France—but a dead negro—many years dead—ough!"

"You'd better take the coffee pot in, Maurice," I said. I saw he was genuinely scared. "I'll lock this door."

"I do not fear the dead, but the dead who walk—with a knife through the jugular—that is not so agreeable. And one who looks like a mummy—yes, that is what he is, a mummy negro. What a house!"

"If you want to go home, Maurice," I told him, "I won't keep you. I won't think any the less of you for going, either."

That touched him on the raw. He drew himself up stiffly.

"But no, to run away! To leave you and the ladies! No, indeed. Only when I go in the kitchen, I leave the door open, eh!"

So we left it at that.

Eleven o'clock found us still by the fire. A wind had risen and was screeching about the eaves of the house. But loudly as it howled, it did not drown the sound of that unholy whispering, nor yet the suggestion of bestial snarling which punctuated it at irregular intervals.

Our conversation died down, till finally midnight found us ourselves reduced to whispering. The effect was grotesque. But the rivalry of whispering was too much. I saw it must stop, so I sprang to my feet with a show of briskness.

"Bedtime! You two girls better go up to bed, and Maurice and I will get some sleep here. If you hear us moving about, don't leave your room. And, of course, we're here, so don't be afraid to knock if you feel at all anxious or hear any suspicious noise."

I thought they were a bit subdued as they went upstairs, but I set an oil lamp in an alcove half up the stairs to their floor, which helped to dispel the shadows. There is always danger in the shadow.

I did not trouble to undress, and lay down on the cot near the door to the hall where I could hear the slightest movement. Maurice lay down also. I heard him sigh once or twice, then his even breathing told me he was asleep. Sleep was not to be mine this night, I had made up my mind to that. I knew instinctively that the crisis was at hand. The atmospheric station had broadcast a danger signal, and I was keyed up to any encounter.

I sent my mind back to past triumphs over the powers of evil, to my handling of that case which came to be called "The Thing in the Chest,"* and to the conclusion of "The Oakdale Ridge Vampire"†; but try as I would, my mind began to wander, my eyelids crept closer. I shook myself awake and fixed my attention on the whispering. Could I read into its indistinct sounds any suggestion of connected speech?

---

* "In Terror of Laughing Clay," Ghost Stories, October 1926.

† "The Vampire of Oakdale Ridge," Ghost Stories, December 1926.

• • •

Suddenly my mind jumped to attention, as though a bugle had been blown in my ear. Could I have been asleep? I sat up, every sense now alert. The wind had gone. The fire was dead—all but a speck of flame flickering in its center. Maurice slept as though dead. I touched him, and he did not move. All was peaceful and quiet. Serenity reigned.

And then in a twinkling I knew everything was wrong, terribly wrong, and that this peace, this imponderable silence which lay upon the house, was a shout—a warning shout of danger!

There was not the faintest sound of a whisper.

Overhead, a faint trickle of sound crept down to me. Someone was moving overhead with utmost precaution.

It took me but an instant to grab my flashlight and slip on the moccasins I use as undress house shoes. As I reached the landing, I was amazed to see Miss Hawthorne come from her room and without hesitation go towards the stairs to the third floor. She carried no light, but made her way without faltering. To all appearances she was walking in her sleep, and I knew there was only one thing for me to do—to follow her and see that she came to no harm.

She went up the stairs, unconscious that I was at her heels, and made for the ladder of the look-out room. She set her bare foot on the first step, ready to go up, and at that moment I noticed she was carrying a cord of some kind in her hand—it looked like the belt of a dressing gown. The suggestiveness of this rope leaped to my mind at once. I had a panicky vision of her body dangling to the hook above, and of my stooping my head to clear the quivering white feet.

Some vile, malevolent influence was prompting her to a death such as had befallen her great-grandfather.

I put out my hand instinctively to catch the sleeve of her silk negligee. As I did so, something disengaged itself from the shadows. I can only describe it as a shadow from the floor which leaped up at me. A horrid odor filled my nostrils and all but stole away my senses, and as I reeled I felt a hand clutch at my throat. A red mist swam before my eyes, as bony fingers searched for my life. And then I felt Miss Hawthorne fall against me, and involuntarily I threw out my arm.

No doubt, the contact of our two bodies produced some disturbing shock. In that instant the compression was gone from my throat.

Miss Hawthorne gave a shudder, and looked at me.

"Whatever—" she exclaimed amazedly.

"You've been walking in your sleep," I said. "I heard you, luckily. You were just going up the ladder here."

"I—how horrible. I might have hurt myself." She looked down at the cord she was still holding, and raised it to the light of my flash. "What on earth—this is the cord from Janet's dressing gown—it's her brother's old one, really—she brought it because it was warmer—what a queer thing to be carrying round!"

"You'd best go back to bed, or you'll catch cold," I told her.

She caught my arm nervously.

"Listen—isn't that Janet calling?"

She ran downstairs, while I followed her. Miss Dunlop was standing at the door of the bedroom.

"Oh, there you are, Margaret! Thank heavens. I had the most horrible dream. I dreamed the old lady came into the room and began trying to pull me out of bed, telling me to go and save you. You were in terrible danger from Hannibal, upstairs in the look-out room, and I couldn't move hand or foot. It was terrible, and she kept shaking at me, whispering in my ear, and I could make out every word: 'Go save her from that devil—he killed Amos—he'd like to kill us all, him and his old idol in the cellar.' "

"Whatever are you talking about, Janet?" said Miss Hawthorne. She turned to me. "Janet must be asleep still."

Miss Dunlop made an indignant protest.

"Sleep nothing. I'm awake now for the rest of the night. What a dream! I feel as if I were pinched black and blue. I never knew anything so real. And being able to make out what the old lady was whispering—such a story!"

"Well, she seems to have gotten over her story at last," I said.

"But why to me?" asked Miss Dunlop. "Why not to Margaret, since she is the old lady's great-granddaughter?"

"I suppose because this negro, Hannibal—a negro slave probably—stood between. Margaret was the center of conflict. One wanted to help her, the other to hurt her because she was a Hawthorne. She was to keep on paying for a sin of the past—some cruelty to the negro, no doubt. The message had finally to be delivered to someone who had a sensitive streak. You have Celtic blood in you, Miss Dunlop, haven't you?"

"On both sides. Irish and Highland Scottish."

"That accounts for your being a receiving instrument. Well, I feel that the show is over for tonight."

"I hope so," said Miss Hawthorne wearily. "I don't think I can stand any more."

"You won't have to," I assured her. "We are near the end now. The things which have happened tonight were the last incidents of the struggle."

I left them at the bedroom door and came downstairs. In some strange way, even the air of the house felt purer. Maurice was still sleeping quietly. That has always appealed to me as perhaps the strangest incident of the whole night.

Next morning, we all went down to the cellar. Miss Dunlop insisted on that, and I was eager myself to test the statement as to the idol. I turned my attention at once to that beam, against which I had placed my hand through the phantom of the old woman. Both Maurice and I tried to move it, but without any success. We attacked the mortar in which it was set, with a crowbar, and after some hours of labor we managed to withdraw the beam. I could not help giving a satisfied exclamation. The concealed end was rudely carved into a hideous image.

"This must have been brought from Africa and built into the house in some way," I said. "You know it isn't at all unlike the idol in that African picture of yours, Miss Hawthorne."

"It's very like it," she said in an awed voice. "I might almost have used it as a model."

Maurice, who had been probing in the recess exposed by the withdrawal of the beam, drew back his hand with a smothered grunt.

"There's something here, sir. Perhaps the ladies ought to go upstairs."

"No!" they protested.

"Well, there's a lot of bones here—a skull with skin on it—and some kind of box."

"Let's have the box, Maurice, first."

He pulled out a brass box, and as he did so the lid fell off the hinges. There was a tatter of old rags in it.

"Treasure!" said Miss Dunlop eagerly. "Oh, Margaret!"

Miss Hawthorne picked the rags out.

"No," she said disappointedly, "just a lot of old stones."

I am afraid I laughed as I picked up the uninviting pebbles.

"When these are cut, young lady, you'll not need to worry for some time. Diamonds, and big ones, too. I wonder who ever hid them away. They must have known you would need them."

"I know who put them there," said Miss Dunlop quietly. "I didn't tell you last night, but it was like seeing a movie in my dream, only when I waked up, I remembered everything. I saw this house, and old Amos and Elizabeth—that was the old lady's name—"

"Why, yes, Janet," cried Miss Hawthorne. "How did you know it?"

"Amos Hawthorne," continued Miss Dunlop, "was a domineering brute. I saw him catch his wife by the throat and frighten her so she could only whisper afterwards. I saw him thrash the negro Hannibal for stealing rum out of the brick storehouse—where the ruins are, and then I saw Hannibal bowing to the idol he kept down in the cellar, making *ju-ju*—that was the word—and then lying in wait for his master. I saw the old man go up to the look-out room and fall from the ladder as the negro caught his ankle. His neck was broken, and I saw Hannibal hang him to the hook so as to make it look like suicide. I saw your great-grandmother, Elizabeth, going in fear of Hannibal until one night he had a fight with another negro, who killed him. It might have been all right if Hannibal had been buried properly, but your great-grandmother with her own hands dug this grave in the cellar—she was a capable old woman—and hid the diamonds and the body of Hannibal there, and sealed up the hole with the idol. I saw her dying a month later, before she could tell anyone. They said it was her throat which killed her, but there were the marks of two hands on it."

Miss Dunlop stopped. Her tones had been those of a prophetess. She pressed her hands to her eyes, and remarked in her usual voice: "Goodness, I'm doing a lot of talking, surely. But it just came back to me suddenly."

I sent the two girls upstairs, while Maurice and I lit a glowing fire in the furnace. Then we pulled out the bones of the slave, together with a rusted knife, also in the recess, and consigned them to the flames. Later in the day, when nothing was left but ashes, we cleared the grate and threw the contents into the sea. Nothing is so purifying as fire and sea.

That was the end of the haunting. The evil lurking in those bones of a murderer, sustained perhaps by some magic inherent in the idol, was banished from the house. And the old woman, having eased her mind of its long-carried secret, was at rest.

The whispering was never heard again. As I said, Miss Hawthorne sold the house, and with the proceeds from that and the diamonds she has gone abroad for a time with Miss Dunlop.

I begged for the African picture, and it hangs in my study, an object of admiration which, I pleasurably reflect, increases in value with each day of my possession.

The Green Monkey
By Silvia Underwood
As told to Rosa Zagnoni Marinoni

It was the fortune-teller's last gift to her friend—a present far more valuable than any earthly keepsake.

THERE IS A REASON FOR ME TO WRITE THIS STORY. I WANT MY GREEN MONKEY.

Have you seen a green monkey?

Has anyone offered to sell you one? If you have bought it (perhaps for the children to play with), for heaven's sake take it away from them! Don't let them tear it up! I must tell you about it: how it came to be mine and—the rest.

The first time I saw the green monkey was many years ago, inside the crystal of Zanzara, the fortune-teller. At the time I was but a slip of a girl, barely able to reach up on tiptoes to peer into the crystal. Zanzara herself seemed young then. I liked her; I ran inside her shack every chance I had. She held a fascination for all of us children down in River Hallow. She named me Silvia, and said that I reminded her of the forest with its crickets, birds and brooks, because I laughed and ran and capered so. She often tousled my hair, and when I was good, very good, she would let me stare down into her crystal. And one day I saw the green monkey there.

I remember asking, "What is that funny animal, Zanzara?"

And she answered, muttering the words in her throat, "That's me—"

I laughed and pointed my finger at her. "Oh, Zanzara, you—a green monkey!" And when I looked again into the whirling shadows of the crystal, the monkey was gone. Zanzara was meditatively patting my hair.

Years passed. I married and moved away to a town where my husband was cashier in a bank. I only wrote to Zanzara now and then.

One summer I went back to River Hallow, and the first person I went to see was Zanzara, My, but she had grown old! You see, I was twenty-eight at the time but she seemed about seventy, I guess. I found her crouched before a fire, although it was summer. She looked at me for a moment tensely out of dimmed eyes, then she rose and flung her arms high.

"Silvia!" she cried and held me close.

I could feel her sharp bones against me.

Everything about the shack was just as it had been years before. There was the crystal, the old, enormous diagram of a human palm, the pictures of skulls nailed to the walls. I sat by the fire and talked to her a long time, feeling like a little girl again. That evening, before I left, she told me she was going to make me a present before I returned to my new home. And she did.

Two weeks later, when I went to say good-by to Zanzara, I found her in the doorway of her shack, as if she had been waiting for me right along. She did not say very much, but when I started to leave, she rummaged in the folds of her shawl and pulled out a loose-jointed, crudely-knitted monkey. A green monkey!

She had knitted the thing herself out of wool yarn for me. She had stuffed it with cotton, sewed into the head of it two yellow crystal beads for eyes, and put in a few red stitches for nose and mouth—and that was the monkey, a reminder of old, happy days.

I all but cried. She had made that thing for me with her own hands—poor old soul!

She handed me the monkey, and her voice quavered as she said, "Keep this, honey; it will remind you of me, when—when I'm gone—"

"Oh, Zanzara," I cried, the tears stabbing in my eyes. "I'll come and see you again. To think you made this for me! A green monkey! Remember—the green monkey—I saw—" I could not finish the phrase.

Zanzara placed a finger on her lips. "Hush," she said. "Someone is coming."

I looked around. No one was in sight. I did not think anything of it at the time—she was old and queer—and I left, hugging that homely thing to my breast. Later I stuck it into my suit-case and when I returned home, I pulled it out and placed it above the door of my living room. There the green monkey sat, balanced on the molding, where I could look at it when I played bridge, or when company bored me.

It was a week later that I learned old Zanzara had died. I cried, and was glad she had given me the monkey.

But you can't grieve long over an old friend that dies, when you have children, a seven-room house and a perfectly good husband who comes home for supper as hungry as a wolf. My duties absorbed all my attention, and I thought very little of Zanzara.

One night, about two months after her death, my husband came home long after the

children had gone to bed, and announced that he was to leave at midnight for a nearby city. He showed me a large envelope, and told me that the bank had entrusted him with an issue of bonds which he was to take to a bank in Kansas City.

As he was showing me the bonds and proudly telling me of the confidence the bank had placed in him, there was a thud at our backs. I turned. The green monkey had fallen from its perch above the door and was lying limp on the rug! I picked it up and put it back above the door, while my husband went to the phone to make a reservation for a Pullman berth.

He soon returned and said the phone was out of order. He decided he had better go to the depot and make reservations right then, to be certain he would not have to sit in a chair-car all night.

As he started to leave, he fingered the package in his coat pocket and remarked: "I dislike to ramble about more than is necessary, with these bonds in my pocket. Guess I had better leave them here till I come back." So saying, he placed the bonds well back in a pigeon-hole of his desk.

He took his hat and left. I sat near the reading lamp, looking over the evening paper. The children were asleep, and I felt cozy and contented—yet, as the minutes ticked by, a strange uneasiness began to crawl over me. I glanced at the clock. Why had not my husband come home? He had been gone over half an hour, and the depot was only four blocks away. What could be detaining him? I walked to the window and looked out. No one was coming down the street. I went back to my chair.

Suddenly, I thought I felt a draft on my back. I turned. No one was in the room. The hall door was closed.

The walls seemed to stifle me. What had come over me?

I tried to shake off my feeling of uneasiness, but I could not. I had that spooky sensation that comes over you when some hidden person is staring in your direction.

My voice was strangely hollow as I called, "Is that you, Spencer?"

No one answered.

My glance traveled about the room, and then focused on the green monkey balanced on the molding above the door. I don't know why, but it did. The monkey was staring straight at me.

From where I sat, its head had always seemed to be turned toward the ceiling, but now those yellow eyes were looking down at me.

Suddenly my hands grew cold. What was that! As I stared at the monkey's eyes, I saw its gaze *shift*. Do you understand? Its eyes traveled slowly from my face to the window back of me! I did not move. Slowly, slowly, I tell you, the eyes again met mine and again drifted to the window! I had to turn and—look toward the window—

There, in the shadow of the room, I saw the long draperies move. They bulged strangely. I looked toward the floor. A pair of black shoes protruded from under the fringe—the heavy shoes of a man!

My body grew cold. A man was hiding behind those draperies and—the green monkey had made me look at them!

I could not move—I could not breathe. A thousand pins stabbed at the roots of my hair. I wanted to scream, but could not. Was that man looking at me through a hole in the drapery?

My horrified gaze traveled up to what should have been the level of the man's face. Through the red curtain I saw the sparkle of eyes! I screamed.

The lights went out. I heard a chair turn over. I felt something push me backward—a hand clutched at my wrist! I frantically pulled away—afraid—afraid to scream. The children!—had they heard?

A hand grabbed at my throat. A door slammed. Then a shriek! A terrible, eerie cry, inhuman in its harrowing dissonance, cleft the span of silence like a thin knife hurled from Satan's wrist. The light came on—

In the sudden glare I saw a man staggering away from me, his eyes like glazed opals bulging from his head! His hands were thrashing wildly in the air—blood trickling from his gaping mouth!

Curled around his neck—I saw—I saw—*the green monkey!*

The man dashed madly toward the window, plunged through it and dived into the night.

I ran to the window. Looking out, I saw him running wildly along the pine trail that led to the river.

A few minutes later, some neighbors and I found my husband lying unconscious on the lawn, stunned by a blow on the head.

When he regained consciousness, he could only remember that as he left the house, a man had jumped out of the bushes and hit him.

On the grass were papers that had been pulled out of his pockets. Fortunately the bonds were safe in the desk.

We also found that our telephone wires had been cut—obviously the man had known of the bonds. He had assaulted my husband and, failing to find them on his person, had come into the house—and I knew the rest.

A search failed to uncover any trace of the man. Where did he go? Who was he? I do not care. I want my green monkey—did anyone find it? Has anyone seen a green monkey? Having heard of my experience—if you have the monkey, you would not want to keep it, would you? Oh, please, if you have it, return it to me! It means nothing to you—it means so much to me. You see, I owe my life to it. Also, I loved old Zanzara.

Selected Bibliography

Ashley, Mike. "Spectral Memories." *Phantom Perfumes and Other Shades: Memories of Ghost Stories Magazine*. Ash-Tree Press, 2000.

Cohen, Lester. *The New York Graphic: The World's Zaniest Newspaper*. Chilton Books, 1964.

Ernst, Robert. *Weakness Is a Crime: The Life of Bernarr Macfadden*. Syracuse University Press, 1991.

Hersey, Harold. "My Friend Fulton Oursler." *The Author & Journalist*, July 1927.

———. *Pulpwood Editor*. Frederick A. Stokes Company, 1937.

Locke, John. "Fulton Ousler: The Magician Detective." *The Magician Detective: and Other Weird Mysteries*. Off-Trail Publications, 2010.

———. "Harold Hersey: Tales of an Ink-Stained Wretch." *City of Numbered Men: The Best of Prison Stories*. Off-Trail Publications, 2010.

Macfadden, Mary, and Emile Gauvreau. *Dumbbells and Carrot Strips: The Story of Bernarr Macfadden*. Henry Holt & Company, 1953.

Murray, Will. "True Ghostly Confessions." *Lurid Confessions*, June 1986.

Oursler, Fulton. *Behold This Dreamer!* An Autobiography by Fulton Oursler, Edited and with Commentary by Fulton Oursler, Jr. Little, Brown and Company, 1964.

———. *The True Story of Bernarr Macfadden*. Lewis Copeland Company, 1929.

Oursler, Will. *Family Story*. Funk & Wagnalls Company, Inc., 1963.

Wood, Clement. *Bernarr Macfadden: A Study in Success*. Lewis Copeland Company, 1929.

Woodbury, Marda Liggett. *Stopping the Presses: The Murder of Walter W. Liggett*. University of Minnesota Press, 1998.

Index

OFF-TRAIL PUBLICATIONS
Specializing in the era of American pulp fiction

THE WEIRD DETECTIVE ADVENTURES OF WADE HAMMOND
By Paul Chadwick
Volume 1: 10 stories, 180 pages, $18
Volume 2: 10 stories, 172 pages, $18
Volume 3: 10 stories, 202 pages, $18
Volume 4: 9 stories, 232 pages, $18

The Wade Hammond stories complete in four volumes. In these chilling adventures, all from the classic 1930's pulps, Detective-Dragnet *and* Ten Detective Aces, *freelance investigator Wade Hammond battles a series of weird enemies. Some of the best of '30s pulp fiction.*

DOCTOR COFFIN: The Living Dead Man
By Perley Poore Sheehan • Introduction by John Wooley
8 novelettes, 178 pages, $16

Weird stories from Thrilling Detective, *1932-33. A former character actor who faked his own death, Doctor Coffin runs a string of mortuaries by night and fights crime at night. One of the strangest detective series.*

SUPER-DETECTIVE FLIP BOOK: Two Complete Novels
From the pulp *Super-Detective*:
"Legion of Robots" (November 1940) by Victor Rousseau • Introduction by John McMahan •• "Murder's Migrants" (March 1943) by Robert Leslie Bellem and W.T. Ballard • Introduction by John Wooley
2 short novels, 174 pages, $18

Super-Detective *started as a Doc Savage-like adventure pulp, then changed format to hardboiled detective. The* Flip Book *features a novel from each of the two phases with intros exploring the historical background. Exciting!*

   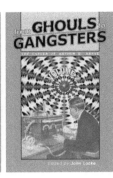 

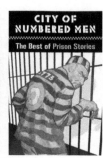

AMAZON STORIES
Volume 1: Pedro & Lourenço
Volume 2: Pedro & Lourenço
By Arthur O. Friel • Introductions by John Locke
Vol 1: 10 stories, 222 pages, $18 • **Vol 2**: 10 stories, 286 pages, $20

Collects Friel's first twenty stories from Adventure *(1919-21), following the strange experiences of two Amazon Basin rubber workers as they explore the jungle. The best of pulp adventure fiction.*

THE GOLDEN ANACONDA: And Other Strange Tales of Adventure
By Elmer Brown Mason • Introduction by John Locke
10 stories, 260 pages, $20

Ten fantastic stories set in the exotic corners of the world, all of them known to their globe-trotting entomologist author. Includes all five Wandering Smith stories from The Popular Magazine; *and five tales from* All-Story Weekly, *topped by the horror-laden two-part saga of Borneo, "Black Butterflies" and "Red Tree-Frogs." All published, 1915-16.*

CITY OF NUMBERED MEN: The Best of Prison Stories
Introduction by John Locke
12 stories, 278 pages, $20

During Prohibition, America's decrepit prisons turned into seething cauldrons of hate and despair: escape attempts, inmate violence, sadistic wardens, grisly executions, and horrendous riots that were beaten back with machine guns and tear gas. . . . all the raw material that famed publisher Harold Hersey needed to launch the hard-boiled Prison Stories *(1930-31). Included are stories from all six issues of this ultra-rare pulp, the startling history of* Prison Stories, *complete cover gallery, and "Harold Hersey: Tales of an Ink-Stained Wretch," the first comprehensive biography of pulp publishing's most colorful character.*

THE MAGICIAN DETECTIVE: And Other Weird Mysteries
By Fulton Oursler
Introduction by John Locke
7 stories, 210 pages, $18

Fulton Oursler was one of the great editors of his time, ruling over the Macfadden publishing empire for two decades. But stage magic was his first love, and, in his heart, he remained a conjurer in a black cape and top hat. In this collection of early fiction, Oursler's bewitching imagination takes flight in tales of magic, murder and mesmerizing mystery. Also featured is an in-depth exploration of the astonishing career of Fulton Oursler.

CPSIA information can be obtained
at www.ICGtesting.com
Printed in the USA
BVHW051000201221
624302BV00002B/13